Praise for author Deb Kastner

"Kastner's latest will grab the reader with familiar characters and engaging dialogue."
—*RT Book Reviews* on *Yuletide Baby*

"Endearing final installment of the Email Order Brides series."
—*RT Book Reviews* on *Meeting Mr. Right*

"[A] sweet second-chance story."
—*RT Book Reviews* on *The Doctor's Secret Son*

"The storyline...[has] a strong emotional edge and true sensitivity."
—*RT Book Reviews* on *The Heart of a Man*

D1047838

DEB KASTNER

The Nanny's Twin Blessings

&

Meeting Mr. Right

HARLEQUIN® LOVE INSPIRED®CLASSICS

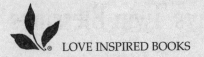

LOVE INSPIRED BOOKS

Recycling programs for this product may not exist in your area.

ISBN-13: 978-0-373-20844-9

The Nanny's Twin Blessings & Meeting Mr. Right

Copyright © 2017 by Harlequin Books S.A.

The publisher acknowledges the copyright holder of the individual works as follows:

The Nanny's Twin Blessings
Copyright © 2012 by Debra Kastner

Meeting Mr. Right
Copyright © 2013 by Debra Kastner

www.Harlequin.com

Printed in U.S.A.

CONTENTS

THE NANNY'S TWIN BLESSINGS 7

MEETING MR. RIGHT 215

Award-winning author **Deb Kastner** writes stories of faith, family and community in a small-town Western setting. Deb's books contain sigh-worthy heroes and strong heroines facing obstacles that draw them closer to each other and the Lord. She lives in Colorado with her husband and is blessed with three daughters and two grandchildren. She enjoys spoiling her grandkids, movies, music (The Texas Tenors!), singing in the church choir and exploring Colorado on horseback.

Books by Deb Kastner

Love Inspired

Lone Star Cowboy League: Boys Ranch
The Doctor's Texas Baby

Lone Star Cowboy League
A Daddy for Her Triplets

Cowboy Country
Yuletide Baby
The Cowboy's Forever Family
The Cowboy's Surprise Baby
The Cowboy's Twins
Mistletoe Daddy

Email Order Brides
Phoebe's Groom
The Doctor's Secret Son
The Nanny's Twin Blessings
Meeting Mr. Right

Visit the Author Profile page
at Harlequin.com for more titles.

THE NANNY'S
TWIN BLESSINGS

"For I know the plans I have for you," declares the Lord, "plans to prosper you and not to harm you, plans to give you hope and a future."
—*Jeremiah* 29:11

As always, to my family—
Joe, Annie, Kimberly, Katie, Isabella and Anthony.
Without your support, there wouldn't be a book.

Prologue

PARENTS OF PRESCHOOLERS ONLINE COMMUNITY
NITY
CLASSIFIED ADS

WANTED: Nanny for three-year-old twin boys.
Two-month temporary live-in position includes stipend, room and board. Assistance in relocation to
Serendipity, Texas, provided. Mandatory two years'
experience with references. Please respond with
resume and salary requirements.

Chapter One

Stephanie Cartwright would have described the Texas prairie in early spring in two words: dry and barren. Endless miles of dirt, rolling hills of dry grass and dark, skeletal weeds, stretching out as far as the eye could see.

The land was a mirror of her heart. Or maybe it was her frame of mind that was coloring the landscape in dreary shades of gray. As if that wasn't enough, she exited her subcompact rental car to find her nostrils angrily assaulted by a strange, pungent odor—no doubt the scent of cows or horses or other livestock.

Did it smell like this all the time? She hoped it was just the direction of the wind adding to the eye-watering stench in the air, because for better or for worse, Serendipity, Texas, was where she'd be living for the next couple of months. As far away from the east coast—and her ex-boyfriend—as she could get. Hidden from the world in a tiny town in the middle of nowhere.

And way, *way* out of her comfort zone.

But it wasn't as if she could turn around and go back home. There *was* no home to go back to. Trying not to breathe too deeply, she clenched her fists and fought for control as her feelings once again vacillated between devastation and anger. At any given moment since she'd boarded the plane for Texas, she had struggled with one of those emotions, sometimes both at the same time.

Her eyes widened as a large, square-headed and very intimidating dog wandered up and situated himself on the wood-planked porch steps to the house where her new employer, Drew Spencer, presumably waited.

Peachy. Another obstacle. Just what she needed....

Stephanie was a nanny. She'd expected to be greeted by children, not canines. She had little experience with animals and had never even owned a pet.

The dog shook his head and licked his chops. He appeared to be welcoming her, though she couldn't be certain. For all she knew he was putting her on the menu.

"Hello there, big guy," Stephanie crooned, speaking in the same soft, gentle tone of voice she used to calm small children. She prayed it would work. "Nice puppy."

The dog's ears pricked. His mouth curved up naturally, as if he was smiling at her, and he wagged his tail with unreserved enthusiasm. Was that a good sign?

"Don't worry. He's harmless." Warm laughter emanated from behind the screen door, startling her.

If she wasn't a twenty-three-year-old woman in perfect health, she probably would have thought she was experiencing a heart attack. Every nerve ending in her body crackled with an unexpected jolt of electricity. She hadn't realized someone was watching her, and her face flamed in embarrassment.

A man who quickly introduced himself as Drew Spencer opened the screen and stepped out onto the porch. "Sorry about that. The four-legged Welcome

Wagon that greeted you is Quincy, the over-enthusiastic pit bull. I should have put him in the house."

"He's very…friendly." Stephanie straightened her shoulders and curled her lips into what she hoped was an inviting smile.

"Very," Drew agreed, chuckling. "He may look like a tough old watchdog, but Quincy is as harmless as they come. If you were a robber he'd invite you into the house and show you where the silver was."

"I'm more interested in your gold," she teased as her gaze locked with Drew's intelligent but darkly shadowed green eyes.

Her breath caught. It was as if the scene had suddenly gone from black-and-white to a rainbow of color. To put it bluntly, the guy was one tall drink of water.

Which is to say, he was *nothing* like she'd imagined him to be.

In the emails they'd exchanged, Drew had seemed staid, rigid and academic—at least on paper. Even the times they'd spoken on the telephone, she'd thought his voice was dull and lackluster, with little emotion or variation in his tone. Somehow she'd imagined he looked the way he sounded.

The man standing in front of her, however, wasn't anything like her mental picture.

Uh-uh. Not even close.

He was wearing a pair of worn but polished brown cowboy boots, crisp blue jeans, a navy button-down dress shirt and a loosely knotted burgundy-colored necktie. He had strong-boned, even facial features, and thick brown hair lightly brushed his forehead. He looked as if he'd be as comfortable on a horse as he was in the classroom. All that was missing was the cowboy hat, and Stephanie had a good notion that he owned one.

There were no dark-rimmed, pop-bottle-thick glasses. No nerdy slouch or nutty-professor grin. Just a long, lean and fantastic-looking elementary school teacher in the guise of a cowboy.

She shook herself mentally, thoroughly appalled at where her thoughts had gone. What difference did it make whether her employer was a gorgeous cowboy or a geeky academic? She was here solely to watch over his children, not to gawk at him, and she knew how important first impressions were.

Specifically, his first impression of her.

She'd intended to appear poised and confident when she met Drew face-to-face for the first time. Not that she generally *felt* composed or self-assured—but she was good at faking it.

Widening her smile, she extended her hand. For a moment, Drew just stared at it as if he didn't know how to finish the gesture. The left corner of his mouth curved up, then down and then into a tight, straight line that matched the unyielding right side of his lips.

Stephanie nearly pulled back her arm. She couldn't tell what he was thinking. Had she botched things already?

Waves of relief washed over her when he finally reached out to shake her hand. His firm, steady grip reassured her, as did the way his mouth finally relaxed, his lips bowing upward in what could almost be considered a smile.

A tow-headed young boy peeked around Drew's leg and sized Stephanie up with a thoughtful stare. She paused, observing the child and allowing him a moment to adjust to her presence before she introduced herself to him. Presumably he was one of her two future charges, and he was a real cutie-pie, with large blue eyes and trim white-blond hair combed over to one side like a miniature Cary Grant.

Stephanie immediately relaxed. Her senses had been jarred by both the dog and the man, but kids she could handle. She was comfortable with the little ones.

She was one of the lucky ones who'd found out early what she wanted to do with her life—care for children, whether it was as a babysitter for her younger foster brothers and sisters, in her first official job as a superintendent at a bounce house or as a nanny for a high-society family. As long as there were children, she was happy.

Eventually she wanted to teach in a preschool and had already gotten her degree in early childhood education, but she had not yet pursued her teacher's certification. For now, she was content being a nanny.

"Who are you?" the three-year-old asked bluntly.

Drew coughed into his hand but she could see he was covering a smile. His eyes lightened for a moment, sparkling with barely concealed laughter. She arched an eyebrow at him, amused at how valiantly he tried to keep a straight face at the nerve of his precocious offspring.

She struggled not to giggle, herself. It was funny. She was glad Drew hadn't corrected the boy on her behalf, as many of her foster parents over the years would have done when their children had misspoken. The child's question was direct, but it was equally as innocent.

Leave it to a three-year-old to get right to the point of the matter.

Stephanie didn't mind. She was used to the straightforward, curious nature of children. She much preferred it, in fact, versus lying, deceitful adults. At least kids were honest.

With a smile, she crouched down to the boy's level, looking him straight in the eye to let him know she was taking him—and his question—seriously.

"My name is Miss Stephanie," she answered earnestly. "And I'm happy to meet you—"

She hesitated, glancing up toward the door, seeking Drew's input on the little boy's name, since she knew she'd be caring for identical twins. Instead, the answer came from a gruff, guttural voice from somewhere behind Drew's right shoulder.

"His name is Matty." Using his cane for leverage, an older, scruffy-faced gentleman Stephanie presumed must be Drew's father inched around him. "He's the bold one. And this sweet little guy," he continued, gesturing toward the child cuddling in his arms with his face tucked shyly into the old man's chest, "is Jamey."

As far as Stephanie could see, the twins were completely identical in looks, but she had no doubt she'd be able to tell them apart once she'd spent some time with them. There were bound to be differences in personality, if not tiny distinctions in their looks.

"Hello there, Matty and Jamey," Stephanie responded as she stood upright. "How are you fellows doing today?"

Jamey curiously peeked out at Stephanie, and Matty laughed and ran around the old man's legs.

"I figure you already know that the rude fellow blocking the doorway and not inviting you inside the house is my son, Drew," the old man continued. "Although most everyone in town calls him Spence, on account of our last name." He grunted noncommittally. "And I, my dear, am Frank. Please come in."

Drew's father winked and flashed an engaging grin, then set little Jamey on his feet and ushered both boys through the door. Quincy the pit bull stood up, stretched lazily and followed the twins inside.

Drew hesitated a moment, the corners of his lips once again curving down as his brow furrowed. He shoved his hands into his pockets and shifted uncomfortably from one foot to another, looking a great deal more like the staid, solemn school teacher Stephanie had initially imagined him to be. Something was definitely bothering him, and she wondered if it had anything to do with her. Why else would he be smiling one minute and frowning the next?

Her apprehension hung almost palpably in the air, on her part, if not on his. He certainly wasn't what she'd expected. Perhaps she wasn't what he'd anticipated, either. Maybe he was wondering how to gently let her down, to send her packing again. But Drew obviously had *some* serious motivation in bringing her here to take care of his twins, something beyond what they'd discussed when she'd interviewed for the position.

She had no clue why he had decided to look so far out of town to find someone to watch his children, and it was one of the first questions she planned to ask him when the opportunity presented itself. Granted, Serendipity was tiny, but it was hard to imagine there were no adequate forms of child care Drew could call upon in a pinch. At the very least, there must be a few teenagers who would be vying to earn a little extra spending money.

So why her?

It was a fair question, and one that she eventually meant to get to the bottom of, but in the end, she realized it didn't matter to her all that much what his motivations were. The point of the matter was that she was here now, and this man had unknowingly offered her a way out of a really bad situation. He'd given her a place to hide from a spoiled, abusive boyfriend who didn't know how to take no for an answer. Drew Spencer's offer to hire her as a live-in nanny from now until the end of the school year was truly an answer to prayer—two months to heal her heart and get back on her feet, to give herself a fresh start.

It wasn't enough that her ex-boyfriend Ryan had torn her heart to shreds—he'd also ripped her home and her job right out from under her. She'd naively given up everything for him, only to find out he was playing her.

She was proud of herself for finding the self-esteem to walk away from a toxic relationship, but that didn't stop her from being a little bit anxious about the way it had ended—Ryan was used to getting his own way, and he was frighteningly possessive. He'd alienated her from everyone else in her life, wanting her all to himself—even though he never had any intention of putting a ring on her finger.

How could she help but look over her shoulder, even knowing she was far away from New Jersey? Ryan had threatened to come after her, and he had power and money behind him to do it. She hoped she'd done enough to keep herself safe.

She needed somewhere secluded and private to regroup and refocus her life, to make plans for her future, though at the moment, she had no idea what that would be—other than finding more permanent housing and a stable job.

In the meantime, Serendipity was a good place to hide.

Drew wasn't overly keen on having a nanny living in his house and getting under his feet. He was already so busy he barely had time to breathe, and he didn't need the added complication of having someone in the way, especially a beautiful woman who smelled like orchids and jasmine.

Unfortunately, he had little choice in the matter. Drew was working off the advice of his lawyer, who had *strongly* suggested he get someone to watch his boys full-time until the end of the school year, particularly since the custody mediation with his ex-wife wasn't progressing well. His lawyer had called it making a *good faith effort* to show he was taking care of the boys.

It had better be good. It was costing Drew a good part of his pension plan. And it was causing him a *great* deal of stress.

Heather had recently been making all kinds of verbal threats about taking the boys away from him, and though none of them had yet come to fruition, Drew still felt as if she was holding him hostage where the kids were concerned.

He knew full well that Heather didn't have any intention of shouldering the responsibility of raising children. She probably planned to pawn them off on her parents, or worse yet, whatever boyfriend she was living with.

Drew's gut felt as if it was filled with molten lead, as it always did when he thought about the callous way Heather had left him—and even worse, how she had abandoned the twins. He prayed he could eventually find forgiveness in his heart for her, but he was human, and forgiveness was a long way off, especially now that she was locking him in a battle for custody of the children.

For Heather, this wasn't about what was best for Matty and Jamey. She was only interested in hitting Drew where it hurt. He couldn't even imagine life without the twins. He would *have* no life without his sons.

And Heather knew it.

"Which name should I call you?"

Stephanie's golden voice slowly penetrated into his thoughts. She flashed him a dazzling smile that exposed both rows of straight, white teeth. "Do you have a preference?"

"I'm sorry?" he asked. His eyebrows rose in confusion as he was mentally jerked into the present.

"Shall I call you Drew or Spence? Your dad said the folks in town call you Spence."

"Oh, yeah. Right. No… Drew is fine."

He didn't know why he was stammering, and he certainly had no clue why he'd just given her the answer he had. Only members of his immediate family called him Drew. The words had just slipped out before he'd had a chance to think about what he was saying, but he didn't correct himself. As a live-in nanny, Stephanie was going to be a part of the family for a while, even if she was everything he *didn't* want in a nanny.

Not outwardly, anyway.

What had happened to the peculiar cross between Mary Poppins and Nanny McPhee that he'd been expecting to show up at his door? Instead, Stephanie had soft, delicate features, high cheekbones, a pretty smile, wave upon wave of sun-drenched, fair hair and warm brown eyes that a man could easily get lost in.

He didn't feel like it sometimes, but he was still a living, breathing man. He was going to trip over Stephanie's beauty every time he looked at her. He'd erroneously assumed, from her upside-down umbrella avatar on the Parents of Preschoolers classified board that she'd be…

Plain?

Homely?

Truth be told, he didn't know what he'd been expecting, only that the woman still waiting on his doorstep was not it.

Emphasis on *waiting*. On his *doorstep*. He ought to kick himself for his discourtesy.

Stepping aside, he gestured for her to go in ahead of him. He averted his gaze from her female sway, but he was unable to keep himself from inhaling the rich oriental fragrance that wafted over him as she swept by. She smelled every bit as good as she looked, which really wasn't helping matters any. He was uncomfortable enough as it was.

There was no sign of his father, but the twins were huddled around the toy box in the living room. They already had several trucks and trains on the floor and were reaching for more.

"One toy at a time, boys," Drew reminded them. "Remember our rule." His gaze shifted to Stephanie. "I tidy up this place at least five times a day, and there are still toys scattered everywhere. They haven't quite mastered the one-at-a-time rule yet, and they're easily distracted."

Stephanie chuckled lightly. "Comes with the territory.

I don't mind at all. *Preschoolers* and *messy* go together like butter on toast."

"Right," he agreed, noting that her expression softened and her shoulders lost their stiffness when her attention was directed at the children.

Offering Stephanie a seat on the couch, Drew positioned himself on the antique chair near the fireplace. Seconds later, Jamey slipped onto his lap and Matty climbed up his back, wrapping his little arms around Drew's neck and practically choking him in the process.

Or was it was Stephanie's smile that was making his throat close so forcefully?

"Have you had dinner? I can make you a sandwich if you like."

"I'm fine," she insisted with the hint of a smile.

"Coffee, then?"

She shook her head, and the conversation drifted to a standstill.

Less than a minute passed before Matty's curiosity got the best of him. The small boy crawled off Drew's back and launched himself at Stephanie, who caught him with a laugh and tucked him next to her on the couch, under her arm. There was a toy airplane in reaching distance, and Stephanie grabbed it, giving it to Matty complete with a *vroom* sound.

To Drew's surprise, Jamey crawled off his lap and settled up on Stephanie's knee, his thumb tucked in his mouth, a habit Drew hadn't yet been able to break him out of.

Incredible.

Drew had never seen Jamey cozy up to a person as quickly as he had to Stephanie. It was as if she'd earned the boys' respect the very first time she smiled. She tickled the boys on the ears and they both squealed with laughter.

"These little men are absolutely darling," Stephanie said, giggling along with the twins. Her eyes were shining, lighting up her whole countenance. She was definitely in her element with the children.

"They're a handful," Drew countered teasingly, though he spoke the truth. He was unable to stop himself from grinning, despite his misgivings about the situation.

"Oh, I'm not worried about that. I love children. I'm happy to be here."

Drew could see that, and he could sense it, too. She had become immediately attached to his kids, and they clearly liked her. He would be foolish to put her off just because she didn't look like the nanny he'd pictured in his head. It was what was inside a person's soul that really counted—like seeing the way his kids had instantly warmed up to her and instinctively trusted her. That spoke volumes about her, in Drew's mind. Kids had a way of perceiving things about people that weren't so obvious when seen through an adult's eyes.

His father picked that moment to hobble across the hallway behind Stephanie. He paused and gave Drew two thumbs-up, grinning and wagging his bushy gray eyebrows for emphasis.

Apparently *he* approved of her—which was an absolutely frightening thought. Whoops. Drew hadn't thought of *that* particular ramification of hiring Stephanie. Pop wasn't viewing her as a nanny for his grandsons, but as a potential future wife for his son. Drew had seen the impish light in his father's eyes before, and it never boded well.

He couldn't imagine how ghastly it would be once his father put his head together with his best lady friend and cohort in mischief, Jo Murphy, the gregarious owner of the Cup O' Jo Café and the town's chief matchmaker.

Nanny or not, his pop and Jo Murphy would see romance where there was none. Before he knew it, they would be pestering him half to death. Stephanie, too, for that matter, and she certainly hadn't signed on for *that*.

"I hope my father won't be too problematic for you," Drew said. "The twins love the gruff old guy, but the simple fact of the matter is that he is getting up in years and he can't do everything he thinks he can. He doesn't require any special physical care or anything. For his age, he's as fit as a fiddle. But he has a tendency to involve himself in matters that don't concern him. You may want to keep your eye out for him so he doesn't cause you any trouble."

He paused and chuckled, but it was a dry, nervous sound rather than a happy one. "Have I overwhelmed you yet? Made you change your mind about working here? I'm sure you're ready to turn right around and hop on the next plane back to the east coast."

"I think I can handle your father," she assured him. "How ornery can one man be?"

"You would be surprised." Drew cocked his head and twisted his lips in amusement. "He's going to be in your way. Constantly. And he has an opinion about everything."

She shrugged. "Doesn't everybody?"

"Maybe, but my father is especially blustery when he gets into one of his moods. Which is often. Just so you know."

"Not a problem," she assured him. "I tend to get along with everybody."

Somehow, he believed she did.

"Boys," he stated firmly, addressing the twins, both of whom by that time were using Stephanie as playground equipment, swinging over her shoulders and sliding down her legs—not that she appeared to mind. The crystal-clear sound of her feminine laughter laced the air like stardust.

Drew gestured toward the hall. "Why don't you two run along now and get ready for bed? I think Pop-Pop is waiting for you. I'll be there in a minute to read another chapter of our story to you."

At least that would keep his father occupied for a while, getting the two squirming, over-excited preschoolers into pajamas and tucked into bed. Drew ruffled their fair hair and kissed each of his boys softly on the forehead before urging them to the back hallway where their room was located.

"Sorry about the interruption," Drew said once he'd herded the twins down the hall. "Bedtime is a real zoo around here."

He returned to his seat and braced his elbows on his knees, ignoring the quivering sensation in his stomach as their eyes met.

He cleared his throat, wondering how to start the conversation. There was a lot she needed to know about why she was here, issues he hadn't felt comfortable discussing over the phone, but that she ought to be aware of if she was going to be working for him.

And he had a few more questions for her, as well.

Like why she'd chosen a temporary position in Serendipity when she'd clearly had a successful career in child care on the east coast. It wasn't *What's a pretty lady like you doing in a place like this?* But it was pretty close. He wasn't sure if he should be prying, yet it seemed an obvious question.

If it was none of his business, she would no doubt tell him so. But something about her expression gave him pause to consider.

With just the two of them in the room, she appeared uneasy—like a cornered animal, with wide, wild brown eyes staring back at him. Though she was trying to hide it, she was clearly uncomfortable sitting here with him.

Maybe she was just nervous about starting a new job in a new town, but somehow he thought it was more than that. He hoped she wasn't reconsidering the position. It had been next to impossible just to find someone suitable for these circumstances the first time around. He didn't know if he would find anyone else willing to do the job.

He fidgeted in his chair, which was unusual for him. Normally, he would just blurt what he was thinking outright. He'd been told on more than one occasion that he was too blunt and outspoken. This might be a good time to work on that defect.

But how did one ease into this kind of subject?

Before he could say a word, there was a knock at the door.

Stephanie jerked in surprise, as her gaze shifted to the door.

"I'm sorry," he apologized, rising. "I wasn't expecting anyone this evening. It's probably my father's friend Jo, although she usually just lets herself in. I'll only be a moment."

Stephanie tried to smile, but the color on her face

had faded into a serious shade of gray. She clasped her hands together in her lap until her knuckles were white.

"Are you all right?" he asked, concerned.

"I'm—yes," she stammered. "I'm fine."

Drew didn't think she looked fine. She looked terrified. And it had something to do with whoever was potentially knocking at his front door.

Even though he barely knew Stephanie, his deep-rooted protective instincts flared. She had nothing to fear. He wasn't going to let anyone hurt her while she was in his house, though he couldn't imagine why anyone would want to. And like he'd said, it was probably Jo Murphy, come to see his pop.

Only it wasn't Jo Murphy.

Drew opened the door to a lanky young man he'd never seen before, certainly not a resident of Serendipity.

A friend of Stephanie's? Or worse yet, an enemy?

"Andrew Reid Spencer?" the boy asked, obviously trying to sound official despite the crack in his voice.

Drew's eyebrows shot up in surprise. Why was the young man asking for him?

"Yes," he replied cautiously. "I'm Drew."

The boy shoved a manila envelope at Drew's chest and was backing up before he even spoke. Drew instinctually reached for the envelope, clutching it to his side as the young man made his pronouncement.

"You've been served."

Chapter Two

Stephanie didn't hear the actual conversation between Drew and his guest. Adrenaline made her heartbeat pulse and pound in her ears in a fierce rhythm, like a roofer hammering nails, drowning out the sound of the men's voices.

At the knock, she'd experienced a startling moment of panic where she'd actually considered hiding behind the couch. She'd been certain that the man at the door was Ryan, that he'd already tracked her down, determined to charm or intimidate her into going back with him.

Which she would never do.

She wondered how long this indeterminable fear would follow her around. Would she ever *not* jump when someone knocked on the door?

She was more relieved than she could say when she realized the visit had nothing to do with her, but she felt guilty that it was at Drew's expense—it didn't take a genius to figure out something had gone wrong in his world.

He slammed the door and returned to his chair, a crumpled manila envelope clenched in his fist. His breath came in ragged gasps and his face was an alarming shade of crimson. Stephanie braced for the detonation she was sure was to follow, for the man was clearly a ticking time bomb.

The explosion never came. Drew yanked at the knot in his tie and stretched his neck from side to side, but he didn't yell, or sulk, or throw anything, which is what Ryan did when things didn't go his way.

Instead, Drew quietly reached into his shirt pocket for his reading glasses and removed from the envelope a crisp white set of legal documents. He released a long, unsteady breath as he silently perused the papers, the worry lines on his forehead deepening. When he was finished, he bowed his head and pinched the bridge of his nose. Stephanie thought he might be praying, but she wasn't certain. Probably staving off a headache, as well.

The pressure in the air around her seemed to intensify as her mind thought up a number of scenarios that Drew might be facing. She wanted to reach out to him but wasn't sure how. When she laid a comforting hand on his forearm, his muscles rippled with tension.

"My ex-wife is suing me for full custody of the twins." The statement was matter-of-fact, but his expression was anything but. Agony flashed through his eyes when he spoke of the woman, and Stephanie winced. She could relate to that kind of pain—of having the person you had expected to spend your life with let you down.

But there was more injury than anger in Drew's gaze. Stephanie couldn't claim to be as noble. She despised what Ryan had done to her, and she hated herself even more for having let him, for getting her priorities so mixed up she couldn't see what was happening to her until it was too late.

But for her, at least, what was done was done, and she was moving forward with her life, starting now.

For Drew, however, it looked as if his troubles were just beginning.

He cleared his throat, his lips moving silently as he searched for the right words. "Obviously, I'm pretty desperate to find adequate child care for the twins," he began, leaning his forearms on his elbows and clasping his hands together. "The boys were in day care with a local woman, but she had to move to Chicago to be near her ailing sister. Her leaving left a big gap in Serendipity, especially for me."

"I'm sorry to hear that," she replied, though in truth she wasn't exactly *sorry*. If the woman hadn't left, she wouldn't have a job. "The boys are three years old, right? Do they attend preschool yet?"

He shook his head. "Unfortunately, Serendipity doesn't have a preschool."

"Oh, my," she responded, her surprise showing in her voice. She would have thought that even as tiny a town as Serendipity would have a preschool to help the little ones with learning readiness.

"I know. It's a huge issue, right? I've been in mediation over custody of the children with my ex-wife, Heather, for some time now, and being able to send the twins to a preschool might have worked in my favor. Right now, I have temporary custody. Heather sometimes visits the kids on weekends. Right after the divorce, that was how she wanted it, but now, inexplicably, she's changed her mind."

He sighed. "I hired you in the hopes that she and

the mediators would see how serious I am about taking care of the twins and would grant me primary custody without getting the court involved." He slapped the legal document with the back of his hand. "As you can see, that's not working out so well for me."

He scrubbed his free hand over his scalp, making the short ends of his hair stick up every which direction. "If my ex-wife has it her way, I won't get to see the twins at all, except for maybe supervised visits. She's claiming I'm an unfit father."

"Why did she change her mind? And why would she be so unwilling to share custody?" Granted, Stephanie had just met Drew, but she'd appreciated what she'd seen so far. No one could fake the kind of love shining from Drew's eyes when he was around his boys, or even spoke of them. He appeared to be a patient and tender father. He was even willing to hire a nanny from out of town to make sure the twins were adequately cared for full-time. If that wasn't devotion, Stephanie didn't know what was.

Besides, the boys needed their father in their lives.

"Two years ago, Heather left me and the kids because she didn't like being tied down as a wife and mother. She's a party girl, and always has been. Staying home on Friday nights just didn't suit her."

"Then why does she want custody of the boys now?"

He scoffed and shook his head. "There's the rub. I don't know. She doesn't want to be tied down with the twins, so it only makes sense that I maintain primary custody. I'm guessing she just doesn't want *me* to have them, because she wants to hurt me. I had no idea she felt so much hostility against me."

His voice was raspy with emotion, and his gaze didn't

quite meet hers. "If she wins in court, the twins will be raised by various relatives and an absentee mother. I'm afraid for them. That's why I have to fight."

"Wow." Stephanie didn't even know what else to say. She'd grown up in foster care. She knew firsthand what it meant to be unloved, to be shuffled from house to house with no stability. She couldn't imagine using those two precious boys as pawns in what was essentially a vindictive game.

"According to this summons, I've got a CFI—a Child and Family Investigator—from the court coming to the house sometime in the near future to scope out the family situation. With all your credentials as a nanny for the twins, I can only hope it will help my case."

"It certainly can't hurt. I'll do whatever I can," she vowed.

"I know I have to trust God with my boys. But sometimes I find it hard to put my circumstances in God's hands. Their whole lives may be affected by what happens next."

That, Stephanie thought, was the closest he was going to get to saying he was frightened, both for himself and for his sons. And she couldn't blame him. She'd heard the stories of court cases gone wrong, where children had been hurt and even killed by misinformed decisions from the judges.

Compassion and resolve welled in her throat. She'd only known the twins for an evening, but that didn't lessen her determination. She would help in whatever way she was able. She wasn't going to let anything happen to those boys—or Drew, either, for that matter, if it was in her power to stop it.

She'd been praying for purpose in her life. Maybe

that's why God had sent her here—for a set of darling twins and their handsome, dedicated father.

Being served legal documents had shaken Drew up more than he cared to admit, and he was a little embarrassed that Stephanie had been there to witness his private humiliation. He made a quick decision to mentally shelve his emotions for now, until he had time to consider his next steps.

"I'm sorry," he apologized, suddenly noticing that Stephanie's eyes were darkened with fatigue. "I'm being insensitive. I should have postponed our conversation until tomorrow. You must be exhausted from your trip."

"I am a little tired," she admitted. "It's been a long day."

"Then let's table this discussion for now and pick it up tomorrow morning. I'll see you to your room and get your bags for you so you can settle in for the night. It's nothing fancy—just a furnished room over the garage—but it has its own entranceway so you won't be stumbling over Pop and the twins when you need some privacy."

She smothered a yawn, making Drew feel even guiltier for keeping her from her rest. Studying her face thoughtfully, he realized that her eyes were puffy and shaded by dark circles, as if she hadn't been sleeping well.

He definitely didn't want to push her when she was already exhausted, but he was still curious about her situation. It occurred to him that moving out here to be a nanny for his twins might have been a last resort for her. No one else had answered the advertisement he'd placed, and with good reason. He wasn't offering much in the way of a salary, especially for someone who'd been a successful nanny in a large east coast town. Who would want temporary employment in the middle of nowhere?

Stephanie Cartwright, apparently.

The question was, why?

"Drew!" His father's loud, gruff voice echoed down the hallway. "The boys are waiting on their story."

"Coming," Drew called back. "Give me a second. I'm sorry," he apologized to Stephanie. "Would you mind waiting a few more minutes while I tuck the boys in?"

She chuckled and gestured with her hands. "I see what you mean about your father. Go. I can wait."

"Bring Stephanie with you," the old man hollered, almost as if were eavesdropping on the two of them.

Drew tensed and turned back toward Stephanie. "Do you mind?" he asked with a quirk of his lips. "Pop's not going to stop until he gets his way."

"No problem, really," Stephanie assured him. "I'd love to spend a little more time getting to know the twins, and I'm sure they're anxious to have their daddy tuck them in."

"Probably," he agreed. Their bedtime ritual had become one of Drew's favorite parts of the day, when his two sleepy boys were all quiet and cuddly. Tonight, however, he doubted they were either, what with all the excitement in the household. Getting them to calm down enough to go to sleep might be easier said than done.

Then again, Stephanie was a nanny. Maybe she had some fresh ideas for rustling rowdy preschoolers into bed and under the covers.

"Drew," his father called again. *Impatiently,* in typical Pop fashion. Stephanie might run for the hills yet.

"Yeah, yeah," Drew replied, winking at Stephanie. "What did I tell you?" he concluded in a mock whisper.

She giggled lightly, which erased some of the weariness from her countenance.

He felt her eyes branding into his back all the way down the hall, and unease once again bore down on his shoulders. He couldn't help but be uncomfortable. What was she thinking about?

How he'd just been served? His apparent failure as a father?

He hoped she could see beyond the legalities to his heart. Being a dad was everything to him, and he wanted to keep it that way. Having her on his side would definitely be a positive factor, especially now that this was going to court.

The moment the twins realized Stephanie had entered the room behind him, they squealed and bounced on their beds. In Drew's opinion, it didn't help matters that she jumped right into the fray, laughing along with them and stirring them up to even greater noise and excitement. The idea here was to calm them down enough to go to sleep.

"Settle down, boys," he instructed gently. "It's already past your bedtime. If you guys want me to read you a story, you need to lie down and cover up. Right now, no excuses."

"But, Daddy," Matty whined, rubbing his bright blue eyes with his little fists. "We're not tired yet."

Drew smothered a chuckle as Matty's objection was punctuated with a big yawn. The boys weren't tired—they were overtired.

"We want to stay up and play with Miss Stephie," Jamey protested.

"It's Stephanie," Drew gently corrected, ruffling Jamey's hair with his palm. "And she'll be here when you wake up tomorrow. She's your new nanny. She's here to take care of you."

Stephanie placed a hand on Drew's arm. "My name is hard to pronounce when you're just learning how to speak. Stephie is just fine."

"Steph-eee," Matty said proudly.

"Very good, Matty," Stephanie praised, causing Matty to straighten his shoulders and sit an inch taller.

Okay, that was weird—or incredible, depending on how he looked at it. She'd only spent a few minutes with the boys, and she already knew Matty from Jamey—and quite confidently, at that. How had she known which twin she was addressing?

He wasn't able to ask how she'd done it, for at that moment the boys launched off their beds onto the floor and began dancing around Stephanie.

"Boys," Drew warned, trying to sound stern. "Bedtime. I'm not going to say it again."

"Grouch," his father grumbled under his breath. Drew and Stephanie exchanged a look.

What did I tell you?

Drew didn't speak the words aloud, but he was pretty sure Stephanie correctly read his expression. Pop was going to be interesting at his best and exasperating at his worst.

Her lips twitched. He thought she might be smothering a laugh. At least she was good-natured about it.

The twins groaned in unison at his spoilsport pronouncement, but they both returned to their beds and crawled underneath the covers. He hated to be the bad guy, but someone had to take control here.

Drew set a chair between the twins' beds and pulled out the Bible storybook they were currently reading together. The book included little finger puppets which Drew manipulated as he told the stories, delighting the boys with his silly moves and goofy voices. At the very least, it usually captured their attention enough to settle them down; but tonight, to his chagrin, their primary focus seemed to be on Stephanie.

"Stephie do it," Jamey announced.

"Yeah," Matty agreed. "Let Miss Steph-eee read to us."

"What a good idea," his father added in a coarse voice. "Ladies first, and all that."

Stephanie's eyes widened at the prospect. She hesitated and cast Drew an enquiring look—ready to step in and read, but not willing to step on his toes.

It was kind of her to think of him, even though he was clearly outnumbered. He had mixed feelings about relinquishing his nightly reading to Stephanie, even once. This was his special time with the twins, their bonding time.

But this was about what was best for the boys.

Overpowering love for his sons billowed up his chest until he thought he might burst from it. By God's grace, the twins had kept him anchored in this world when he might otherwise have drifted away. They filled his life with purpose.

He turned his face so Stephanie and the twins couldn't see what he was feeling as he faced the truth. He was in no mental condition to read out loud, and he didn't want the boys picking up on his concern. Stephanie was their new nanny. It would be good for her to start bonding with Matty and Jamey as soon as possible.

Who knew when that case worker was going to visit? His shoulders tensed and sent sharp jabs into his neck just thinking about it. The relationship between Stephanie and the boys had to look natural, without pretense.

Which actually made it pretense. He felt mortified even to think that way.

In any case, the boys were clearly anxious to enjoy her interpretation of the present story, perhaps even with the finger puppets, if she was willing.

"I guess it would be all right for Miss Stephanie to read to you," he conceded, surrendering both the chair and the book to her.

"Okay," she agreed, her dark eyes shining and a sweet smile on her face. "But only this one time. You like it best when your daddy reads to you, right?"

Both boys nodded in response to her animated question and Drew shook his head in amazement. Stephanie had somehow managed to put an enthusiastic spin on something that would otherwise have been uncomfortable and demoralizing for him.

It was almost as if she'd been able to read his thoughts and empathize with his feelings, which was an uncomfortable notion. The last thing he needed right now was a woman in his head.

"So, where are we?" Stephanie asked brightly.

Not you. *We.*

The way she instantly and effortlessly integrated herself into the family was unsettling, to say the least.

"Uh, Noah, I think," he answered, smothering the catch in his voice by feigning a cough.

Stephanie might not have noticed his forced enthusiasm, but his father raised a suspicious eyebrow. Drew pretended not to notice.

He sat on the edge of Jamey's bed and pulled the little guy into his lap, and then urged Matty to come cuddle with him, as well. Maybe this wouldn't be so bad, after all, being able to sit here with the boys in his arms.

"A long, long time ago, there was a man named Noah. God told him he had to build an ark—that's a big boat," Stephanie began, holding the book so everyone could see it.

Drew had to admit Stephanie was a good storyteller. Even his father was enthralled, hobbling over and perching on the edge of Jamey's bed next to Drew so he could watch the story in action.

Stephanie was vivacious and animated and brought the story to life with the little finger puppets. If he was being honest, she was a far better storyteller than he. And this was clearly not her first time using finger puppets. She was a natural.

She must have often read books to the children she cared for in New Jersey, or maybe even for a library story time. He could see her doing that, captivating other little children with her storytelling as much as she was with his own kids right now.

He really didn't know that much about her, beyond what he'd read in her resume. There were a lot of blank spots in her history, more than words on paper would be able to convey. He'd have to remedy that if she was going to stay.

Wait.

What was with the *if*?

Of course she was going to stay. He had invited her. *Hired* her. No room for second thoughts now.

With effort, Drew turned his attention back to the story. Stephanie had given each boy one of the finger puppets and was drawing both of them into the action, retelling the story she'd just read to them with their own words and their own character voices.

Why hadn't he ever thought of that? The kids would retain the Biblical account much better if they were actively involved.

That sealed it—Stephanie was definitely going to be good for the boys. Maybe it was good that he *had* hired a nanny, even if it was only temporary, until the school term ended and he could be home with the boys for the summer, or at least until he'd had that court hearing at the end of May.

The twins retold the story several times, and then Stephanie tucked the puppets away and replaced the book on the bookshelf. All of the adults gathered around and listened to the boys recite their prayers as Drew tucked them in, pulling their comforters up under their chins and kissing each of the boys on the forehead.

Stephanie's face turned a pretty shade of pink when Matty named her specifically and asked God to bless her. Drew closed his eyes and prayed right along with his sons. Their family, the nanny included, needed all the prayers they could get.

Afterward, he retrieved Stephanie's bags from the rental car and made sure she was comfortable in the room above the garage. Before becoming Stephanie's quarters, the room had been his study, where he often went to read or grade papers after the boys were asleep. But when he'd decided the best thing for his family was a full-time, live-in nanny, giving her the room over the garage only made sense. He'd removed a file cabinet, relocated a couple of bookshelves and made the addition of a queen-size bed and a dresser. Voilà—comfortable living quarters.

Of course, that was from his perspective—which even he had to admit was unembellished and completely male. He had no idea what Stephanie would think of the room. He didn't know her well enough to guess, and he didn't know what kind of conditions she'd come from, what she might have to compare it with.

No doubt she'd experienced more opulence than he could ever afford. After all, her last position was for a wealthy political household in New Jersey. Did her parents have money? What kind of living had she made as a nanny? How different were city accommodations versus what he could offer her in Serendipity?

He scoffed and shook his head at his own extraneous thoughts. He was going to short-circuit himself worrying about the dozens of unanswered questions whisking around in his brain, and he had enough to be anxious about already.

Like Heather, and being served with legal papers.

Drew took a much-needed breath of fresh air on the back porch. Quincy needed his nighttime outing, anyway, so Drew figured he might as well take a few minutes to see if he could get his whirling mind to quiet down a little, but he ended up ruminating on how his life had come to this point.

His ex-wife had taken his heart and trampled on it. He'd tried to save his marriage, even seeing a counselor, but he couldn't do it alone. All his prayers and actions had been for nothing. Heather didn't want to be a wife. She'd balked at the notion of being tied down to house and home.

To his surprise and dismay, Heather hadn't even wanted to see the boys, except for the occasional weekend. And even when she'd planned to spend time with them, she'd often been late. Once she hadn't bothered to show up at all, and Drew had been left with two disappointed three-year-olds to console.

Now she suddenly wanted full custody? He'd never felt so powerless. Didn't the courts usually side with the mother?

What could he do that he wasn't already doing? Jamey and Matty were in a difficult and possibly dangerous situation, since he suspected Heather would neglect them even if she won custody, leaving them with their maternal grandparents at best, or any one of her string of boyfriends at worst. And there was nothing he could do to stop the chain of events that was unfolding.

Except the fact that he'd hired Stephanie. He prayed that having a nanny for the boys would make a difference at the court hearing. He didn't know how else to show something as intangible as love and devotion.

Shivering, he folded his arms and sighed. It wasn't the cold night air getting to him, but rather the chill inside his chest.

There was one thing he could do. On his own, he was bare and vulnerable. But he wasn't on his own. God in His Providence would take care of the twins. He had to believe that. God was in control of his future, and his sons' well-being. His children were protected in the palm of the Master's hand.

Drew bowed his head and thanked God for His many blessings. He had health and a home, and bounteous food on the table. He had family—his father, for all his gruffness, and his precious twins.

And he had Stephanie, the woman who might make

the difference between his being able to secure custody of his twins or not.

God bless them all.

Chapter Three

Why did the house smell like bacon?

Drew awoke to the sizzling smell of a hot breakfast and his stomach immediately growled in protest. He hadn't had a real, home-cooked breakfast since...

Well, it had been a long time.

He shrugged on jeans and a T-shirt, not bothering to check his appearance in the mirror. His curiosity about what was happening in the kitchen trumped the urge to take extra time to spruce up before presenting himself to the world—or rather, to Stephanie.

Drew walked bare-footed into the kitchen, where he discovered Stephanie at the stove flipping pancakes, while Pop and the twins waited impatiently at the table, forks in their hands and expectant looks on their faces. Someone had set a basket of fresh strawberries on the table and both of the boys sported telltale red-stained faces.

"Good morning, Drew," Stephanie greeted as he entered the room and tousled his twins' hair.

"Morning," he echoed absently as he tried to take in the full extent of what was happening.

Stephanie was dressed in gray sweatpants and a loose-fitting pink T-shirt and had her sun-gold hair swept back in a ponytail. Even in casual clothing, she was strikingly beautiful, especially because she appeared at ease and in her element with giggling children in the room.

At home. In his house.

In the week since she'd arrived to supervise his sons, the whole house seemed to be more orderly and less stressful. She was paradoxically full of energy and yet able to create a calm, tranquil atmosphere in the house when need be. The boys loved her, and he had no qualms about having the twins stay in her care while he taught at the elementary school. He might not have known Stephanie for long, but he trusted her.

She'd apparently scoped out his pantry at some point during the week. Not only had she found all the ingredients to make breakfast, but she was wearing his *Don't Mind the Fire: Everything is Under Control* apron that he used when he grilled outside.

"Pull up a seat," Stephanie continued cheerfully. "Your pancakes are almost ready. I hope you're hungry. I made a lot of them." Her voice was as bright as sunrise on a spring day, which only served to rattle Drew's nerves even more. Ugh. He wasn't a morning person on the best of days, and this was not his best day.

"Look, Daddy. It's a kitty." Matty pointed to his plate. Sure enough, there was a pancake shaped in the form of the little boy's favorite animal.

"Really cool, buddy," he said. Fairly creative, he had to admit. Breakfast art. "I don't think I've ever seen an animal pancake before."

"Me, too. Me, too. Stephie made it," Jamey informed

him, pumping his little arms in excitement and pointing at his own plate. "I got a mouse."

Stephanie's sparkling brown eyes met Drew's as she chuckled and glanced over her shoulder. "I gave it my best try, anyway. A kitty's tail is a little bit more difficult than mouse ears, and I'm not an artist on my best day."

"You don't hear anyone complaining," his pop said, in an unusually chipper voice. Stephanie's presence had seemed even to have worked on the grumpy old man.

Drew directed his gaze to his father's plate, amusedly wondering if Stephanie had made Pop an animal pancake. Like maybe a porcupine. But he seemed to be happy devouring his silver-dollar half-stack.

"What is all this?" he asked, wondering if he sounded as disconcerted as he felt. It was as if he was a modern-day man stepping into a 1950s appliance advertisement.

Fortunately, Stephanie didn't seem to notice his agitation. She just smiled and gestured to the skillets on the burners of the stove.

"It's just what it looks like. The twins said they were hungry for breakfast, and I thought I might as well cook for everybody. It's not any harder to whip up a meal for the whole family than it is just for the boys. I hope you don't mind. I asked your father if it would be okay and he said it would be fine."

He shrugged and shook his head. "No problem."

Truthfully, he didn't know how he felt about Stephanie taking over the kitchen. She fit into his family like fingers in a glove, and he wasn't sure he was comfortable with that. It was too cozy. Too personal.

Like the sweet family gatherings he'd always hoped for and pictured in his mind but had never quite had. Reality was blinding. And now Stephanie was bridging that gap with her smile and a batch of pancakes. With what appeared to be effortless grace, she flowed into the current of their family, seamlessly blending with them as if she'd been there all along.

"I take requests," she joked, waving her spatula around like a drum major marking time with a baton. "No promises, but I'll give it my best shot. An animal? Your favorite sport?"

"Plain pancakes are fine. What Pop's got on his plate looks great." He felt awkward being waited on in his own kitchen by a woman he'd invited to his house. She wasn't exactly his guest, but he hadn't hired her to cook and clean, either. He hoped she knew that.

"A full stack for you," she amended. "You're still a growing boy."

"I'm going to be, if I start eating a full-size breakfast every day."

"It's important to start the morning with a good, nutritious meal, don't you think? It gives you energy and sets the tone for the day."

Stephanie was certainly setting the tone *this* morning. Clear skies, sunny and warm. What a counterbalance to Drew's current partly-cloudy-with-a-chance-of-rain attitude.

"If we're talking about needing some energy, I'm going to require a solid jolt of caffeine," Drew added, smothering a yawn.

"I think we can include a cup of coffee or two with your meal, as long as you eat everything else on your plate and drink a tall glass of orange juice." She set a steaming mug of coffee before him and he took a long, fortifying sip.

"Because it's nutritious," Drew repeated, mimicking Stephanie without mocking her.

She slid him a smile that affected him more than he would have liked.

"Tritious," Jamey repeated, shoving a large strawberry toward Drew's mouth.

"That's right, Jamey," Stephanie encouraged, sounding just as proud of the young boy as Drew was, even though she had no vested interest in his children beyond being their nanny.

Drew barely dodged the squished-up fruit Jamey was aiming at his face and regarded the boy thoughtfully. Jamey was his shy one. It took a while for the boy to open up, and he didn't usually speak around people that he didn't know, especially adults.

But Stephanie was different. Jamey already trusted her, and Drew had to admit, if only to himself, that he could see why. She already knew which twin was which and was able to address each of them by name. Most people couldn't tell the boys apart, even after they'd been together for a while.

And her ease with the boys wasn't the only conquest she'd made. She'd even won over his ornery, cantankerous father, which was no easy feat.

"*New*-tri-shush," Matty corrected, even though the word was new to him.

Stephanie set a plate piled high with pancakes, bacon and eggs in front of Drew. For some reason seeing this well-rounded meal right in front of him convicted him of his own lapse in parental aptitude.

Nutrition hadn't exactly been the word of the day where Drew and the kids were concerned, especially recently. An image of the blueberry toaster pastries and quickly peeled bananas that he usually served on busy school-day mornings flashed through his head, followed by a gut-tightening wave of guilt.

When had convenience food become the extent of their morning routine?

He had to hand it to Stephanie—this was the first really *nutritious* breakfast the twins had had in ages. He, too, for that matter. Pancakes, scrambled eggs, crispy bacon and a large pitcher of orange juice. His mouth was watering already.

"Nice to have a woman in the house," his father commented gruffly, loud enough for the neighbors in the next county to hear. He grunted and shoved another large forkful of eggs into his mouth. "Yes, ma'am, this is the bee's knees."

"Why, thank you, Frank." Grinning, she flipped the last pancake onto a plate. "I'm certainly outnumbered here, guys to girls. Even Quincy is a boy." She set the platter of remaining pancakes in the middle of the circular oak table and tickled Matty on the ear.

The boy squealed and wiggled in his chair.

"Me, too! Me, too!" Jamey insisted. Those seemed to be his favorite two words lately.

Stephanie chuckled and moved around the table, leaning over Drew's shoulder so she could tickle both boys at once. "It's a good thing I have two hands."

Drew closed his eyes, trying not to breathe, because if he did, the warm, spicy fragrance of her perfume was going to get to him. He'd always been a sucker for orchids and jasmine. Maybe it was the appeal of the foreign scent to his down-home-country nose.

Whatever it was, he didn't need the distraction, and he was relieved when she moved away and went back to the stove to remove the last few pieces of bacon she'd been frying.

"How do you know which boy is which?" he asked, desperately trying to stay cool and collected, at least on the outside. "Most people have difficulty telling the twins apart. Did Pop help you figure it out?"

"Didn't need to," his father replied, before Stephanie could say a word. "She had it right from the get-go."

"I've never had a problem with twins," she answered, leaning her hip against the counter. "Matty has a little dimple on his chin," she said, gesturing toward the boy in question, "and Jamey here has just the hint of a cowlick on his forehead." She leaned forward and ruffled Jamey's hair.

"Incredible," Drew murmured under his breath. He was impressed. Stephanie certainly had a keen eye for children. *His children.*

"So for lunch, I was thinking we could take in a burger at Cup O' Jo as a special treat to the boys."

In truth, this wasn't so much about the boys. This was about getting over the hurdle of Stephanie meeting Jo Murphy, who owned the café. His strategy was to get to Jo first and try to convince her *not* to play matchmaker.

Which probably wouldn't work, but he had to try, anyway.

"Cup O' Jo?" Stephanie queried. "Is that a coffee house?"

Drew chuckled. "It's *the* coffee house. You've never had coffee until you've tried a Cup O' Jo." He chuckled at his own joke. "They have hot coffee, iced-coffee and everything in between."

Not that he'd had many fancy gourmet coffees in his lifetime to compare it to. He wasn't very adventurous when it came to trying new foods and drinks. He preferred the tried and true. Steak and potatoes. Black and bold. It suited him.

"My mouth is watering already," Stephanie assured him. "Caramel frappés are my favorite."

"And Jo's niece-in-law Phoebe makes the best cherry pie in Texas," his father added, smacking his lips. "Maybe in the whole U.S. of A. We've got us a world-class pastry chef right here in Serendipity."

For once, his father wasn't exaggerating. Phoebe really *was* a world-class pastry chef. How she'd ended up in Serendipity and married to Jo's nephew Chance was beyond Drew's comprehension.

Strangers seldom came to the small town, and even more infrequently stayed. Family roots in Serendipity grew as long and thick as an old cottonwood tree. Few were pulled up, and even fewer were planted. As in Stephanie's case, visitors usually had a specific reason for visiting and left soon afterward.

"It's Saturday, so we aren't going to see the usual lunch crowd," he continued. "But there's still bound to be a few regulars catching a meal there. And, of course, you'll meet many of the town folk at church tomorrow."

Her eyebrows rose, but she didn't say a word.

He hesitated and cleared his throat, realizing he hadn't even asked her about her religious preferences before blurting out that last statement. Now he'd put her on the spot.

"Er—I mean, if you'd like to go to church, that is. I didn't mean to presume. What I intended to say was that most of our neighbors attend services on Sunday. It would be a good chance for you to meet everyone, and for people to get to know you, as well."

"Of course," Stephanie agreed, with a smile that put him at ease and stirred him up at the same time. "I'd like to go with you tomorrow. Thank you for asking."

Feeling more on edge than she cared to admit, Stephanie reached for the nearest breakfast plates, all of which were satisfyingly empty, and began stacking them into a sink full of warm, soapy water. The Spencer family seemed to have liked the meal as much as she'd enjoyed cooking it.

The one thing she'd been worried about was how Drew would react to her taking over his kitchen, but so far he hadn't said anything negative about it. In fact, he was as vocal as Frank and the twins in praising her cooking skills and appreciating her efforts.

She didn't even want to think about how things might have gone if for some reason Drew had taken offense to her actions, if he'd become angry at her poking around his pantry without her asking him first.

She'd always been that way—caring what other people thought of her, wanting to keep the peace. Her desire to please others came from a deep-rooted need in her childhood. Foster children—especially older ones— were easily overlooked, even in the best-meaning of families. Many of her peers in the juvenile system had acted out as a way to get attention—taken drugs, joined gangs, got in fights, committed crimes.

Stephanie had taken another route to getting noticed—trying to please everyone all the time. Getting straight A's in high school when she was really a B student at heart. Keeping her bedroom immaculate when her nature was to be more cluttered and disorganized.

Being the perfect girlfriend long after all of the signs pointed to a disaster-ridden relationship.

What had she been thinking? It was thoroughly humiliating, that she'd been so desperate for a family of her own that she'd only seen Ryan's charm and the wealth. She'd convinced herself to overlook the glaring inconsistencies in Ryan's words versus his actions, blinded herself to who he really was just because he was a handsome, rich man who could have his choice of women.

He'd chosen her, and she'd thought it meant something. She thought he would propose to her. She thought they were in love, so she'd made excuses for him when he lashed out in anger, when he bruised her body as well as her pride.

But she was a victim no longer. Ryan couldn't hurt her anymore. She just had to ignore the cloud of trepidation still hanging over her head until it went away on its own.

"I didn't hire you to cook and clean for us, you know." Drew's warm voice came from behind her, disturbingly close to her left ear, and she jumped in surprise. "You're a nanny, not a maid."

"Oh, that's quite all right," Stephanie assured him. "I don't mind at all. I enjoy doing a few tasks around the house while I work. I can keep a steady eye on the boys and tidy up a bit at the same time. Multitasking is my specialty."

"Then let me help you, at least," he said, slipping in next to her by the sink and taking the plate she was rinsing out of her hands. "You gather the dishes from the table, and I'll rinse them and stack them in the dishwasher."

"Sounds like a plan." She was glad to be able to

move away from him to scoop the silverware from the table. Everything about Drew oozed masculinity, from the strength of his hands to the way his biceps pulled against the sleeve of his T-shirt. Her shoulder would fit right under his, were he to reach out to her. When he'd stepped up next to her, she'd immediately inhaled his brisk scent—an intoxicating combination of soap and man.

How could she even notice Drew that way? She *definitely* didn't want to go there. She was not in any big hurry to get her heart broken again. Besides, Drew was her employer.

In her head, it was easy to tick reason after reason why she shouldn't see him that way, but that didn't stop the awareness flowing through her when he stood at her side.

She supposed it proved she was still alive, at least. There was a time after her breakup with Ryan where she'd seriously wondered if she would survive. And now she was here, with a job and sustenance and a place to lay her head. God was good.

"You had a funny look on your face when I first opened the door last week," Drew said conversationally. "What were you thinking—apart from wondering if my dog was going to eat you, that is?"

She drew in a surprised breath. "You mean, about you? Honestly? I didn't expect you to be a…well, a cowboy, for lack of a better term."

"Ha!" he chortled. "And I didn't expect you to be…" His face turned an odd crimson color and his lips curved first into a frown and then into a grim line. "Well, it doesn't really matter what I thought. Do you like baseball?"

Now *that* was an abrupt change in conversation if she'd ever heard one.

What *had* he thought of her? Somehow she didn't think she was going to find out any time soon.

"That depends," she answered, tilting her head up to meet his gaze. "Watching baseball or playing it?"

He arched an eyebrow. "Both, I suppose."

"I'm not big on watching baseball on television, although I don't mind catching a game if someone else is watching it. I've seen a few Yankees games live. That was fun. I especially liked the hot dogs."

"That's the twins' favorite part of live baseball, too," Drew said with a chuckle.

"See? We have a lot in common already."

"And playing? How are you at hitting a curve ball?"

That, Stephanie thought, depended entirely on what kind of curve ball was being thrown. The ones life had been pitching her lately had been beaning her in the head. But she supposed he was asking about the real kind, the one with a literal ball. "If you want to challenge me to play, I'm down with it—and I'll warn you right now, I'm the woman to beat."

"Intriguing. I'm going to put your words to the test, you know. The twins are on a T-ball team, and they'll want you to practice with them. They'll probably want you to come cheer them on at their games, too."

"I would love to," Stephanie answered sincerely. In her experience, being a nanny and being a cheerleader often went hand in hand. Anything she could do to instill in her charges the self-esteem she lacked as a child was worthwhile in her book.

"Most Saturdays I take them out to practice in the

park," Drew continued. "I'm not sure we'll get to it today, but maybe next weekend we can bat a few balls."

At the word *park,* Quincy whined and pawed at Drew's leg. He laughed and scratched the dog behind his ears. "You can play, too, Quincy."

She smirked. "Your dog plays baseball?"

"He makes a formidable outfielder. He'll retrieve the baseball no matter where it goes and bring it back to us. That way we don't have to run around and pick them up."

"I can't wait to see it."

Chapter Four

Drew leaned back in his chair, folded his arms and watched the new nanny sharing lunch with his children. He'd already wolfed down his own burger and was sitting with an empty plate in front of him.

He'd never expected that there would ever be a time in his life where it would be in his best interest to hire someone out of the family to care for his kids. Not in Serendipity. It just wasn't done that way here—not to mention he'd thought he'd be a married man for the rest of his life and have a wife at his side to help care for the children. But things being what they were, he had to admit he was impressed with Stephanie, even if he'd had to dip into his meager retirement account to pay for her.

Anything to keep his kids.

Boisterous, red-headed Jo Murphy, the owner of the café, sashayed up to them with refills on all their drinks. As usual, she was right on top of things, anticipating needs and meeting them before a word could be spoken.

"You almost spilled my coffee," his father complained as Jo refilled his cup.

"Oh, hush, you," Jo said, swatting at him with her

free hand. "I did not, and you know it. I've poured more cups of coffee than you've taken naps," she teased merrily, "and that's saying something."

Both of them shared a laugh, their gazes locked on each other. Drew wanted to roll his eyes. It was always like this with his father and Jo.

As far as he was concerned, they ought to just admit they had feelings for each other and tie the knot, but he doubted that would ever happen. They had this odd, mutual sparring war going on between them, but it was comfortable, and he supposed it was okay for them to keep it that way.

Stephanie was looking at the old couple speculatively. Drew was sure she could see what was obviously going on. The secretive smile on her face gave her away.

After a moment she turned her attention back to the boys. Matty and Jamey were definitely benefiting from her attention. She'd convinced them to eat sliced apples with their burgers instead of their usual French fries, simply by indicating that that was what she was ordering, too. Even though she'd only recently come into the boys' lives, they appeared anxious to emulate and impress her.

"Eat your hamburger, sweetie," Stephanie encouraged Matty, who, as usual, was mostly just pushing his food around on his plate and turning his sandwich into a big, sloppy mess.

To Drew's surprise, Matty did as he was told.

The first time. No counting down. No scolding.

Stephanie simply spoke and Matty listened. She seemed to have an instinctive understanding of how to get his sons to cooperate.

Or, to be more precise, Matty *half* cooperated. He

took the burger part of the hamburger and shoved the whole thing into his mouth.

Stephanie laughed. "Not all at once, sweetheart. You don't want to choke on it."

"You really have a way with children." His compliment was sincere and for once he didn't trip over his tongue.

"You ought to see me with babies," she responded glibly, and then blanched, her eyes widening. "I—I mean, wh-what I meant to say is that I've had a lot of experience with young children," she stammered. "Most of it isn't on my resume."

"Firstborn of a large family?" Drew guessed, pushing aside his plate so he could rest his arms on the table.

He'd been an only child himself, so he had been clueless about how to care for babies when the twins had come along. It had all been trial and error with him, from the bottles to the diapers.

"Families, plural," Stephanie corrected, pressing her lips together. "I was a foster child, a genuine product of the system." She glanced at the boys to make sure they were busy eating and not listening to the adult conversation. "I was in six foster homes before I hit my eighteenth birthday."

"I'm sorry." He didn't know what else to say. It had obviously taken its toll on her, and he guessed her foster years hadn't been good ones.

"No need. I managed all right. At first I resented it when I got stuck babysitting the little kids in the family I was staying with, but somewhere along the way I realized I actually *liked* taking care of children. I studied hard in high school and worked as a nanny while I pursued my bachelor's degree in early childhood education." She took a breath, trying to smile, though it didn't reach her eyes. "And there you have my entire life in a nutshell."

He cocked his head and raised an eyebrow. "Somehow, I don't think that's all there is to the story. I imagine there is much about you I have yet to learn."

As soon as he said the words he knew they hadn't come out the least bit like how an employer should talk to an employee. He'd been trying to make her feel better, and he was being borderline flirtatious. Guessing from the attractive pink shade slashed across her cheeks, she'd thought the same thing.

In Drew's mind, that left Stephanie with two options. Flirt back, or shut him down.

Her gaze dropped to the table and the crimson staining her cheeks phased into a cherry red. "Nothing I want to talk about. Not yet."

Remorse hit him hard and fast. He hadn't meant to put her on the spot. He'd only been joking. Or, at least, half joking. He really did want to get to know her better.

What was she hiding? Was it cause for concern that a woman with her credentials and background would apply for a relatively low-paying position in a small town in the middle of nowhere?

He was sure she had her reasons, but they were none of his business. He decided right then and there that he was going to keep his curiosity to himself—and try not to put his foot in his mouth again.

None of this was permanent. It was just a means to an end. Stephanie was a godsend, and his lawyer seemed to think her presence might mean the difference between him being able to keep custody of his boys or them going to live with their unstable mother.

"Okay, boys," Stephanie said brightly, as if nothing were wrong and he hadn't just stuck his nose where it didn't belong. She laid a hand on Jamey's shoulder. "I don't know about you, but I'm stuffed. What do you say we get up and walk off some of the delicious food we ate?"

She was referring to returning home on foot, just as they'd gotten there. Serendipity was such a small town that it only had one main street with a three-way intersection at the middle worthy only of a stop sign. There wasn't a single stop light in all of the town.

The Spencers lived close enough to make the trek into town on foot, even the preschoolers. Drew walked to work most days, unless the weather was particularly hot or cold.

Three women a little younger than Drew entered the café, chattering and giggling loudly amongst themselves. He'd gone to high school with these ladies, and they were some of the friendliest people he'd ever known. They'd be thrilled to meet Stephanie, and he hoped she might cultivate some friendships in town, as well.

He would have called the ladies over to introduce them to Stephanie, but he knew he needn't bother. They would approach just as soon as they'd seen that there was a visitor in town, without him having to do anything special to attract their attention.

And he was right. Within moments of entering the café, Samantha Howell, whose parents owned the local grocery, glanced in their direction and her eyes lit up with interest.

"A diet cola for me," she called back over her shoulder as she made a beeline for the new figure in town. Drew smothered a grin. He didn't know who, exactly, was going to do the ordering, because as soon as the other ladies—Alexis Granger and Mary Travis—saw where Samantha was heading, they forgot about their drinks and followed their friend to Drew's table.

"Hey, Spence," Samantha greeted warmly. "You didn't mention any relatives coming to town to visit."

Ha! He grinned despite himself. Samantha was fishing—and none too subtly, either. He found it amusing just to let them dangle for a moment, even if he was appalled by the direction in which the conversation was obviously headed. Because as soon as they knew Stephanie wasn't a relative....

"Sam, Alexis, Mary," he said, pointing to each woman in turn. "Meet Stephanie Cartwright. She's the twins' new nanny. She only arrived in town about a week ago."

"O-o-oh," Alexis purred, lengthening the syllable. "And how did we not hear about this? Where are you staying, Stephanie?"

"With Drew," she replied with a friendly smile. "I'm watching the twins full-time, and I've taken up residence at his house."

Drew nearly cringed when he saw the spark of interest in his friends' eyes. They didn't say it aloud—for a change—but he knew exactly what they were thinking.

"In an apartment above my garage," he jumped in, amending Stephanie's statement, not that it would do any good now that certain ideas had been planted in the women's heads.

Small town. Beautiful woman. Single dad. They could connect the dots, even if the picture they created was completely off the mark.

Now it was *his* face turning red.

"I didn't even know you had an apartment over your garage," Alexis commented. "How many times have I been to your house now? And I had no clue."

"It was my study," Drew explained, exasperated. "And it's just temporary," he felt inclined to add. "To help my boys make a smooth transition, you know?"

He didn't have to say what kind of transition they were making. Everyone in town knew of the demise of his marriage.

And he didn't mention the Child and Family Services Investigator or the court date. His business was his business. He sometimes spoke to Jo Murphy, who was like a mother to him, but otherwise he preferred to keep his private life to himself. Jo was ordinarily the root of the gossip tree, but she also knew when to keep silent.

The women chatting at his table? Not so much.

Affectionately known about town as the Little Chicks, they would have the news of Stephanie's arrival spread throughout the town before the day was done. Which was both good and bad.

Good, in that Stephanie would likely be approached by many curious friends and neighbors at church tomorrow, her Christian brothers and sisters who would be there to support her if she needed it.

Bad, because now it was highly likely folks were going to get the wrong impression before even meeting her. The young ladies meant well and they were genuine in their friendship, but they hadn't earned their high school moniker Little Chicks for nothing. In this instance, their "cheeping" would be heard loud and clear from one end of the town to the other. Drew doubted it would take as much as a whole day for the news to spread about Stephanie's arrival.

Which meant going to church might turn out to be diving into a feeding frenzy, with Stephanie as the bait. People would not only want to meet Stephanie, but they would want to see her with Drew—to get the *real* story on why she was in town. Everyone would have a theory, and some of them wouldn't be pretty.

He shouldn't have expected any less. His ex-wife, Heather, had grown up in Serendipity. She and Drew had attended school together, although she'd been much more popular than he'd ever been. He was studious and academic, while in high school she had been the tri-county rodeo princess four years running.

People remembered her, and they remembered Drew's tumultuous relationship with her. A few even knew the truth about why the marriage had ended. But for those who didn't, he wasn't ready to besmirch her name with the gritty details of their breakup, even if she deserved it.

He doubted this hiring-a-nanny-from-out-of-town thing was going to slide through, however. It was just a little too out of the ordinary. People in Serendipity looked out after their own, and Heather had been one of their own, even though she'd moved away from the town after the divorce.

Drew was a third-generation Serendipity native. To hire Stephanie was like waving a red flag to tell everyone that something was out of sorts.

"They seemed nice," Stephanie commented as Alexis, Samantha and Mary picked up their diet colas and went on their way.

"That's a polite way of saying it. They're very—unreserved. Probably the most forward and social of the folks you'll encounter here, though most everyone is friendly to a fault. We affectionately refer to them as the Little Chicks."

"Because?" Golden eyebrows arched over her warm, brown eyes. Their gazes met, and his breath hitched tight in his throat.

Drew coughed into his hand to dislodge the uncomfortable feeling, but it stubbornly remained. "When they get together, they become so animated it starts to sound like chirping. The football team came up with that moniker for them in high school, and to their misfortune, it just stuck. Permanently."

"Hmm," Stephanie replied thoughtfully, her gaze seeking the door where the ladies had just left. "Well, as long as they don't mind, I guess."

Drew was taken aback by the comment. He sat back in the booth and rubbed his chin pensively.

"Honestly, I hadn't thought about it that way," he admitted with a rueful shrug, feeling a little callous that the thought *hadn't* ever crossed his mind. "But they're all good with it, at least as far as I know. They got a lot of attention in high school being the giggly girls they were, and the three of them are best friends to this day, so something good must have come out of it."

Stephanie's gaze dropped to her plate. She picked up an apple slice and bit the end off of it.

"In high school, I was the studious girl with few real friends, the one who often sat alone at the lunch table and actually did her algebra homework."

Drew couldn't believe that, not for a second. It wasn't just that she was beautiful, although there was certainly that, high school being the fickle place that it was. Had she been an ugly duckling who'd later developed into a swan?

Even if that were true, there was so much more to Stephanie than her looks, so much she had to offer. She was beautiful on the inside, as well as the outside. She was generous, and warm and caring. She was a little shy, maybe, but he couldn't imagine that friends wouldn't flock to her.

She offered him a weak smile and shrugged.

"Be careful, boys," she said, laying a gentle hand on Matty's shoulder.

Jamey and Matty had taken out their little Matchbox cars and were making roads between their plates and glasses, complete with the sounds of racing and swerving.

"Mind Stephanie," he agreed. "You don't want to accidentally spill your milk."

Stephanie stacked the plates and arranged the silverware and the glasses for easy pickup. "The service here is exceptional. We never had to ask for a refill or an extra condiment or anything. Jo anticipated our every need."

Drew's lips curved upward. "Small town."

She leaned forward and caught his eye. "During the time we've been in the restaurant, Jo has greeted every single person in the room by name."

Drew chuckled. "That's not all she knows—she's into everybody's business—in great detail. And she's not afraid to ask customers about their personal lives. But she's the most kindhearted person in the world and she is like a second mother to much of the town."

Stephanie reached for her purse and laid a generous tip on the table.

Drew protested with a shake of his head, but Stephanie insisted. "You paid for the meal. Leaving the tip is the least I can do."

It wasn't as if this was a date. The furthest thing from it, in fact. He flexed his fists and breathed deeply.

Call him old-fashioned, but it still grated against his consciousness to let a woman pay for anything when he was out for a meal with her. Stephanie was a strong, independent woman, and he respected that. But still. It might be his male pride flaring, but Stephanie was a lady and he was going to treat her like one.

She paused, almost as if she suspected he would protest.

When he didn't, she smiled. "Are we good?"

He shrugged and nodded briefly. "Sure. We're good."

But when Stephanie turned to herd the children to the washroom to clean up, he swiped the tip from the table and returned it to the pocket of her purse, replacing it with his own money.

A man had to live up to his standards, after all.

Stephanie was slightly nervous and very excited about going to services at a church where she didn't know anyone.

For one thing, although she considered herself a Christian, she had hardly ever been inside a church, much less attended a church service—at least in the traditional sense. She'd been to a few weddings and funerals, but that was the extent of it.

At first it was because her foster family wouldn't allow her to get away. She'd only been to camp meetings with her friends during the summer break.

She'd accepted Christ at one of their altar calls, but had never followed up the way she should have. She got caught up in college and Ryan, and…well, if she was being honest, there *weren't* any good excuses for why she hadn't joined a church once she had turned eighteen and was out on her own.

She just hadn't.

She was curious about what a small-town church service was like. She pictured it being cozy and welcoming, rather than closed and cliquish. The people she'd met in Serendipity so far had been gracious and friendly.

But even so, Drew had built it up to the point where it was an enormous hurdle in her mind. The idea of meeting practically an entire town all at once was a little intimidating, especially for her. She wasn't the most outgoing person in the world. She was a natural with kids, but adults, not so much. That Drew would be at her side reassured her a little, but she was still nervous.

She needn't have worried. The moment she and Drew walked through the doors of the church with Frank and the twins, she heard her name being called.

"Stephanie," Mary called, gesturing for her to join their group. "We're so glad you could make it."

"Go," Drew said. He'd had his hand on the small of her back to guide her in the door, and now he gently pushed her forward. "I'll get the boys to their Sunday school class."

Stephanie timidly entered the women's circle. "I'm happy to be here," she said, and meant it. Even though the vestibule of the church was far more crowded than she had imagined it would be, her nerves seemed to have fled as soon as she'd come into contact with the three genial women. Somehow they seemed like old friends.

"We need to make a plan," said Alexis. "How many people have you met so far, Stephanie?"

"A handful, counting you ladies."

"All right, then. I say we start at the front door and

work the room clockwise." Alexis glanced at her watch. "There's twenty minutes before the service starts. If we keep the introductions short, we ought to be able to make a full circle by then."

Stephanie's nerves jolted back to life. "Everyone?" she croaked through dry lips.

"I think we're overwhelming her," Mary said, pressing a hand to Stephanie's shoulder. "Maybe we should start with a few people and go from there."

Alexis looked disappointed, but Samantha smiled and nodded.

"Take it easy on me, girls," Stephanie said, holding up her hands palms outward.

"Of course," Samantha agreed, and then pointed to a nearby table that was loaded with finger foods. "There's Pastor Shawn swiping a powdered donut while no one is looking. He probably thinks he needs a good sugar high during his sermon."

"Perfect. Let's start with him," Alexis exclaimed.

Stephanie wasn't certain she wanted to start with the pastor of the church, but the three women expertly guided her through the maze of people to the table where Pastor Shawn stood, quietly munching on his treat. He was quite a bit younger than Stephanie would have expected a pastor to be, and handsome in his own way—if one was supposed to call a pastor handsome. He looked as if he might have come from a military background, with flat-top, short cut blond hair that reminded her of a Marine.

"Pastor," Alexis said, giving him a friendly hug as they approached. "This is Stephanie Cartwright. Drew Spencer hired her as a nanny for his kids."

"I'm sure you'll be a great help to them," he answered, extending his hand to Stephanie with a genuine smile. "I'm Pastor Shawn O'Riley. If you need anything, don't hesitate to ask."

"Thank you. I will."

"How long have you been a nanny? Do you enjoy your work?"

"Yes, sir, very much. I got my Bachelor of Science degree in early childhood education. I worked my way through school as a nanny, and continued in the profession even after I graduated from college. Eventually I'd like to teach preschool, but I'm perfectly content at the moment watching over Drew's adorable little twins."

The gleam of an idea appeared Pastor Shawn's blue eyes. "Maybe you can teach preschool here in Serendipity."

Stephanie tilted her head in surprise. "I thought there wasn't a preschool."

Pastor Shawn shrugged nonchalantly, but there was something in his gaze that seemed serious. "Not yet. Maybe you could change that. Never forget that you have something unique to offer—here in the town, and to the world."

"Have you ever taught Sunday school before?" Alexis queried. "Mary is the volunteer in charge of rounding up teachers, and we're always short. What do you say to teaching the three-and four-year-olds, Stephanie?"

She shook her head. "I'm only going to be here for a couple of months. It's a temporary position, just until—" She was going to say until Drew cleared up the custody issue, but she wasn't sure he wanted people knowing about that. "Until the end of the school year," she said instead.

"Do what you can when you can. You are exactly

where God has called you to be," Pastor Shawn said. "That's the title of my sermon today. Well, not exactly. I'm paraphrasing."

"Even though I'm not staying in town?" Stephanie wasn't sure she should be questioning the pastor about the sermon before he'd even preached it, but she was definitely interested in the answer.

"God's placed you right here, right now, for a purpose. It's your job to figure out what that purpose is, and then to act on it."

Samantha rolled her eyes. "Pastor Shawn always makes it sound so simple. If it were that easy, there'd be a lot more harmony in the world."

"Amen to that," Pastor Shawn agreed, reaching for another donut and popping it into his mouth. "Well, I'd best be going. I need to robe up before the service."

"Okay. Where to now?" Alexis wondered aloud. "Pastor Shawn took up an awful lot of our time."

Stephanie was still trying to digest what the pastor had told her. She'd been so busy looking over her shoulder into her past that she hadn't been living in the present. She realized that it was high time she did.

"Are you ready to go into the sanctuary?" It wasn't a female voice who asked that question. It was male. And it was Drew.

"Oh. We didn't have time to introduce her to everyone yet." Alexis sounded dejected.

"You ladies can continue your little tour after church, in the fellowship hall," Drew said with an amused chuckle.

"I'll catch you later," she told the Little Chicks as Drew took her elbow and guided her toward the sanctuary.

Frank was already seated on the far right rear section marked for handicapped people. Sure, Frank walked with a limp, but Stephanie hardly considered him handicapped. With his cane, he could probably beat her in a footrace if he put his mind to it.

Not surprisingly, Jo was sitting with him, her head close to his as she whispered something in her ear. They sure did make a cute couple.

Drew led her to the second row to the left and gestured for her to go in before him. Immediately, he knelt down and bowed his head, his lips moving silently as he prayed.

For a moment, Stephanie simply sat on the pew by his side, watching him and wondering what he was praying for.

It felt a little awkward for her to kneel down beside him, since this was her first real experience with church, but she ignored her discomfort as she folded her hands in front of her and opened her heart in prayer.

After speaking to Pastor Shawn, she had a lot to pray about. Living in the present, having a purpose. It was all pretty overwhelming. How was she supposed to find out why God had brought her to Serendipity and what she was supposed to do here?

Peace flowed through her as she continued to kneel in prayer. She might not know all the answers, but she was exactly where she needed to be to ask the One who did.

Chapter Five

By the time Stephanie had been with the Spencers for three weeks, they'd established a fairly predictable routine. Stephanie had never been happier taking care of children as she was with Matty and Jamey. The Spencers included her in everything from family devotions to board games. Sometimes she almost forgot she wasn't family.

Drew didn't treat her like hired help. He regarded her as an equal, with respect and courtesy. He was a gentleman from the tip of his hat to the heel of his cowboy boots, and his reading glasses and necktie in between. He didn't look down on her, as Ryan had.

Ryan came from a rich family and thought everyone was below him, her included. And she'd let him treat her that way. He'd insisted she quit her job, not because it was beneath her, but because it was beneath *him*.

And then, as it turned out, *marriage* was beneath him—at least, marriage to her. He'd wanted the milk without the cow, and that was something she could never do. So she'd left. Or maybe she had run away.

She didn't like to think of the past, and purposefully

pushed her memories back whenever they surfaced. She refused to live in fear. As Pastor Shawn had reminded her, she couldn't serve God by living in the past. She needed to embrace the now, and that was exactly what she intended to do.

Though she'd settled comfortably into the household, she hadn't yet had an official tour of the town. When she commented about it, Drew promised to show her the sights on Saturday. She found herself looking forward to the outing—as much to spend time with Drew as to see the town close up.

Thus far, she'd only visited the church on one corner of Main Street, and Cup O' Jo on the other. She thought it would be fun to walk the length of the town and see what all of the other old buildings looked like. Drew had promised the twins they'd play baseball in the park afterward, so everyone was happy.

Once they reached the square at the center of the town, Stephanie paused, taking a moment just to enjoy Serendipity's unique ambiance. The town had been built in the late 1800s, and she imagined it looked nearly the same as it had back then.

As they wandered down the town's solitary main street, Cup O' Jo Café, Emerson's Hardware and Sam's Grocery caught her eye. Nearly every shop, all built with rugged clapboard, had a personal name attached to its shingle. The air smelled slightly of what she thought must be horses—and maybe cows—but oddly, it was no longer an unpleasant odor for her, and it wasn't as if she could see any livestock around, although she'd seen more than a few animals while making the short trek into town.

Of course, there was the quaint, small white chapel

at the end of the way, with its red doors and a pointed steeple with a bell and its ability to hold far more people than it looked capable of. She wondered if they ever rang that bell for Christmases or weddings.

Their feet echoed on the wood-planked sidewalk as they continued down the street. The three old men in bib overalls congregated in front of Emerson's hardware store waved as they passed, and a few children of various ages ran through the streets playing a game of hide-and-seek, but for the most part there wasn't much action, especially for a Saturday afternoon. Stephanie could not believe how quiet it all was.

"There's not much to show you," Drew said, sounding as if he was apologizing for the town—or rather, the lack of one. "In Serendipity, pretty much what you see is what you get."

"I like what I see," she assured him.

She wouldn't admit that her statement encompassed the good-looking man walking next to her who was wearing boots and a cowboy hat and looking very pleased by her comment about his town. His kids were cute. And the way he devoted himself to them, being an attentive father, was very attractive, perhaps because she was a nanny and making sure children were well cared for was her living.

So maybe she did like what she saw. She supposed she could add that small addendum—to herself.

"I haven't noticed any schools around," she remarked as they strolled along the wooden sidewalk. "Where is the elementary school where you work?"

"The town is kind of shaped like a T," Drew explained, pointing to the only side street off the main thoroughfare. "Main Street here is our major cruising district," he joked, "but you'll find the police and fire stations down that way, along with a small library and two school buildings. We have one for the elementary kids, and then the middle and high schoolers share a building. There's a football field between them, but for the most part, our kids' sports teams use the community center to practice and play."

"That sounds a little cramped."

Drew chuckled. "Sometimes. But you've got to remember we're only talking about a population of eight-hundred-some-odd people. I imagine the class sizes where you're from are a bit larger than here in Serendipity."

"Much larger. Thirty-five to forty students per classroom."

"Wow. I have eleven."

"Eleven what?"

"Students in my fifth-grade class," he clarified.

"Seriously?" Stephanie was starting to picture an old one-room schoolhouse with Drew teaching up front, a ruler in his hand and a cowboy hat on his head. "Even my online college classes had more students than that."

"What we lack in numbers we make up in sincerity," he informed her, feigning an affronted sniff. "Virtually every adult in town graduated from Serendipity High School—home of the Panthers—and they all have a vested interest in both our competitive sports teams and our musicians. We also have a formidable debate team," he teased with a wink.

"Oh, now you're talking," Stephanie responded, maybe a little too enthusiastically. "I was on the debate team in high school."

"Really?" He sounded as if he didn't believe her.

She tilted up her chin, not that the gesture made much of a difference, since he was so much taller than she. "I'll have you know that not only was I *on* the debate team, but I was team captain two years running."

If she sounded animated when she spoke of high school debate, it was with good reason. She had hoped touring with the debate team would help her break out of her painfully shy shell, and it had. She'd made new friends and had even found a date to her senior prom through debate.

"Are you trying to tell me that arguing is your forte?" Drew smothered a grin by coughing into his fist.

"Not arguing. Logic," she replied tartly. Which was true, even if *none* of her recent actions contained the least bit of logic.

"The words *logic* and *woman* do not belong in the same sentence," he informed her, trying to keep a straight face. Instead, he ended up outright laughing— so much so that it took him a moment to regroup. "But seriously," he continued, swiping his fingers over his eyes as his lips continued to twitch, "if you want to volunteer to coach debate while you're here, I'm sure the high school team would welcome your expertise."

Her eyes widened. "Are you serious? Just like that?"

"Just like that. Why are you surprised?"

"Having the credentials to work with children, especially in a school setting, is more complicated in New Jersey. I'm a nanny, not an educator."

"I thought nannies *were* educators. It seems to me you've already taught my boys a lot and you've only had them for a few weeks."

"Well, thank you, I think. But teaching preschoolers and teaching high schoolers is hardly comparable."

He lifted an eyebrow. "No? You'd be surprised. You'll have less trouble with the preschoolers."

She chuckled. "Probably. I'd like to give back to the community while I'm here, but I think I'm better suited for something like the preschool Sunday school class than a high school debate team."

"I'm sure Pastor Shawn will be happy to hear that. It's going to be a striking loss for our debate team, though."

Her gaze snapped to his. "I said *like* Sunday school. Don't go telling Pastor Shawn I've discovered my calling."

His eyebrows rose, and he cocked his head. "Haven't you?"

Without answering, Stephanie broke her gaze away from his and reined the boys in so they wouldn't dart out into the street after a couple older children who chose that moment to run past them. She hadn't seen a single car go by, but it still made her nervous.

Drew gestured with his chin. "It's okay. You can let the boys go."

"Into the *street?*"

He chuckled. "Sometimes I forget you come from somewhere where there are cars on the road."

"And—what? You all ride horses?" she teased.

"Well, yes, ma'am, we do," Drew said in a comical accent that was nothing like his genuine soft-spoken drawl. "See right there? We've got a hitching post and a watering trough and everything—right in front of the bar."

The *bar* he was so playfully indicating was Jo's café, but to Stephanie's surprise, there really *was* an old hitching post and watering trough in front of it, which she hadn't noticed before, maybe because it blended in so well with the town's old-West flavor.

"Well, I'll be," she murmured under her breath.

"Yeah. See? I told you so."

Jamey came around from behind her and vaulted upward into her arms. The move caught her off guard, but she managed to catch him underneath the shoulder blades and swing him around in a circle.

"I won't doubt you again," she promised.

Matty squealed and lunged forward, his hands in the air. "Me too, me too, me too!"

Stephanie obliged the small, wiggling boy, laughing along with him as she swung him around in the air.

"Is it always so quiet around here?" she asked, gesturing to include all of Main Street.

Drew held his hands out for Matty, who crawled from Stephanie's arms into his, while Jamey attached himself to Stephanie's leg and didn't look as if he was going to let go anytime soon.

"We haven't reached the park yet. That's where all the action is on Saturday afternoons. And you've already experienced Sundays at the church."

Oh, yes. She had. After that first week, she'd resolved to attend every Sunday service with Drew. The last week's sermon was as interesting and relevant to Stephanie as the first week's had been, and she was excited to go again tomorrow and hear what new insights Pastor Shawn had for his congregation.

"And let's not forget the parties. Serendipity throws whopping shindigs. Generally for anything and everything they can find to celebrate."

Stephanie wasn't the party type, but she thought she might like to go if Drew was with her. She knew lots of the town people now. She already considered the Little Chicks dear friends.

"Maybe I can attend one before I have to leave town."

His eyebrows rose and his gaze turned pensive. "I'd like that. I mean, I think you'd like it. May Day is coming up. Some of the ladies from the church organize a fairly large social event every year. Flowers and Maypoles and tons of food. They even crown one lucky lady May Queen." He made a face. "Except for the food, it's not really my cup of tea, but I'd be happy to take you, if you want."

Before Stephanie could answer him, Matty and Jamey sprinted off down the street. Stephanie quickened her pace to catch up with them.

"Not so fast, boys," Drew called, but the boys didn't appear to hear him. Stephanie's breath caught when the boys rounded the corner and darted out of sight.

"Not to worry," Drew insisted, laying a hand on her arm. "The park is just around the corner. They'll be crawling around on one of the jungle gyms by the time we get there."

"I'd still feel better if I could see them."

Moments later they rounded the corner and reached the park themselves. Stephanie had to admit she was impressed. As Drew had said, there was a large greenbelt that might have covered the expanse of a city block, had they been in a city.

Serendipity might be small in size, but it was big in heart. The playground equipment looked as if it had been pieced together—a little wood here, a little plastic there. A few steel pipes and girders. There was no real architectural plan that Stephanie could see. It wasn't *pretty.* But it was definitely made with love. The important thing where children were concerned was that it was safe and functional, and that there was a lot of it.

This park fulfilled all three of those requirements.

And it was a good thing, because there were a lot of kids. Skipping, swinging, playing, laughing children swarming over the playground equipment like ants.

Drew hadn't been kidding when he'd said this was how Serendipity townsfolk spent their Saturday afternoons—congregated at the park. Kids of all ages squirreled over the playground equipment while adults assembled in small groups where they could speak with one another and still keep one watchful eye on the kids.

And he'd been right about the twins, as well. Matty and Jamey had already each climbed aboard one of a circle of spring-loaded "horses" painted in primary colors. The boys' little arms and legs pumped furiously as they rocked their steeds.

Neighbors and friends smiled and waved as they approached. Several people called greetings specifically to her. It was amazing how fast she'd become enmeshed into this community. She felt more at home here than she had anywhere else she'd ever lived. She had to remind herself that this was only temporary, that she wouldn't be staying for long.

A woman carrying an infant in a lime-green sling was the first to draw near. Stephanie recognized the duo as Cup O' Jo's official baker, Phoebe Hawkins, and her baby, Aaron. Drew greeted Phoebe with a kiss on the cheek and then excused himself to speak to a friend.

Stephanie hadn't had much of an opportunity to speak with Phoebe before now, but it didn't bother her that Drew had left her alone to speak with the woman. She'd heard a lot about Phoebe from Frank. Phoebe had been a world-class pastry chef, but had somehow managed to end up married to a local man—Chance Hawkins, Jo's nephew.

"It's nice to see a new face in town," Phoebe said with a welcoming smile.

"Um…thank you?" What was the correct response for that?

Phoebe laughed, a light, cheerful sound without the least bit of censure or guile.

"By that I mean to say, until you showed up in town *I* was considered the last *new face* in town, and I've been here almost two years. You've been taking the heat off of me." Her pretty mouth curved into a frown as she surveyed Stephanie's dismayed expression. "Oh, don't let me frighten you. People around here are the greatest."

"I know. Just a couple of weeks in church and I already feel like I'm part of the community."

"The townspeople have a way about them, don't they? I don't think I've ever come across friendlier people. I spent years traveling the world learning to cook, but no place compares to Serendipity.

"I heard you're taking care of Drew Spencer's twins," Phoebe commented, gently bouncing the baby boy in her arms. Stephanie wondered how the whole town seemed to know about her, even though she had yet to meet everyone. The town gossip tree seemed to be especially sturdy in Serendipity.

"You're not a relative, are you? Please tell me you're not Drew's cousin or something." Phoebe cast Drew an appreciative glance that seemed to say, *"I'm happily married, so everyone should be as happy as I am—and Drew's perfect for you,"* and then turned her gaze back on Stephanie.

"I'm not a relative," Stephanie verified. She wasn't completely ignorant of what Phoebe was thinking, and she decided she ought to stop that train before it started. It wasn't the first time she'd felt that vibe from someone in the town—the Little Chicks all seemed to be pushing her toward Drew, and even Frank made a couple of remarks that suggested he thought she'd be better suited as Drew's wife than as his twins' nanny.

"There's nothing romantic about the reason I'm here," she continued quickly. "I'm the nanny, and nothing more—and it's a temporary position, at that. For some reason more than one person in this town seems to think I'm here to marry him, not take care of his kids."

"I know, right? Like a mail-order bride or something." Phoebe rolled her eyes. "Right idea. Wrong century."

Phoebe put her at ease, and Stephanie chuckled. "He needed someone college-educated and here I am. I'm only here until the end of the school term, when he'll be able to watch the boys himself."

"Temporary, huh? Believe me, I'm the last person on the planet who would want to put pressure on you—I've been right where you're standing. But I'm warning right now that the rest of the people in this town aren't going to leave you alone." She gazed meaningfully at Stephanie. "You and Drew are too easy a mark for folks to pass on. They don't have much live entertainment around here, so they make it up."

"Lovely," Stephanie murmured, only half joking. She glanced at Drew. He had his back to her and was speaking to a couple of men that looked to be around his age. She had to admit Drew was an attractive man—tall, broad-shouldered, even-featured. She could see how someone might make the mistake of thinking she was interested in him in a romantic way. Who wouldn't find the single dad attractive?

But she wasn't here for a relationship, and he certainly wasn't in the market for one. She had to wonder how *he* was going to feel about all this potential matchmaking? The pressure would be intense, especially because these were his friends and neighbors, people he'd known all his life. He was clearly still recovering from a nasty divorce. The last thing he needed was the community pushing a romantic involvement between him and his temporary employee.

"Is there anything I can do about it?" She didn't realize she'd asked the question aloud until Phoebe chuckled and shook her head.

"I can only tell you what happened to me. Let's just say I lost that particular war." She kissed her baby on his dark-tufted head, her gaze filled with adoration. Aaron responded by gurgling and pumping his long legs, his breath coming in short pants as he stared back at her. He was clearly excited to have his mama's attention, and she cooed back at him.

He was an adorable baby, and Stephanie had to cross her arms against the compelling urge to reach for him. It was as instinctive to her as breathing.

Phoebe must have sensed her feelings, for she pulled little Aaron from the sling and offered him to Stephanie. "It seems like this little bruiser grows bigger every day. He's getting heavy for me. You want to hold him for a minute?"

"Oh. Yes, please. He's just gorgeous." Stephanie appreciated Phoebe's kindness more than she would ever know. She held the squirming bundle of joy close to her heart and burrowed her cheek next to his, breathing in his baby scent. There was nothing like it in the world.

Someday, God-willing, she would hold a baby of her own. Several, if she had her way.

"I wish I could tell you that you were going to get away from Serendipity without losing your heart, but I'm afraid I'm living proof of it working the other way around."

"So figuratively, at least, you lost the fight? It doesn't look like you mind too terribly much."

Phoebe laughed. "Oh, no. Not at all. Quite the opposite, actually. I hadn't the least intention of starting a relationship when I came to Serendipity. Like you, I had a temporary position. I was just looking for a break from my crazy schedule back home for a while." She sighed with contentment. "Instead, I found a home here. I fell completely and madly in love with Chance. One minute we were working together, and the next we're married with two children—Aaron and Lucy, his daughter from his first marriage."

"That won't happen to me," Stephanie assured her. "Like I said, I'm only passing through town." For a moment, she wondered what it would be like to stay in Serendipity, to make it her permanent home.

The idea took a moment to settle, but it quickly took roost. What *would* it be like to live in a place like Serendipity, where everyone knew her, where friends and neighbors really cared?

Did she have something special to offer in return, as Pastor Shawn had said?

Was it possible, as the pastor had suggested, that she could make her dream into a reality and start a preschool in the town? Even the thought of it nearly overwhelmed her. She was finding it difficult to catch a breath. But she couldn't simply set the notion aside, no matter how hard she tried.

Phoebe flashed her a knowing glance, as if she had discerned information Stephanie was not privy to. "That's what I said, too. I'm living proof that love can creep up on you when you least expect it. And Serendipity—it grows on you. If you're not careful, you'll be woven into the fabric of the town so tightly that you can't be cut away from it. I'm just warning you."

"Warning her about what?" Drew asked, rejoining the ladies.

Phoebe looked amused, but to Stephanie's relief, she deflected Drew's question. "I was just telling Stephanie here how Serendipity tends to grow on you."

"Does it, now?" Drew drawled, his gaze narrowing as it moved between the two women.

"Are you taking her to the May Day picnic next Saturday, Spence?" Phoebe asked, her voice bubbly with excitement.

Really? Stephanie cringed. She thought Phoebe was going to be on her side, but it looked as if she was already trying to set the two of them up. Phoebe had certainly made it sound as if she was pushing Drew to ask her out on a date.

Drew sighed, sounding taxed. He must have caught on to the sudden influx of underhanded matchmaking ploys, as well. He was clearly stressed about something.

"Of course. I started to explain about the party, but then we got to chasing the boys and our conversation got derailed somewhere along the way. So what do you think, Steph?"

Her heart started pounding erratically, which was ridiculous, since he *wasn't* asking her out on a date. If he had been, she would have had to say no. But since he was only asking her as a friend and an employee, she felt obligated to accept.

Obligated. And she was just going to keep telling herself that until she believed it.

"Yes. I'd enjoy that. Are you going to be there, Phoebe?"

"Oh, definitely. The whole family will be there. The whole *town.* Even more people than Sunday's regular church crowd. If you haven't been introduced to everybody in Serendipity, you'll be able to meet them next Saturday at the May Day picnic."

Drew looped a half Windsor through his necktie and adjusted it without looking in the mirror. As was his habit, he wore a tie to school every day. He might be a small-town teacher, but he took his job seriously— maybe too seriously—and always tried to represent the children in his care to the best of his ability. That included the way he dressed—slacks, an oxford shirt and a necktie.

Even on a Monday morning, when he was exhausted. He hadn't been sleeping well lately. Knowing a case worker was going to show up at his door any day now.

When he entered the kitchen, Stephanie was already there, serving up scrambled eggs and toast to his father and the boys. She had his *Everything is Under Control* apron wrapped around her tiny waist again, but this time he wasn't as jarred by the sensation of seeing her dressed in his apron as he had been that first time.

In fact, she looked as if she belonged in his kitchen, and he was comfortable having her there. And it wasn't some kind of misogynistic male chauvinism making him feel that way.

It was the look on his boys' faces that sold him. Even his father wasn't complaining for a change. She really did have everything under control.

"Eggs and toast, coming right up," she said, *way* too brightly for seven o'clock in the morning. He'd never get used to living with a cheerful morning person.

Not that he was going to need to.

"Thanks, but I don't have time to catch breakfast this morning," he said, waving away the plate heaped with steaming eggs that she offered him. He glanced at his watch and frowned. "I'm already late. I have two new bulletin boards to set up before class."

"You can't leave without eating. It's my secret recipe, guaranteed to put a smile on your face."

While the eggs looked and smelled tempting, *she* was the one putting a smile on his face. His breath caught in his throat when their eyes met. She challenged him with her warm brown gaze. It was almost enough to make him back down.

"Yummy," Matty agreed. Jamey just kept eating.

"How long will it take you to eat—all of two minutes? I've got a meeting this morning with the Little Chicks to help plan games for the kids for the May Day picnic, and you don't see me running off without eating."

She pleaded with her eyes just as much as with her smile, blinking just rapidly enough to cause his heartbeat to rise in synch with her eyelashes. It was *totally* not fair for her to use her feminine wiles that way.

"Give the woman a break and eat the food," his father growled.

Drew looked from one to the other of them and

sighed. "Oh, all right," he finally conceded, only because he knew he could eat the meal and be on his way faster than he could get out of the house arguing about it. He took the plate Stephanie offered and sat down at the head of the table. "I'll eat, if it'll make you feel better."

"It'll make *you* feel better," she insisted. "How you fellows got along before I arrived is a mystery to me." She slid into the chair next to Drew and picked up her fork.

"Bananas and toaster pastries," his father grumbled.

Drew hoped he could avoid a close scrutiny of his pre-Stephanie nutritional principles. He'd learned a lot since she'd started joining the family for meals.

"I was hoping I'd have the opportunity to speak to you about the educational system in Serendipity. Since you're a teacher, I thought you might be able to shed light on a few questions I have," she said with a soft sigh. "But I guess I can wait until you get home from work."

One look at the disappointed expression on her face and Drew decided his bulletin boards could wait.

"Ask away," he said, shoveling a forkful of fluffy scrambled eggs into his mouth. He was startled by how good it tasted. What had she put into the eggs that made them so good?

"What I'm most curious about is why there is no preschool in Serendipity. Doesn't the town see a need for early childhood education and pre-kindergarten reading readiness?"

He paused and wiped his lips with his napkin. "The children in our school district perform well above the national average on state exams, so it's never been what folks would consider a huge detriment not to have a preschool for the children. Most of the kids get some help at home. But even so, I personally think a preschool would be a real blessing to the community, and I've lobbied with the town council for just that very thing for years."

"That surprises me." She paused, and then her eyes widened as she realized how her comment had sounded. "Not that you are aware how essential a preschool is," she amended, "but that there isn't one. It seemed to me that there were quite a few preschool-aged children at the park the other day."

Drew nodded. "There are. And now that my own boys are preschool-aged, I realize more than ever what a gap there is in the formal learning structure. But right now it's all we can do to keep the elementary program running well. There's just not enough funding available, so according to the town council, the preschool will have to wait."

He shook his head. "There always seems to be something on their list that appears to be more critical, at least in the short term. I'm not judging them. The town council is made up of gracious volunteers, and I wouldn't want the job myself. They have a tough time deciding how to keep Serendipity up and running."

"That's too bad." Stephanie tilted her head and pursed her lips, her expression speculative.

He wondered what was going through her mind, and then decided he didn't really want to know. The less involved he was with this woman, the better. He was already getting in too deep as it was. More and more he found himself thinking about her when he least expected it—and that was a distraction he did *not* need right now.

Besides, she appeared to snap out of whatever was bothering her quickly enough. When she smiled, it was with her eyes as well as her lips. She made what was almost a purring sound from the back of her throat and stood, moving to the sink and rinsing off her plate.

"Well, at least I'm around for the time being, for the twins, anyway. Readiness is as natural a part of a preschooler's daily life as breathing. You just have to pay attention so you can take advantage of those opportunities."

Drew sighed. "That's a great disadvantage of being a single parent. What with my work I sometimes don't feel like I'm around enough. I can't take advantage of all those teachable moments."

"Don't worry about the twins," Pop reminded him. "Stephanie's not the only one who does teachable moments. I'm here twenty-four/seven, and I'm perfectly capable of caring for those boys. I love them. And I expect I have a thing or two to teach them, too."

Drew knew that particular bullet was aimed right at his head. His father still hadn't forgiven him for hiring a nanny from the outside when the older man lived at the house, even if his dad liked Stephanie for dozens of other reasons, most of which Drew didn't want to think about.

"I know you love them, Pop. I have other reasons for having Stephanie with us."

His father grunted and spread his newspaper. "Well, you kids do whatever you want. I have a date today."

"A date?" Drew's eyebrows rose. "With who?"

Pop lowered his paper enough to pin Drew with a scowl. "Like you don't know."

"Jo Murphy?"

"Hmmph," was his father's only answer.

Stephanie chuckled.

"Since when did you start calling an outing with Jo a date?" Drew demanded, unwilling to let this go.

"You have a problem with that?"

"Well, no." He didn't have the least bit of a problem with Jo Murphy. He loved her like a second mother.

"It's not a *date* date," his father insisted, backtracking. "Best you keep your nose out of my business."

"I think it's lovely," Stephanie crooned.

She would.

Drew remembered that he was late and started shoveling food into his mouth as quickly as possible, barely chewing between bites. Matty and Jamey stopped eating to watch their father's foray into bad table manners.

He swallowed and cleared his throat. "Sorry," he apologized contritely. "I'm being rude."

His father grunted his agreement, but Stephanie just shrugged, her mouth tugging upward in amusement.

"It's just that—I really am in a hurry. Boys, stop gawking at me and start eating." He was in his own kitchen, in his own house, explaining his actions as if *he* was the preschooler.

He pushed his plate away, despite the fact that he'd only eaten half the eggs and only one slice of toast. He was flustered and disconcerted and he was going to be his own man—even if that meant going hungry.

Chapter Six

Wednesday evening found Drew and Stephanie doing housework. He'd received a call from his lawyer that the Child and Family Investigator would be coming by sometime in the next couple of weeks. He'd tried not to show how distressed he was, but Stephanie had grown to know his moods too well.

She also knew he didn't like to talk about his feelings. Instead, she had graciously suggested they thoroughly clean the house so he would feel a little more confident about the case worker's visit.

He'd never known a woman as kind and sensitive as Stephanie. She knew just what to say and do—not only with him, but with the kids. It concerned him a little bit that the whole family was beginning to rely on Stephanie for more than just simple child care during the weekdays. She'd become a staple of their household. He didn't want to think about how upset the twins would be when she left.

And he most certainly didn't want to think about how *he* was going to feel when she left.

He finished mopping behind the refrigerator, huffing and puffing as he carefully slid the large appliance back to its original position. Wiping the sweat off his forehead with his shoulder, he leaned his forearm on the end of the mop and surveyed his work.

The worn white vinyl kitchen floor showed years of wear. He couldn't get some of the scuff marks and scratches out no matter how hard he applied himself. Using information he'd gathered on the internet, he'd stripped the buildup with vinegar and then covered the area with a thick coating of shiny floor cleaner, but he wasn't happy with the results. Now he was wondering if perhaps he hadn't used the most reliable sources. Information gleaned from the internet was hit or miss at best.

Stephanie peeked her head around the corner where the kitchen met the living dining room. "How is the kitchen coming along?" she asked brightly, but didn't give him the opportunity to respond. "Your floor looks nice. I dusted all the furniture and pictures and polished all the wood with some wax I found in the closet. Now the whole house smells like lemons."

She'd pulled her hair back into a ponytail, making her look even younger and fresher than she usually did. It was a stunning reminder of how different they were—Drew was older and wiser, neither of which necessarily was a good thing.

Used goods, so to speak. And she deserved better than that.

She'd clearly been applying herself to her labors, for her face was flushed with exertion and a few tendrils of wispy hair had escaped her elastic and were curling against her hairline, wreathing her face in gold.

She'd never looked more attractive. Or more completely off limits.

It escaped him why he had to keep reminding himself over and over again why he *shouldn't* be noticing her as a woman. Clearly, he wasn't nearly as strong-minded as he'd imagined himself to be. Put a pretty lady under his nose and she might as well be leading him by it—like a bull with a ring through his snout.

"Thank you for helping me out. I feel better now knowing that at least the case worker is going to find a clean, organized house when she comes."

"Don't ever be afraid to ask if you need an extra hand with something. I like to be useful. It makes me crazy to sit around and do nothing." She shrugged. "Since your dad and Jo have the boys locked in a serious game of Candyland, I really don't have anything better to do, anyway. You're rescuing me from dying of chronic boredom."

She gave him an encouraging smile that flickered into a flame in his stomach and lit his insides with warmth.

"I'd be nervous, too, if it was me and my children under the microscope," she murmured, reaching for his hand. "But don't worry. I'm sure the case worker will be more interested in how attentive you are as a father to the boys—and you *are* a great father, by the way— than by whether there are any dust bunnies hidden in the corner. Which, for the record," she continued, teasingly waving her dust cloth under his chin like a flag, "there aren't."

Even under the stress he was feeling, she managed to make him smile, which was just one more reason of many to like her. He was pretty sure he'd smiled more in the past few weeks than he had the entire year before that. After Heather had left him, he wasn't sure he'd ever smile again, and now look at him—grinning like a fool.

Maybe he was a fool. But it felt good, anyway.

"I had the rugs cleaned a couple of months ago, which got out most of the big stains. If we run a vacuum over the carpet and wash the living room windows, I think we'll be good for the night."

"Great. Where can I find your vacuum? I'll get that, and then after you finish the kitchen, you can take care of washing the windows. I don't do windows," she joked, using the old cliché.

Drew chuckled and gestured toward the floor he'd been mopping. "Yeah, this vinyl is pretty much hopeless. At least I think I can get the windows clean, if I apply a little elbow grease. Like the rest of the house, I'm ashamed to say it's been a while since they've had a thorough cleaning. I feel overwhelmed just keeping up with work and the boys. Cleaning house somehow seems pretty far down the list."

"Understandable."

At least she didn't chide him. "The vacuum is in the hall closet, buried somewhere behind our winter coats. If you dig deep enough you should be able to find it with no problem."

"I'm on it." Stephanie disappeared around the corner and Drew turned back to his work, applying yet another coat of vinyl cleaner on the floor for good measure. If a little product made it shiny, a lot ought to make it gleam, right?

Stephanie must have found the vacuum without incident, for a few minutes later he heard the telltale hum of the motor. The kitchen floor was as good as it was going to get. He might as well go do something truly productive. He grabbed a bottle of glass cleaner and a roll of paper towels and joined Stephanie in the living room.

She was laughing at something, her beautiful brown eyes shimmering with delight. He quickly saw why. She was playing with the dog.

Quincy had never been a big fan of vacuums. In fact, he was a big chicken when it came to being around any loud devices. He usually tucked his tail and ran and hid underneath one of the beds.

But today he'd apparently decided the vacuum cleaner was attacking Stephanie, and he was having none of it. Quincy valiantly charged at the machine, lunging and nipping at it to keep it away from his beloved mistress, who, over the course of the past few weeks, had become the dog's favorite person on the planet.

It had become a game between the two of them— Stephanie pushing the vacuum out and Quincy chasing it back in again. The woman was clearly having at least as much fun with it as the dog was. Her laughter was contagious.

"I see you have a new BFF," Drew said with a chuckle as soon as Stephanie shut off the machine. "Quincy was certainly ready to take on the vacuum cleaner for you. Normally he's terrified of vacuums, just so you know how special you are."

Drew's throat closed as he said the words and he swallowed. Hard.

"My knight in furry armor." She crouched and wrapped her arm over the dog's neck, scratching his broad chest with her fingers. "Who could resist a face like this?" Laughing, she planted a kiss on the dog's forehead.

"I can tell you like dogs. And you appear to have the same amazing affect over them as you do on children."

"I've never owned a dog," she said with a tinge of sadness.

"No?" He was surprised, since she was so good and natural with Quincy.

"I lived in a series of foster homes growing up, and then in the dormitories while I was in college. I could have had a small dog at my apartment after I'd graduated, but Ryan—my ex-boyfriend—didn't like animals."

Ex-boyfriend. He heard the catch in her voice and saw her wince, almost as if she were being struck by an invisible hand. Was this Ryan the reason she'd left New Jersey and come to Serendipity?

Drew already didn't like the guy. Whoever this exboyfriend of hers was, he'd clearly hurt Stephanie, which didn't set well with Drew.

And what kind of a man didn't like animals, anyway?

"Maybe someday, though," she continued wistfully. "I'd love to have a dog, if I ever settle down permanently."

He could easily see her settling down, with a house and a dog and children of her own. If he didn't know anything else about her, he knew this—that she would be an excellent mother someday, caring and compassionate and dedicated, just as she was with his boys.

"To tell you the truth, I've been praying about maybe staying in Serendipity."

His heart jolted into his throat. How could a man be alarmed and relieved at the same time? And yet that was exactly how he felt.

What was she saying? That she wanted a more permanent job offer?

He turned away from her, not wanting to meet her

gaze until his emotions were under control. He didn't want her to see how confused he was.

He couldn't give her a job even if he wanted to, and he admitted there was a large part of him that *did* want her to stay with him. And, of course, the boys wanted her to stay.

But he was already making a painful dent in his retirement account just to have her here now. He couldn't extend her stay indefinitely, no matter how well she got on with the twins.

But there was far more to it than that—something much harder for him to admit. If she stayed then he was going to have to confront his attraction to her, feelings he'd rather avoid if at all possible. He didn't want to have to admit he was falling for her.

Even to himself.

Well, *that* wasn't the reaction Stephanie had imagined she would receive. Not from Drew. Up until this point, he'd been very supportive of her. She hadn't expected him to turn away from her.

His less-than-stellar response to her idea of staying in town put an instant damper on her mood. Talk about a killjoy.

She didn't know what she expected. Maybe just that he would think it was a worthwhile idea to consider, or that he was happy that she might be staying.

She frowned. It was just an idea, not yet even fully conceived. She didn't need his permission, or his support, to stay in town, but deep in her heart she'd hoped for both. She'd met a lot of people here in Serendipity, many of whom she now considered her friends, but there was no one she felt as close to as she did to Drew.

He was her employer and the twins' loving and committed father, but she'd anticipated that he was much more than that. She'd thought—hoped—he was her friend.

There were times when he'd even been flirtatious with her. Deep inside she'd wished perhaps—

But, no. She wouldn't allow herself to go there, even in her mind. Obviously she was setting herself up to have her heart ripped in two again, and how stupid was that? If she'd learned anything from last time, it was that she shouldn't give her heart lightly.

"What do you mean you want to stay?" Drew asked bluntly. He was being his usual self—solemn and straightforward about everything. The image of the staid academic entered her mind. He might look like a cowboy, but clearly he was an uptight school teacher at heart. It would have been laughable if it wasn't so serious.

Unfortunately, it was serious. This was her life she was talking about, and whether he encouraged her in her decisions or not, she wanted him to know all the facts.

"It's just something I've been tossing around," she began. "I've been speaking with Pastor Shawn. He's encouraged me to get involved here in town. I'm helping Mary with the Sunday school kids at church this weekend, and I've helped with the planning for the May Day picnic. I've made a lot of friends here, and quite frankly, I don't have anything or anyone to go back to on the east coast. No house, no job. Nothing."

His gaze turned compassionate as he searched for the right words. "I remember you saying you were a foster child, so you have no family, right?" His eyes and the gentle tone of his voice didn't match the furrow in his brow, which marred his otherwise handsome face. "Friends?"

"A few." No one close. No one she could turn to in a crisis, which she'd only discovered when she'd become suddenly homeless and not a single one of her *friends* had a spare room to offer her. There was no one who cared enough to reach out to her and lend a hand.

The truth was that Ryan had forced her to alienate all of her friends, and all of his friends took his side when she broke things off him.

"I don't want to be on that coast, never mind in the state," she admitted, feeling the heat of shame rush to her cheeks, leaving her hands and her feet cold—and her heart like ice. "Back in New Jersey, my ex-boyfriend Ryan is a member of the old-money Forsythe clan. They have the ability to throw their weight around and make my life pretty miserable." Ryan would throw *his* weight around, probably literally, but she wasn't sure she wanted to say that yet. "I'd certainly have difficulty trying to get another job within their sphere of influence, which extends pretty far."

"I get what you're saying," he stated thoughtfully. "And I'm sorry things worked out for you that way. I really am. But I have to wonder how Serendipity is going to be any better for you in the long run. There are other places you could go. Wouldn't you be better off in a larger city?"

When she sighed, he reached for her hand, covering her cold fingers with his warm ones.

"I'm not trying to rain on your parade," he continued. "I know I think too black-and-white sometimes. I'm just trying to be practical. There aren't any families with substantial amounts of money around here, not anything remotely like they'd need to hire a full-time nanny. There are no millionaires or oil barons among this crop of simple folks."

"I realize that," she admitted.

"Frankly, it'll be difficult to find a job in your field, or even close to your field. You could do day care, maybe, if you can get a mortgage on a large house."

She shook her head. "I don't have that kind of money. Not nearly enough to put a down payment on a house, even in Serendipity."

"You're creative. I'm sure you'll come up with a solution to your problems."

His encouragement warmed her heart. "There must be some way for me to get by," she murmured, more to herself than to Drew. "I'm willing to work hard."

"Yeah, I know you are," he agreed. "But doing what? Working as a waitress at Cup O' Jo?"

"I don't know. Maybe. Like I said, at this point it's only conjecture. But there's more."

He raised his eyebrows and nodded for her to continue.

"I would like to start a preschool here," she admitted softly. "I see the need, and I think I have the skill set to fill it."

"If anyone can do it, you could."

She sucked in a breath. He had shocked her again, this time by his encouragement.

"I have a bachelor's degree. I should have no trouble getting teaching credentials in Texas. I have some administrative experience from when I worked as a supervisor for a bounce house as a teen. And if anything good came out of my relationship with Ryan, it is that I've seen how rich people raise money. I know how to generate community awareness. I've been to quite a few charity fundraisers. I think if we ask the right people, we can get the money we need to start the school."

"Wow. You've put a lot of thought into this."

"And prayer. More than you know. I'm only in the beginning stages of my planning. There's still a lot to do, working out the logistics and so on, but I wanted to tell you now, so you can pray with me." She sighed softly. "I've never really sought the Lord's guidance for my life before. This is all very new to me."

He didn't say anything. He just stared at her, his expression unreadable.

"What?" she asked when she couldn't stand the silence any longer. "You think I'm an idiot with a whacked-out scheme, don't you?"

"No," he responded so quickly that she knew he was telling her the truth. "I think you're incredible."

Did he really mean that?

She searched his eyes, which had darkened to a deep jade. He was so close she could feel his warm breath on her cheek. His fingers brushed the sensitive spot at the nape of her neck.

She reached up and brushed her palm along his jaw.

"Thank you for believing in me," she whispered.

And then she kissed him.

Chapter Seven

"I guess my son is a little bit brighter than I thought he was," came a low, gruff voice from somewhere out of the scope of Drew's present realm, which consisted only of Stephanie. Her lips. Her exotic scent. The sweet softness of her skin as he cupped her face in his palm. His heartbeat was hammering so hard in his ears that he almost didn't hear his father speak. It was no surprise to him that he was a little slow on the uptake.

Stephanie, however, wasn't. She bolted out of his arms and across to the other side of the sofa as if he'd electrocuted her. She covered her cherry-red cheeks with both hands and groaned.

Not that he was any happier about the situation than she was. He wanted to pull her back in his arms, which would be the absolute worst thing he could do at the moment.

This was a worst case scenario, and he was pretty sure Stephanie knew that, too. He had absolutely *not* wanted to be interrupted in a private moment that he would rather no one except he and Stephanie know about.

"Not a word, Pop. Not one word," he warned, knowing full well his threat wouldn't stop the old man from saying exactly what he thought of the situation.

He caught his father's gaze and silently pleaded with him. *Please don't embarrass Stephanie.*

Drew didn't care about himself. He was used to the old man's blunt speaking. But Stephanie's face had gone from bright red to an alarming white, and she looked as if she'd like to shrink into the plush fabric of the burgundy-colored sofa and disappear.

And it was all his fault. Drew shouldered one-hundred percent of the responsibility for getting caught in this situation. She might have initiated their kiss, but if she hadn't, he knew he would have.

The spark between the two of them was set to blaze no matter who struck the match. And he should have known better. Instead of sharing a special moment just between the two of them, they'd now announced whatever fledgling feelings they might have for each other to the two biggest gossips in the town, and all without saying a word.

So much for older and wiser. He wasn't some slaphappy youth riding on too many hormones. He was a single father with two boys he would always put first—*always*—but especially now, with court-appointed social workers breathing down his throat.

He couldn't and shouldn't *date,* and he wasn't ready to court a woman. It was *because* he cared for Stephanie that he had to nip this relationship in the bud. She might think staying in Serendipity was good, for now. And he had no doubt she was completely sincere in her aspirations to build a preschool in town.

But dreams had a funny way of being crushed by

life. He had ten years on her—ten years of learning the bitter truth about reaching for the stars.

Falling back to earth hurt. A lot.

He wanted to spare her and protect her from that pain. And, while he was at it, he ought to protect her from his father's teasing.

Unfortunately, the most obvious way he could think of doing that was going to hurt her feelings—for now. But in the long run, she'd thank him for it.

"Did you finally come to your senses, boy?" his father asked, groaning as he gingerly lowered himself into the forest-green armchair and stretched out his feet onto the matching ottoman. "All I have to say is—good for you. It's about time you came around."

Drew frowned, knowing that was not even *close* to all his father had to say on the matter.

"Don't be ashamed, dear," Jo said, settling in on the couch next to Stephanie and patting the younger woman's knee. "I can see that you're blushing, but you needn't worry. We've all been hoping and praying that you two would get together."

Drew didn't know who the *we all* was, and he figured he probably didn't want to know. He had to stop this train—fast. Pumped with adrenaline, he verbally stomped on the brake as hard as he could. "You're mistaken, Jo. We're not together."

Jo just chuckled. "No, of course not, dear. Your father and I just imagined what we saw when we walked into this room a minute ago."

"What you saw didn't mean anything. We just shared a kiss. Don't read anything into that that's not there."

He saw Stephanie flinch, and he knew he had wounded her with his blunt and purposefully callous words, but he didn't know how else to handle the situation. She probably thought he was a royal jerk—and he was. But she could not possibly imagine the things that would happen to her if he did not end this right now.

Pop and Jo wouldn't waste a second before telling everyone in town that Drew and Stephanie were a couple. News would spread like a wildfire and then Stephanie would have no relief from the pestering. Jo served meals at the café. It wasn't difficult for Drew to imagine her bringing this juicy new morsel of relationship gossip into the conversation at every single table she waited.

And if the folks in town thought they were a couple—watch out. As well-intentioned as they might be, they would be endlessly throwing the two of them together. If Stephanie really did stay in Serendipity, she'd end up being miserable, and it would all be his fault.

"Stephanie is only contracted to stay until the end of the school year," he stated firmly, "or until I've retained custody of the boys. Whichever comes first."

He didn't say that she might stay in town indefinitely. Now didn't seem the right time to bring that up.

"Right," Stephanie agreed softly. To her credit, she straightened her posture and her expression. "Don't forget, I'm just an employee. Drew is my boss."

Jo laughed briskly. "That doesn't mean a thing, sweetie. Not in Serendipity. Besides, it sure didn't look like an employer/employee relationship when we walked in. Bosses and employees have been getting married practically since Noah landed the ark."

"Married?" he exclaimed, with probably more emotion than he'd shown in a good while. "It was a mistake, and it will never happen again." Drew wondered how he sounded. Probably not very convincing—he wasn't all that confident it was a one-time thing himself. He wasn't even sure he wanted it to be.

When he was around Stephanie, his head never moved as fast as his heart. The yearning to pull her into his arms and keep her by his side was incredibly strong. But chemistry was impulsive, and he was not an impulsive man. The last time he'd followed his heart had ended in disaster, save for the two beautiful boys who had come out of the relationship.

He could not do it again. And he would keep telling himself that until he believed it.

Someone had delivered an anonymous basket of flowers to the Spencers' door step this morning, reminding everyone that this was May Day, Serendipity's celebration of spring.

It didn't feel like spring to Stephanie. Not if Drew didn't want her here, which he'd been pretty clear about. Not in his house, and not in Serendipity. He was sending her packing at his earliest convenience.

Okay, so he hadn't said quite that much. He'd said that their kiss meant nothing and that she was only his temporary employee. As far as Stephanie was concerned, that amounted to the same thing.

She pulled her hair back into a loose ponytail and applied a bit of eyeliner and a light coat of mascara, mostly to try to hide how puffy her eyes looked again this morning. It had been three days since Drew had openly stated that their attraction to one another was a mistake, and she was still struggling with her emotions.

She was determined to be strong and composed during the days, with Drew and the boys always around, not to mention the many other people about town that she had met. She didn't want anyone to know her heart was breaking. She felt like an idiot for letting herself become vulnerable to a man again.

She'd thought Drew was different, but he'd just done what Ryan had done—stomped on her heart, and her pride.

But no way was she going to let *him* know how deeply he'd affected her, so she pulled her emotions inward and presented a smiling face to the world.

Nighttime was a different story. In those moments between sleep and wakefulness when she was all alone, the pain of rejection and of unrequited feelings would bubble up inside her. Sometimes she was just too tired to tamp her emotions back down and she ended up shedding a few tears. All she could do was hope that in the morning, her makeup would cover all the signs of her midnight distress.

She supposed it was nice to *know* she was being rejected outright, and not have to guess at it.

But she didn't regret kissing him, even if he hadn't experienced the kind of bolt-of-lightning revelation she had had when their lips met.

For her, it was a game-changer.

All that stuff she'd said about staying in town and starting a preschool was true. But now she realized there was more to the equation. Much more.

She was falling in love with Drew.

If he had been willing to admit he had feelings for her, or if nothing had happened between them in the first place, then she could easily see herself staying in town.

But if Drew didn't want her in Serendipity, that was a different story. Maybe she was simply too emotionally battered to fight any more, but she didn't think she had the strength to move on without literally *moving on*.

Only she was having a hard time picturing herself living anywhere except Serendipity. But it was equally as difficult to picture herself somewhere without Drew and the twins.

Stephanie picked up the duster she'd left on a shelf in the hall closet and moved toward the mantel of the fireplace in the living room, dusting over it the same way she'd done every day since she and Drew had been caught in a compromising position by Jo and his father. Not that there was anything left with dust on it. She just needed something to do, a way to keep busy to keep from going crazy with her thoughts.

Today was May Day, and she was supposed to be looking forward to a fun Serendipity picnic. Instead, she dreaded it. It was like stabbing an already open wound to watch the happy people of Serendipity enjoying themselves while she wasn't even sure where her life was going in the next thirty days.

If she didn't have to go, she probably wouldn't, but she'd been put in charge of running the preschool and toddler games, so she had to be there. Besides, Matty and Jamey would be disappointed if their Miss Stephie didn't attend the festivities with them.

The boys were in the corner entertaining themselves by emptying the entire toy box, spreading toys from one end of the living room to the other. She usually tried to enforce Drew's one-at-a-time rule, but today she didn't care if the boys made a mess. It would give her something to clean up, and it was keeping the twins happy.

Since they'd be gone most of the day, Drew was the kitchen, trying to get his weekend grading done before they had to leave. Hence another reason to dust—to stay out of his way. They hadn't really spoken about what had happened, and after a few days, Stephanie assumed he didn't want to talk.

As for herself, she was too afraid of blurting out her feelings if she was provoked. And since she knew that nearly anything would provoke her—a grimace, a smile, silence, the word *hi*—she thought it was better just not to take the risk of being around him.

Frowning at her own weakness, she turned back to her dusting—and her thoughts.

Why couldn't Drew at least admit there was an attraction between them, even if he didn't want to pursue it any further? They were adults. They should be able to talk about it.

But he'd called their moment together *nothing*.

And she should be able to deal with that.

So why couldn't she?

Because, she finally managed to acknowledge to herself, Drew meant something special to her. She was only now beginning to realize just how much.

The feelings she'd thought she had toward Ryan now seemed the essence of weakness and immaturity. Her ex had taken advantage of the fact that she struggled with her self-esteem. He'd seen the way she tried to please everyone and he'd used that to his advantage. He'd used *her*.

And despite the fact that he'd been studiously avoiding her all week, deep down she knew that Drew was everything that Ryan wasn't. He might not want to talk about what happened between them. He might be blunt, and sometimes not cushion his words. Yet for all that he was respectful and deeply caring in his own way.

Like so many of the folks she'd met in Serendipity, he was a committed Christian who worked out his faith in his life rather than merely giving lip-service to it. He was a phenomenal father—he'd walk over broken glass for his kids, and then turn around and walk back again. And despite the good-natured bickering between the two men, Drew clearly loved his father—enough to bring him to live in his home when he could no longer care for himself on his own.

And one other thing…he was a great kisser. Strong, yet gentle, just like everything else about him.

No two ways about it—Stephanie was falling for him. And, for reasons he wouldn't go into, he didn't feel the same way about her.

So the question yet remained…could she stay in Serendipity, where she'd be constantly running into him? Could she hazard the possibility of having to watch him fall in love with another woman, maybe even marry her and bring her home to be the mother to his kids?

She'd been asking herself the same questions all week, trying to picture herself living somewhere else other than Serendipity, or more specifically, at the Spencers. She'd never before been invited into real, active family life. Her past employers had never welcomed her into their lives—she had been nothing more than a servant, and she had been treated like one. Even her foster families had kept her on the fringes of their daily lives, never really warming up to her and letting her in.

Living with the Spencers had given her a taste of what it meant to care for other people, and have them care for her. What it meant to be a family. It wouldn't be easy to walk away.

She tried to picture her Saturday mornings alone

reading a newspaper rather than sharing in the intimate devotions and prayer time that she now shared with the family over the breakfast table, hearing Drew gently leading his little ones through the Scriptures. It was difficult to imagine not being around to read the boys a book at night, which had become a mainstay in the Spencer household ever since she'd arrived. Even Drew had said how much he enjoyed listening to her create voices for all the characters she was reading about.

She supposed she could read a bedtime story to the children of another family, but the thought of that nearly broke her heart. She had fallen in love with the rowdy, tow-headed boys, and even cranky old Frank held a place dear to her heart.

But all of that meant nothing without Drew.

The doorbell pealed and Stephanie brushed stray tendrils of hair off her face with the back of her hand. She assumed it was Jo here to visit Frank, though usually the woman let herself in with no more than an obligatory knock.

Stephanie checked her watch. It was only mid-morning. Jo was usually busy at the café at this time of day, cleaning up after the breakfast crowd, especially on Saturday. And today was May Day. She'd be scurrying around trying to organize the dozens of dishes Cup O' Jo would supply for the picnic.

It didn't appear that Drew heard the door, or else he was expecting her to get it. He was probably grading papers or planning lessons for the upcoming week. He tended to be really focused when he was working, to the point of shutting everything else out.

No matter. It wasn't as if she was super busy and

couldn't be interrupted. In fact, she welcomed the disruption of her depressing train of thought.

She pulled the door open without looking to see who it was. "Come on in. Coffee's on."

"Thank you so much," said an unfamiliar female voice in a moderated but scratchy low tone. "Coffee would be nice. One cream, two sugars. What can I say? I like mine sweet."

A tall, thin woman Stephanie guessed to be about fifty years old stepped into the house as if she owned it. For all that she was no-nonsense in her attitude and her expression, her clothes were at the height of fashion and she had a blue streak colored into the one of the underneath layers of her highlighted brown hair. The streak was nearly invisible until she brushed her hair back behind her ear—which she did, probably unconsciously, a few moments after she'd entered the house.

Stephanie was positive she hadn't seen this woman around town, which could only mean one thing.

She was the Child and Family Investigator.

Chapter Eight

"Is Drew Spencer here, please?" the woman queried in a businesslike tone. "I've been sent by the court to speak with him."

What was Drew's case worker doing here—on a Saturday, and apparently unannounced? Stephanie was certain Drew would have mentioned it if he thought she'd be coming around.

Stephanie looked at the duster in her hand, her ratty blue T-shirt, gray sweatpants and purple toe socks, and then—last but definitely not least—the toys the twins had strewn from one end of the living room to the other. There was no possible way to hide any of that.

She groaned inwardly, hoping her distress didn't show on her face. Never let the enemy see you sweat, and all that.

At least she'd put Quincy in the backyard. Otherwise the case worker might have had the kind of welcome she herself had had the first time she'd visited the Spencers. That particular meeting might not have gone as well with this woman as it had with her. Who knew if the investigator liked dogs or not?

This was Drew's worst nightmare come to life. He'd talked about being caught off guard, and this situation definitely qualified as that.

"Uh," she murmured, buying a moment to think, "please have a seat on the sofa while I run to the kitchen and get you that coffee." She gestured toward the couch and spurred herself into action. She needed to warn Drew before he accidentally waltzed into the living room and had a heart attack.

Drew looked up from his papers as Stephanie skidded into the room, sliding on her socks. Drew had overdone it just a little bit with the vinyl cleaner and the floor was out-and-out slippery. She was aiming for the cupboard where the coffee mugs were housed, and she grasped the counter for support, adrenaline causing her breath to be quick and uneven as she turned to face him.

He was as casually dressed as Stephanie had ever seen him—jeans and a tattered, grease-stained white T-shirt that looked as if he'd been working under the hood of a car with it. His feet were bare. There was a day's worth of stubble on his chin, which was actually quite attractive, if she'd had time to admire it. He was usually so conscientious about being clean-shaven. His hair looked as if he'd been scrubbing his fingers through it, which he probably had been, since he was clearly deep in thought. When he looked up, his reading glasses magnified the brilliant green of his eyes.

"What's up?" he asked, tapping his pen on the table. "You look like something scared the life out of you. Did you find a spider on the windowsill or something?"

A *spider?* First of all, she was absolutely fine dealing with bugs. And secondly, the woman currently sitting in the living room was much, *much* worse than the average, run-of-the-mill insect.

She pressed her knuckles onto the table and leaned toward him. "Okay, I don't want you to panic, but—"

"What is it?" he broke in, standing abruptly to his feet. "Is it one of the boys?"

She put a hand to his chest to restrain him from darting out into the living room before she finished her explanation.

"No, it's not one of the boys," she assured him.

He sighed and slid back into his chair. "Good. You really had me worried there for a second."

"It's your case worker."

"What?" Again, he stood abruptly to his feet, this time nearly knocking over the glass of orange juice he'd been drinking. "Here? Now?"

"Unfortunately, yes." As calmly as she could under the circumstances, she took a mug from the cupboard and filled it with steaming coffee, then put a dollop of cream and two healthy spoonfuls of sugar in it. It probably wouldn't help, but perhaps she could sweeten the woman. "That's who was at the door a minute ago."

"We don't even have time to pray," he said, blowing out a frustrated breath and running his palm back over his hair. "We're not ready. I'm not dressed for it."

Stephanie had lived in plenty of large, metropolitan areas, where most of her guy friends put a lot into how they looked, but for Drew, it was different, more organic. His trademark shirt and tie, unusual for the town's blue jean dress code, set him apart, said a lot about him as a man. She knew it would really bother him to appear in his present attire.

Not to mention his entire future with his kids was at stake.

And she wasn't in any better condition. She sighed, looking down at her own super-casual outfit. What a disaster.

"Well, she's already seen me, so there's no help for that. I've been made. But I can serve her the coffee and give you a moment to clean up."

He hugged her so tight it knocked the wind out of her, and then pecked her squarely on the mouth. "You're the best, Steph."

And then he was gone, dashing out the back door of the kitchen, which led…outside. She wasn't sure exactly what his plan was, but now that she thought about it, the only entrance to the hallway, and thus his bedroom, was through the living room, which is where the case worker was presently located.

Drew would just have to come back in the way he'd left and deal with the reality that the case worker was going to catch him in jeans and a T-shirt, sans shoes.

"Sorry for the wait. Here's your coffee," she said as she reentered the living room, realizing that she still didn't know the woman's name.

Instead of taking the seat on the couch she'd been offered, the court investigator was down on the floor playing choo-choo train with the twins—short skirt, high heels and all.

Stephanie breathed a sigh of relief. Any woman who would take the very probable chance of getting a run in her black stockings just to play toys with a couple of preschoolers couldn't be all bad.

At the sound of Stephanie's voice, the woman smiled

and stood to her feet, looking amazingly graceful as she moved. She made Stephanie feel like all thumbs.

"Thank you," she said, taking the coffee Stephanie offered her and finding a seat on the sofa, only to exclaim and jump up again, reaching behind her for the sharp-spined green plastic stegosaurus that had fallen in-between the cushions.

"Oh, my!" Stephanie exclaimed, reaching for the errant toy. "I'm so, so sorry. This place isn't usually so untidy. Boys, pick up your toys, right away."

She hoped the twins couldn't hear the sheer panic in her tone. She hoped the *case worker* hadn't heard the panic in her tone.

"Don't apologize for the toys," the woman said. "I don't usually make it a practice of stopping by unannounced, especially on a weekend. I just happened to be driving through Serendipity today."

She paused, and Stephanie couldn't help but raise an eyebrow at that unlikely scenario.

"I know, right? I was on my way home from another appointment, a special case—farther out even than this town. Since I was close, I thought I would save myself the trouble of having to drive back out here another day." She shrugged. "It was a last-minute decision, or else I would have phoned. I hope I'm not inconveniencing you too much. And I'm Eileen, by the way."

"I'm Stephanie Cartwright, the boys' nanny. My little charges here are Matty and Jamey Spencer." Thankfully, Jamey wasn't acting quite as shy as he usually did, and was staring at Eileen with open curiosity. Matty was his usual boisterous self, which, she supposed, was good. She probably shouldn't be trying to analyze the boys' reactions the way Eileen would see them, but she couldn't seem to help herself. "Their father, Drew—"

She was going to say *will be along any second now,* but he stepped out of the back hallway and cut her off.

"Is right here. Eileen, I'm so sorry to have kept you waiting."

Stephanie had to consciously stop herself from gaping. Drew had appeared looking—and smelling—fresh out of the shower. He had slipped into a green oxford shirt, black slacks and his cowboy boots, with a necktie and a sports jacket for good measure.

He glanced at Stephanie and his eyebrows furrowed for just a moment as they shared an unspoken *close call.* She smiled and brushed her fingers across her cheek, reminding him that *he* should be smiling, because otherwise she thought he might forget. He pasted a smile on his face and gave her an almost imperceptible nod, then took a seat on the antique chair near the sofa.

"I was just telling your nanny here that I happened to be passing through town today," Eileen explained. "I hope it's okay that I stopped by on a Saturday."

"No. Yes. Of course. That's fine," Drew stammered.

Stephanie prayed as hard as she ever had. She didn't know how interested God was in minute details, but if He was, she hoped He'd help Drew take a breath and calm down.

"You have a lovely home here, and I'm very impressed with your boys," Eileen commented. "I had a few minutes to interact with them while Stephanie was getting coffee."

"Thank you. I—"

Drew looked toward the twins. His eyes widened and he swallowed. Twice. Then he yanked on the knot of his necktie as if he was choking—definitely not a good sign. "What happened in here?" he squeaked.

Stephanie jumped in before Drew had the opportunity to completely lose his composure. "If I were to guess, I'd have to say Hurricane Jamey and Matty the tornado." She turned toward Eileen, feeling as if she needed to explain. "This is entirely my fault. I should have had them putting one toy away before they took another one out."

Drew's rules—the way he wanted things done. If she'd listened to him, the house would be a shining example of family harmony right now and not an accident within a catastrophe.

Not to mention how that made *her* look, as a so-called professional—as if she hadn't been paying attention to what the boys were doing and didn't know how to keep order. What kind of nanny was she, anyway?

"Please don't apologize," Eileen said for the second time. "Believe it or not, it's nice to see a nice, normal family for a change, in all their chaos and madness. Many times people are so nervous about me coming around that they present to me picture-perfect households with cardboard-cutout pictures of family life."

Eileen chuckled and gestured with her hands. "Families are messy. From what I can tell, your boys are very well-adjusted. There's a lot of joy to be found in a box full of toys—or should I say, an *empty* box."

Eileen's laughter appeared genuine enough, Stephanie thought, and the shine in her gaze encompassed all of them. *Don't overanalyze the situation,* she mentally coached herself. She found herself reading something into Eileen's every word and gesture, but it was incredibly hard not to, what with Drew's family life—his sons' futures—hanging in the balance.

"So I understand you are a fifth-grade teacher," Eileen stated, turning to Drew.

"That's correct," he affirmed.

"Tell me a little about the work you do."

As Eileen pulled Drew into conversation, Stephanie took the opportunity to gather the boys around her.

"What do you say we put some of these toys away?" she asked in a secretive voice that got both the twins' attention.

She dropped to her hands and knees and gathered some blocks in her arms. In her experience, children responded better to joining into an activity than in being told what to do and left to their own devices. And at the moment, giving her mind and her hands something to do seemed like a pretty good idea.

"Matty, you get the dinosaurs," Stephanie whispered, allowing the boys to enjoy the conspiratorial atmosphere, even if that same air was making her a little bit nervous. "Jamey, please pick up the cars. I'll put away the rest of the blocks, and that should about do it."

"Cars," Jamey repeated, and then picked one up and thrust it up under her chin. "Green."

Succinct and to the point, like his father. No mincing words.

"That's right, Jamey. It's green. What color is this one over here?" She pointed to a red car.

"U-u-m," Jamey said, frowning in concentration. "It's…orange!"

"Close, sweetheart." Stephanie wasn't sure whether Jamey's mistake was in recognizing the shade, or rather because his favorite color was orange.

She surreptitiously glanced at the case worker to see if she was watching her interaction with the children— which was completely appalling, once she thought about it. She didn't want this to become some kind of drama with the kids playing parts.

It wasn't as if she was staging a program for Eileen to see—at least she hoped she wasn't. Case worker or no case worker, this was about the boys. Colors and numbers were games they played every day, preschool readiness in the form of fun and laughter.

"Okay, Jamey," she said with an encouraging smile, holding up the tiny car. "Try again."

"It's red," Matty exclaimed, not waiting to be invited into their little game. Matty had already mastered his colors and was working on numbers and counting.

"That's right, little dude," she affirmed, not wanting to shut the exuberant preschooler down in his tracks. "Can you find me five dinosaurs to count?"

Matty nodded and began lining up his dinosaur crew on the rug beside her. Stephanie turned back to Jamey and picked up another car.

"Blue," answered Jamey, before she could ask the question.

"Woohoo, buddy! Way to go. And look at Matty with his dinosaurs. You guys did great." She high-fived Jamey and then Matty, giving each of them a special moment of attention.

"Pound it," Jamey exclaimed, offering her his knuckle. Laughing, Stephanie *pounded* it. She learned something new every day, and the importance of pounding it after high-fiving had been one of the first things Matty and Jamey had taught her.

Eileen was chuckling, as well, so apparently she'd

been watching their interchange, or, at least, the last part of it.

That said, she wasn't taking any notes. Stephanie was shocked. The woman hadn't even brought in a briefcase or portfolio. For some reason Stephanie had expected her to be scribbling her thoughts about them on one of those long yellow legal pads like lawyers used.

Instead, Eileen was just observing. How could she possibly make an accurate report without taking notes? How would she remember what she saw? Was it possible she'd get her details mixed up? She said she'd seen another family earlier in the morning.

Stephanie didn't know, and she couldn't ask. All she could do was hug the kids tight, wait and pray that the court would rule in Drew's favor.

Chapter Nine

Forty-five minutes. Forty-five minutes of sheer agony and torture. At least, that was how Drew saw it. The knot in his gut hadn't loosened at all, even though Eileen was now headed to her car and was preparing to leave. He stood at the door and watched until she had pulled away and her vehicle was no longer visible. Only then did the tension in his shoulders and neck begin to ease.

"So what happens now?" Stephanie asked softly, stepping up beside him and resting her hand on his elbow. She, too, was staring out the door and down the road.

"According to my lawyer, we wait."

"For how long? Do they mail you something, or do you have to go to court to find out what the case worker thought?"

"My lawyer will receive a report of the case worker's *findings,* and will email it to me. Then, if necessary, we'll start planning a strategy for the courtroom."

He growled in frustration and scrubbed his eyes with his fingertips, resentment swelling like thunderclouds in his head. He was incensed that this situation was so completely out of his control. He'd worked overtime to be ready for the case worker and he'd still been caught off guard.

"I *hate* this," he rumbled. "I hate that I have to *plan a strategy* in order to keep custody of my sons. This is not the way it's supposed to be."

"No, it's not," she agreed. "And then having some case worker—a complete stranger—come to your house to sit and stare at you and ask a whole bunch of questions was pretty unnerving, I have to say."

He turned toward her, basking in her warm brown gaze, which told him better than any words she could say that she really did understand and sympathize with his situation. She was probably the only one who could. She'd been right there beside him throughout this crazy day.

He framed her face with one hand and brushed his thumb across the velvet softness of her cheek. He wanted to kiss her again. Desperately. Was there any better way to show his appreciation, which he could never put into words?

Bad idea.

He dropped his hand to his side, using every bit of the willpower he possessed to step away from her. She was like flame to a moth. He was going to get burned if he wasn't careful. Or worse yet, he would hurt her.

"You were absolutely fabulous today," he told her, his voice unusually husky.

She looked dazed, and he couldn't tell what she was thinking. He cleared his throat.

"I don't believe I would have made it out of there in one piece if it hadn't been for your quick thinking."

"Thank you, but I don't know about that."

He leaned his shoulder against the door frame and folded his arms against his chest, mostly to keep himself from reaching out to her again. "Believe me, you were outstanding."

"I do have one question—how did you get from the backyard into your bedroom?"

His lips twisted in amusement. "If you have to know, I climbed through my window," he informed her.

"You—"

She burst out laughing, putting a hand to her neck and throwing her head back merrily. "Now *that* I would have liked to have seen."

"It was quite undignified, and I'm glad there was no one there to witness it."

"You cleaned up pretty good. I think you made a decent impression with Eileen," she said, fanning herself with her hand to tamper her amusement.

"You think?" The cords of muscle in his neck tightened. With all the fun he'd been having bantering with Stephanie, he'd forgotten his predicament. It had only been a moment, but for that short amount of time, he'd let go of his fear.

He honestly didn't have a clue how things had gone with Eileen, only that all his preparation—cleaning the house from top to bottom and making sure all the kids' toys were organized and put away—had been for nothing. And the interview itself was nothing like he'd expected it to be.

But he had to let it go, or it was going to eat him alive. Good or bad, the experience was over and there was nothing left for him to do about it.

Except, as he'd told Stephanie, *wait and pray.*

* * *

Stephanie didn't think that even the May Day picnic would be able to take her mind off the harrowing morning she'd had, but she found it was actually nice to be around neighbors who did not want to talk about anything more pressing than how thankful they were that the day of the picnic turned out to be sunny.

She hoped Drew would also be able to relax a little bit, but she could see the lines furrowing his brow from where she was sitting, a good twenty feet away from him. He was smiling and she heard him laugh from time to time, but she knew him well enough now to be able to see how he was really feeling, even when he was trying to present something different to the world.

She wondered if he could see the same in her.

Someone had erected a Maypole in the center of the park, and many of the older kids were winding and unwinding the colorful ribbons that flowed from the top of the pole.

Maybe a little preschool action would get her out of her own funk. She opened the box at her side. It was a fishing tackle box, full of makeup.

"Who wants their face painted?" she called loudly. Immediately several children, Matty and Jamey included, were running toward her and shouting. Now *this* was what living was all about. Maybe that's what Pastor Shawn meant when he said to find your purpose and then act on it.

She had a heart for these precious preschoolers. She just had to figure out a way to make what was in her head work out on paper, and then in brick and mortar, and whiteboards and storybooks.

For a good hour, she painted butterflies and cat whiskers onto little children's faces. Mary came to help her, and soon they'd managed to paint the face of every child who wanted it.

Alexis and Samantha were busy leading the older children in sack races and three-legged races. Stephanie had heard of such things, but the reality was so much better. And then when some of the adults took the places of the children, the scene actually stoked her to laughter.

Where else but in Serendipity would grown men tie their legs together and hop around hooting and hollering like little kids? She couldn't remember enjoying a festivity more in her life, in spite of the fact that she'd had such a stressful morning, or maybe because of it.

People had been sampling many of the food dishes all through the afternoon, but now it was time for everyone to settle down on their blankets and eat a full meal. Frank joined Jo at a table set up for the older folks, and Drew and Stephanie and the twins shared a blanket spread across the manicured lawn.

Pastor Shawn gave a blessing, and then everyone dug in. Stephanie had brought fried chicken and brownies. Jo had explained how she needn't bring a whole meal for the family, just something to share. The women had set up one of their traditional thirty-yard spreads, a length of folding tables that really did measure thirty yards. Stephanie was amazed by the fact that the whole thing was covered with various types of dishes, everything from salad to dessert.

Stephanie was relieved that she and Drew seemed to have lost some of the tension from earlier. She didn't know whether it was from going through the stress of the investigator visiting, or whether it was that the boys were with them, but she was glad she and Drew were back to small talk, at least.

She was just finishing up a piece of Phoebe's famous cherry pies when Pastor Shawn stood up to make another announcement.

"Now as most of you know," he said in his preacher's voice, which easily carried across the park, "we have one more tradition here at our Serendipity May Day celebration. Alexis, will you please come do the honors?"

Stephanie's most outgoing new friend took Pastor Shawn's place, with Samantha by her side. Samantha's arms were behind her back, and Stephanie assumed they were about to hand out some kind of prize for the games today.

"Every year the ladies of the church elect a very special woman to be named May Queen. This honor belongs to a person who graces us with new hope to our community, the way spring brings new hope to summer."

Alexis paused for effect. "Today, I'm pleased to announce that our new May Queen is… Stephanie Cartwright!"

Stephanie's mouth dropped open. Her shocked gaze flew to Drew's, but he didn't look all that surprised. In fact, he was the first to applaud. Everyone else was quick to join in as Samantha retrieved a floral wreath from behind her back and proceeded to crown Stephanie with it.

She didn't know what to say. Tears streamed from her eyes. She certainly wouldn't have expected herself to be in the running for May Queen. This was a community award, wasn't it?

As she looked around at the people she now considered her friends and neighbors, she realized it *was* a community award.

And she was a part of that community.

Since it was late on a Saturday night and the kids were tucked soundly in bed, Stephanie was working on the particulars of opening her new preschool. She'd eaten dinner with the Spencers and read the boys a couple of books at bedtime, but now she was alone in her apartment, very much enjoying being up to her ears in the beginning stages of her dream.

Painting faces on all those precious kids during the May Day celebration two weeks ago had made her more excited than ever to make that dream a reality. She could feel it, so deep inside her heart that her pulse virtually sang from it.

She'd shifted that dream into overdrive since May Day, working on the various details of her preschool every chance she got, often late into the night.

Legal forms and notebooks full of preliminary research stood in precariously leaning piles on her desk and around her laptop computer. She'd left curriculum catalogs spread along the foot of her bed—quite messy for someone who had once forced herself to be a chronically neat person.

It felt good to let go of others' perfect expectations of her and just be *herself,* rather than constantly worrying that she was letting someone down.

She realized that she probably should be actively seeking some other type of temporary employment in Serendipity, not to mention a place to live, but she just couldn't bring herself to put any real effort into it.

But she knew her current arrangement wouldn't last.

The case worker had come and gone, and school would be out for the summer in a couple of weeks. Drew hadn't yet heard the outcome of the investigator's report, but that was bound to happen any day, at which point a court date would be set. He knew she was planning to stay in Serendipity, so even if he needed her to testify in court, he'd know where to find her. There'd be no reason to remain with the Spencers once school was out for the summer.

Which meant Drew would soon be broaching the subject of her leaving. She was surprised that he hadn't already. She supposed she could speak up herself, but quite frankly, she didn't want to.

Why would she, when she was so content?

She absolutely adored Matty and Jamey. There were no other children on earth who had ever touched her heart the way they had. If she hadn't had enough of a reason to want to start a preschool here in Serendipity before, she had it now—for the boys.

Frank kept her on her toes and laughing, especially when Jo was around. As far as Stephanie was concerned, those two needed to stop their bickering long enough to find their way to the altar and get hitched. If ever there was a couple who belonged together, it was Frank and Jo.

And as for her feelings for Drew—they hadn't changed, except to grow stronger. Sometimes she'd catch him looking at her and think he might be softening toward her, but then he'd back off and turn all reserved again.

Which left the two of them at an impasse.

She scoffed to herself and straightened the nearest stack of papers. Mulling over her feelings for Drew wasn't going to do her any good. As it was, her thoughts were interrupted by the man himself knocking at the door.

"Come on in," she called, swinging her chair around to face the door. "It's open."

"You're starting to sound like a local. I'm sure you locked your doors in New Jersey."

She tilted her head up to him, her gaze burning into his. She just wished he could try to understand how she felt. *Fitting in* was something she'd never had before.

But how could he understand? He'd grown up in a loving family and within the close-knit Serendipity community. He had no idea what it was like to grow up feeling absolutely alone in the world.

She decided it was time to bring up the subject they'd both apparently been avoiding.

"I don't suppose Serendipity has a newspaper? I need to pick one up so I can take a gander at the current want-ad section."

"We had a paper at one point. It went out of business a few years ago. Anyway, there weren't any want-ads in it. At least not the kind you're looking for."

"Not for an apartment *or* a job? Surely employment positions have to open up from time to time somewhere in Serendipity. I'm not too picky. Will work for food."

Drew shook his head. "Most of those kinds of transactions are word-of-mouth around here. No sense spending money for an ad in the newspaper when you can advertise in church for free. Besides, you have a place to live."

Taken aback, her eyes widened. "I do?"

"Well, hello—where do you think you've been sleeping these past few weeks?"

"Yes, but my contract with you is almost over. I'm

sure you'll hear from the case worker soon, and unless she needs to visit again, my role in that drama is finished. I'm happy to stand up as a witness for you in court, but you don't need me still living here for that. Not once the school term has ended."

He lowered his head and quirked his lips. "Like you said, your contract isn't up. Yet. So don't be too hasty getting a new job. Like the Bible says, don't worry about tomorrow, it'll take care of itself."

"I don't think I've ever heard that verse before. Pastor Shawn's wonderful sermons have inspired me to start reading the Bible, but I haven't gotten very far. It's a lot to take in, with so-and-so begetting so-and-so and so on."

Drew grinned and leaned his broad shoulder against the door frame. "Started in Genesis, did you?"

Stephanie's eyes widened. "Isn't that where you're supposed to start a book? At the beginning?"

"Well, sure, but the Bible isn't just any book. Not to go into any deep theological discussions or anything, but I find it's helpful to read parts of the Old Testament and the New Testament at the same time. I have a schedule that helps me read through the whole Bible in a year. I could make a copy of it for you, if you'd like."

Stephanie nodded, her heart welling at the way he showed he cared, even when he was trying to stay distant from her. "That would be nice. Thank you."

Thank you didn't seem to be good enough. She was so grateful that God had led her to work for Drew, a man whose faith showed clearly in his daily life and his spoken word. Drew had helped her in so many ways, and not just to get away from a bad situation in New Jersey. She'd never be able to express her appreciation to him.

He shifted, hooking his thumbs into the front pockets of his jeans. "I'll be sure and get that for you. In the meantime, you might want to start reading the Book of Matthew. You'll find that verse we were just talking about not too many chapters in."

His blue jeans and dark gray T-shirt were a welcome change, though she was used to seeing him without shoes—they were the first thing to go once Drew stepped into the house after work. The man leaning on her door frame in casual clothes, his hair rumpled and a dark shadow of whiskers across his jaw, wasn't remotely like the nerdy academic she'd imagined before she'd come to Serendipity.

She liked the shirt-and-tie Drew, but she thought she almost liked the casual Drew better. He looked as if he was ready to mount a horse and ride off into the sunset—except maybe for his lack of boots.

"Horse?" Coming slowly back to earth, *horse* was the only word Stephanie heard Drew say.

"I beg your pardon? Something about a horse?"

"Well, sure. If you're going to stay in Serendipity, you have to learn how to ride a horse."

"Hmm," she said, suspicious of his motives. "So I can tie my old nag to the hitching post in front of Cup O' Jo?"

He chuckled. "Something like that. You up for it? Tomorrow? We can either take the kids with us, or else it can be just you and me."

Something about the way he said *just you and me* made her stomach flutter. Was she getting mixed signals from him, or was it all in her imagination?

Was there hope, or was she just setting herself up for another bad fall?

Chapter Ten

Drew settled himself down on the front porch steps and leaned his palms back against the wood planks. Matty and Jamey were wrestling around in the dirt in front of the house. Pop had gone to get Jo so they could watch the boys while Drew and Stephanie went riding, but the old couple hadn't yet returned. The boys were wiggly and rambunctious at the best of times. Drew couldn't be expected to keep them corralled indefinitely. They were kids, and kids wanted to play.

"I really didn't know what to wear to go horseback riding," Stephanie said, skipping down the stairs of her apartment. "I don't have cowboy boots, so I guess sneakers are going to have to do, yes?"

"Ah. No. Sshh!" Drew protested, but it was too late. The twins had heard the words *horseback riding*. He had forgotten to tell Stephanie that he hadn't mentioned to the twins where they were going. The boys loved horseback riding and he didn't want to disappoint them.

Now, it looked as if he wouldn't have to. The twins were already jumping up and down and cheering about going on *their horseys*. And while Drew might have been tempted to weather the storm and leave them with Pop and Jo, anyway, he knew Stephanie had too soft a heart not to take the boys with them.

And here he'd really been looking forward to having some time alone with her.

"Oh, hey, little dudes," she said, reaching down to hug both of them at the same time. "I didn't realize you guys were going with us."

"Yeah," Drew said, groaning. "Neither did I."

Stephanie was already rounding the boys up and herding them inside. She certainly had an amazing way with them. And it wasn't just the boys. She'd reached each and every member of his family. With her pancake breakfasts. Her cheerful morning personality. The way she threw herself so completely and with such joyful abandonment into any project she wanted to accomplish, from dusting the mantel to playing board games with the boys.

He owed her a lot—far more than he was able to pay her in a salary. Which was a stress in itself. He'd almost reached the end of the meager savings he'd set aside for that purpose. If he had more—

If he had more—what? He would ask her to stay on as the nanny? He shook his head. That didn't seem quite right.

"I have a great idea!" Stephanie exclaimed, snapping Drew out of his thoughts. He had to smile when she became animated about something. The woman had boundless energy, and such an upbeat personality that a man would have to be made out of stone not to respond to her.

"What do you say we invite Pop-Pop and Auntie Jo along for our ride?" she asked the twins. Jo was the designated aunt to every one of the town's children, Drew's own boys being no exception.

He groaned again. When he'd first suggested this little outing, he'd been anticipating a more intimate situation, just him and Stephanie.

Alone.

Not that he begrudged his sons tagging along. He would never do that, and he knew Stephanie wouldn't, either.

But Pop and Jo?

Talk about a way to ruin a date—or whatever it was. Those two would undoubtedly talk nonstop throughout the whole ride—bicker, actually, knowing the two of them. Putting Pop and Jo in the same county was one state too close. He loved the older folks, but—

"Hey, are you okay? You have an odd look on your face, like you ate something that didn't agree with you." Stephanie ushered the boys inside the house, encouraging them to go put on their *cowboy clothes.* "Do you still want to go horseback riding today?"

"No, no. I'm fine. And obviously the boys are excited."

"I hear a *but* in there."

"But inviting Pop and Jo? Really?"

"That's the best part!" When she smiled, her whole countenance lit up. He was almost inclined to agree with her, just to keep seeing that look on her face.

He shook his head and chuckled. "You can't honestly believe that."

"Oh, dear," she exclaimed, a frown worrying her lips. "Your father isn't in any condition to ride a horse, what with his bum leg and all, is he?"

"Ha!" Drew burst out. "Don't let *him* hear you say

that. The old man's been riding longer than he's been walking. He's better on horseback than he is with his cane—although he may be just as dangerous."

"Oh. Good, then."

"I'm still unclear how adding Pop and Jo to our little excursion can be considered the *best* part."

Her sly grin explained more than her words ever could, and Drew broke out in another round of laughter. "Matchmaking. Turnabout is fair play."

"I have no idea what that means," she informed him, although he suspected that she did. There was no way she could possibly have missed all the times Pop and Jo had pushed them together, trying to merge them into a couple. The persnickety old folks weren't exactly the most subtle individuals on the planet.

"Don't you?" he prodded.

She pretended like she didn't hear him and continued her own train of thought. "If ever two people should be together, it's Jo and your father."

"That's a scary thought."

Again, she ignored the sarcasm in his comment. "We just have to figure out a way to make them admit they care for each other. That ought to be simple, right?"

He crossed his arms. "If you say so. Personally, I think you'd have better luck tying two cats together by their tails. You'd probably get scratched less, too."

"You have no faith in the power of love."

"Hmph." His arms were already folded, so he crossed one ankle in front of the other. If he could have crossed anything else, he would have. This whole *power of love* conversation was frightening the socks off of him, and it wasn't just because they were discussing getting his

Pop and Jo together on a permanent basis, as terrifying as that thought might be.

He scuffed the tip of one boot against one of the porch's rough wood planks and then lifted his tan Stetson, brushed back his hair with his fingers and planted the hat back on again, this time low over his brow.

"Are you ready to ride, or what?"

Stephanie wasn't anywhere near ready to ride a horse. She'd never been close to one of the creatures in her life. She wouldn't have ever imagined that she would come to enjoy the pungent odor of horseflesh and hay that assailed her nostrils as she entered the dimly lit stable, but she'd come to associate the smell with Serendipity. As her love for the town grew, her appreciation for the scent of livestock grew, as well. But that's where her pleasure ended and her panic began.

She hadn't realized that horses were so large in person. She'd only ever seen them on television, and they didn't look quite so large with actors riding them.

She couldn't even see over the shoulder of the enormous mare Drew had given her to ride. It reminded her more of an elephant than an equine. Was he seriously expecting her to mount this thing?

He had to be joking. He'd given her the biggest, tallest horse in the stable.

Frank and Jo were already mounted on their own trusty steeds, and Drew was helping the boys onto their horses, as well. The older couple had been thrilled to be invited along on the family outing. Drew's phone call had caught them before they left Cup O' Jo, so they met Drew, Stephanie and the boys at the town stable, where Drew rented out horses for them for the day.

Stephanie set her jaw. If Frank and Jo could get on their horses, so could she, she thought, determined not to make a fool of herself. She stared at the stirrup as if it was a mountain she must scale.

How was she supposed to get her leg extended enough to lace her foot through one stirrup, much less find the momentum to swing her other leg up and over?

She'd seen it done in the movies, and the actors always made it look easy. There must be a trick to it, and she would just have to figure out what it was.

She grabbed the stirrup in both hands and lifted her left foot, hopping around on her right one until she was finally able to thread the left through the leather.

She was certain she was going to break something—probably her neck. The saddle horn looked like her best chance for leverage, so as soon as she was sure she could maintain her balance for a moment, she grasped for the top of the saddle, breathing a sigh of relief when her fist closed tightly around the protruding leather.

Success. Now it was just a matter of getting enough of a start to be able to pull herself up and over.

She took a deep breath and counted down.

Three. Two. One.

Before she could so much as hop, skip or jump, she found herself floating in midair, with no stirrup or saddle horn in her reach to help her balance, only a pair of strong hands at her waist. A moment later, she found herself upright on the saddle, her legs dangling off either side. The horse shifted underneath her and she squealed and lunged for the mare's mane, but she needn't have bothered, for Drew hadn't yet released his hold on her waist. It was both reassuring and unnerving at the same time, having him holding her this way.

"Slide your other foot into the stirrup, grip with your knees and lean back on your heels for balance," he instructed briskly, sounding a little amused.

She wasn't surprised. She must have looked like an utter fool trying to mount the horse on her own. She realized she probably should have waited for his help to begin with, but she still had a little pride, although she suspected that by the end of the day, she wouldn't have enough vanity left to fill a tea cup.

She was vitally aware that Drew was still touching her, making sure she stayed upright in the saddle while she found her equilibrium. She thought she had her balance, but she appreciated his gentlemanly kindness and attentiveness just the same. It was nice of him not to allow her to take a very unladylike nosedive.

Perhaps she was enjoying his attention a little more than she ought to be. She had to remind herself that they were trying to play matchmaker for Frank and Jo—not each other. It was easy to get sidetracked with him looking up at her that way. She glared down at him, but she couldn't find it in her to put any real feeling behind it.

"You could have at least warned me before you launched me up like a rocket," she grumbled good-naturedly. "You took ten years off of my life just now."

"You looked like you needed a little help," he drawled.

"A *little?* You select the biggest horse in the barn for me and you think I need a *little* help? What am I missing here?"

"I picked Juliet because she's the gentlest horse in the herd. She wouldn't go much beyond a trot if there was a nest of hornets on her tail. You're perfectly safe with her."

"Well, that's a relief." She couldn't help the note of friendly sarcasm that accompanied her statement.

"Are you two going to sit here blabbing all day or are we going to have us a trail ride?" Frank demanded, pulling his appaloosa alongside Stephanie's bay.

"I've still got to saddle up Romeo," Drew informed him. "You guys go ahead and lead the horses out to the corral. I'll be along shortly."

Jo, who was leading the twins' horses by their halters, reined her horse toward the stable door. "Get a move on, old man," she shouted over her shoulder. "Drew can tack up faster than you can get your old nag out this door."

Frank grunted and nudged his horse into a walk. "Always tellin' me what to do," he groused at no one in particular as he followed Jo and the boys out.

Stephanie watched them leave without as much as flinching a muscle. She was afraid even to breathe, as she had no idea what types of movements might possibly startle her horse. Drew had placed Juliet's reins into her hand before he'd disappeared into one of the stalls, but he'd left out some vital pieces of information. She had a few questions about this riding business, things she needed to know *before* she shifted this horse into gear.

Like how to steer. And more importantly, how to *stop*. She had a sudden vision of Juliet running at breakneck speed through an overgrown field—with Stephanie hanging on for dear life.

A trip to the emergency room might be a fine way to bring Frank and Jo together, but it wasn't Stephanie's idea of a good time.

"Hey, sweetheart," said Drew, leading his horse out of one of the far stalls. He walked his now-saddled black toward her. "Why aren't you out with the rest of the family?"

Her heart lurched into some sort of up-tempo Latin beat at the casual way he included her in his family unit, though she knew he was probably talking off the top of his head and didn't mean anything by his words. She'd been tagging along with them for several weeks now, so she supposed it only seemed natural.

But *sweetheart?* Was that off-the-cuff, as well?

"Um, let me see here," she answered blithely. "Maybe because I haven't the slightest idea what I'm doing. I've never even been near a horse before, never mind attempted to try to ride one. Where is the ignition, again?"

Laughing, Drew mounted and pulled his horse in front of her. "Don't worry about that. Just sit back and enjoy the ride. Juliet will follow Romeo anywhere."

Drew clicked his tongue and Romeo danced to the side and then moved forward. Stephanie waited for her own mount to follow, but Juliet just snorted and tossed her head, refusing to move an inch.

"Drew," she called quickly, before he, too, disappeared from view. "This isn't working."

Drew pulled back, glanced behind him and laughed. "Loosen up a bit on the reins, sweetheart. You've got a good *whoa* going on there."

"Oh." It took her a moment just to recover from his easy grin and the way he'd called her *sweetheart* again as if it was the most natural thing in the world. If this was going to be a habit with him, she thought she liked it. He had her world in a tailspin. But right now she needed to concentrate on following his advice.

He leaned back in the saddle, tipped back his hat and winked at her. She decided she definitely liked the casual Drew, the one in jeans and a cowboy hat and old, scuffed riding boots.

Her left hand was fisted over the reins, and she could immediately see what Drew was trying to tell her. The lines were tight from Juliet's mouth to her fist. Taking a deep breath, she released the death grip she'd been holding on the saddle horn and used her right hand to loosen the reins through her fingers, hoping they wouldn't slip from her hands.

"That's better," Drew encouraged. "Now nudge her with your heel."

Stephanie hardly touched her foot to Juliet's side. "Giddy-up, horsey," she quipped, feeling ridiculous.

Drew pulled his horse around in a circle so their mounts were side-to-side.

"She has to feel it," he explained. "Like this." He leaned over and grabbed her ankle, and then dug it into the horse's side with surprising force.

Stephanie gasped, certain that Juliet was going to bolt. Instead, the mare just whickered and plodded forward at a pace even Stephanie could handle.

"There you go. See?" Drew was very encouraging, considering she put the R in rookie when it came to horseback riding. "You're riding a horse."

"Not as well as your three-year-olds," she replied tartly, but she sat a little taller in the saddle just the same, and lessened her hold on the saddle horn—at least marginally.

Drew pulled his mount ahead of her, and this time Juliet did, indeed, follow Romeo, outside the stable door and into the corral where the others were waiting.

"Thought you guys might have gotten lost," Frank grumbled. "Or stopped for a little kissy-face."

"Frank!" Jo scolded.

"Pop!" Drew protested at the same time.

Stephanie just blushed.

With a rumbling, self-satisfied chuckle, Frank urged his mount forward, leading all of them out of the corral and down a well-worn grassy path. The boys followed, and then Jo, Drew and finally, Stephanie.

She didn't mind bringing in the rear. For one thing, no one could see her awkwardness in the saddle. And for another, it gave her a good excuse to watch Drew from behind.

And what a view it was. Just as she'd suspected the first time she'd seen him, he cut a fine figure on a horse—tall and lean and broad-shouldered.

While she was already starting to feel saddle sore, Drew moved as one with his mount. Unlike Stephanie's horse, Drew's black was skittish and full of power, yet Drew held him completely under control, the animal's power leashed by man. It was as if Romeo was an extension of him, and it was a beautiful thing to watch.

He was a beautiful thing to watch.

She was falling for him. Hard. It wasn't as if she could deny her feelings anymore, and she wasn't sure she wanted to. It was far more than just their intense initial attraction, or the potent, almost palpable chemistry between them.

She was intrigued by every single thing about him. The way he always dressed up to go out, yet went barefoot inside his house. The way he chewed on the arm of his reading glasses when he was deep in thought. The tender way he brushed his sons' hair off their foreheads when he put them to bed at night. The kiss they'd shared, a magnetic and wonderful moment she would never forget.

She no longer believed he thought what had happened between them was *nothing*. Privately, she believed he'd been trying to protect her with his unusual and unendorsed chivalry.

She knew he was fresh from a painful divorce. His child custody issue was the biggest thing on his mind—and rightly so. She wouldn't expect any less from a man so completely committed to being a good father for his twins.

But when all was said and done, after Drew was able to walk away with a clear conscience and could look toward his future, she was still going to be around. If God was willing, Drew Spencer and his wonderful family would always be a part of her life.

And if God especially blessed her, a big part.

"Can we run the horses, Daddy?" Matty asked excitedly as they all drew up in a field.

"We want to run," Jamey echoed.

Oh, no. Stephanie definitely did *not* want to run, or gallop, or whatever it was called on a horse. And hopefully, neither did Juliet.

"Please, no," she said aloud, speaking both to Drew and to her horse.

Drew guided Romeo around in a small circle and grinned. His smile alone was enough to warm her heart, stoking it into a tender glowing flame. "Are you sure you don't want to try a trot? It's a lot of fun."

She knew he was teasing her rather than pressuring her, so she shook her head and laughed. "Thank you, no. Count me out. Juliet and I will be just fine staying right here to wait for you."

"I do believe I'll hang back and keep Stephanie company," Jo said, her usually exuberant voice sounding strained, at least to Stephanie's ears. Frank must have heard it, as well, for he pulled around and trotted his horse to Jo's side, a deep frown lining his face.

"Are you okay, honey?" he inquired in a voice that was surprisingly gentle, especially for Frank. "You sound like you've got a thorn in your shoe."

Well, that sounded more like the old man she knew.

"What I have," Jo informed him, stretching forward in the saddle, "is a bogus hip. And at the moment, that lousy piece of metal is giving me all sorts of grief."

Stephanie hadn't realized that Jo had had a hip replacement. What was the woman doing up on a horse? That had to be painful.

"You're a stubborn woman," Frank said, sliding off his mount and limping to the side of Jo's horse, lifting one stirrup to adjust the girth on her saddle. Stephanie privately thought that in a fair race, Frank was equally as stubborn, which was what made it so fun to watch the two of them going at it full steam.

"I'm just sore. And who wouldn't be, at this age? An old woman has the right to grumble now and again."

"Not in front of me, you don't," Frank retorted. "My poor ears can't handle that sort of thing. You'll give me a headache."

Which, translated, Stephanie thought, meant he'd really been worried that Jo might be hurt. But, of course, he'd never admit it.

"I'm fine," she insisted. "I just need a moment to catch my breath."

"Before we even started, I asked you if you were up for riding today," Frank accused, narrowing his eyes on Jo. "You said you were. I don't know what you were thinking, woman. You shouldn't have come. You're going to really hurt yourself one of these days and I may not be there to help you."

Jo glared at him. "Don't you even think about telling me what I can and can't do, Frank Spencer. Not now, and not ever. I've been riding horses all my life. No stupid hip replacement surgery is going to keep me from doing what I love, and neither is some obstinate old man."

"When the good Lord was handing out common sense, woman, you must have been standing behind the door."

Jo laughed. Stephanie was amazed at how they got along with each other, saying things no one else would dare.

"And you were running the other way," she countered.

"I could have run back again just as fast. I'll have you know I was the master of the hundred-yard dash in my time."

"Sure. At field day in elementary school."

Stephanie's attention began to drift. She knew there would be no stopping the two older folks once they got going, and they were on a roll now. Besides, she wanted to see what Drew was doing.

She turned in her saddle and looked behind her, no longer completely terrified that her horse would bolt as soon as she shifted her weight.

Drew had taken the boys a little way off and was allowing them to *run*. Actually he had them at a slow trot, but the twins were still bouncing around in the saddle. So much so that, if it was anyone else but Drew watching them, Stephanie would have been afraid one of the boys might take a tumble and hurt themselves. But she had complete confidence in Drew, and the utmost faith that he knew exactly what he was doing, both with the horses and with his sons. The twins were perfectly safe in his capable hands.

Drew glanced up and she waved. When he tipped his hat in response, her heart fluttered and it took a moment for her to catch her breath.

She'd never felt like this with Ryan, even before he'd turned abusive. He was always pushing her, too hard and too fast, and she'd unconsciously held back.

Now she knew why.

Drew followed the boys back over to where she waited with her mount, and she assumed they would all be ready to head back home, but Frank and Jo didn't seem to notice Drew's return, or if they did, they ignored it. The two older folks were deep in conversation, their mounts side by side. Frank was leaning his hand on the back of Jo's saddle as he spoke closely into her ear.

Drew reined in close to Stephanie and smiled as he realized the direction her gaze was directed. "How goes the matchmaking?"

"Uh," she responded blankly. She'd been concentrating most of her resources on learning to ride and staying in the saddle. And what was left of her attention kept drifting to Drew. She'd completely forgotten her ulterior motive for going on this horseback outing had originally been to force Frank and Jo together as a couple and compel them to admit their feelings for each other.

Fortunately, they seemed to be doing just fine coupling off on their own, although in their typical back and forth way.

Stephanie wasn't sure they'd ever truly admit to having feelings for each other.

"I'm afraid I'm failing in that regard," she admitted. "I don't think we're any closer to seeing a wedding in their future than we ever were."

"Don't feel bad. You wouldn't be the first to be unsuccessful in that endeavor. Maybe those two simply aren't meant to be together. They both live with family. Maybe it's better that way. Family won't kick them out when they get annoying."

"And yet it's clear they care for each other," Stephanie added thoughtfully. "You should have heard how concerned your father was when he thought Jo might be hurt. It was really touching."

"Touching?" Drew parroted, chuckling and patting Romeo on the neck. "I don't know about that."

"Daddy, Daddy," Matty exclaimed as he bounced forward on his horse. "Pop-Pop and Auntie Jo are holding hands."

The way the little boy said it made Stephanie laugh. *Holding hands* may as well have been *flying to the moon to eat green cheese.* Completely impossible and equally as unappealing in the eyes of a three-year-old boy.

Matty was loud in his exuberance and excited by his finding—loud enough for Frank and Jo to hear what was being said. Frank spurred his horse a comfortable distance away from Jo, but not before Stephanie had switched her gaze their direction and had seen the truth.

Frank and Jo really *had been* holding hands.

Interesting.

Drew must have seen it, too, because he began sputtering and gasping, trying to harness his amusement.

"Shush now, Matty. It's not polite to talk about what other people are doing."

"They love each other," Jamey insisted, pulling back too hard on his horse's reins and causing his sorrel to toss her head.

Matty was exuberant in his haste to one-up his twin brother and make his final observation.

"They should get married."

Chapter Eleven

Pop and Jo had gone ahead with the kids, leaving Drew and Stephanie alone to walk their horses back to the stable.

"It's really nice out here," Stephanie remarked, gesturing at the rolling meadow before them. "There's something wonderfully stark and majestic about Texas. The spring wildflowers peeking through the dry grass are absolutely lovely."

The wildflowers weren't the only gorgeous thing in this field, but all he said was, "Texas is a beautiful place."

In truth, he had nothing to compare it to. He was Texas born and bred, and proud of it. He'd even attended college within the Lone Star State. He'd never seen a reason to go any farther.

"I'll be honest with you…. I didn't notice the beauty of Serendipity when I first drove in." She looked sheepish for a moment. "To me it looked dry and barren. Of course, I hadn't been out of the metropolitan areas much back on the east coast. Now that I've been here awhile,

I think I would balk if I went back to all the black asphalt the city has to offer."

"I know what you mean." He tipped his hat back with his palm and studied her, thinking about how she'd blossomed under country life. She was just blooming—her cheeks a healthy rose and pure delight in her eyes. She didn't even notice his gaze on her because she was too busy enjoying the nature around her. She brought a new kind of beauty to Texas—not just in her outward features, but in her heart.

She glanced at him and the color in her face heightened. "Well," she said softly, "as lovely as this is, we probably ought to be heading back. I'd hate for the twins to tire Jo and Frank out too much. Jo's been a trouper, but I think the horseback ride might have been too much for her. If you ask me, she looked peaked there toward the end."

See, now here was why Drew was so attracted to her. She always put the needs of others before her own.

Sometimes too much, in his opinion. She was probably right about the boys tiring the old folks out, but was it completely selfish of him to want a little more time with her?

Alone?

Or maybe that was the real issue. Maybe she was uncomfortable being alone with him. Which wasn't surprising, he supposed. He knew he'd hurt her pretty badly by denying there was anything between them. Now that he was considering if there *could* be, he wondered if it was too late.

"I'm sure Pop has everything handled," Drew assured her. "He's really good with the kids. And for all his griping, Jo is super important to him. He won't let her overdo it."

"Do you think your pop is maybe softening toward the idea of something more serious with Jo?"

"Maybe."

"It's all on your father's shoulders, you know. If it was up to Jo, she would have had him standing at the end of the aisle a long time ago, tuxedo and everything. She's in love with him, you know."

Her expression took on the dreamy quality that Drew noticed most women had about them whenever they talked about engagements and weddings. Usually he would have balked and spurred his horse for the hills, no matter whose wedding they were talking about.

What had changed?

"I think he might feel the same way about her." It half frightened Drew to think about his father being serious about a woman. It *completely* frightened him that *he* might be getting serious about a woman.

About Stephanie.

As they turned their mounts for home, they rode together side by side, enjoying an easy conversation about nothing in particular. As daunting as his emotions were, he waited to feel uncomfortable. He *wanted* to feel uncomfortable.

But it didn't happen. He was suddenly extremely grateful that Stephanie hadn't listened to his nonsense about leaving Serendipity. She belonged here every bit as much as he did. His heart was singing. He could breathe again. For the first time in forever, he felt alive.

The next Saturday, Drew and Stephanie were enjoying a lazy afternoon sitting out on the porch, speaking in hushed tones from time to time, but mostly just enjoying the fresh air and the late-spring weather.

Stephanie was working on some paperwork, something to do with the preschool, he imagined. He was ostensibly grading papers, but he kept glancing over at Stephanie. He wanted to say something to change the dynamic between them, but how did a man apologize for the callous way he denied their relationship to others?

He'd just returned to his grade book when Matty charged out the front door screaming at the top of his lungs, tears flowing down his face.

"Help Jamey! Help Jamey!" He kept repeating the same phrase over and over.

Stephanie immediately crouched to his level and opened her arms to him. "What's wrong, honey? Where is your brother?"

"In there. In there. He can't breathe," the distressed little boy sobbed. "He's choking."

Drew's pulse jolted to life and painful shots of adrenaline surged through him. He was right at Stephanie's heel as she scooped Matty into her arms and darted for the living room. Panic lengthened his steps and his heart roared in his ears. He prayed as he went, even before he knew what, if anything, was wrong.

God knew, and that was what was important. Drew felt more inadequate than confident in his job as a parent, especially as a single parent. Confusion and disorder were the words of the day with his two unruly preschoolers. There always seemed to be one crisis or another rearing up around the house.

He knew he shouldn't be worried. It was probably nothing—a simple cough or a sneeze, or even Jamey playing a trick with his brother. But something in Matty's demeanor set off alarms in Drew's head. He instinctively sensed that this time it was something different. Something serious.

Should he call 911?

In a matter of seconds, a dozen scenarios crossed Drew's anxious mind. He'd heard of children swallowing toys or suffocating themselves with plastic bags. He prayed through his worried thoughts, but that didn't lessen the sheer terror of the possibility that his son was hurt.

Lord, protect Jamey.

Drew had always been careful not to let the twins play with toys that weren't specifically made for their age range, and he was absolutely certain there was no plastic of any kind lurking around at their level.

Drew rounded the corner into the living room just after Stephanie. Jamey was hunched over on his knees on the floor, nearly motionless, one hand at his throat, the other across his midsection.

He was definitely choking, but Drew had never before witnessed anything like what he was seeing now. He'd expected Jamey to be hacking and coughing and rolling over and pounding at his chest.

The reality was infinitely more terrifying.

Jamey wasn't making a sound. He opened and closed his mouth convulsively, but there was no gasping, no wheezing. Not so much as a squeak.

And he was turning blue. Not the heated red of adrenaline-fueled panic, but a frightening purple-blue from a lack of oxygen.

Drew fumbled for the cell phone in his pants pocket, knowing even as his fingers closed around it that it would take too long for the paramedics to show up at the house.

Jamey couldn't breathe. He needed help now. He was already starting to waver and sag toward the floor, his usually bright blue eyes glazing over.

"Jamey? Can you hear me, son?" Drew rushed toward Jamey and dropped to his knees in front of the boy. He held his own breath, waiting for a response.

Anything to give him hope.

But the boy didn't react to Drew's words. It didn't even seem as if he was aware Drew was there. He was quickly losing consciousness, and Drew didn't know what to do about it.

His heart screamed in his head as he reached for Jamey and waited for the emergency operator to pick up. He hoped they'd be able to talk him through whatever measures were needed to get the boy breathing again.

What was the best course of action? Should he try and do some kind of modified Heimlich maneuver? Should he turn the boy upside down? Pound him on his little back?

Would that make things worse or better? What about CPR? Or was that only for when a baby's heart stopped?

Drew didn't know. He didn't have any answers, and he certainly didn't want to do the wrong thing and make it worse. It ripped him apart to feel so helpless, and yet he couldn't act for fear of making a mistake.

"Here," Stephanie said, her voice surprisingly calm and collected as she thrust Matty into his arms. "Take Matty."

Her gaze willed him to hold it together. The intensity in her eyes gave him a new sense of hope and strength. "Stay on the line until you get an operator and do what you can to send those paramedics out here as soon as possible."

Just like that, Stephanie took control of the situation. She knelt down behind Jamey, wrapped one arm diagonally across his chest to support him and placed the other one at his back. There was no pause, no hesitation, as she leaned him forward and pounded him firmly between his shoulder blades with the heel of her hand.

Drew winced with every one of the five firm strokes he counted, but he trusted Stephanie's instincts. She'd been trained in first aid. He hadn't. And now he wished he was.

Why hadn't he thought about this before? What if Stephanie wasn't here to perform the maneuver?

He'd be useless and panicking. That's what.

"Come on, little guy," Stephanie urged. "Breathe for me."

She placed her fist under his ribcage and gave five quick thrusts.

Still nothing.

"Stephanie?" Drew croaked out.

Why wasn't it working?

Stephanie didn't appear to hear him, but Drew didn't repeat her name. As much as he needed answers, he understood why she didn't respond. Her entire focus was on Jamey, and that's where Drew wanted it to be. She had returned to thumping him slowly and rhythmically on his back.

"Come on, little man. Cough it up." Her encouragement sounded upbeat to Drew's ears. He was panicking to the point of hysteria, but she appeared in control of the situation, or at least as much as a person could be.

Please, God, let it work.

Suddenly Jamey heaved violently and a small green square launched from his throat onto the carpet several feet away.

The boy rolled into Stephanie's embrace and wailed in fright.

Drew had never heard such a welcome sound.

"Thank you, God. Thank you, God. Thank you, God," he murmured over and over again.

He rushed forward and swept Jamey into his arms, closing his eyes to pinch back tears and reveling in the feel of the boy's arms wrapped so tightly around his neck that his own air was cut off. He kissed Jamey's face and his shoulders and his hair until the boy was squirming to be released.

Reluctantly, he set his son on his feet. The boy rushed to his twin and the two of them immediately started playing with their preschool-aged train set, the one with big wooden wheels and a caboose.

It was as if nothing had happened—as if Jamey had forgotten his traumatic experience already. By the time the paramedics arrived, he'd probably have moved on to yet another toy, with the joyous, limited attention span of a three-year-old boy.

Drew shook his head in amazement. Children were so resilient. Much more so than he was. This was one day he wouldn't forget. *Ever.* He hoped he never had to experience that level of sheer terror again in his life.

He'd learned a valuable lesson today. He could have lost his son because of his ignorance. He planned to sign up for the very next child CPR class available, even if he had to drive for an hour to find one.

If it hadn't been for Stephanie...

He was so thankful for her presence here today that

he knew he'd never be able to find the words to express it. He'd been so caught up in the fact that Jamey was breathing again that he hadn't noticed Stephanie's response. She was still sitting on the floor, her hands braced on her knees and an incomprehensible look on her face, somewhere between relief and queasiness.

"There aren't words," he started, but then stammered to a halt. There really *weren't* words that could convey what he felt, how grateful he was that she'd been here at the house.

That she'd saved his son.

She shook her head and wouldn't meet his eyes. "I'm glad he's okay."

"He's *alive*," he amended, emotion swirling through him and tightening his throat. "Because of you. And don't say it was nothing. It's *everything*. My sons mean everything to me."

He moved to her side and reached for her. Her fingers were quivering, and she was clearly trying to catch her breath.

Drew was confused by the sudden change in her demeanor. Only moments before, she'd been so calm and collected. So in control.

Now she appeared vulnerable. Fragile.

"Sorry," she apologized briefly. "I think my nerves just kicked in."

Drew didn't consider his actions—he just wrapped his arms around her waist and tucked her in close to his chest. The spice of her perfume didn't smell so foreign anymore. It was uniquely Stephanie. He closed his eyes and, in a moment's diversion, lost himself in the scent.

In her.

She shivered. He rubbed a hand along her back, mak-

ing the same comforting noises he did with his sons
when they needed soothing. And then he heard her snif-
fle. He leaned back, seeing the tears in her eyes.

"It's all good," he said, his voice low and husky. He
brushed his thumb across her wet cheeks, drying her
tears. "I don't think Jamey is any worse for the wear."

"Thank God," she replied. "But what if it hadn't
worked? What if he'd—"

She didn't have to finish the sentence.

Drew swallowed around the lump in his throat. "But
it did work. And Jamey is fine, thanks to you. Look at
him playing in the corner. He's happy."

"Yes, he is," Stephanie agreed softly. "And so am I."

His heart welled as he met her gaze. "Really?"

"Really."

Stephanie crouched and reached for the slimy green
square projectile that had clogged Jamey's throat. The
paramedics had arrived within minutes of Drew's call
in to them, and the whole house was alive with noise
and confusion.

Wet. Sticky. Gooey.

Hard candy?

How had Jamey gotten a hold of hard candy?

"What's all the racket?" Frank Spencer demanded
gruffly as he limped into the room, a scowl burrowing
his brow. "Can't an old man get a decent nap around
here?"

Stephanie was surprised Frank hadn't heard Matty's
terrified cries. Apparently he'd been awakened by the
sirens, or else by the ruckus of the paramedics entering the house.

Two men briefly introduced to Stephanie as Zach

Bowden and Ben Atwood had rushed to the living room to check Jamey out. He appeared to have recovered from the incident without harm, but the paramedics wanted to be certain before they headed back to the station.

"Not now, Pop," Drew warned, his attention only marginally on his father. He was sitting crouched on his knees, holding Jamey on his lap as Zach examined the boy's lungs with a stethoscope.

"What's wrong with Jamey?" Frank demanded. When Drew didn't answer, the old man turned to Stephanie.

"Would you like to explain to me why we have paramedics in our living room?"

"I'm wondering the same thing," came a high, warble-like voice from the door. Jo rapped twice on the open door. It was a formality, since everyone already knew she was there because she'd spoken first. She confidently entered the house of her own accord before anyone invited her in.

"I was on my way to the café when I saw the ambulance pass by. You may be the lawyer, Frank, but I'm the official ambulance chaser." She chuckled at her own joke.

Frank didn't look amused.

Drew welcomed the new company with a brisk nod. "Hey, Jo. We had a little mishap with Jamey."

A *little?* Stephanie's heart had stopped beating for a full minute while she'd worked on Jamey. She'd never been so frightened in her life. That hardly qualified as trivial, though she knew Drew didn't mean it that way. She knew from the look on his face that he'd been even more terrified than she was.

"Zach? Ben?" Frank would not be put aside. He

pounded his cane on the hardwood floor like a judge with a gavel. "What's wrong with Jamey?"

Jo shuffled to Frank's side and looped her arm through his. "Patience, old man," she chided gently. "I'm sure they'll tell you as soon as they know anything." She flashed pointed looks at the two paramedics.

"Can you open your mouth for me, little buddy?" Zach asked Jamey. "I need to take a look at your throat. See my flashlight?" The paramedic waved the beam on the floor around Jamey. "I'm going to use this little stick here to help me keep your tongue down, okay? And then I'll look inside your mouth with my light."

Jamey burrowed his face into Drew's chest. He kissed the top of his son's head, his gaze welling with compassion and love. A minute went by as Drew patiently encouraged Jamey to let Zach take a look at him.

"You get to keep the stick afterward," Zach bribed with a grin. He handed the tongue depressor to Jamey to allow him to get familiar with it. "If you're a brave boy and let me look in your mouth, I'll even throw an extra one in for Matty."

Matty shrieked in delight and Jamey suddenly looked a little more interested in conceding. Stephanie chuckled. Pleasing his twin brother was obviously important to Jamey, for he finally assented with a reluctant nod.

"Open wide and say aaah," Zach instructed, gently using the tongue depressor as he shined the flashlight into Jamey's mouth and examined his throat.

"That's my boy," Drew encouraged, patting his son on the back.

Zach pronounced Jamey good and, as promised, handed the tongue depressor over to him. Ben supplied Matty with an identical stick. Before shuffling the boys off to the corner to play, Drew managed to get the sticks away from them, promising them he would help them make puppets.

"His lungs sounded fine," Zach informed the anxious audience of adults. "His throat looks a little red and tender, but nothing serious that I could see. What was it that he choked on, anyway?"

Stephanie held out her hand, palm up. "A piece of hard candy. He must have tried to swallow it and it lodged in his throat instead."

"Hard candy?" Drew exclaimed, his voice tight. "I don't keep any hard candy in the house."

Frank made a strangled sound from deep in his throat and his face went from cherry red to ash gray. He brushed a hand across his hair, causing white tufts to spring to attention.

"It was me," he admitted in a stifled tone. "This is my fault. I'm completely to blame."

Frank's usual outwardly stern nature was now turned on himself. "I could have been responsible for killing my own grandson."

"Frank, dear, take a seat and lower your voice. You don't want the boys to hear you." Jo's voice no longer held that sweet, flirtatious tone to it. She was all business. Even Frank couldn't say no to her.

Not that he intended to. For once, he didn't have a sharp, witty comeback. He looked his age, his face weathered and pronounced wrinkles around his eyes and lips. His breathing was coming in short, strained gasps, and Stephanie thought he might be close to collapsing.

She rushed to the old man's side and, with Jo's help, assisted him to a seat on the couch. She reached for the educational magazine lying on the coffee table and began fanning the old man with it.

She'd expected him to protest, at least a little.

Leave me alone. I can do it myself. That was typical Frank.

Instead, he appeared to welcome the women's help, sighing loudly and squeezing Stephanie's hand to convey his gratitude to her.

"I had the candy in the pocket of my sweater," Frank explained gravely. "You know how Jamey is—he's always trying to pickpocket my lip balm. I really thought that was all he was doing. If I would have known he was—"

He inhaled harshly and then coughed and hacked, jamming his hand into the pocket of the tattered sweater he always wore as if to check for the candy.

"Maybe I really am going senile."

"Nonsense," Jo replied, clucking her tongue at him. "You're the sharpest tool in the shed and you know it. Now stop blaming yourself for something you didn't mean to do, you hear?"

Drew crouched in front of his father and laid a comforting hand on his knee.

"It was an accident, Pop," he said gently, his gaze full of compassion and understanding.

Drew was an extraordinary man, and a loving one. Kind and tender, yet strong and enduring. Stephanie could barely breathe around the emotion swelling in her throat.

"Don't blame yourself, Pop," Drew continued. "It just happened. The Lord has His reasons."

"Yeah," his father agreed, pinching his lips and cringing. "To scare some sense into a stubborn old man who ought to have known better."

"Can't disagree with that one," Jo quipped, feigning a knock to his head with the palm of her hand. "Never in my life have I ever met as stubborn a one as you, Frank Spencer. God has His work cut out for Him getting you to bow the knee to Him."

"Oh, hush, woman," Frank replied, the tender expression on his face at odds with his words. "Me and the Lord, we get along just fine. We've got us an understanding."

And then, just like that, the world was okay again, all thanks to a little help from Jo Murphy. Stephanie probably would have coddled the old man, which she now realized would have been the worst thing she could have done. Frank felt guilty enough. Sympathizing with him would have just made him feel worse than he already did.

Jo and Frank settled in together, probably trading barbs, and Zach and Ben had packed up their supplies and shook Drew's hand in turn, preparing to head out.

"It all turned out for the best," Zach said with a grin. "Thank the Lord that Jamey is safe and sound. Hopefully you guys can take it easy for the rest of the day. Y'all have had enough excitement this morning to last a good, long while."

"I owe a debt of gratitude to Stephanie for saving the day," Drew announced loud enough for everyone to hear. "If God hadn't sent her into our lives, I don't even want to think about where we'd be right now."

Jo beamed at Stephanie. "But He did, didn't He?"

One corner of Drew's lips crept upward. Stephanie

found the look very attractive, but then, she found nearly everything Drew did these days attractive.

Her face warmed from all the attention, but she had to admit it felt wonderful to be noticed. And for some inexplicable reason, the fact that it was Drew who had praised her only made her feel that much better. Her stomach flitted around like a dozen butterflies at the thought of anyone who needed her for anything.

A good man who needed *her* to take care of his *family*.

She'd rushed into this job head-first, more concerned with running away from everything she'd known than about where she was going. She hadn't given much thought as to what lay ahead.

She was thinking about that now.

About a wonderful fifth-grade teacher with the weight of the world on his shoulders, his adorable twins, a cantankerous old man and a vivacious redhead—and yes, even the dog.

As if on cue, Quincy's wet nose burrowed under her elbow. His black muzzle looked as if it had been spray-painted in a perfect circle on his otherwise-tan body. He cocked his square head at her and whined softly, his large brown eyes and the funny, dependable smile on his face somehow making her feel as if everything was right with the world.

"Hey, are you all right?" Drew's deep voice resonated into her consciousness.

Her heart jolted. "I'm fine. Just nerves from the adrenaline, I guess."

He shook his head and his pensive green eyes flickered with emotion. "You had a curious look on your face just now."

She probably had the doe-eyed look of a teenager with her first crush. She certainly felt that way.

"No…really. I'm okay," she assured him.

Without taking his gaze from hers, Drew reached a hand out to stroke the dog's neck and instead covered her hand with his. "Quincy here doesn't seem to think so, and I've discovered he's rarely wrong in cases like this."

Stephanie chuckled at the idea of the dog knowing what she was thinking. In any case, Drew was trying to make her feel better—and it was working.

"No fair, you guys teaming up on me like that," she protested, shaking her head and grinning.

He tilted his head. "Can't resist us, huh? Too cute for you?"

Stephanie's face flamed. If only he knew.…

"I think we should all go to the café and get some supper—take everyone's mind off of what happened. We're all a little shaken up by the events of the day. Food and prayer are always the best answers to whatever ails you—not necessarily in that order." Jo laughed. "Go ahead. Admit it, Stephanie. Doesn't a big, juicy hamburger sound delicious right about now?"

"Jo, I don't think—" Drew started, but he was interrupted by his father, who'd shuffled up only a few moments before, curious as to what everyone was talking about.

"Don't bother arguing with her." Frank wedged his way between Drew and Jo. "The belligerent old woman always gets what she wants in the end."

"And don't *you* forget it, old man," Jo responded, jauntily tossing her chin.

"How can I, what with our weddin' coming up?"

"What?" Drew and Stephanie exclaimed at the same time.

Frank chortled. "You heard me, son. I'm a stubborn old man, but I'm not stupid. It's high time I step up for the woman, don't you think?"

"Well, y-yes, I—" Drew stammered. "You just took me by surprise."

"You ain't the only one," Frank murmured.

Stephanie didn't hesitate to throw her arms around Jo and exclaim her delight. "I prayed," she said. "I'm so excited. Congratulations! I'm so happy for you both."

"Thank you, dear. The scare today reminded us that every day God gives us on this earth is precious," Jo explained. "We oughtn't be wasting it when we could be loving it."

Stephanie's breath caught in her throat as she glanced Drew's way, but he wasn't looking at her. She hadn't a clue how Drew felt about what had been said, but she knew how she felt.

She was in love with Drew Spencer. That was the high and low, the long and short of it.

She wasn't exactly wasting her days as a nanny to the twins, but now she recognized that she wanted more.

She wanted Drew to be in love with her.

"Lunch is on me." Jo's voice rose so everyone in the room could hear, even the paramedics, who were loading their gear in the ambulance. "Burgers all around, and chocolate shakes for the twins. That means everybody— even you boys," Jo said, indicating Zach and Ben.

Zach jogged back up to the doorway, his expression disappointed. "We'd love to, but we're on call. Besides, the men back at the station would be jealous if we took you up on your offer."

"You know that's no excuse. Y'all come around and I'll fix something up for the whole gang."

"Yes, ma'am," exclaimed Ben, his head appearing from behind Zach's shoulder. He rocked his fist forward and smacked his lips. "Best call of the day, by far."

"I'll make it worth your while," Jo promised with a hearty chuckle, expanding her smile to include Stephanie.

"It sounds like we can't refuse," Drew said, laying his hand on Stephanie's shoulder and casting her an amused glance. "Who's up for a burger?"

Chapter Twelve

By the time they'd all eaten a good meal at Cup O' Jo and returned to the house, everyone was back in good spirits again. Jamey was roughhousing with Matty as if nothing had happened, and everyone else was wearing marked expressions of relief and gratitude.

Frank and Jo watched over boys, already playfully bickering about the size of the wedding and how long they should wait before tying the knot. Stephanie joined in the animated conversation while Drew checked his email, a daily habit for him—mostly for work-related reasons, although he didn't really expect to get anything on a Saturday.

He certainly didn't expect to hear from his lawyer. But there it was, in black-and-white on his computer screen—an email from his lawyer with the investigation report attached.

He'd been waiting for this moment. He'd been praying about it, desperate to find the peace he knew he would never feel until he heard the results of the investigation. But now that the report was here, he felt sick to his stomach. He swallowed hard against the burn in his throat and squeezed his eyes shut, trying to contain the apprehension exploding in his gut.

"Drew?" Stephanie approached and laid a comforting hand on his shoulder. "Are you okay?"

He jerked his chin toward the computer screen. "The C.F.I. report. It's here."

Her grip on his shoulder tightened and her expression flooded with concern. "Bad news?"

He gasped for a breath, which came out sounding raspy and ragged. "I don't know yet. I'm afraid to open it."

She nodded, stooping down to look over his shoulder at the computer screen as if to confirm what he had already told her.

"Stupid, huh?" he murmured, looking down at his hands, his fingers still resting on the keyboard.

She shook her head. "No, not at all." She used her palm to tip his chin so he could see the sympathy in her gaze. "I completely understand. The twins mean everything to you. Of course you're terrified." Her compassionate brown eyes welled with tears. "It's frightening how much hinges on this one person's opinion. I know it's the judge who ultimately decides, but I imagine this lady's report will have a lot of influence."

He groaned, pressed his lips tightly together and nodded miserably.

"And I'm not helping, am I? What an inconsiderate comment to make right now. I'm so sorry."

"You're only saying what I'm already thinking in my head." And in a way, her speaking the words aloud *did* help, knowing there was someone who understood how he was feeling right now—and who cared enough to root him on. He'd never needed support as much as he did at this moment. He reached for her hand and grasped it tightly, threading his fingers through hers.

"What do you need me to do?" Her voice had taken on the same quality it had when she'd been saving a choking Jamey—calm, collected and in control. Now he was the one choking, and Stephanie was once again coming to the rescue, just as she had earlier that day with his son.

"Could you ask Pop and Jo to take the boys outside for a while?" He didn't want any of them to see him cry, and he thought he might just, no matter which way the pendulum swung on the report.

He didn't want Stephanie to see him cry, either, but he couldn't find the strength to send her away. He needed her there, just so he wouldn't be all alone. "And then you'll come back?"

She nodded briskly. "Of course."

Drew downloaded the report while Stephanie ushered his family outside, but he didn't open it. Neither did he read the letter his lawyer had sent along with the attachment. He still felt unprepared, not ready even to discover what he was dealing with.

What had the case worker said about them? What if the report was negative? Would he be in danger of losing his children?

Eileen had caught them all off guard the day she visited, from his mad dash scurry around the side of the house and through his bedroom window so he could get dressed appropriately, to the toys the twins had strewn from one end of the living room to the other.

The only constant in the equation was Stephanie— her steady influence with Eileen and her reassurance that everything had gone as well as could be expected.

Now they both would know if that was, in fact, the truth.

"Well?" she asked, slipping back through the front door after seeing that the kids were busy playing on the lawn. "How is it?"

He grimaced. "I still haven't read it yet."

"Oh." She looked surprised. "Okay."

"Will you do me a favor?"

"Anything." She hadn't hesitated a second before answering. "Whatever you need."

"Pray with me?"

"Of course."

He reached for her hands, and together they knelt on the hardwood floor, their foreheads close as they petitioned the Lord for strength and wisdom to deal with whatever they were about to face.

When they finished praying, Drew felt marginally better, although he was still scared to death. But at least he'd taken a moment to seek God's presence, and remind himself that no matter what the social worker had said about them, God was ultimately in control of what happened. The Lord would never stop taking care of Matty and Jamey.

Drew reached for the Bible he kept next to his desktop computer. "I need to hear this right now. Will you read it for me?"

He turned the dog-eared pages to chapter twenty-nine of the book of Jeremiah and cleared his throat. He felt a little awkward. He wasn't a preacher, and he didn't usually read Scripture aloud outside of family devotion time. "Um, this is Jeremiah 29:11. *'For I know the plans I have for you,' declares the LORD, 'plans to prosper you and not to harm you, plans to give you hope and a future.'"*

"Well, I say amen to that," Stephanie murmured, squeezing his hand. "Our future—and the twins' futures—are in God's capable hands."

"Right." Drew glanced back at the computer screen, the flashing cursor pounding with the beat of his heart. "We should probably get on with it, then."

"Okay."

"But Stephanie?"

"Hmm?"

"One more favor?"

"Sure. Of course. Anything."

"Read the report first yourself, and then read it aloud to me. I know it's not going to make any difference on the outcome, but it might be easier for me to hear coming from you."

She hesitated. "Are you sure? This is such a private, personal matter. And you—"

"—need your help. Please, Stephanie." His voice cut out halfway through her name. He hoped she wouldn't make him continue to beg.

Her wide gaze met his. She looked unsure of herself, but after a moment, she nodded. "All right, then. I'd better get started, then."

He stood and offered her the chair he'd been seated on and then stood behind her, one hand jammed into the front pocket of his blue jeans and the other leaning on the back of the chair. The cords of his neck and shoulders strained with tension.

Her lips pursed as she carefully scrolled through the document—pages upon pages of information with bold paragraph headings and asterisked lists. She didn't say a word as she read, although she occasionally nodded or made indistinguishable sounds from the back of her throat.

Fire burned through his veins. He was in agony. The sheer length of the report couldn't mean good news, could it? The case worker hadn't even taken any notes while she was at the house. How had she been able to write in such detail about them?

It wouldn't take that many words for Eileen to say she thought they were doing well as a family. The only reason she'd have needed to write at length was if she'd found issues she thought needed to be addressed, right?

He held his breath, wishing Stephanie would read faster, yet relieved that the words on the screen were too blurry for him to read without his glasses. He wanted— needed—to hear Stephanie's summary before he read the whole report on his own. She would let him down easy, prepare him to face whatever was written within the letter.

Even when she finally reached the end of the document, she didn't say a word. Instead, she rubbed her chin thoughtfully and then clicked back to the lawyer's email and started silently perusing that.

Why wasn't she saying anything?

Was it so bad she didn't want to tell him?

Was he in danger of losing his boys?

He pressed his fingers to his incessantly throbbing temple, sure his head was going to burst at any moment. Try as he might, he was unable to get his thoughts to slow down. He paced away from the desk, pivoted and stalked back, feeling like a caged tiger. Feeling like his chest was going to explode from tension.

After what seemed like forever, Stephanie swiveled

the chair around and looked up at him, her expression unreadable. All she said was, "Okay."

"What?" Drew pleaded. "What did Eileen say? Are the boys going to be safe? Am I going to be able to fight to keep them with me?"

He had a million other questions for her—like what the case worker had thought of their living situation and her opinion of him as a father, if she thought he was able to care for his children.

But all that paled in comparison to one thing—what was going to happen to the twins?

"She said," Stephanie murmured as she stood and reached for his elbows, and then slid her palms down his forearms until her hands were clasping his, "that from what she observed, you are an incredible father who is doing a fantastic job raising his two sons."

The adrenaline surging through him had him literally quivering. His legs nearly gave out from underneath him. He dropped to his knees, taking Stephanie with him.

"Thank God. Thank You, Jesus." Tears streamed from his eyes, but he didn't care. He pulled Stephanie farther into his embrace and kept thanking God aloud for His grace.

She wrapped her arms around his neck, brushing her fingers through his hair and beaming at him through the tears in her own eyes.

"That was the paraphrased version of the report," she said when he allowed her to get a word in edgewise. She laughed softly and hiccupped back a tear. "You'll probably want to read the whole thing yourself, now that you know that it's good news. Considering the fact that

Eileen didn't even take notes, she sure wrote a novel-length report."

"You noticed that, too, huh?" He stood gingerly back to his feet and pulled her up with him. His smile was so wide it was making his face ache, but he didn't care. If he could have grinned any wider, he would have.

The twins were safe!

Or at the very least, he and his lawyer now had a powerful legal tool in their battle for full custody.

"Oh, and by the way," she added, pressing her soft palm against his cheek and beaming up at him. "Your lawyer says he's already heard from your ex-wife's counsel. Apparently they want to set a meeting. Your lawyer seems to think you won't have to go to court at all."

Drew's mood skyrocketed. He whooped and reached for Stephanie's waist, lifting her off her feet and spinning her around and around.

Her laughter was like a meteor shower, threads of brilliant light. When he stopped twirling her and set her back on her feet, their eyes met and locked, and his breath caught at what he saw.

Though she was clearly happy for him—and with him—he detected a hint of sadness in her gaze.

He couldn't imagine why, on a day filled with so much happiness. He only knew he didn't want her to feel that way. This was one of the best moments of his life, and he wanted to share the exhilaration he was feeling with her. He wanted her to feel his joy.

He didn't think about it—there was nothing to think about. There was only the glowing warmth of his heart, the same feeling he wanted to be inside her heart, too.

His gaze dropped to the luscious fullness of her lips, and then to the rapid rhythm of her pulse beating along the line of her delicate neck. He brushed the tip of his finger along that spot on her neck and felt her pulse jump. The spicy, exotic scent of her perfume wafted around him, making his head spin and his heart hammer.

He took his time, hovering his lips over hers, enjoying the experience of her warm breath mixing with his, bonding them together even before their lips met. This wasn't some merely physical attraction overcoming a man's good sense. This was the kind of love he knew he would only find once in a lifetime, the kind of feeling strong enough to trump even his own stubborn stupidity.

He slanted his head and deepened the kiss, satisfied when she immediately responded.

How could he *ever* have encouraged her to leave? He knew better now. He needed her in his life. He'd never felt this way about any woman, even Heather, and he wasn't about to let her go.

He just needed to figure out a way to humble his own pride and ask her to stay.

"What's all the hollering in here?" Frank boomed, rushing in the door as quickly as his cane would allow. "Is everyone all right?"

"Whoa," he said, coming to such a quick stop that Jo, who'd been right on his heels, nearly plowed into him. "Watch out, woman. Can't you see what's going on here?"

Drew reluctantly broke off the kiss, but he wouldn't allow Stephanie to squirm out of his arms.

"I do see," Jo replied. "And it's about time, if you ask me. Now we can all do some celebrating."

Stephanie turned a shade of bright red. "Yes, we can."

When the twins came running in, she elbowed him just enough to let him know she was truly uncomfortable with the situation. He supposed he had to agree. He needed to make his intentions known to Stephanie before the twins witnessed any public display of affection between them. He didn't want to confuse the boys.

When he released her, she ran straight forward, squealing as she hugged Jo around the shoulders and gave his father a big smacking kiss on the cheek. "We have the best news."

Wait for it, Drew thought, a little bit amused because both Pop and Jo thought Stephanie was going to announce that she and Drew were a couple. If everything went well, that would happen soon enough. In the meantime, he was enjoying how this was playing out. Pop and Jo had jerked his strings enough times.

Stephanie beamed. "A celebration is definitely in order. The C.F.I. report came back and Drew passed with flying colors!"

"That wasn't what I meant," Jo said, shaking her head and chuckling, "but that is certainly good news. Does that mean he gets to keep full custody of the kids?"

"We think so," Stephanie answered, and Drew bit back a grin. She'd said *we.* He wondered if she was aware of it or not, or whether it was just instinctual. Either way, he'd take it as a good sign. "Drew's lawyer says that Heather's counsel has asked for a meeting. He seems to think that means we won't have to go to court."

There was that *we* again. From the knowing grin on Jo's face, she had noticed it, too.

"And about the other news?" Jo pushed.

Stephanie's gaze jerked to the twins, and then to Drew. "What news? There is no other news."

"So we're back to that again, are we?" Frank said.

"Take a tip from my book and stop wasting time. God's only given you so many days, son. Don't waste 'em."

Drew didn't know why his father was directing his comments at him. He wasn't the one denying that there wasn't anything between the two of them.

"I think we have more important things to concentrate on right now," Stephanie insisted. Her face was still a bright shade of red, and Drew realized that maybe they were all pushing too hard on her. Maybe if they backed off and gave her room to breathe, she'd be more inclined to admit she might still have feelings for him.

"I think I have a bottle of sparkling cider in the pantry," Drew said, taking the heat off of Stephanie. "I've been saving it just for this day."

"Do we get some, Daddy?" Matty asked, running forward and swinging around his leg.

Drew laughed at his progeny's selective hearing. If he'd been told to pick up his toys, he would have feigned being too far away to hear. But Matty and Jamey loved the bubbles in sparkling cider.

He tousled Matty's hair. "I think it would be okay if you have a glass today. It's a very good day. Jamey, do you want some, too?"

"Yes, yes, yes," came Jamey's excited reply.

"And how about you, Miss Stephie? Are you up for a glass?"

Stephanie had been staring out the window, her arms folded, but now she turned with a steady, genuine smile and a clear, unfettered gaze.

She ran up mimicking the unsteady gait of a preschooler and cried, "Yes, yes, yes. *Please.*"

Chapter Thirteen

"I've been thinking about solutions for you, now that your temporary position with me has almost ended," Drew informed Stephanie as she returned from running errands. He'd apparently been waiting on her, for he'd stepped out from the side of the porch as she approached the front door and had scared her half to death.

Especially because she'd kind of been trying to avoid him for the past couple of days. Frankly, she wasn't sure what to do with him. He went hot and cold on her faster than a bad faucet.

"Is that right?" she murmured. She had been thinking about solutions for herself, too, but she hadn't come up with anything concrete, as of yet. She figured the first thing she needed to do was find housing, and then she would look for a job—beg Jo for a part-time waitressing position, if she had to. She'd spread the news that she was looking for a new place to live around church, but so far she hadn't had any offers.

Drew nodded, looking quite proud of himself. "Yes. I think you should stay."

"In Serendipity?"

"In my garage."

She couldn't have been more shocked if he would have thrust her finger into a light socket. He'd said over and over again that this position had to end, that he couldn't afford to have her living with them anymore.

But his gaze was serious. Determined.

Her breath caught in her throat. "What? I'm not sure I understand what you are saying."

He shrugged as if it was nothing, but it wasn't *nothing*. Her whole world was spinning around the axis of his answer.

"How else can I spell it out for you? I think you should stay with *me*. With us—me, and Pop and the boys."

"Oh. I—"

"Before you say no, consider how much the boys have come to depend on you. They've kind of gotten used to you being around all the time. Our house won't be the same without you, *Miss Stephie*. And not just because you make top-of-the-line kitty pancakes, either, although the kids love those."

"You know I'll visit the twins a lot, even after I'm not living here anymore."

"I'm not sure that's enough." He held his hands up before she'd even thought of anything to say. "I want you to know that I'll do everything I can to help you start a preschool here in Serendipity, even run for town council if I have to."

Her heart felt as if it was going to beat out of her chest. He was saying the words she'd longed to hear— or almost. For so long he'd been persuading her to leave.

Now he was asking her to stay. But she needed to know why.

"That's very generous," she replied.

"Not as much as you think," he said with a dry chuckle that almost sounded nervous.

"Okay." He hadn't said as much, but she felt there was a condition coming up, and she tensed for it. This wasn't quite the way this scene had played out in her head.

She had to admit it…she'd thought of it. Of Drew asking her to stay. But this wasn't what she'd prayed about and hoped for.

This wasn't any kind of romantic proposition, based on flowery sentiments and feelings that would rival late spring on the Texas prairie. This sounded more like a business proposal.

"I'm not in a position to offer you an actual job, because I can no longer afford to pay you a salary. I know that's what you were looking for—I heard you mention it in church. But the room above the garage is just going to sit there empty after you move out. Since you're planning to stay in town while you get your preschool underway, it seems ridiculous for you to have to look for other accommodations. You're already settled in right here. You may as well stay with us."

"Okay," she said again. She wasn't assenting to his idea as much as acknowledging it.

"You're welcome at our table as often as you can make it. While I can't afford anything in the way of salary, we have plenty of food to go around. Maybe we can make the terms of your room and board some kind of exchange for watching the twins once in a while? They've been begging me to let you stay, and I hate to let them down."

So this *was* a business arrangement. His voice was the controlled tone of a professor, asking for help on behalf of his sons. His proposition hadn't come from any deep feeling on his part, but motivated from not wanting to see his twins hurt.

And she was an idiot to have even thought for one moment that it might be otherwise. She was getting really good at misreading signals. When would she learn that to a man, a kiss or two didn't mean a commitment? Even to a man she respected as much as she did Drew. Clearly she'd read too much into the time they'd spent together.

And that was that. She took a deep breath to calm her racing pulse.

She wasn't the woman of Drew's dreams. She was the nanny. It was as simple as that.

Or, at least, it ought to be. With her, it never would be—but that was kind of beside the point now, wasn't it?

And the worst thing about it was, she wouldn't hesitate a moment to take him up on his proposition, even now that she knew exactly what it was. Even with offering her room and board, he was offering her way more than he would receive in return by having her babysit for him once in a while. She felt guilty considering it. But she wasn't going to turn him down.

"I have a couple of ideas on ways you can make some cash while you're working out the details of the preschool. I wouldn't object at all if you wanted to take in a couple of kids at the house, to babysit over the summer. Your reputation precedes you. You won't find any problem locating a few parents who need day care for their children, as long as you keep the prices reasonable."

"Of course." What did he think, that she would charge New Jersey prices in a Serendipity market? Surely he knew her better than that by now.

"We can announce it at church. Or if you don't want to go that direction, I'm sure you can get a part-time job at the café. Jo's always willing to help a friend in need."

"I accept." He sounded as if he was going to go on forever, trying to set her up so she would stay and help him out with the twins.

He didn't need to continue. She was prepared to do all that and more—clean his house, wash his car…whatever was necessary in order to stay with him, and with his family. She loved every single one of them.

It would break her heart every day to be with Drew and not *be* with him. But wasn't that better than nothing?

He probably didn't know how much he was asking, but she knew how much she was willing to give.

Everything.

For a moment there Drew had thought he'd made an enormous mistake offering her room and board like a tenant, when she was so much more to him. But he'd panicked when he thought of her leaving, even so much as to move down the block, and he felt he needed to be serious in convincing her to stay.

Because if she left, his heart would go with her.

Down the street, across town or across the continent. Wherever she was, that's where his heart would be.

He thought it preferable just to keep her under his roof, even if the arrangement wasn't exactly ideal. Conflicting emotions churned through him as he glanced across the truck cab at Stephanie, but she was looking out the passenger side window.

They'd gone to Sam's Grocery to stock up on supplies. He hadn't expected her to go with him, but she'd insisted. She'd said she needed to feel as if she was doing more to carry her weight, and since she enjoyed shopping, that seemed like as good a place as any to start.

As if she knew he was looking at her, she turned her head. Her eyebrows arched as their eyes met.

"Are there sugarplums dancing in your head?" she asked, pursing her lips in amusement.

He nearly swerved the truck at the look in her eyes. "I beg your pardon?"

She laughed. "Never mind."

He glanced at her and back at the road. If he didn't pay more attention to his driving he was going to get them in an accident, even if he was the only truck on the road. "You say the oddest things sometimes. I can't keep up with you."

"Yes, but that's why you love me."

He stomped on the brakes and turned to face her. "What did you say?"

Her face turned beet-red and she averted her gaze out the passenger-side window. "Nothing." She paused a moment, and then added, "What a colossally dim-witted thing to say."

He didn't think so. He thought those were the best words he'd ever heard in his life. She'd said "love." She'd only been teasing, but it was the truth. He *did* love her. And if the pretty blush on her cheeks was anything to go by, he thought she might care for him, too.

It couldn't get much better than that.

But it could get worse.

Drew immediately noticed the sporty blue Mustang parked in front of his house, even before Stephanie did. A sharp pain spiked in his gut like an ice pick. He didn't know *anybody* in town who owned a car like that. He knew that the fellow was from out of town even before he was close enough to read the rental plates. The guy must be loaded to rent a car like that, considering how far away the nearest car rental place was. He would have had to have driven for miles, and a car like that would guzzle gas.

"Oh, no," Stephanie murmured, burying her face in her palms.

"What?" Drew asked as his body surged with adrenaline. "Who is he?"

Three guesses, and the first two didn't count.

"Ryan. What is he doing here?" Her voice was laced with panic. Drew couldn't imagine how she felt.

What *was* the guy doing here? He had no more business in Stephanie's life. Drew was going to tell him as much and get him out of here as quickly as possible. He was glad his father had taken the twins out for an afternoon at the park. He wanted to be able to concentrate all his resources on getting this man out of here as quickly as possible.

"Your ex-boyfriend," he ground out, keeping his eye on Stephanie to monitor her reaction.

It wasn't a question. They'd talked about Ryan a lot. He knew enough about the guy to dislike him, just for hurting Stephanie. Her reaction now only served to crank his protective instinct into higher gear.

Ryan wasn't going to hurt Stephanie again.

He turned off the ignition and reached for her hand. He didn't know what to say, so he didn't say anything, waiting for her to take the lead. Only now did he realize just how much he should have *already* said, whether or not he'd thought she'd be ready to hear it. She should have known how he felt about her. But now it was too late to make up for that mistake.

She was trembling, but when she looked up and met his gaze, it was with the calm strength and determination that he so admired in her.

"I've got this one," she assured him, almost but not quite smiling.

"Are you sure? Because I can send the guy packing, if you'd rather. You wouldn't even have to talk to him."

That's what *Drew* would rather do, to be sure. If he could keep Stephanie from having to relive what was clearly one of the most difficult times in her life, he would. He'd step between her and Ryan and protect her from the kind of heartache he had known with Heather. Stephanie was even braver, because Ryan had been physically abusive. Just to meet him face-to-face had to be the hardest thing she'd ever done in her life.

But she wasn't asking him to step in and fight her battles for her. She was a strong and capable woman, more even than he'd realized until that moment. She was facing down her own past, and her own pain, with more courage than he'd ever shown with Heather.

She tilted her head thoughtfully. "As pleasant as the idea of having you pound him to pieces sounds, I think I'd better take care of this one on my own. I don't know why Ryan is here, but I can guarantee you that he won't be staying long."

Stephanie squeezed his hand and exited the cab, walking toward Ryan with her head held high and her shoulders back. If Drew wasn't mistaken, Ryan was in for a giant surprise. Stephanie wasn't the same woman she'd been when she'd left New Jersey.

She was going to tell Ryan off. Drew only wished he could be around to hear it.

Or maybe that wasn't how this was going to go down.

She *had* been in love with the man…enough to want to marry him. He'd been abusive and over-possessive—could he intimidate her back into his arms? Drew watched as he greeted her animatedly and kissed her on the cheek. She didn't rebuff him as Drew half expected her to do.

What if Ryan was here to make amends? What if he wanted to rekindle their relationship? What if she decided to go back with him?

If Drew could have kicked himself he would have. Why hadn't he taken advantage of the time they'd had alone together today to speak what was really on his mind, to tell her how much he loved her?

Fool.

Stephanie was nodding to Ryan, and then a moment later she was heading back toward the truck. She opened the driver's-side door and leaned her forearms against the top of the frame, smiling down at Drew in a way that made his stomach flip over.

"Just so you know, I'm going to bring Ryan up to my room for a bit. He's flown in all the way from New Jersey to talk to me, so I figure I'll give him the dignity of hearing what he has to say."

"I see," he said, trying not to grind his teeth. He didn't want to know what Ryan was going to say, but he had the gut-wrenching suspicion that he already did.

This was worse than a nightmare. This was a competition, and every male instinct he had wanted to fight for this woman. Maybe not physically, but at least in his heart.

Which was, he realized with a sudden twinge of dejection, virtually all he had to give. Side by side, there wasn't one thing he could offer Stephanie that would even remotely compare to the world of luxury Ryan could provide.

A meager country existence on a fifth grade teacher's salary versus mansions and sports cars and culture. There was no competition in that. The younger man won hands-down.

Ryan was here, wasn't he? He'd flown all the way in from New Jersey to attempt to reconcile with her, or, at least, that's why Drew assumed he was here, and he had to admit that was a point in Ryan's favor. Stephanie had changed. Maybe Ryan had changed, too. Maybe he'd gone to therapy or something. Could abusers ever get beyond that stage?

Drew pounded his fist against the steering wheel. This wasn't stacking up well for him, at least not in his mind.

But the big city life wasn't what she wanted anymore, was it? She'd left Ryan for a reason. And he had broken her heart. He'd physically beat her. She wouldn't go back to him that easily, would she?

She said she loved being in Serendipity, and she certainly cared for his twins. That much Drew knew for certain. She wanted to start a preschool, but he supposed she could do that anywhere—and probably with a lot less effort, if Ryan got behind her and financed her dreams.

Drew wanted to pull Stephanie aside right then and there, take her in his arms and kiss her until she understood how he really felt about her. If only he'd figured that out for himself before he was thrust into a situation where the truth had smacked him in the head....

He wanted to know if she could possibly feel the same way about him, if he had what it took to make her happy. He wanted to give her a diamond ring, even if it took what was left of his meager pension fund to do it.

Last, but definitely not least, he wanted to pack Ryan back in his fancy sports car and point him to the nearest airport.

But that wasn't for him to do. It had to be Stephanie's decision, made without his influence. It was how *she* felt about Ryan that counted here.

He brushed her cheek with his palm. "Whatever happens, Stephanie, I want you to know I'm here. You're safe, do you understand me?"

Her expression was solemn and unsmiling, but she leaned her cheek into his touch. "Thank you. You'll never know how much that means to me."

Stephanie wasn't comfortable bringing Ryan into her living quarters. The room above the garage was her personal space, her private haven, and having him there seemed as if it was spoiling the atmosphere. It didn't feel that way when Drew visited, but she felt safe with Drew.

Ryan was a different story entirely. The only reason she could stand to be in the same room with him was because she knew Drew was down at the house waiting for her. One scream from her and he'd come running.

Ryan couldn't hold a candle to Drew. Drew was the best man she'd ever known, and he was the man she wanted to spend her future with.

It was past time to put her emotions out in the open, be an adult and own up to them.

But first she had to deal with Ryan.

"I'd offer you something to drink, but as you can see, there's no kitchen in my apartment."

He gave her a look that was just a hair short of a sneer. "Really? Not even a mini-fridge?"

"That isn't necessary. I take meals with the Spencer family at the house."

"At the *big* house?" he asked with a snicker. "Who is Spencer? Your employer? That hick cowboy I saw driving you around."

Stephanie bit her lip and gave him a clipped nod.

"You've been hiding out here for over two months? How did you stand it?"

"I don't need to hide from you anymore," she said and realized it was true. She wasn't afraid to stand up to Ryan. "I've been working. What do you want, Ryan?" she asked bluntly. She'd learned a few tricks from Drew. Straight-talking was one of them.

"I should think that would be obvious. I came for you." He stepped forward so he was looking down on her, one of his old ploys. It used to work.

She straightened and looked him in the eye. If he thought he was going to intimidate her, he had another think coming. There was a time in her life when she would have been unsettled by his high-handed behavior, by his money, his clout…and his fists.

Not now. He couldn't hurt her. He'd wasted a trip. And the quicker she told him so, the quicker she could throw herself into Drew's arms where she belonged.

"How did you find me?" she asked, knowing even as she said the words that Ryan's power was in his money. "I didn't leave a forwarding address."

"No kidding." He shook his head in an almost violent gesture. "Did you think you could just leave me like that? That I wouldn't find you?"

Her mind flashed back to the fear she'd once lived in

and a moment of panic ensued, but she quickly brushed it off, remembering Drew's presence nearby.

"I can't believe you left me." He sounded like a little boy. His voice was almost a whine. He was four years older than she was, but he seemed so immature, especially compared to Drew.

She'd never even loved this man. She hadn't known the meaning of the word. She'd been afraid of him perhaps, and she'd been afraid of being alone. Now she knew she was never alone. God was always with her.

"I'm sorry you've made the trip for nothing. I'm not interested in returning to New Jersey, with or without you."

Ryan's eyebrows shot up, and he actually had the nerve to look surprised. Offended, even. She should have guessed that was how he would react.

But then he nodded, as if he'd come to a sudden understanding. "Oh, I get it. You have some kind of legal obligation to the dude in the truck. You always were a stickler for those kinds of details."

Stephanie wanted to stop him before he got out of hand, but Ryan never gave her the chance. When she opened her mouth to protest, he held out his hand.

"Hush," he barked. "Don't worry about it. I'll take care of it. I'll go down and talk to the guy," he promised with a self-assured nod. "I'm sure we can work this out. And if talking isn't good enough for him, I can always get my lawyers involved."

"No lawyers. Ryan, please," she pleaded, thoroughly exasperated with trying to explain herself to what amounted to a brick wall. "Listen to me just a second."

He flashed her his playboy smile and ran a palm over his neatly-trimmed hair. "Well, you need to hurry if we're going to catch a flight back to New Jersey tonight."

She noted that he didn't apologize for the way he'd treated her before, for the anger and the abuse. For treating her as if she were inferior to him. He had the nerve to wonder why she'd left New Jersey in the first place?

He'd always been controlling and domineering, which was part of the reason Stephanie was not entirely surprised to see him when he showed up at Drew's curb today.

He probably *didn't* understand why she'd left. And now he thought he could come down here and she was just going to waltz back into his arms as if nothing bad had ever happened between them?

She didn't think so. She wasn't sure what he was offering—or what he thought had changed—that he'd suddenly come seeking her out. He might just be here because he didn't like to lose what was his.

Frankly, she didn't care. Her life was here. In Serendipity.

With Drew.

"Look, I'm not sure how to get through to you, but I'm not going anywhere with you. Yes, I had a contract with Drew, but it's up now. And besides, it was a verbal obligation, not a legal one."

His face reddened, and his hands clenched into fists, a sure sign he was getting agitated.

She paused and leveled her gaze on him. "Let me be perfectly clear. I'm staying in Serendipity because I love it here and I want to make it my home, not because I'm obligated by anyone to do so."

His expression was a combination of sheer disbelief mixed with a healthy dose of distaste. He was a snob in the worst way. Stephanie wondered how she could only now be seeing him for the man he truly was.

"You've got to be kidding me. You love this *town?*" Then he stopped and his eyes narrowed with contempt. "Don't tell me. It's that cowboy. *He's* the real reason you want to stay in the middle of nowhere."

"That *cowboy* happens to be an educated teacher, and I'd appreciate it if you didn't speak about him in that manner," she retorted.

"Educated?" Ryan mocked. "Stephanie, you aren't thinking straight. What can that man give you? Horses? Pigs? A miniscule house and a dozen children? Come on. That's not the life for you."

Stephanie thought of the twins, and of how very little Ryan really knew about her.

"And what about you, Ryan? What can you offer me? Pain and humiliation and heartbreak? You don't know a single thing about me. I'll take the *pigs* and the horses." She couldn't help it if she emphasized that one word just a little bit.

"You really are in love with this guy, aren't you, Stephanie?" Ryan said scornfully, sounding shocked. She, on the other hand, wasn't stunned by the revelation at all.

"Unbelievable."

She was thinking the same thing—how unbelievably blessed she was.

"Why?" she asked. "Because I learned the meaning of faith and family and fell in love with a wonderful man? A man who treats me with respect and kindness, I might add." She looked him square in the eye. "I don't call that unbelievable. I call it a godsend, and I thank

Him every day for allowing me to be a part of Drew's life, and the lives of his family."

"I see you've found religion, too."

"Not religion. God. Another benefit to living in Serendipity."

"God. Religion. Whatever. You're out of your mind, girl, you know that? I offer you the world and you turn it down." He scoffed at her. "Well, it's your loss. It wasn't like I was going to marry you, anyway. Take that back to your hick cowboy."

Chapter Fourteen

Drew nearly burst the door down. He knew he shouldn't be listening to a private conversation. He didn't exactly *mean* to overhear what was being said, but since he had, he was outraged about the way Ryan was treating Stephanie. He nearly dropped the tray of iced-tea and cookies he'd been bringing to her and her guest when he heard how unpleasant the young man was being.

So much for Texas hospitality. The sooner Ryan Forsythe left, the better, as far as Drew was concerned.

And then he'd heard Stephanie's bold proclamation. Of course, she didn't know he'd heard what she said— but that only made her declaration more special to him.

She'd said she loved him.

His heart was soaring and his mind was racing. The first thing he was going to do when he got Stephanie alone was to kiss her senseless.

And then he was going to ask her to be his wife.

After he threw Ryan out on his ear. The man was clearly not good at taking hints. Even when she'd directly informed him she wasn't going back with him, he hadn't backed down. Drew had a feeling she hadn't seen the end of the annoying Richie Rich with his slick hair and his sports car. Not unless Drew did something about it.

He backed down the stairs and returned to the kitchen without delivering the snack. If he wasn't mistaken, he'd just heard the end of the conversation between Stephanie and her ex-boyfriend. It was only a matter of time before Ryan would come to him. All he had to do was sit back and wait. A confrontation was looming in the distance, and Drew was more than ready for it.

Just as he suspected, a few minutes later there was a knock at the door. He barely had the screen open before a furious Ryan burst through, looking not nearly as neat and refined as he had been earlier. Apparently being rejected and not having things go exactly as he had expected them to had knocked a little bit of the wind out of his sails.

If Ryan wasn't careful, he was about to get a lot more than just the wind knocked out of him. Drew just needed a few minutes with the man to set him straight about a few things, one way or the other. He prayed God would help him keep a cool temper and sort this out without physical violence, even if his first inclination was to grab the kid by the ear and teach him how to speak to a lady.

The moment he and Ryan began to face off, Stephanie burst through the door, out of breath. "Ryan, please don't bother Drew. There are children in the house. You need to leave."

"Not until I've spoken to Mr. Green Jeans, here," Ryan insisted.

"He can tell me whatever he thinks I need to hear, and then he can be on his way. It's all right, Stephanie,"

Drew assured her. "The boys are out with my father. I can handle this."

"Yeah. Like you handle her?" Ryan asked with a callous chuckle.

Drew wondered if anyone could see the steam shooting from his ears. "I beg your pardon?"

"I get it. I do," Ryan insisted. "She's nice on the eyes. It's hard not to notice her. A bit of a step up for you, though, isn't she?"

Well, Drew couldn't argue with that.

"I just came in here to warn you about your dear *Stephanie*. You need to know the truth about her, dude," Ryan continued. "Before you get in too tight."

Drew went stiff, trying to breathe through his nose to quench the urge to clench his fists and deck the man. It wasn't easy to restrain himself from at the very least coming out and ripping Ryan to pieces with his words. As an educated man, it would be a simple thing to do.

Turning the other cheek was easier when it was his face being slapped. But when someone offended the woman he loved, it was a different story.

"You've got to watch her like a hawk," Ryan insisted. "Frankly, it's better if you don't get involved with her at all. She's an opportunist. Take it from me. I don't know exactly what she's got on you, dude, but whatever you're offering her, take it back." He shrugged. "I know firsthand how she uses men and then dumps them flat to move on to new prey. She'll take advantage of you if you let her."

Stephanie made a strangled sound and slapped a hand over her mouth, and then went running from the room. Drew reached out to stop her, but he missed.

"Stephanie, wait," he called, but either she didn't hear

him or she ignored the sound of his plea over her sobs. He knew Stephanie hadn't had her sights set on Ryan's money. That wasn't what she wanted out of a relationship. All she'd managed to take out of her relationship with Ryan was a few black eyes, and frankly, it was all Drew could do not to give Ryan one now for lying through his teeth just to be cruel.

When he turned back, Ryan was smiling—a downright sinister grin, as far as Drew was concerned. Ryan knew exactly what his words had done, and the kid had the nerve to be proud of it. In fact, Drew realized that was exactly what the other man had aimed for in coming here to talk to Drew in the first place.

It wasn't to warn him. It was to hurt Stephanie.

"You don't get what you want one way so you think you'll just try another, huh?" Drew didn't care if Ryan heard the unveiled threat in his voice. He was furious, and it would be better for Ryan if he knew it.

Ryan's smile became an uncertain frown. Maybe he hadn't expected the old *hick* to have the guts to stand up to him.

He was wrong on that count.

"I don't know what you're talking about."

"Oh, I think you do."

"Well, she had it coming, then." Ryan smirked.

"You besmirch the name of an honest, respectable woman and you think it's funny?" Drew set his jaw. Control was difficult, but he reminded himself that being able to think his way through things and not simply act with brute force was what set him apart from a man like Ryan.

"Honorable? Who even says that word anymore?"

"I do, that's who. And now, I suggest you remove

yourself from my house before you say another word about Stephanie, or anything else, for that matter."

Ryan had the audacity to sneer at Drew, so he took one step, and then another, toward the young man, moving forward until he was looking down on the kid, or rather, glaring down at him. It didn't take long for Ryan to become intimidated and duck his head, cowering like the coward he was.

"As a matter of fact," Drew continued, "I don't just want you out of my house. I want you out of Serendipity. The whole state of Texas, for that matter. And don't even think about coming back."

"Why would I want to come back *here?* I'm so done with this place."

"I'm glad to hear it." Drew opened the front door and pointed to Ryan's fancy rented sports car. "Now, go."

Stephanie was packing her suitcase. She could have screamed at the top of her lungs and it wouldn't have drowned out the rushing sound in her head.

After what Ryan had just told Drew, she had no doubt that it was time for her to leave. Oh, Drew wouldn't throw her out on her ear straight away. He was too nice of a man for that. But even if he didn't immediately take Ryan at his word, the accusations would eventually take root and grow.

Why wouldn't they? Every single thing Ryan had said was true.

She *was* an opportunist, however unintentional. She'd never meant to be a burden on him. But how could Drew not see the way she was using him—his house and his hospitality—as a stepping stone to achieve her own goals and dreams? He had just offered her *free* room and board, and for little more than watching his beautiful children now and again, which she would have been glad to do, anyway.

If that wasn't taking advantage of him, she didn't know what was. She didn't mind watching the twins. She'd be heartbroken when she no longer could. But she had no illusions about who was getting the better end of the deal here, and it wasn't Drew.

She tensed when she heard a knock on her door. If it was Ryan again, she didn't know what she was going to do.

She quickly wiped her tears from her eyes with the corner of her sweater, hoping they wouldn't give her away. The last thing she needed was for Ryan to see her cry. He'd get all the wrong ideas about it and start putting pressure on her again to come away with him.

"Ryan, please. Just leave me alone," she said as she swung the door open.

"Ryan's gone," Drew said, standing at the doorway with his hands in his pockets. "I sent him packing."

Stephanie sighed and brushed a stray tendril of hair off her forehead. "Thank you for that."

He cleared his throat. "No problem." He didn't step through the threshold, but he did glance over her shoulder. "What are you doing?"

Good old Drew, blunt as always. Her mind flashed back to her first day here, and Mattie's *Who are you?* Now she knew where the little man got his straightforward nature from—his father.

Tears sprang back to her eyes and she swallowed a sob.

"I'm packing. I promise I'll call the airline first thing in the morning to get a flight out of here."

He frowned and leaned against the door jam. "And why would you do that, exactly?"

She was going to start bawling again if he kept peppering her with questions. "You know why."

"Because of what Ryan said."

"Yes, because of what Ryan said," she repeated, hurt and exasperated at having to spell it out for him. "You heard him. I'm an opportunist. You can't deny that I've taken advantage of you."

His gaze darted away, as if he'd been blinded by a camera's flash.

That proved it, then. No doubt about it. Ryan's words had gotten to Drew.

Not that it mattered in the end. Even if nothing Ryan said got to Drew, it had gotten to her, and she was still going to leave. Why had it taken Ryan's coming here for her to realize the great extent to which she'd taken advantage of the man she loved?

"Stephanie." Drew's fingers caressed her cheek, turning her gaze toward him. He was looking right at her, and there was no anger or betrayal in his gaze.

There was—something else.

"Do you think I've used you by having you take care of the twins at all hours of the night and day?" he asked gently.

"No, of course not. That's what you hired me for."

"And the fact that I added my pop into the mix? You didn't feel taken advantage of then?"

"Not in the least."

"What about all the cooking and cleaning you did so I'd be ready for the case worker to visit? Surely that bothered you."

Stephanie moved back to the bed and started folding

clothes to put into her suitcase. She didn't know where Drew was going with this, and her heart was aching. Her hands needed something to do. "No. It didn't bother me. You didn't force me to clean for you, I offered. I told you I was happy to do it, and I was."

"Were you? And yet you somehow seem to think that I'll resent you for being here, if not now, then later."

She shook her head, even if that was exactly what she'd been thinking. "Eventually you'll feel that way. You're too kind for your own good, offering me a place to stay and food to eat free of charge."

"Then I rescind my offer."

She hadn't expected that. It was as if he slam-dunked her and then threw her out of bounds. She lost her ability to take a breath, and her throat burned with emotion.

"I'll be gone as soon as possible," she whispered, unable to look him in the eye. She stuffed the rest of the pile of clothes she'd been packing into the suitcase without folding any of them. There was no chance whatsoever of stopping her flood of tears now.

"I will no longer be providing your room and board for free," Drew repeated succinctly. "There are new conditions."

"Conditions?" Now she was confused. She'd thought he was showing her the proverbial door, if not the literal one.

"Right. I'm going to expect you to keep playing with the twins every day, and reading to them every night before bed. Hand puppets and everything. You'll need to tuck them in at night, and fix any boo-boos they incur during the day. I'll expect you to have tissues and bandages on your person at all times."

Stephanie didn't know what to say. She was in complete and utter shock.

"And you'll have to continue to put up with my father, at least until he and Jo get married and move in together. I know that's asking a lot, but there you have it."

"And if I agree?" She didn't know how she even got the words out. Drew was offering her a second chance to prove herself. She wasn't going to let him down. He'd get all he asked and more. She would never be a burden to him.

"If you agree, I will fulfill my side of the bargain—to provide room and board and help you get that preschool of yours started."

"Then I accept."

His eyes widened and he reached for her hand. He actually looked surprised—and very pleased. Ryan's words must not have had the impact on Drew that she'd originally thought they had.

"You accept?" he asked as if he wasn't sure he'd heard her right.

"Yes, of course. I'd be crazy not to. If you really want me to stay here, I'll continue to be the twins' nanny for as long as you want."

"I—you," Drew stammered. He was a man of few words, but he was rarely at a loss. He cleared his throat and tried again. "I really want you to stay here," he repeated.

When he squeezed her hand, she smiled and nodded.

"But not as the nanny." His smile was so broad and encompassing and hopeful that her heart stirred despite her best efforts to remain impassive. She really did love this man, with every beat of her heart.

"Nanny doesn't quite have the right ring to it," he said, pursing his lips thoughtfully.

"Child care provider?" she offered, wondering why it mattered what she was called. This was Serendipity. Nobody went by titles here.

"I was thinking more like *wife*."

"Drew?" she questioned, afraid she had heard wrong. Her heart was hammering so loud in her ears that she couldn't be certain.

"If you're really willing to marry a cowboy teacher who can't afford to offer you more than a tiny house and a dozen children, then I promise I will be the best husband you could ever imagine. I will love you with everything I have, and protect you with my whole being."

"You forgot the horses and the pigs."

He looked confused. "What?"

"The horses and the pigs. Ryan seemed to think that was part of the deal if I married you. That might be a deal breaker if you can't provide them."

"I think I can manage to get you a horse, if you really want one. But pigs?" Laughing and whooping with joy, he swung her around in circle. When he set her down, he pressed his forehead to hers and gazed into her eyes. His green eyes were gleaming with unabashed love.

"I know I'm asking a lot," he murmured. "Not just for me, but for the twins. You'll become a wife and a mother and a daughter-in-law all in one quick trip down the aisle. Although I can't promise you it will be easy, I guarantee you'll be greeted by that much more love when you make this house your home."

"I didn't even know what the word meant until the day I joined the Spencer household. My life really started on that day, Drew. And then I fell in love with you, only to think it was all over for me when Ryan showed up tonight."

Drew shook his head and tightened his arms around her. "Never, my love."

Somehow when Drew had been swinging her around, they had knocked the suitcase off the bed. Multicolors of fabric pooled around their feet. Before she met Drew she might have considered the haphazard pile of clothes a mess. Now it looked to her like an ocean of rainbows.

Besides, there was plenty of time to tidy up later—after they'd sealed their love with a kiss.

Epilogue

Thirteen. Fourteen. Fifteen. Stephanie counted heads as the children lined up to come in from recess. Fifteen lovely children from ages three to five, all a part of her first-ever Serendipity preschool class. Teaching these kids was better than anything she could have imagined when she'd first conceived the project in her head.

With Drew's help, they not only had the community behind them, but the church. Preschool was being held in the fellowship hall. They'd even allowed her to put up colorful bulletin boards depicting colors and numbers and days of the week, as well as the Bible stories she illustrated every afternoon.

"Story time, children," she called, moving to take her place in the center of the circle so the kids could gather round.

Suddenly she felt a tug on the bottom of her sweater. She looked down to find Matty's big blue eyes staring up at her, with Jamey ever-present at his side.

"Yes, boys?" she asked with a smile. Her love for them had only grown in the months she'd been married to their father.

"We were wondering," Matty began.

"Yes?"

"Do we have to call you Miss Stephie here like the other kids do, or can we just call you Mama?"

"I'd like to know the same thing, little man," said a warm tenor voice from behind Stephanie's shoulder.

Stephanie whirled around, a smile on her face and her heart welling. She wondered if it would always be like this, the tender feelings that were stoked to life every time she heard Drew's voice or saw his handsome face.

"Drew!" she exclaimed. "What are you doing here?"

Drew leaned down and pressed a kiss to her forehead, then pulled a plain brown paper bag from behind his back. "I thought I'd stop by and bring my lovely wife her lunch. You were in such a hurry this morning that you forgot it. Besides, it was a good excuse to see you."

Stephanie beamed at her thoughtful spouse. There was no one like him in this world.

Matty tugged on the corner of her shirt, reminding her that she hadn't yet answered his question.

"I think Mama will be fine," she said with a catch in her voice. She reached for the boys' shoulders and pulled them close to her. With a smile that said more than any words, Drew stepped forward and wrapped his arms around them all, completing the family.

Her family.

* * * * *

Dear Reader,

It's been a lovely journey to Serendipity, Texas, for me, and I hope for you, too.

Like Stephanie, I have struggled with the issue of self-esteem all my life. I've made the mistake of trying to find my worth through my own good deeds and through what others might think of me. It was only after Christ entered my life that I came to see that through God's plan and purpose for me, I can find out who I truly am, and be happy with myself. True esteem begins and ends with Him.

I hope you'll be encouraged by Drew and Stephanie's story to seek out God's promises and plans for you. God's vision is so much clearer than ours, and His designs so much better!

My thoughts and prayers are on the readers of this book, and hearing from you is a great blessing to me. Please email me at DEBWRTR@aol.com or leave a comment on my fan page on Facebook. I'm also on Twitter @debkaster.

Keep the faith,

Deb Kastner

MEETING MR. RIGHT

You are the light of the world. A city that is set on a hill cannot be hidden. Nor do they light a lamp and put it under a basket, but on a lampstand, and it gives light to all who are in the house. Let your light so shine before men, that they may see your good works and glorify your Father in heaven.
—*Matthew* 5:14–16

To my grandchildren, Izzie and Anthony.
My heart "beeps" for you both.

Chapter One

Dear Veronica Jayne,

I can't believe we have less than two months until our online Spanish class is finished. Have you given any more thought to picking a mission organization? We need to get our applications in soon. I've been seeking the Lord's will on it, but I'll admit I'm dragging my heels a little bit until I know for sure where you are planning to go.

Speaking of our Spanish class, we need to start thinking about how to wrap up our team project. Your idea for our PowerPoint presentation rocks. The Benefits of Knowing Spanish on the Mission Field. It's perfect because we're both going into stateside missions and there are so many Spanish-speaking folks here in America. We'll get an A for our work on the project, and it certainly won't hurt us to know all about the missions that need our skills when we're working on our applications.

By the way, what I've seen of the script you've written is awesome. Keep it up! I'm still gathering and integrating charts and graphics to go along with the explanations you've presented.

I've got to say, this collaboration is surprising in more ways than one. I'm so happy that the professor placed us together as a team. We work well together. I trust you—especially because the team project is nearly half of our grade. Not only that, but I've made a new friend, which trumps any school grade, even an A+.

I'm glad that friend is you, Veronica.

Sorry—I'm starting to sound lame. It's late, and I'd better wrap this up. I have an early day tomorrow.
All the best,
BJ

At least I can look forward to working on that project with BJ, Veronica Jayne Bishop, known as "Vee" to everyone in Serendipity, Texas, thought to herself. *Because the other man I have to work with today is driving me nuts.*

"I cooked dinner last night." Vee crossed her arms, leaned her hip against the counter and glared at the paramedic Ben Atwood, who lounged casually on a folding chair. His legs were stretched out in front of him, crossed at the ankles, and his fingers were laced through the thick ruffle of dark brown hair he wore long enough to curl around his collar.

Their gazes locked. Ben's eyes were arguably his best feature. Displaying both amusement and intelligence, they were a compelling mixture of green and bronze and contained what looked like a purely and disarmingly friendly luminescence that most women would easily get lost in.

But Vee wasn't most women. And she wasn't buying that oh-so-charming demeanor for a moment.

She scoffed inwardly. She knew just exactly what was behind that sparkling gaze, and it didn't bode well for any woman with a lick of sense in her—just ask her dearest friend Olivia Tate, who knew firsthand how unreliable Ben's handsome smile could be. It still rankled Vee every time she thought about it.

"I'm just sayin'—" Ben started to explain, but Vee didn't allow him to finish.

"What? That because I'm a woman, by definition I should do all the cooking at the firehouse? Benjamin Atwood, you know perfectly well that each of us is responsible for one evening a week in front of the hot stove, men and women alike. The fact that I'm the *only* woman who works for this fire department makes your attitude all that much more reprehensible. You're welcome to step into the twenty-first century anytime now."

There was a flash of irritation in his eyes, but it vanished as she watched.

"Okay, first of all, only my mama calls me Benjamin," he drawled, his gaze sparkling as a smile crept up one side of his lips. "And second, that wasn't what I was about to say at all."

He lifted his hands level with his shoulders to show he was harmless. "If you would have let me finish, I would have been able to make my point."

She narrowed her gaze on him suspiciously. "And that would be?"

He chuckled. "Only that I'm the world's worst cook, while the lasagna you made last night was mouth-wateringly delicious." He tilted his head and a shrug rippled across his broad shoulders. "It was supposed to be a compliment."

She arched a brow. His expression was absolutely earnest and without the least bit of guile, so why didn't she believe him?

Let me count the ways, she thought to herself.

Because the man was a chronic liar. And a cheat. He used his charm to get what he wanted. She couldn't trust him or his winsome smile any further than she could throw him, and because he was a good two-hundred pounds and she a mere one-twenty, that wouldn't be very far.

"No, really," he insisted. "I know it's my turn. Look," he said, swinging off his chair with sleek, catlike grace and reaching for a paper grocery bag on the counter. "See? I came prepared."

Vee peeked skeptically over the rim of the bag. "Cans of chili? What kind of dish are you preparing with that?"

His grin widened. "Chili."

She snorted and shook her head. "Why did I even ask?"

"*Slow cooker* chili," he amended, his brow dancing. "My own secret recipe."

"What makes it a secret?" She had to ask. She really didn't want to make small talk with the man, but she had to admit she was curious.

The bronze in his eyes danced with the green. "If I told you, it wouldn't really be a secret, now would it?"

"Seriously? Do you want me to leave the room while you prepare your *secret* recipe?"

"I'll let you in on it," he acknowledged in a pseudo whisper, "if you promise you won't breathe a word of it to any of the guys."

Vee nodded grudgingly. She didn't like the idea of sharing anything with him—not even a secret—but she couldn't resist a mystery. She watched carefully, curious to see what Ben would add to canned chili to make it his *special recipe,* something her fellow firefighters might find especially unique and tasty.

Vee wondered if Ben's recipe was something his mother had taught him, and then her heart gave a sudden, jagged tug, twisting painfully as she was once again reminded of her own mother's recent passing, just six months ago.

Would it ever get any easier? She would be fine one minute—or at least she'd convince herself she was all right—and then the next she'd be struck by a sharp-toothed edge of grief that made her nearly double over.

"Need help?" she offered, her voice raspy as she fought to control her emotions. She refused to let what she was feeling show on her face. Busy hands and an engaged mind helped her not to dwell on the unpleasant emotions sparring inside her.

"Nope," he replied, turning to plug each of the slow cookers into separate outlets.

Vee stared at his back, letting out her breath when she realized he didn't have a clue that she'd just fought an emotional battle and had barely come out unscathed. This was one time she was thankful for the man's insensitivity.

"As you so enthusiastically reminded me," he continued, tossing a glance over his shoulder, "it's not your day to cook. I've got it covered."

He was right, of course. She *had* just declared that it wasn't her turn to cook. In fact, she'd made a big stink about that very issue. But willingly offering her assistance wasn't the same thing as being expected to do all the work. Besides, it made her antsy to sit around doing nothing.

"At least let me open the cans for you," she insisted, reaching into the paper bag and grasping a can.

He shrugged. "Suit yourself."

She opened several sizeable cans of chili and handed them off to Ben, who scooped the contents into three large olive-green slow cookers that looked like they were throwbacks from the seventies—which they probably were, come to think of it. The men at the firehouse often used the slow cookers to heat their food, allowing them to throw together simple meals that made large portions—the two main requirements in any firehouse kitchen. The boys had hearty appetites, especially after they'd been working out with extra PT—physical training—as they were doing today.

Ben and Vee had been left to cover the firehouse. In case of an emergency, they would be first on call. It was part of their duties as volunteers for the tri-county emergency team. They were each paid a small stipend, but nearly everyone, with the exception of Chief Jenkins, had second jobs to support themselves, Vee included. She worked in the gardening department at Emerson's Hardware. She knew Ben worked at his uncle's auto garage as a mechanic, using the paramedic training he'd learned in the National Guard as a volunteer for the county.

Ben stirred the contents briefly, took a whiff, groaned in anticipation and covered each pot with a glass lid.

Vee raised a brow. "I thought you said you have a special recipe."

"I said I have a *secret* recipe. That's not exactly the same thing."

Vee shook her head. Now she was really confused. "Okay, then…what's the secret? I didn't see you add anything to the beans."

"Exactly." Ben crossed his arms over the broad muscles of his chest, a movement that highlighted his large biceps—which was probably exactly what he'd intended.

Vee remembered him as being rather scrawny and easily overlooked in high school, but he certainly made up for that now. Women flocked to the man like pigeons to a piece of fresh bread. He had the build of a magnificent sculpture, every plane and muscle clearly defined, flaunting the many hours he'd spent in the gym—but sadly enough, he knew it. It was no wonder he drew attention to his physical assets—especially since he so clearly lacked anything emotional or romantic to offer.

"Come again?" she asked, pulling her gaze away from his upper arms.

"I didn't add anything. So you see, that's my *secret*."

Vee didn't want to react. She definitely didn't want to encourage him in any way. But how could she not laugh at the utter ridiculousness of the situation? "So let me get this straight. Everyone else adds herbs and spices to the chili to doctor it up, and you, by contrast, just serve it right out of the can."

His grin widened to epic proportions. He certainly looked pleased with himself. "Brilliant, huh? I'm not too keen on onions and tomatoes, anyway," he informed her, making a face like a five-year-old boy being served brussels sprouts. "Give me good, plain beef steak any day of the week."

"Or chili?"

"Or chili," he agreed with a clipped nod. "I told you I'm a horrible cook. I don't even trust myself to add things to the food that comes out of a can. I wouldn't want to subject anyone else to what qualifies as my attempt to make homemade food from fresh ingredients. No doubt what I'd cook up would be nothing short of a blooming disaster—food so spicy you'd burn your tongue to a crisp and your eyes would water until you couldn't see out of them, or on the flip side, food so bland it'd put you to sleep.

"If it doesn't come out of a can or a bottle, I'm helpless. If I lived in a bigger town I'd order takeout every night. As it is, Cup o' Jo Café and the deli at Sam's Grocery get a lot of my business. I actually enjoy my shifts at the firehouse because I get to eat decently, something a little bit closer to home-cooked."

Vee crinkled her nose. Granted she hadn't been working here very long, but she wouldn't classify any of the food she ate at the firehouse as *decent*. Acceptable at best, and barely palatable at worst. Cans of plain chili might be a promotion from what she was usually subjected to.

"And I visit my mama every Sunday afternoon," he added, more as an exclamation than an afterthought. "She enjoys cooking for her son, and naturally I'm keen to eat whatever she makes for me."

"Spoiled," she quipped, but she nodded in approval just the same. He might be a player with the women he dated, but she knew he took good care of his parents, which Vee had to admit was a small mark in his favor.

Not enough to erase the black smudges, but perhaps a small offset.

"A little," he admitted. "But mostly I'm just being a dutiful son."

"I'm sure your parents appreciate that, especially your mother." Her voice cracked a little on the last word, and she scolded herself for being so transparent in front of him. But she couldn't help remembering how blessed she had felt to have had the chance to spend time with her own family, before her mother's recent passing. Now her dad kept to himself, and neither she nor her two brothers could help him get beyond his grief.

Ben regarded her with a thoughtful frown. "I'm so sorry for your loss. It must be difficult for you, losing your mother."

"What? No. I mean, thank you. At least I know she's with the Lord."

"Yes," he agreed. "Your mom's faith was a real inspiration. But it still must be hard on you, having her pass so suddenly."

She didn't know whether she was more surprised by Ben's openness or the fact that there was a genuine note of compassion in his voice. She knew he was a church-going man, but then, so was almost every man in Serendipity. Attending church didn't necessarily mean he was a man of faith.

"It was difficult to lose her," she admitted, wondering how they'd gotten on such a serious topic—how he'd turned the conversation and gotten her to talk about herself. She didn't know why she continued, but she did. "It's still difficult. To be honest with you, I don't quite know how to respond when someone says they feel sorry for me."

She shrugged away the statement, wishing it could be simple to shirk off the turmoil of emotion teetering near the edge of her consciousness. She didn't like feeling as if she were on the verge of an emotional breakdown all the time. She preferred to keep her feelings locked tightly away.

"It's a good thing that you're close to your family. There's nothing wrong with that. And despite my loss, I'm still blessed to have my father and brothers, although we don't get together as often as I'd like now that we're all grown up and living away from home."

"Right. There's a change in family dynamics when we reach adulthood. How does Cole like the Navy?"

"Are you kidding? He was born for service," she said, cheering up a little at the change of topic. Cole was the middle of the three Bishop children, the one who was always causing mischief of one sort or another—often involving his naive little sister and leading her into trouble. Now those days seemed pleasantly nostalgic.

"Cole was always one of the tough guys, and serving the country in the military suits him. Same with Eli. He was playing cops and robbers from the time he could walk," she commented of her oldest brother. "I guess it's lucky for us he ended up on the *cop* side of the equation."

Ben chuckled at her weak attempt at humor. "And you, the firefighter."

"Me, the firefighter," she agreed. "But I never played with matches. No correlation there."

"Never?" he asked, a curious gleam in his eye. "Come on. You can admit it. I won't tell."

She gnawed thoughtfully on her bottom lip, wondering how much she should divulge. Was he baiting her, or was this a sincere attempt on his part to be civil? She decided to take a chance on him. A very *small* chance.

"I might have lit a twig on fire…once or twice, when I was little."

One side of his mouth crept upward in an appealing half smile, the one that sent the single female population of Serendipity all aflutter. "Now we're getting to the good stuff. If the fellows here at the firehouse ever learned that you—"

"But you said—"

Jerk.

"Your secret is safe with me," he assured her. "I'm just teasing. I won't say anything. Besides, if that's the worst of your record, I can assure you that you're lagging far behind me."

"Is that right? How so?"

He returned to his folding chair and leaned his elbows against the long table. His gaze met and locked with hers. "We all have some skeletons in our closets, don't you think? I'm every bit as human as the next guy."

"Really?" Was he sorry for the mistakes he'd made, the way he'd hurt people like Olivia? As far as she knew, he'd never apologized. And even if he had, he'd done some truly callous things in his past, things Vee was slow to forgive.

"I'm just saying my secrets are probably, shall we say, more *interesting* than yours?"

If he thought of his secrets as "skeletons in the closet" then they were probably nothing she would want to know. Her own best, most closely held secret was light and bright and made her grin every time she thought of it. In this case, she highly doubted that any one of his secrets could rival hers. She smothered her grin behind her fist.

Lighting a few pine twigs on fire with a magnifying glass in the sunshine didn't even begin to cover the mysteries she was hiding in her heart. Her mind immediately flashed to the wonderful internet relationship she was building with BJ. She'd met him through a college-level online Spanish class. They'd been paired up together for a project and had been emailing each other daily for the several weeks since. She'd started anticipating his emails, and reading them had become the best part of her day.

That she'd never seen him in person was just a trivial detail. They weren't officially dating or anything—it wasn't probable that she could form a truly romantic relationship in cyberspace—but they'd often spoken of working at the same mission, more and more as the days went by—and who knew what would happen then?

BJ definitely qualified as a *secret.* She hadn't told a single soul in Serendipity about him, not even her best friend, Olivia. It might be pride, or even embarrassment at the fact that the closest thing she had to a real relationship was a cyber Prince Charming, but right now, this minute, BJ was hers and hers alone. Her heart warmed just thinking about him.

She realized Ben was staring at her speculatively and a blush rose to her face. It was disconcerting to realize his gaze could affect her, even if what she was feeling was discomfiture.

"You look like you're deep in thought," he teased. "Anything else you want to 'fess up to?"

Like she'd tell him.

She tossed her chin and scoffed dramatically. "Wouldn't you like to know."

"You'd better believe it," he agreed, his grin deepening to reveal his dimples. His eyes sparkled.

She took a deep breath, mentally coaching herself to relax her shoulders. The warmth spreading from her chest to her face had nothing to do with Ben, she assured herself, but it still disquieted her.

Ben was a flesh-and-blood man sitting directly opposite her. She could reach out and touch him if she wanted to—and that was the problem. Even if Ben hadn't been someone she disliked on principle, teasing and flirting just weren't her style. She knew that had to be the reason why she'd gotten through so many years without a serious relationship.

But online was a completely different story. BJ was safe because he wasn't entirely real, so she didn't have to be nervous when they chatted. She could share her enthusiasms and talk freely with him, sometimes even flirt a little. As a result, she felt closer to him than to most of the people in town she'd known all her life. People like Ben Atwood.

She may not have met BJ in person, but she knew he was kind and thoughtful with a heart driven toward helping others. She didn't have to see him face-to-face to know all of that.

She also could see exactly the kind of man Ben was. He was right before her eyes.

A heartbreaker.

Chapter Two

Dear BJ,

I'm still working on the script for our project. I haven't had time this week to do much more than try to keep up on the reading assignments, much less work on the draft. It's that time of year again. My schedule is filled to the brim with flowers, flowers, flowers.

I love planting seeds in the springtime. Winter has borne down upon the land, harsh and unforgiving, but seeds hold the fresh promise of spring inside them. It's humbling to hold such future magnificence in the palm of my hand. And then to clip the blooms and arrange them into beautiful bouquets—could there be anything lovelier?

On another topic, what are your thoughts about the Sacred Heart Mission to America? I've been researching them and I've learned that they're usually right in the middle of the action, building shelters and offering both physical and spiritual aid for folks affected by hurricanes, tornadoes or floods.

I don't know about you, but that's what I'm looking for—to be where people need me. I can't imagine anything better than to minister to others during their hardest struggles, and I know you share the dream. I'm sure your skills in the medical field will be highly valued.

I'm anxious to hear your thoughts—school wise, mission wise, and anything else you care to add.

Faithfully waiting,

Veronica Jayne

Ben snapped his laptop closed and grinned. He could always count on an email from Veronica Jayne to have him smiling from ear to ear. Beautiful Veronica Jayne, his refined, gracious flower girl, his very own My Fair Lady. Even her name was feminine and graceful. He didn't have to see a picture of her to know she was exquisite. Her elegance shined through every word she wrote. In a word, she simply charmed him.

He'd finished his morning workout early in his rush to get home and see if Veronica Jayne had replied to his email, so he decided to use his extra time to walk over to his folks' house to see how they were faring. He'd missed the previous weekend's Sunday dinner because of an emergency call. Though his parents were in perfect health, they were getting up in years and Ben still worried, despite their protests. He wanted to make sure everything was going well—and maybe catch a bite to eat, if he timed it just right.

As he strode the short distance to his parents' residence, he mused about last night, when he'd been kicking back with Vee Bishop at the firehouse. He was surprised at how much she'd had to say to him—usually she went out of her way to keep her distance. But last night, she'd opened up—just a little. Her cryptic response to his question about what secrets she wasn't revealing intrigued him, even knowing it was none of his business whatsoever.

Frankly, he was surprised she hadn't told him so herself.

When he'd started mindlessly carrying on about the theme of secrets, he'd half expected her to blow him off completely. That or blow *up* at him. He was fairly certain she didn't particularly like him, although exactly why that was he couldn't say. She'd been short with him on more than one occasion in the past.

But in this instance, she *hadn't* blown him off, nor had she become angry. Instead, she'd gracefully sidestepped the whole subject, which intrigued him far more than if she'd become annoyed. What she did or did not care to share with him was none of his business. They might have lived in the same town all their lives, but in truth they didn't even know each other particularly well.

While he was fairly certain he'd rattled her with his tactless digging, for once he seemed to have avoided making her angry. He wished he knew how he'd dodged the bullet this time—usually it seemed like everything he did upset or offended her, even if she rarely vented her feelings out loud.

He increased his pace as a shiver ran through him. He'd be the first to admit he had trouble speaking to women. They were a complete enigma to him in every way, and he put his boot in his mouth more often than not. His appalling trail of failures with the list of women he'd dated proved that point in a major way.

The only consolation was that his very cluelessness usually convinced his ex-girlfriends that he hadn't meant any harm. In most cases, he'd been able to charm his way back into being friends. But any attempt to charm Vee only seemed to make her angrier.

Vee was a tough nut to crack. She intimidated him with the way she pulled her hair back into a stark bun that defined her cheekbones into sharp lines, not to mention the incessant way she was always scowling at him with a permanent frown etched into her features whenever he was around. That he'd gotten her to laugh once or twice during their exchange the night before was definitely the exception to the rule. Maybe he was making some progress.

"Progress" just made him think of the other projects in his life—like his plans for mission work, for example, and the online Spanish class he was taking to prepare.

But most of all, he thought about the plans to meet and hopefully date his beautiful Veronica Jayne.

No one in Serendipity knew of the developing relationship with his internet classmate. Not his paramedic partner Zach Bowden. Not his friends. Not even his parents. He supposed that deep down he just wasn't ready to share her yet.

What a sweet secret to have.

Ben grinned to himself as he reached the one and only intersection off of Main Street, glanced both ways and crossed over to the other side. Serendipity, with its population of less than a thousand, didn't even merit a stoplight and just barely bothered with three-way stop signs. There was seldom traffic to watch out for, and today was no exception.

In fact, it was an unremarkably quiet day in Serendipity, with most folks going about their business as usual. Even the three retired men in their matching bib overalls who usually congregated in front of Emerson's Hardware in their wooden rocking chairs were nowhere to be seen.

With nothing interesting to view on the horizon, Ben's mind shifted to Veronica Jayne and the unlikely development of their cyber relationship. It had started innocently enough, emailing each other back and forth about their combined class project. After a while the conversation had drifted to chattering about weekly assignments, and before he knew it, they were talking personal issues—sometimes *very* personal issues, especially when they'd discovered they had the same plans for stateside mission work.

He'd been praying for his future wife for some time now, and if he was being honest with himself, the thought that Veronica Jayne might be *that* woman had crossed his mind more than once, even if they'd agreed they wouldn't pursue anything romantic until—and if— they met in person.

Frankly, it was easier keeping Veronica Jayne at a distance, on the other end of cyberspace, where he wasn't as apt to screw things up. He didn't exactly have a stellar track record where women were concerned.

He'd been a skinny, awkward teenager who was often embarrassed and humiliated by school bullies, a boy who hid in his uncle's auto garage to avoid having to deal with his callous peers, never mind girls his age, who would either ridicule or ignore him. Girls simply weren't interested in boys like him. His mother had told him not to worry, that his day would come, but he hadn't believed her.

Then, in a desperate attempt to get away from everything and everyone he knew, he'd enlisted in the Army National Guard Reserves. He'd bulked up and put on a uniform, and that had changed *everything*. He'd returned to Serendipity to find the women—those same girls who'd thumbed their noses at him in his youth—all grown up and fawning over him.

He was the first to admit he hadn't handled it very well. What could he say? He was a guy, and the attention of pretty ladies went straight to his head. Being as inexperienced as he was in the world of women, he knew he'd made quite a few mistakes along the way.

How was he supposed to know that after two or three dates, a girl would assume that they were dating exclusively and that he wasn't seeing anyone else? He hadn't even been looking for a serious relationship—not then, anyway—despite the impression he'd apparently given. He'd quickly learned that women had certain ideas in their heads, and they weren't very forgiving when he didn't catch their unspoken implications.

Which he rarely did. He didn't know how to guess how a woman thought. He hadn't known then, and he certainly didn't know now.

No, he'd had enough of all that, thank you very much. Perhaps that was why the idea of finding someone *outside* Serendipity sounded so appealing to him. Someone who didn't know what he'd been like as a kid. Someone unaware of his recent screw-ups in the love department.

If he left Serendipity, he could reinvent himself into anything he wanted to be. A tough guy or a dashing charmer. Sensitive or daring. It was a heady notion. But there was more to it than that. He truly felt called to make a difference on a scale he could never achieve in his small hometown. He wanted to get involved in difficult and often perilous stateside mission work, perfect for an adrenaline junkie like him who wanted to be part of an organization that ministered to people, body and soul.

At times he even dared to imagine the possibility of having a classy, incredible woman working at his side— a strong, independent, caring, Christian woman ready and able to both handle the worst and pray for the best.

It wasn't completely beyond the realm of possibility that this woman was Veronica Jayne. In their emails, her dreams and future plans and goals matched his, and their personalities melded perfectly, each playing off the other's strengths.

But that was online.

Reality? Well, that was probably nothing more than empty space. Would he even know her if he passed by her on the street? Would they connect on that kind of level?

He was almost certainly grasping at straws. If anything ever *did* happen between them, and that was a big *if,* Veronica Jayne eventually would learn everything about him—including his past, which he was still ashamed to think about. Then there was the fact that he had perpetual grease under his nails from working as a mechanic. And the fact that he lived in a miniscule Texas town—he had the impression, though she'd never stated outright, that she lived in a big city.

If he took her home, his mother would no doubt bring out his baby pictures and his yearbook, which would only serve to further humiliate him. One look and Veronica Jayne would discover what a gawky, pimple-covered youth he'd been. Too tall for his skinny physique and all elbows and knees.

He wasn't sure he was ready for that. Anyway, he was getting way ahead of himself. They'd never met in person. Who knew if they'd even like each other when that time came, much less in any kind of romantic capacity? He must be getting soft in the head.

The moment he rounded the corner onto his parents' cul-de-sac, he noticed the black truck parked in his parents' driveway. The back end was loaded with red bricks and multi-colored rocks of various shapes and sizes and bags upon bags of soil and fertilizer. It wasn't an old truck, but it wasn't a new one either. It had some wear—definitely a sensible working vehicle. And though it looked vaguely familiar, he couldn't immediately put a name to the owner. He was fairly certain he hadn't serviced it at the auto shop recently, yet he could picture the vehicle in his mind, sans contents. So where did he know it from?

One way to find out.

He heard someone singing before he even reached the front porch. More telling, it was a *female* singing, or humming rather, and it definitely wasn't his good, old-fashioned country mother, unless she'd developed a sudden propensity for something that sounded suspiciously like classical music to Ben's untrained ears.

Instead of approaching the front door, his curiosity led him around the side of the house to see whose pretty, richly husky alto laced the air with Beethoven, or Bach or whatever it was.

When he got his first glance of her, he nearly stumbled with surprise.

Vee Bishop.

What was she doing here? She hadn't mentioned visiting his parents when they'd been talking the prior evening.

She had her back to him, her slender figure accentuated as she stood on tiptoe on the top rung of a stepladder, precariously reaching for a flowerpot that dangled just out of her reach on a hook next to the patio door. She thought she was alone, as evidenced by the fact that she was humming aloud to the tune of the small mp3 player she had clipped to her belt.

"Beethoven?" he called. With his mind busy creating and discarding reasons why Vee might be in his parents' backyard, he realized only *after* he'd spoken that she couldn't have seen him approach and that the sound of his voice might startle her. She'd managed to unhook the basket with the tips of her fingers, but she didn't have the basket firmly in her grasp and she over-reached her mark at the sound of his voice. Wavering in a futile attempt to balance herself, she put one hand out to grasp for the wall, but nothing was there to stop her from falling backward. She squeaked in dismay, and her arms flailed wildly as she attempted to right herself against the ladder.

Ben acted instinctively, darting forward to sweep Vee into his arms before she hit the pavement. He barely felt the weight of her frame as he protectively flexed his biceps to curl her into the safety of his embrace, but he was intensely aware of the moment she wrapped her arm around his neck. The hook of the hanging basket she'd managed to hold on to dug deeply into his shoulder. The sensation didn't register as pain, maybe because his adrenaline was so high. Her free palm rested against his chest, directly over his rapidly beating heart. He wondered if she could feel the pounding staccato rhythm of his pulse.

Crazy woman. What had she been thinking? It was

a good thing for her that he'd arrived when he did. He hoped she realized that he had barely averted a disaster.

She could have had broken bones. Been knocked unconscious. Suffered a concussion. He could easily tick a dozen frightening scenarios off on his fingers.

He didn't immediately release her, giving them both time to get their bearings. For a moment she just stared up at him, her cheeks flushed a pretty crimson. Her dark eyes first flared with surprise and then simply sparkled with what Ben suspected was mirth, though he couldn't imagine what she considered to be funny in this situation.

"Mozart," she informed him, wriggling out of his grasp as if she only now realized that he was still holding her up. She stood to her full height, but even so, the top of her head didn't reach Ben's shoulder. "And you should be ashamed of yourself, sneaking up on a person that way. You nearly scared the life out of me. I could have really been hurt there!"

"I didn't sneak," he responded, trying to keep his jaw from dropping. Why was *she* chewing *him* out? She should be eternally grateful for his efforts on her behalf. "What I *did* was save you from a major catastrophe just now. You should be thanking me, not railing on me. And you should know better than to stand on the top rung of a ladder. It's dangerous."

"It's just a step stool," she rejoined with a scowl. Now *that* was a familiar expression from her, especially combined with her backing away from where his outreached hand tried to offer her some support. Although she'd landed in his arms and had not—thanks to him—taken a digger on the ground, she brushed off her jeans as if she'd hit the dirt on both knees.

"Maybe," he conceded. "But you're still begging for an accident by name. In case you're not aware of the rules, you're not supposed to stand on the very top rung of a ladder, step stool or otherwise. You can't balance that way. Didn't anyone ever teach you better?" He kept his tone light and hoped his words sounded like banter and not a reprimand.

It partially worked. Her frown eased a little, though it didn't go away. She rolled her eyes and took another step back. "Are you kidding? With an overprotective dad and two big brothers, I've had every lecture in the book and then some."

"Any reason why this lesson didn't stick?"

She tilted her head thoughtfully and shrugged. "Sometimes they do, sometimes they don't. I'm pretty independent. I've been told I'm stubborn, too, if my brothers have an opinion about it."

Her response seemed serious, and she was still frowning at him. Ben wasn't sure what to say or why the woman was so determined to be angry with him when he'd just saved her from breaking her neck.

He shifted from foot to foot, measuring his words before speaking to the overly testy woman. Speaking suddenly felt like a new and difficult skill, one of which he was nearly incapable. He hadn't yet sorted out words in his brain, much less found the faculties necessary to utter them from his lips, before she spoke again.

"Climbing to the top rungs of ladders is just one of many of the perils of being short," Vee explained. She waved the hanging basket in front of him. "At least I got the basket, thank you very much."

"Right," he agreed, but he was shaking his head. "We wouldn't want you to have to climb back up on that ladder and risk putting life and limb in danger again." He paused and cocked his head, staring at her speculatively. "So tell me why, exactly, are you stealing flowerpots from my parents' backyard?"

Her frown deepened, and for a moment he worried that she'd taken his teasing seriously. She was always pretty quick to think the worst of him. To his relief, she relaxed after a moment instead. "Of course I'm not trying to steal anything. Your folks asked me to come here to do a little spring landscaping for them."

"Why would they do that? If they want some work done, I can do it for them."

That, and the fact that of all the people on the planet they'd chosen to work on their yard, it had to be the one woman he had trouble working with at all. And he *would* be working here, now that he'd discovered his parents' plan. But there was no reason why Vee had to stay. All he had to do was to talk his parents out of this decision, which shouldn't be that difficult, right? Then Vee could go on her merry way.

Her eyes widened and she stared at him like he was slow on the uptake. Could she really blame him? He was still reeling from the nearly averted disaster of catching a plunging-to-the-pavement woman. His heart was still pounding heavily in his chest, stoked by adrenaline. He couldn't set it aside as easily as she appeared to have done.

"It's my job, remember?" she pointed out in a pithy tone of voice. "I work at Emerson's Hardware. Lawn and garden. Ring a bell? I know I've waited on you at least a few times over the years."

"No, of course I know you work at Emerson's," he said, quickly backtracking. Was she making fun of him?

"What I meant was, why are you *here,* in my parents' backyard, trying to release flowerpots from their hooks? They didn't mention any gardening projects. I'm surprised they didn't consult me first."

"Why would they?"

Ouch. She had a point, and she hadn't made it softly, either.

His parents didn't need *his* permission to landscape their yard, but it disturbed him just the same that they hadn't asked for his help. He was more than willing to lend a hand. And seriously, what could Vee do for them that he couldn't do himself?

"I can dig in the dirt as well as anyone. For *free,*" he added with extra emphasis. His parents were paying good money when they didn't need to be.

Her dark eyebrows rose in perfect curves. "I'm a landscaping specialist, you know. There's a lot more to it than just digging in the dirt. Apparently your parents seem to think I'm needed here."

"Apparently," he repeated, absently rubbing a spot on his temple that was beginning to throb incessantly. He didn't get many headaches, but he had a feeling that today might be the exception.

"You don't believe me?" She gestured toward the sliding glass door that led to the dining room of the Atwoods' house. "Be my guest. Ask your mom why she hired me."

It wasn't that he thought she was lying when she'd stated that his parents had hired her. He just didn't want to accept it. The real problem here, as he was well aware, was that his pride was wounded. He knew it shouldn't matter that they'd hired, of all people, Vee to do their yard work, but that knowledge scraped across every self-righteous nerve in his body.

Did his parents think he wasn't up to a simple landscaping job? Did they think Vee could do it better?

Honestly. How hard could it be to plant a few flowers and trim a few shrubs? They could have at least asked him if he wanted to do it before they called on outside help. He was certain he could do at least as good a job as Vee.

"If you'll excuse me, I'll be back in a moment," he said, gesturing to the back door. "I want to speak with my mom for a second."

"Sure," she agreed. "I'll be here, planting my flowers and humming my Mozart."

"You do that. And try not to fall off any step stools while I'm gone."

"I'll keep that in mind."

As Ben entered the house through the sliding glass door, familiar sights and smells enveloped him. He breathed deeply and released the tension corded through his neck and shoulders. It was amazing how comforting it was simply to step into the house where he'd spent his youth. Entering his home was like being wrapped in a cozy blanket, not only for warmth but for reassurance.

"Mom?" he called as he wiped his feet on the welcome mat by the door. "It's Ben. Where are you?"

"In the kitchen, honey."

He should have known that's where she would be. His mother was always in the kitchen, baking things from scratch. Cooking was her hobby, and she was excellent at it. She spent hours every week poring over cookbooks and magazines trying to find new dishes to try or new twists on old favorites. It wasn't until Ben was an adult that he'd really learned to appreciate the work she did.

He inhaled deeply and groaned with pleasure. The whole house smelled like cinnamon and fresh bread. If he was lucky, she was baking his favorite rolls. His mouth was watering already.

"What's wrong?" she asked as he entered and before he'd said so much as a single word. His mother was like that—naturally intuitive where her children were concerned. So why hadn't she realized he'd be bothered by her landscaping plans?

"I saw Vee outside," he said, trying for a conversational tone, though he doubted he succeeded.

"Oh, yes. Isn't she a dear, willing to work on our yard even when it's nippy outside? She said she likes being outside, whatever the weather. I really like her. Smart and sensible. And she's a cute little thing, too, don't you think?"

Ben's gaze widened. Whatever else he thought of Vee, he'd never categorize her as a *cute little thing*. Fearless, maybe. Spirited, definitely. But cute?

Not only that, but if he wasn't mistaken, it sounded like his mother was hinting at something beyond simply drawing his attention to the fine work Vee was doing. His mother had been trying to set him up with women since the day he turned twenty. Apparently she wanted grandchildren, and the sooner the better.

But Vee? That was definitely pushing the limits, even for his mother. Vee had never made any secret of the fact that she didn't care for him, and someone as perceptive as his mother had to have noticed.

As if to make it up to him for the suggestion, she pushed a dessert plate loaded with freshly baked cinnamon rolls in his direction. He poured himself a tall glass of milk and settled down with his favorite treat. At least he had timed *that* right.

"Are you having trouble with your yard?" he queried before popping a large chunk of cinnamon roll in his mouth. "Why didn't you come to me for help? I would have been happy to have done your project for you."

His mother's gaze widened in surprise at the change of subject and then narrowed on Ben. "I see," she murmured, not taking her eyes off of him.

He sunk a little lower in his chair at the maternal look she was giving him. It was *the look,* the one that brought down many a child. Ben might be a full-grown man, but it still affected him.

"I'm just asking."

His mother nodded thoughtfully. "Do you have training in landscape architecture?" She paused for less than one second. "No? I didn't think so. That's why I hired Vee," she explained smoothly, wiping her hands on the frilly green apron tied at her waist.

"Did you see the pretty tulips and daffodils already blooming out front next to the dogwood tree?" she continued. "That's Vee's work. She planted a few bulbs for us last fall. It made such a difference in the front that when spring arrived, we decided to hire her to rework our backyard, too. I'm very excited to make more changes in our yard. Your father and I have been talking about doing it for years, but it never seemed like quite the right time. I'm finally going to have the garden I've always wanted."

"I'm as good with a shovel as anyone," he insisted. "Surely I can plant your seeds and tend to your flowers for you. I'm happy to help. You don't need to pay anybody."

"I think I do. It's more than just planting and watering—Vee is designing it all to look just right. I've seen some of the work she's done for our neighbors and I love it. Plus, she has the know-how to pick the right plants to match the weather and amount of shade, to make it all as little work for me to maintain as possible. And that's just the flowers. She has equally wonderful ideas for the vegetable garden. This is how I want to spend my money, Ben. I want everything perfect so your father and I can relax and enjoy ourselves in the backyard. Vee has all kinds of lovely ideas for the backyard and the garden." His mother's face brightened and she slapped both hands on the counter in her exuberance. She was apparently really excited for this garden of hers.

"But if you're eager to help, then that's wonderful," his mother exclaimed. "I may even ask you to build me a gazebo after all the landscaping is finished and my garden is planted. And I'm sure Vee can use you today, too. Most certainly you can do the grunt work—digging in the dirt, like you said. You did enough of that as a young boy. I'm sure you're an expert by now. That will give Vee more time to focus on the brainwork and not have to get her lovely hands so dirty. Bless you, sweetheart, for offering to help."

He hadn't exactly offered, but what else could he say when his mother leaned across the counter and kissed his cheek with unbridled enthusiasm? He didn't want to let her down, especially since he'd run off at the mouth so much today already.

She knew exactly what she was doing, too—forcing

him into this situation, knowing perfectly well that he could not and would not turn her down.

Oh, well. A little dirt never hurt anyone, right? Working with Vee, though? That might be another thing entirely.

Chapter Three

Dear Veronica Jayne,
You know why you're so special? You challenge me to look at the world around me through new eyes. To me, planting anything is just—well—digging in the dirt.

I tend to see life around me that way, too—in black-and-white. It's only since I've been writing to you that I've started to see colors blooming in my world. You're my flower girl.
All the best,
BJ

"Did you get everything straightened out with your mom?" Vee asked as Ben returned to the back patio. Not that she really had to ask to know how the conversation had gone. Even with only a sidelong glance, she could see that his face was the color of a ripe cherry.

"If by 'straightened out' you mean my mother set me in my place and told me to keep my mouth shut and help you dig, then yes. I've definitely been straightened out."

"I didn't mean to cause any problems for you, Ben."

He arched a brow as if he doubted her good intentions. "No, of course you didn't. It's my own blustering that got me into trouble. I may be a thirty-year-old man, but Mama won't take any sass from me."

Vee's throat burned and she quickly turned her gaze from his, blinking rapidly as memories of her own mother overwhelmed her again.

The recollections made her want to laugh.

And cry.

Maybe both simultaneously.

She pulled in a ragged breath, but the air seemed sharp, piercing her throat and lungs. Not a day went by that she didn't think about her mother. She'd be all right for a while, and she even felt like she could function normally most days, but then grief would sneak up and reappear out of nowhere, jumping out from behind her back and wrenching her heart in two once again.

This was one of those times, and she was mortified that Ben was here to witness it once more. Dealt with the sudden blow of emotions she was unable to handle, she would have turned away to hide them, but Ben gently stayed her with his large, callused hand as he grasped her elbow.

"I did it again, didn't I?" he murmured in an unexpectedly tender, soft tone. "I have a bad habit of sticking my boot in my mouth." Ben was a rough-edged man, and in Vee's opinion, not a very nice one, so the sympathy pouring from his gaze surprised her. "I'm truly sorry about your mother, Vee."

He didn't say anything else. In her experience, people tended to chatter when they were uncomfortable with a situation, but not Ben. He just stood there, strong and silent, waiting for her to gather herself together. She wasn't sure how he'd figured out where her thoughts had gone, but she was grateful to him for giving her the moment she needed to compose herself.

But composure failed to come. Despite her best intentions, tears welled. She fought and nearly lost herself to the blaze that was burning in her throat and behind her eyes.

She wasn't a bawler. She'd learned long ago that crying didn't get you anywhere—not with two big brothers around to tease her about it. If anything, breaking into tears only made things worse, so she'd learned not to do it. Her brothers had literally thrown her into the deep end of the pool and expected her to swim. They'd taught her to be tough. She was a Bishop, and Bishops were a strong lot.

But in this case, reminding herself of her heritage didn't seem to help. Nothing did. She wasn't sure if she could keep her tears from falling despite her best efforts.

Ben slipped his arm around her shoulder and pulled her into a close embrace. The comfort of his rock-solid chest and the steady sound of his heartbeat somehow reassured her.

Depending on someone else, even for a moment, was unfamiliar to her. And she couldn't believe that the person she was leaning on was Ben Atwood—possibly the least reliable person she knew. She squeezed her eyes closed and tried to breathe slowly, fighting desperately against the urge to let loose the roaring broil of her emotions and bawl into Ben's chest. She barely restrained herself from wrapping her arms around his waist and hugging him back.

She couldn't break down. Not here. Not now. Not in front of Ben. Bishops were strong people, she reminded herself again. They didn't let anything get the best of them, not even a grief that felt like it was ripping her apart.

She sucked in another big gulp of air and backed away. The sudden sensation of warm fur crisscrossing her ankles in a figure eight caused her to jolt, but she was careful not to step on whatever it was that was twirling around at her feet. She looked down to find a large gray poof-ball rubbing against her and purring louder than the engine on her truck.

"Is that a cat?" she asked with a chuckle that came out as half a sob. She hitched her breath.

Ben leaned down and scooped the ball of fur into his arms, brushing the hair back from the feline's face with the palm of his hand. Vee could barely make out eyes and a black button of a nose.

"This," Ben said, "is Tinker. And you should feel privileged. He's given you quite an honor. He doesn't usually take to people he doesn't know very well."

As he said the words, the cat sprung from his arms to hers. She caught him with an exclamation of surprise.

"Warn me, next time, will you, kitty?" She tucked Tinker under her chin, oddly comforted by the vibration of the cat's purr and the warmth of his fur.

"I never had a kitten," she said, stroking Tinker's soft, downy fur. "Or a dog. My mom was one of those people who thought all animals should stay outside in the barn."

Another hiccup.

Ben jammed his hands into the front pockets of his jeans and rocked back on his heels, not speaking but urging her on with a smile.

"I had a hamster once, though, when I was about nine. Alvin the hamster. He'd run on his little wheel all night long. That sound was like a lullaby to me. I slept so soundly when he was around."

"Tinker is a second-generation Atwood cat," Ben explained, reaching out to tickle Tinker under his chin. "His mama was Belle. Tinkerbelle, actually, but most of the time I just called her Belle."

"Oh, my," exclaimed Vee, putting two and two together. "Please don't tell me that this poor boy…"

"…is Tinkerbelle the Second. In my defense, I was a teenager at the time, and kittens weren't a big deal to me. I was too busy worrying about my social life, which… well…" He cut himself off and gave her a charming smile. She noticed it looked a little strained around the edges, as if he disliked thinking back on those memories but was trying to hide it. "I gave him his moniker without actually bothering to see if it was a he or she, and my mother didn't correct me. I think maybe she was trying to teach me a life lesson. Tinker here got the bad end of that deal."

"Poor Tinker," Vee said on a long, counterfeit sigh, stroking the cat from the top of his head to the tip of his tail, causing his purr to rumble even louder. "It's a wonder he still associates with you at all."

"Yeah," Ben agreed with a self-deprecating shrug. "You're probably right about that."

Tinker started wiggling, and Vee reluctantly released him to the ground. "I think Tinker is giving me a nudge. I suppose I've had enough of a work break now. Your parents aren't paying me to talk. I should get back to planting flowers."

She turned, then paused, her shoulders tensing as she realized she'd returned to a touchy subject for Ben. Was he going to belittle her efforts again—tell her once more how little he valued all her careful planning and design work? She shouldn't have been surprised that he had no appreciation for her craft, yet she had still felt hurt at his clear dismissal earlier.

"Where would you like me to start digging?" Ben asked, surprising her when he reached for a nearby shovel.

Vee released a quiet breath. Gardening was her comfort zone, her sweet spot where she could let go of everything else and just be thankful to God for His beautiful creation. Some might see it as just "digging in the dirt," but for her, working with flowers brought Vee her greatest joy.

Did she want to share that with Ben?

Not really. But if putting him to work meant he'd stop giving his mother a hard time, then what choice did she have? Maybe if he could see how dedicated she was to the task, he'd realize that her work truly was important—to her, if not to him.

She pointed to the flower beds on opposite sides of the screened-in back fence, and then at the large plot she'd lined out with stakes and thread marking a place for the garden.

"If you'd please break up and turn the earth for me, I'd appreciate it. I'll bring you a bag of compost so you can fertilize as you go."

"I'll get it," he offered. "It's in the back of your truck, right?"

"Yes, it is." She hesitated. "I hate to have you make two trips, but can you also bring back some potting soil for me? I brought new annuals, mostly petunias and mums, to plant in the hanging pots."

Ben assented with a nod and strode away. Vee's gaze

followed him until he turned the corner of the house. Then she propped her hands on her hips and surveyed the property, ticking off projects in her mind. The flower beds would be the home to a dozen new rosebushes, and the garden still needed to be seeded with vegetables. Several decorative pots for the back porch awaited her attention, too.

Now, where had she been before Ben arrived?

Oh, right. The hanging basket. Falling into Ben's arms. How could she have forgotten that so easily? It was not her most graceful moment. Her face flamed just thinking about it, so she redirected her thoughts to the tasks at hand.

She was gathering a variety of hanging and standing flowerpots into a line on the porch when Ben returned to the backyard, a twenty-five-pound bag of potting soil under one arm and a fifty-pound bag of fertilizer slung over his other shoulder. She hadn't expected him to bring both bags at the same time. He was probably trying to show off his strength, but the gesture was lost on Vee.

Okay, so maybe it wasn't quite *lost* because she'd obviously noticed. It was hard *not* to notice the solid muscles across his arms and shoulders. But a good man was made up of more than his muscles, and she knew what kind of man Ben was.

Ben had broken her best friend's heart. Olivia had stayed in bed for a week depressed and crying over their breakup, which was all Ben's fault. Vee wasn't in any hurry to forgive him for that, no matter how good he looked in a T-shirt and jeans.

"Where do you want it?" Ben asked. He nodded his square chin toward the bag of soil under his arm.

"Right here is fine," she answered, sweeping her arm indistinctly toward the ground at her feet.

Grunting with the effort—or possibly just for the effect the sound gave—he dropped the bag of potting soil where she'd indicated and then lowered the fertilizer bag near the closest flower bed.

"I'd appreciate it if you'd do the flower beds first," she said, deciding there was no reason not to be civil with Ben since he'd offered to help—as a non-paid apprentice. "I've got a dozen rosebushes in the back of the truck that I'll be planting in those beds today."

"Yeah, I noticed them when I was getting the soil. Do you want me to bring those back here for you, too?"

"Eventually. For now, just dig."

"Pink and red," he said, sounding like he was just making conversation. "Did you pick out those colors, or was it my mother?"

"Your mother, actually. I've planned most of the landscaping colors palette, but she specifically asked for red and pink roses. Red for love. Pink for gratitude. She said it would remind her every day to be thankful for her family."

"That sounds like my mother," Ben murmured.

"I'll get these planters finished and then we'll worry about the rosebushes. After that you can turn the earth for the garden and I can start seeding behind you," she said, pulling on her gardening gloves and picking up a trowel.

She reached for the first tray of yellow mums and easily fell into her task. She'd organized the flowers and seeds according to the layout print she'd prepared of the Atwoods' backyard. She'd spent a long time planning what would go where according to the palettes she'd created. She loved seeing the way the colors came together to make a final product she could be proud of and the Atwoods would enjoy. It was her artist's canvas, available for everyone to see and appreciate.

Ben let out a low wolf whistle as he surveyed her print. She hadn't realized he was standing over her shoulder. He was supposed to be digging.

"That looks complicated," he commented. "And here I thought we were just playing around in the dirt."

"It's a lot more than that," she fired back before taking a deep breath and reminding herself that she'd decided to be civil. "It's actually quite interesting, or at least it is to me. The vegetable garden itself is determined by what your mom and dad want to grow, of course, but you get a better yield, not to mention a better aesthetic experience, if you know which vegetables should be planted next to each other for optimum growth and health. We're going to do green beans, snap peas, carrots and tomatoes for starters."

She gulped in a breath of air and continued enthusiastically. It didn't take much for her to warm to her subject. "As for the hanging baskets, I not only consider which blossoms develop well in this area, but also the arrangement of color palettes…"

She hadn't realized she'd launched into a full-throttle landscaping lecture until she noticed the pensive look on Ben's face. Clearly his mind had wandered, and she flushed at the realization that she'd probably been boring him to tears.

"And…you really don't care a whit about color palettes. Sorry. Too much information," she said with a wince and a guarded chuckle. "I forget that not everyone is as ardent about gardening as I am."

"Don't apologize. I am interested. It's just that what you said reminded me of a friend of mine who—"

He broke off his sentence as suddenly as he'd started it, his eyes widening to enormous proportions, as if he'd almost said something monumental, something he'd regret. He definitely looked a little green around the gills.

"A friend of yours who…?" she prompted, curious as to why he had stopped speaking so suddenly. She usually wasn't the nosey type, preferring to mind her own business and give others the same courtesy. But he'd started it, and now she wanted him to finish.

"She—er—works in flowers. I can't really tell you much more than that, I mean about her career." He turned his back to her and scanned the flower bed. "Is it all right if I just rip into this bag any way I want, or is there a secret procedure I'm not aware of?"

Clearly he was deflecting. Vee was tempted to press the issue just to stir things up a bit, but she refrained. Once he'd finished breaking Olivia's heart, Ben's female "friends" had become no business of hers.

"No special instructions," she informed him. "Just try to open it so too much of the fertilizer doesn't spill out all at once."

"Got it," he said, flashing her a smile.

Who was this elusive *she* who worked with flowers? Vee wondered in spite of herself. He sounded as if he truly cared for her, whoever she was. Maybe he'd learned his lesson and matured some. Or maybe he'd met a woman who hadn't immediately fallen prey to his charms, and it had forced him to actually put some effort into a relationship. But if that was the case, this woman must really be something special. She would have to be a classic beauty. Vee could almost picture the woman—long, flowing blond hair and perfect makeup that accentuated deep cheekbones and a perfect chin.

The exact opposite of Vee, in other words. No one could call her heart-shaped face *classic*. The dimple in her chin marred any chance for that. At best, she could be called pretty—but it wasn't the sort of pretty anyone noticed. She was way too easily overlooked for reasons that had nothing to do with her diminutive height. Her strength was her intelligence, not her beauty, and men didn't line up at the door to date smart women. At least in her experience—or lack of—they didn't.

Which mattered *why?*

She scoffed inwardly and turned her mind back to her work. She wasn't going to consider any other possibility except that she might be nursing her own curiosity. And even that felt inappropriate. She shouldn't care one bit about Ben or about any women that he knew and might care for.

At the end of the day, Ben was still the man who'd broken the heart of her best friend. That hadn't and wouldn't change. Unfortunately for Ben, Vee had a long memory, and though she knew God would want her to forgive him, she just wasn't there yet.

It might have been easier if Ben had hurt *Vee* and not her friend. She could shake off an injury to herself, but going after someone she loved—that was stepping over the mark. She tended to go all mama tiger on anyone who hurt her friends and loved ones.

And by "anyone" she meant Ben.

Vee shook her head and jammed the trowel into the bag of soil, perhaps a bit more forcefully than was absolutely necessary. With a renewed effort, she set to work, trying to keep her mind focused on the task at hand and not the man turning the earth just a few feet to her left.

To her surprise, she and Ben worked well together. After Ben had turned the soil, they retrieved the rose-bushes from the truck. It was nice to have an extra pair of hands. Planting went smoothly and much quicker than Vee had anticipated.

Then they moved their combined attention to the plot for the vegetable garden. Ben flipped over the dense spring turf and mixed it with fertilizer while Vee followed along behind him, planting seeds with her trowel.

They didn't speak much, but that was just as well. Vee didn't know what to say to him, and she hated it when she felt like she needed to chatter just to fill up the space. She wasn't much for small talk.

Before she knew it, the entire afternoon had passed and the sun was starting to make its descent in the west. Vee glanced at her watch and was surprised to find it was after six o'clock in the evening. Where had the time gone?

"I think it's about quitting time," she said, tapping the face of her watch. "I'll be back to finish what's left tomorrow. I appreciate all your help today. I wouldn't have gotten nearly this far without you."

Ben wiped the sweat off his forehead with the edge of his shirt, then rubbed his palms together and grimaced.

"What's wrong with your hand?" she asked, reaching out to examine his left palm.

"It's nothing. I just got a couple of blisters." Stubbornly, he drew his hand into a fist to prevent her from examining it.

"Let me see." He refused at first, keeping his hand tightly clenched, but she ignored his protests and gently worked his fingers open so she could scrutinize his wound.

"See? It's not so bad," he muttered through gritted teeth. "No big deal."

"Maybe not," she answered in a conciliatory tone, "but you need to clean your palm so it doesn't get infected. You stay there," she said, pointing to a porch chair. "I'll be back in a jiffy."

She entered the house through the sliding door in the back and brushed her shoes against the welcome mat. "Excuse me, Mrs. Atwood?"

"You're still here?" asked Ben's mom in surprise as she entered the room. "I would have thought you'd have something better to do on a Friday night than hang around here, especially if you're not on call at the fire station. Don't tell me there's no fancy date with a handsome hunk?"

Vee blushed so hard she thought her head might pop. "No, ma'am. Not tonight."

Not *ever,* actually, but Vee didn't see the need to elaborate on the subject.

Ben's mother chuckled lightly. "Their loss."

"Yes, ma'am," she agreed, becoming more embarrassed by the moment. She decided to change the subject before it got completely out of control. "I was wondering if you had any rubbing alcohol or hydrogen peroxide that I could use. Ben has a few blisters on his hands, and I'd hate for them to get infected."

"Of course. My son isn't used to shoveling dirt, poor dear. Why don't you sit down for a moment while I get them for you?" His mom sounded more amused than concerned by her son's dire plight. She gestured to a chair at the dining room table, but Vee politely declined.

Despite the woman's kindness, Vee decided it was better for her to remain standing on the mat where she wouldn't accidentally make a mess with her dirty clothing.

In less than a minute, Ben's mother returned with a bottle of rubbing alcohol, a roll of gauze, a handful of large cotton balls and a tube of antibacterial cream, delivered with a perceptive smile.

"There you go, hon. Everything you need to patch my boy up right."

"This ought to do it," Vee agreed warmly. Ben's mother was one of the most pleasant women she knew. "Thank you so much, Mrs. Atwood."

"Never a problem. You tell Ben that his mother said that he ought to wear gloves next time."

Vee chuckled. "Oh, don't worry. I will." How nice, to have his mother's permission to rub it in a little bit, both literally and figuratively.

Laden with her impromptu medical kit, she returned to where Ben waited, tucked onto a porch chair with his legs extended before him, crossed at the ankles. His head was back, his eyes were closed and his chest was rising and falling evenly. Vee thought he might be asleep and wondered if she ought to wake him, but when she approached, his eyes, with those thick, long eyelashes that only men ever seemed blessed with, fluttered open.

His gaze narrowed on her tentatively when he saw the bottle of rubbing alcohol in her hand.

"Rubbing alcohol? That wouldn't have been my first choice." He sounded none too thrilled about it.

"Don't be a baby. Now put out your hand."

Ben frowned but allowed her to pry the fingers of his left hand open, palm upward.

Vee doused a cotton ball in rubbing alcohol, cupped

his hand in hers and began dabbing at the red, angry blisters that covered his palm.

"Ow," Ben complained, trying to pull his hand out of her grip. "That hurts."

Vee persisted in wiping the wounds, ignoring his protests. "If you insist on pulling away like that, it's going to take a lot longer to get this done."

"You're enjoying this, aren't you?" he asked suspiciously. "You're making it hurt on purpose."

Was he teasing her? Maybe. She couldn't tell, so she went for a neutral—though truthful—response. "Of course not. I would never do that."

Vee carefully wrapped his hand in strips of gauze so he couldn't accuse her of further assaults on his person. "There. All better. Just keep it clean, okay? Doctor's orders."

"Hey, are you forgetting who the paramedic is here?"

"Fine, then—mother's orders. If you don't like it, take it up with your mom. She's the one who gave me the supplies to get you bandaged up. And if you don't keep that gauze clean, you'll be answering to her."

"Do you really think I can do that? I work with cars, remember?"

"That could be an issue. I don't know how you're going to avoid grease when you're tinkering with a car engine. I suppose you'll just have to do the best you can."

"I will," he promised, but under his breath he muttered, "I'm glad you're a firefighter and not a nurse."

"That makes two of us. I didn't try to hurt you on purpose, but I'll be the first to admit my bedside manner is a little rough."

"A little?" He chuckled and shook his head. "If that's what you're like when you're trying to help me then I'd hate to think of the damage you could do if you really were trying to hurt me."

Hurt you like you hurt Olivia? Vee thought to herself. He must have noticed the shift in her expression that accompanied the new direction of her thoughts because he quickly changed the subject.

"Now that the work's done—the planting and the bandaging—would you like to stay for dinner? I know I told you I can't cook, and I can't, but even I can manage to throw a couple of steaks on the grill without ruining them. Mama usually ropes me into grilling for her when the weather cooperates, so I'm guessing that's probably what she has in mind for today. We've got plenty of room at the table for one more, and I'm sure my parents would love for you to stay and visit the family."

"I should be offering *you* a steak dinner for all the help you've been to me today. I wouldn't have gotten even a quarter as far along as we did together."

"No problem. I was glad to help. It was for a good cause. And we do work well together."

He sounded as surprised as she felt. Vee shivered in what she thought must be discomfort, though in truth she didn't dare identify the emotion. Is that what Ben thought, that they *worked well together?*

"As for dinner," she said and then paused. She already had other plans. Not an in-person date with a handsome hunk who wanted to take her to dinner or out to the movies like Ben's mother had suggested, but definitely the next best thing. Those *plans* in question were calling to her, tugging at her heartstrings to make short work of leaving and hurry along to Cup o' Jo Café.

But then there was Ben, with his convincing half smile and dancing gaze. She hesitated.

Vee couldn't believe she was tempted, even for a moment, to stick around and share a dinner with Ben and his family—but she was. No wonder Olivia had fallen for the man hook, line and sinker. Ben could be very charismatic when he wanted to be.

Nice, even. And he was good-looking, no denying that fact.

Which was *exactly* why she had to say no.

She took a deep breath and plunged in before she lost what was left of her mental faculties and caved to his suggestion.

"I'm sorry, Ben," she murmured, pausing only for a moment at his crestfallen look. If she didn't know any better, she would think he actually cared what her answer would be.

But that wouldn't change it. "As much as I'd love to share a meal with you and your parents this evening," she continued, "I already have other plans."

Chapter Four

Dear BJ,

This week has been very tough for me. Sometimes I just feel like I need to let my hair down—do you know what I mean? I'm so guarded all the time, worrying about what people think of me and, even more, what they expect of me. I'm afraid I might not be living up to everyone's standards.

It's stressful keeping everything bottled up inside all the time. It would be nice to be able to see things differently for a change, from another point of view. From a different set of eyes.

Oh, who am I kidding? I am what I am and that's all...well, you know. I'm starting to sound like Popeye now. Terrific. Who ever knew that he was such a sage?

I guess I should just accept the way that God made me and not try to make myself anything different. I might feel like a distinct person inside my heart, but people don't see that, do they?

That's never going to change. I'm never going to change.

It's just that when I read your emails, I feel...well,

differently about myself. Stronger. I wish I could be as easygoing as you obviously are.

I downloaded the graphics you sent me. They're really good! I'm attaching a revised script that incorporates the photographs, so we can begin preparing the final presentation. Let me know if you have any modifications you'd like me to make.

Faithfully,
Veronica Jayne

The rich smells of roasted coffee, nutmeg and baked apples warmed Vee's nostrils as she entered the Cup o' Jo Café. She inhaled deeply and the tension she always carried around in her shoulders and neck was immediately soothed by the colorful, welcoming atmosphere. The familiar quiet buzz of the other patrons talking as they sat in booths enjoying a hot meal heartened her. Cup o' Jo had been a regular hangout for Vee growing up, and even now it was her go-to place when she needed a lift in spirits.

Or a computer with internet service. Tonight, she needed both. She couldn't wait to see if BJ had replied to her last post.

Jo Murphy Spencer, the owner of the café, approached in her usual exuberant way, her red curls bouncing and her smile beaming. The woman never failed to put Vee at ease, no matter how she was feeling when she walked in the door. Jo, with her wacky T-shirts, observant nature and ear for the latest gossip, was like a second mother to most of the town. Vee suspected the older woman knew more about her than most of her friends and neighbors did, but she was okay with that. There was no one better than Jo for doling out sound advice, solicited or not.

"Vee, dear," Jo exclaimed, waving the purple dish-cloth she held in one hand. "Have you come to spend some time on the internet for your Spanish class, or shall I seat you at a table for a nice home-style dinner?"

Vee felt her face warm and hoped Jo didn't notice the flush of her cheeks. Not much chance of that, though. Jo was extremely perceptive. She was bound to see that something was off, but to Vee's relief, Jo did nothing more than raise a curious brow.

She was here for the computer, all right, but despite the fact that she had an assignment due the following day that she needed to type up and submit, her Spanish course was the last thing on her mind.

"I'll just slip in behind the computer in the corner if that one's available," Vee said, indicating what looked like an open spot in the straight line of tables across the back wall.

"Coffee? Or do you want something more substantial to feed your brain while you work?"

"A caramel latte would be nice."

"Skinny?"

"No, I think I need the real thing tonight," Vee said on a sigh.

"Coming right up," Jo said, tossing her rag onto her left shoulder and bustling over to the service window be-hind the counter. "I need a big slice of apple pie, Phoebe, dear," she called.

"But I didn't—" Vee started to protest.

Jo waved her away. "On the house, dear. You look like you could use a little something to perk you up, and there ain't nothing like a slice of one of Phoebe's famous pies to do just that."

Vee chuckled and nodded. It was useless to try to

argue with Jo when the woman had her mind set on something. All that would do was delay the inevitable. Besides, Vee had planned on ordering dinner here eventually, and apple pie was her favorite.

Tonight, she would start with dessert. After the day she'd just had, she thought she deserved it.

She weaved her way through the tables to the back corner, greeting everyone she passed. Serendipity was a small town. Everybody literally knew everybody— and usually knew everybody's business—which was part of the reason Vee was so hush-hush regarding her own plans for the future and most especially her potential internet sweetheart. Even her closest friends might accidentally blurt out the truth if they knew about it— which was exactly why they didn't.

Sliding in behind the computer, she wiggled the mouse to bring the screen out of sleep mode and signed on, first to the college website where her Spanish class was held, and then onto her private email account. Were anyone to come around to speak to her, she could easily toggle the screen so her class work covered her email and save herself from any possible embarrassment or awkwardness.

It was a clandestine moment. She felt almost as if she were taking part in a spy novel. Secret messages. Covert engagements.

Even if they *were* only online.

It was still fun. And perfectly harmless, right?

Vee's heart raced when she saw that there was a message from BJ. She had nearly a hundred other emails— mostly junk mail mixed with some from friends and classmates—but they went unnoticed as she clicked the one and only link of true importance to her.

Dear Veronica Jayne,

I'll take a look at the revisions you sent for class later tonight, but right now I'm more intrigued by what you said about yourself. I've been thinking about you a lot recently. I think you should do it. No, really, you ought to do it! Put your hair down, I mean, figuratively speaking. Or maybe literally, too, for all I know.

Do you wear your hair down all the time? That's how I picture you. Long, cascading hair. Pretty eyes. Flowery dresses that course around your ankles in waves.

Am I close? Or am I putting you on the spot?

Even without being able to see you, I can tell what a wonderful person you are. God made you special, Veronica. You need to believe in yourself more—and allow others to believe in you, as well.

I know I do.

Take care,

BJ

Vee leaned back in her seat and smoothed her hair back into a knot at her neck as she let out a deep breath that she hoped was not as audible as it felt.

BJ thought she was *special*.

They may not have ever met in person, but he *cared* for her. If Vee's face had been pink-stained before, it was no doubt a flaming red now.

Her heart and her mind were all over the place, fluttering and diving and soaring. Was it a slip of the fingers? Was any of this real? Could she have feelings for a man she'd technically never met?

She'd heard stories of internet romance, of course, but could it seriously happen to her? Could she truly meet Mr. Right online? She highly doubted it, and yet there was a small part of her that hoped for it to be so.

BJ was good to her, not to mention *for* her. Without even trying, he encouraged her to admit to her true feelings about herself and the world, emotions she usually stuffed way, *way* down inside her heart and mind.

How did he do that?

It was unsettling but in a good way. No one else knew her private thoughts and feelings the way he did.

But *cascading hair? Floral dresses?* What could be further from the truth? Would he be disappointed if they met in person and he learned that she was so far from what he had imagined?

No one except her own family had ever seen her wearing her hair down, in a literal sense. She'd been wearing her hair in a knot since the beginning of junior high school when the popular girls had picked on her for being a tomboy. In Vee's contrary way, her defense had been to be exactly that, and so from then on, her thick, dark hair was always pulled tightly into a bun at the nape of her neck.

But that was a long time ago. She wasn't facing junior high drama anymore, so what did the way she wore her hair even matter anymore?

Maybe BJ was right. Maybe she should—

"Hey, Vee." Ben's rich baritone voice startled her and she bolted upright in her seat as if she'd touched a live electrical wire. "I'm surprised to see you here. Didn't you say you had plans for dinner tonight? I thought maybe you had a date or something."

"Ben," she exclaimed, laying a hand on her racing

heart as he slid into the chair across from her. Her pulse roared in her head as, in a panic, she clumsily moused over the *X* that closed the browser completely.

Well, that was smooth. She'd been so lost in her thoughts that she hadn't seen him standing next to her. How long had he been there? Had he seen the email?

She'd probably drawn attention to herself with all of her jumping and jerking, but if he suspected anything was amiss, he didn't say so.

As a matter of fact, he didn't say anything at all. He just leaned his elbows on the table, staring at her over the top of the computer monitor, his bronze-green eyes unreadable. Vee wasn't sure how long it was until Jo arrived at the table with a serving tray in her hands, but her interruption was an unquestionable relief. Vee hadn't realized she was holding her breath until Jo spoke and dissolved the tension in the air.

"Coffee and fresh apple pie for each of you," Jo said, disrupting the silence as she served them.

"Thank you, Jo," Ben said, squaring the plate of pie in front of him and picking up his fork. "This looks delicious. But, uh, what about dinner?" he asked, directing his question toward Vee. "Is pie going to do it for you? No wonder you're so tiny."

Vee straightened her spine and tipped her chin. So what if she was small in stature? It wasn't from eating dessert instead of her regular meals. She glared at him.

Jo, as always, could read Vee well enough to pick up on the tension and interrupted once again. "Meatloaf, mashed potatoes and green beans are the house special tonight," she tempted. "My nephew makes a mean batch of home-style potatoes and gravy."

Ben and Vee nodded simultaneously, and Vee realized just how hungry she really was when her stomach growled at the offering. She'd been so distracted by BJ's email that she hadn't been paying attention to her rumbling tummy.

If *she* was hungry, she realized belatedly, then Ben must be famished. He'd pulled more than his share of the weight helping her break in the soil for the garden. It was still tough this time of year.

"What happened to your steak dinner?" she asked as soon as Jo left the table to put in their orders. "I thought you and your parents had something going."

He shrugged and shook his head, causing a dark curl to fall forward onto his brow. The right side of his mouth twitched upward. "As it turned out, my parents already had dinner plans with another couple," he explained. "Apparently they're following some reality television show or other together. Can you imagine? I would never have pegged my parents for something like that." He chuckled. "Anyway, I didn't want to eat alone, so here I am. And you?"

"I have a date."

He raised a brow.

She couldn't help but chuckle. "With my computer. I've got some…stuff I need to catch up on." That was vague enough, right?

"Landscaping?"

She shrugged noncommittally. She was a dinosaur who still did most of her landscaping the old-fashioned way—sketching by hand—but Ben didn't need to know that.

"I've got to say I'm impressed by that *stuff.* I had no idea that planting a garden could be so complicated. Or so interesting."

"Not to mention fun," she added, warming to the conversation. "Come on, you can admit it. You enjoyed digging in the dirt with me. Isn't that every little boy's fantasy come to life?"

His eyes widened and his gaze danced, and she realized that her words *might* have come out sounding flirtatious—which of course wasn't her intention.

She was suddenly aware—*very* aware—of the tension, like an electrical charge in the atmosphere between them. Something had shifted. Changed. *Warmed.* And she couldn't break her gaze away from Ben's to save her life.

It was Ben who finally looked away, taking a slow, deliberate sip of his coffee. His smile, however, did not disappear. If anything, it grew stronger.

"So, then," he asked casually, "did you want me to find another table for dinner? I'd hate to bother you if you're—busy."

She wanted to say he should leave. She knew she *should* bow out gracefully. He'd generously given her that out on a platter. And yet… And yet. He'd been generous with his time today, and his efforts on helping her with the gardening. He'd been patient and hardworking. Companionable, even.

"No, of course not. Please stay."

This was way, *way* better than steak. Not the meatloaf, though that was good, too, but mostly it was the company Ben was keeping. And he couldn't have been more surprised than if he were enjoying a meal with Attila the Hun.

Vee Bishop usually took a swipe at him at every turn, but tonight he was discovering that she could be warm and sweet when she wanted to be. He'd always known she was an intelligent woman with a great deal of inner strength, but spending time with her, both gardening and at dinner, had enlightened him in more ways than one.

He'd always considered her a little bit edgy—which she definitely was—but it hadn't even occurred to him to wonder about what else went on in that tough-girl brain of hers, that there might be other sides to her that he was missing.

Not until today, anyway.

"My sister Kayla's coming into town for a few days," he commented before forking a bite of mashed potatoes into his mouth and groaning in pleasure at the delightfully creamy homemade texture. "She's bringing my two nephews with her."

Vee made a surprised sound from the bottom of her throat. "To be honest, I didn't even remember that you had a sister until you said something just now."

"No, you probably wouldn't. She's several years older than me, so you wouldn't have been in any classes with her. She moved away just out of high school—out of state, actually, to California—to get a political science degree from Stanford. After that, she was off at law school and once she passed her bar exam, she was immediately swept up by a hotshot San Francisco law firm. I'm incredibly proud of her, of course, but I do wish I could see her and the kids more often. She rarely gets home, and I don't get much of a chance to go visit her in California. Of course, my mom and dad are thrilled to be able to see their grandsons again."

"I'm sure. Are you planning anything special for your nephews while they're here?"

"I'm looking forward to tossing a football around with

the boys. Kayla's a single mother, so they're always raring to play sports when they visit home. And the church carnival is coming up. I expect they'll enjoy popping balloons with a dart and maybe winning a goldfish in a plastic bag for their effort, if memory serves me right."

"Which I'm sure your sister will appreciate," she added wryly.

Ben chuckled. "You're probably right about that one. I can't imagine that toting goldfish back to California is in Kayla's short-term plans—or her long-term plans, for that matter. I'll most likely have to keep them at my apartment, where the boys can visit them when they're in town."

"That would be nice of you." She gave him a speculative look, as if she was trying to figure him out. It made him uncomfortable, and he cleared his throat.

"I don't mind. I can be a responsible pet owner—now. Not like when I named Tinker or anything. I wouldn't forget to feed the fish if I put them in a glass bowl on my counter." His mind drifted to a happy memory from his own childhood. "I remember as a kid how excited I was to attend the church carnival every year. It was such a big moment in my life, throwing a ring around a pop bottle and winning a prize."

"I remember being at the carnival, too," admitted Vee. "Although I don't think I ever ringed any pop bottles. I'm not sure I ever won any prizes to speak of."

"I'll have to win one for you this year at the carnival, then. Maybe a big stuffed teddy bear or something." With his impulsive streak—the one that had gotten him into trouble more times than he could count—he'd spoken before he'd even taken a moment to consider what he was actually saying.

Now, judging from the stunned look on Vee's face, he had to find some way to backpedal.

"You probably don't want a stuffed animal," he continued, but that only seemed to make things worse. Vee turned an alarming shade of red. "I imagine you aren't the type of woman to have a room full of bears and unicorns."

She had taken a long pull of her water right as he began speaking, and now she choked on it.

"And…I should shut up now," he finished.

She sputtered and shook her head. "Your nephews," she gasped when she was able.

"Right. I was telling you about Felix and Nigel. They both want to hang around with me at work. They're at an age where they're in complete awe of what I do."

"Being a paramedic? I'll bet. With all the bells and whistles—literally—it's pretty exciting stuff."

Ben cracked a grin. "I meant my job as an auto mechanic, actually. They want me to let them get under the hood of a car and get lowdown and greasy. You know how little boys are."

Her gaze softened. "I remember. My brothers were like that, too. They were always coming to the supper table covered head to toe with dirt, and Mama wouldn't let them sit down to eat until they were clean right down to under their fingernails."

Suddenly self-conscious, Ben clasped his hands into his lap underneath the table. The dirge of being a grease monkey was the complete inability to get his hands clean, especially under the nails, no matter what products and brushes he used. Although that might be fun for a nine- and seven-year-old boy, it was not so much for a thirty-year-old man having dinner with a pretty woman.

Even if she was a woman who didn't like him.

"You have the oddest expression on your face," she remarked, her dark brows closing in over her nose as she eyed him questioningly. "What are you thinking about?"

"Grease," he blurted, cringing as he returned his hands to the tabletop. As embarrassing as it might be to have dirty nails, he'd hardly be able to finish his meal without using his hands. He suddenly pictured himself diving headlong into his mashed potatoes like a man in a pie-eating contest, a thought that gave him an inward laugh. Somehow he expected that might be even more conspicuous than a little stubborn grease on his hands.

To his relief, Vee merely chuckled at his blurted exclamation.

"That would be one of the hazards of your job, I suppose. I've got a similar problem myself sometimes, so I'm not one to complain. You'd be amazed how filthy I can get when I garden all day, jamming my hands into potting soil and dirt, even with protective gloves on. You shower and scrub, and still all the grime doesn't quite come off."

Her answer, and the affable laughter that followed, put Ben immediately at ease—at least until another unpleasant thought popped into his head.

What would Veronica Jayne think about having dinner with a man who couldn't even get his hands clean?

When Ben pictured some well-into-the-future dinner date with Veronica Jayne, it was in some classy, expensive restaurant where a coat and tie were mandatory and the prices weren't even listed on the menu.

It would be nothing as simple as enjoying a good old-fashioned home-style meal at Cup o' Jo, like he was now with Vee, that was for sure. The very thought of taking

Veronica Jayne to an upscale restaurant such as he suspected she was accustomed to made the hair on the back of his neck stand on edge.

He'd have to wear a suit. With a *tie*.

His throat constricted involuntarily, nearly cutting off his air, and he heaved in a deep, ragged breath to compensate. Christmas and Easter church services were the *only* times he subjected himself to the misery of a sports jacket and necktie. Ugh and double ugh with a cherry on top.

Keep breathing, he coached himself. He was getting way ahead of himself here. It wasn't like he and Veronica Jayne were going to be going on a date *anywhere* anytime soon, if at all. At this point their relationship hardly qualified as a romance. It was a warm friendship…with potential. The prospect of romance was there, even if the reality wasn't.

"I'm glad you don't mind the grease," he said, forcing his mind back to the woman seated across from him. Vee deserved his full attention, especially now that they were official dinner partners. How he had gone from trying to hide the grease under his nails from Vee Bishop to practically walking down the aisle with Veronica Jayne was beyond him. He mentally shook himself to put himself back in the game.

"Not a problem." When Vee smiled at him—truly, fully smiled at him for the first time he could remember—Ben felt it all the way to his toes, and for a moment all of his thoughts about Veronica Jayne and dinners in expensive restaurants faded completely.

Which came as a surprise even to him. What could that possibly be about?

He was grateful, he supposed, that she hadn't up and

left him at the dinner table with his wandering mind and greasy fingernails.

Yeah. That was it.

Grateful.

It couldn't possibly be more. Could it?

Chapter Five

Dear BJ,

Thanks for the note and the encouragement. Take whatever time you need to modify the content I sent you for our project. You're the presentation-software whiz, after all. At the end of the day, you've got the harder part of the undertaking—putting it all together cohesively. Once again I'm thankful I got paired with you.

I've been praying about what you said, and I have decided that I'm actually going to do it! I'm really going to put myself out there for a change and see what happens, though let me tell you, it was no easy decision for me to decide to expose my true self for others to see. I can't even put into words how nervous I am, but I know you're right. I can't keep living this way. I can't serve God to the best of my ability if I'm too busy worrying about what other people think about me. I've got to get over it once and for all. The truth is, I've had walls up nearly all my life.

You're the one who has finally helped me break them down. Thank you for that.

Truly yours,
Veronica Jayne

When Vee decided to do something, she never did it halfway. Go big or go home, as the saying went. If she was going to change her appearance and let people see the *real Vee,* she was going to do it right.

Hair. Eyebrows. Nails. The works. Frankly, it sounded horribly uncomfortable at best, and blatantly painful at worst. But she was committed now, and that was that.

It was Tuesday, and she had the day off both from Emerson's Hardware and the fire station, so she decided to head for Amarillo, hoping to be able to pick up the most important facet on which her entire plan hinged—and the one thing she absolutely did not have.

A dress.

When Vee was little, her mother had put her in frilly dresses for special occasions, but once she got old enough to pick clothes for herself, dresses and skirts simply weren't going to happen. Not in her wardrobe. She'd always worn slacks, even to church services, including weddings, funerals, Christmas and Easter. She wasn't a girly-girl, and she'd never seen the point of owning a dress if she was never going to wear one. Dresses weren't her style.

At least not yet. Maybe it was like her habit of pulling back her hair—a relic of a choice she'd made years ago, a choice she might be ready to outgrow. She'd never know unless she tried. And tried *quickly* because she only had a week to pull the whole thing—or rather, pull *herself*—together.

Every year on the Saturday before Easter the police and fire departments, in conjunction with the ladies' charity group from church, hosted a special dinner for the less fortunate in Serendipity and the surrounding areas. It was one of the highlights of the year for Serendipity. The town folk were always generous in their donations, and the meal was generally an enormous success. This would be Vee's first year in the middle of the action.

Less than one week wasn't a good deal of time to make any kind of personal transformation, much less the kind of makeover Vee had in mind, and she was all on her own in this. No fairy godmother to wave her wand like in the story of Cinderella. Not her friends. She knew better than to let them in on it. If anyone so much as cracked a joke about what she was doing—and they would—she knew herself well enough to know she'd bail on her plan.

So that left no one, not even her mother to help her. And oh, how that fact burned through her chest. How much easier this would be if Mama was still around to put the finishing touches on Vee herself.

Still, she reminded herself, she wasn't completely alone. She had the Lord, and in the long run, He was really the reason she was doing this at all. Hopefully through Christ she would discover the courage to find herself amid all the fluctuation in her life right now and be able to anchor herself in God for the long haul, including stateside mission work.

Lately, she'd been clinging to the verses in Matthew 5, especially verse 16. *Let your light so shine before men, that they may see your good works and glorify your Father in heaven.*

Wasn't that exactly what she was trying to do? Let her light shine? Step out from behind the shields she'd used to protect herself from ridicule or rejection and let the world see who she truly was?

Those verses filled her with renewed hope and peace—and most of all, courage. She knew she couldn't do this herself—but then, she didn't have to, did she? She had God in her corner, and what more could a woman ask for?

She started humming an old Sunday school ditty that had abruptly come to mind. Before she knew it, she was singing the silly children's song out loud, tapping her fingers on the steering wheel in time to the music.

"This little light of mine, I'm going to let it shine, let it shine, let it shine, let it shine."

Or she was going to try, in any case. She might end up glowing no brighter than the muted headlights on her old, reliable truck, but by golly, she was going to give it her best shot or die of embarrassment trying.

Her happy, sunshine-filled day lasted until she got about ten minutes out of town, when the engine on her customarily peppy little black truck suddenly sputtered and wheezed like an old man with a cold.

"Oh, no," Vee groaned aloud, glancing down to check the dashboard panel. She'd filled the gas tank just before she'd left town, and she had recently checked the fluid levels for the oil and antifreeze.

What could be wrong?

Please, God, let it be nothing.

But it wasn't nothing. It was *everything,* apparently. Which just figured. Every light on the panel suddenly blinked red, and then she no longer felt the power of the transmission beneath her feet. Holding the steering wheel tightly, she carefully guided the truck to the side of the road with what insignificant momentum was left in it.

Great. Just what she needed—to have her truck break

down in the middle of nowhere, on a highway that was rarely used even by commercial vehicles. Add to that the fact that this was really her only day to spend an entire afternoon in Amarillo searching for the perfect dress.

Not her best day.

With a loud, exasperated sigh, she slid out from behind the wheel and marched forward to open the hood, leaning forward and peering inside to see if she could discern any problems offhand.

Which, of course, she couldn't, and she didn't have any notion of why she'd looked at all.

Like she knew the first thing about engines. Who was she kidding? All she knew how to do was change the oil and check the fluid levels, and she wasn't particularly skillful at those two things. She absently rubbed at her forehead, where a throbbing headache was rapidly developing.

At least she wasn't being stubborn about it. Calm, cool and sensible. That was Vee. It took her less than thirty seconds to acknowledge the truth. She was officially stranded and it was time to call in for reinforcements.

She mumbled under her breath as she fished her cell phone out of her back pocket and checked for reception, only to find that there were no bars.

Not one, single, solitary bar. She growled in frustration. Of course there was no reception on such a tiny stretch of uninhabited road. Why would there be?

Why was this happening to her, especially now? Couldn't she catch a break just this once? But then, why should this time be any different than the others for her? Nothing was ever easy for her. It never had been. Scaling brick walls had become her specialty, both literally and figuratively.

She sighed again, even louder this time. At this rate she would have to flag down a trucker—assuming, of course, that one would drive by. More than likely she'd be sitting on the road for quite some time.

Not exactly how she'd planned to spend her day.

Holding her cell phone as high as she could reach in the air, which wasn't saying much at her five feet two inches, she walked around in ever-increasing circles, watching for bars to appear in the corner of her phone, turning this way and that in an unscripted cellular-tower dance that left her feeling silly and embarrassed.

If someone saw her now, how they would laugh, watching her waving her phone in the air as if that would somehow make any difference in the signal strength. It was a hopeless cause, as well she knew.

She'd just decided to return to her truck and wait for a Good Samaritan to pass by when a single bar flickered in the upper-left corner of her phone.

"Yes!" she exclaimed, freezing in place so she would not lose the signal. "Hold it…" she squeaked, "please, God, let the signal hold until I can dial someone to come pick me up."

She paused, her arm still extended high in the air. Now that she finally had a connection, she wasn't sure who to dial. She didn't have a phone book handy to call the auto shop back in town, and her brother Eli was working his shift at the police station. He'd probably come get her if she asked, but she didn't want him to neglect his duties, and it wasn't like it was an emergency for 911.

At least, not yet, it wasn't. The future remained to be seen.

At length, she settled on calling her father. She knew he hadn't left the house much since her mother had died, but she was certain he'd make an exception for her.

However, after speaking to him and tossing around a few other options, they decided that it would be better for him to call Derek's Auto Garage where Ben worked and have them meet her here with a tow truck. They'd be able to bring her truck back into town with them and not leave it temporarily abandoned on the side of the highway.

The sooner they started fixing it, the sooner they would be finished. Vee groaned at the thought of an expensive car repair bill. Yet another stress point she didn't need right now, but since she used her truck for work, it was a necessity to get it fixed as soon as possible.

The sun was shining and it was a nice, temperate spring day in Texas, so Vee yanked down the tailgate of her truck and perched herself, legs swinging off the edge, to wait for the tow. She wished she had a book to read. Who knew how long it would be before the tow truck showed up? Her best guess was that she was a good twenty miles from town, and tow truck drivers were notorious for taking their own sweet time. She figured she might as well enjoy the fresh air while she waited.

In truth, it was little time at all. She was surprised when a scant fifteen minutes later she heard the rumbling of a tow truck thundering down the highway.

She was even more surprised to find that it was Ben Atwood behind the wheel, accompanied by two black-haired, green-eyed boys. Of course, she'd known that he worked at his uncle Derek's garage, but she had no idea that he was the tow truck operator, too.

She smiled at the wiggling youngsters as Ben pulled his truck next to hers. Even a casual observer could see the kids were clearly related to Ben. They must be his nephews, Vee thought.

Ben pulled in front of her and then backed the tow truck close enough to hook Vee's truck up to it.

"Hey, Vee," he greeted as he stepped out of the cab. "Having a little engine trouble, are we?"

"Apparently," she answered mildly, tongue in cheek. "Thanks for coming so quickly, although I've got to say that I'm surprised to see you here. I didn't know you drove the tow truck," Vee commented as she watched him fasten the chains from one vehicle to the other.

"I don't," he replied, flashing his generous smile. "Not usually, anyway. My uncle has a kid who generally handles tow jobs. But as it happened, I was the one who picked up the phone when your father called, and once I found out it was you…" His sentence drifted to an awkward halt.

Once he'd found out it was her…

What?

He'd made a special trip just to come to her rescue?

"You—uh—have a smudge of grease on your…" He cleared his throat. "Here. Just let me get it." Before she could react, he'd reached forward, gently brushing at her forehead with the pad of his thumb. She held her breath.

"There, then. That's better." Ben swiftly returned his attention to attaching her truck to the towline. His face was flushed a deep copper color, and Vee wondered if the shade was a mark of exertion or uneasiness. His curly brown hair brushed haphazardly across his fore-

head, as if he'd been running in the wind, giving him
an appealing boyish charm. She couldn't help but notice
that those enormous biceps of his were straining against
his black T-shirt as he worked, only this time he wasn't
showing off for her.

At least, she didn't think he was.

Either way, she had to appreciate him as a man. There
was no doubt he was strong and attractive, whether he
was wearing his paramedic uniform or, as he was now,
in blue jeans and a T-shirt. With those amazing green-
bronze eyes of his, he was beyond a doubt the best-looking man she'd ever known. She suspected he'd stand out
anywhere, but especially in a small town like Serendipity. Certainly he had no shortage of women to date in
town.

Which was exactly why she didn't like him. He went
through women like bunny rabbits went through carrots,
using his razor-sharp teeth to chomp them up and then
spit them out. For the first time, she wondered if maybe
it wasn't entirely his fault. She was willing to give him
at least the hint of the benefit of the doubt, since the
women in question practically fell all over themselves
to be with him. Of course, that was no excuse for treating them badly, but it had to be a little overwhelming to
have so many people want to be with you.

Not that she would know what that felt like.

She apparently scared men silly. Either they didn't
like her looks or her attitude. Or both. And she wasn't
about to apologize for either, even if she *was* considering
making a few changes. In any case, she certainly hadn't
been overwhelmed with potential suitors.

Not now. Not ever. So why was Ben paying special
attention to her?

That was the question of the hour.

He abruptly raised his head and cocked a brow. He'd obviously realized that she'd been staring at him, a fact that she hadn't been aware of until the moment their eyes met. He didn't comment on it, though that adorable half-grin of his snuck up one side of his lips, accentuating the dimple in his right cheek and the cleft in his chin. He managed to look both boyishly charming and utterly masculine at the same time.

"I do appreciate this." She had trouble finding the right words to express her gratitude. Maybe because so many other emotions were skirmishing for prominence inside her mind and heart.

"My pleasure," he responded, opening the passenger-side door of the tow truck. "Okay, tough guys. Scoot to the back and buckle up," he ordered his nephews, whom he introduced as nine-year-old Felix and seven-year-old Nigel. It took a moment for him to rein in the squirrelly boys and make sure they were safely buckled into their seats, but then he turned his attention back to Vee. "I hope you don't mind that I brought the kids along for the ride. They wanted to see what their uncle Ben does all day."

Vee didn't mind. Not at all.

The ride back into town was definitely interesting—and informative. For one thing, the boys' presence kept her from the awkwardness of having to be alone with Ben. As a side note, it was interesting to watch him interact with his nephews. The boys hung on his every word as he explained in an age-appropriate fashion how the towing process was executed. He genuinely listened to their questions and answered them carefully. Maybe most telling of all, he laughed out loud at their childish attempts at humor, especially when they were aimed directly at him. He was definitely a man who could take—and make—a joke.

It came as a great surprise to her that Ben was such a natural with children, although she didn't know why he wouldn't be, now that she saw him with his nephews. Both boys clearly desired to emulate him, even going so far as to mimic his gestures, like the way he brushed the curl off his forehead with the back of his palm, or the way he half shrugged with his left shoulder when he was agreeing with something.

As far as Vee was concerned, he got two thumbs up as a male role model, at least in this setting. If Ben brought the boys along on a date, they'd see a whole different side of him...but that was hardly likely to happen. Besides, it was clear that Ben was careful to moderate his behavior so that he didn't say anything that might confuse the boys or set a bad example, which meant that he probably wouldn't let them anywhere near his social life.

A half hour later, they were back at the shop and Ben had unhooked her truck from the towline.

"You want me to see if I can take care of this now?" he asked, popping the hood and leaning in to get a closer look at the engine. "I can't promise I can make a quick fix. Most engine repairs take at least a couple of hours of labor time. Sometimes more like days, especially if we don't have the parts on hand."

She glanced at her watch and shook her head.

"No, that's okay," she affirmed. "I'm obviously going to have to change my plans, so there's no rush."

Not today, anyway. There was no point in trying to make it to Amarillo and back now, not with the sun already halfway down in the west. She'd have to make her excursion another day, and it would have to be soon. Not that she could count on having another free day between now and Saturday. She might have to come up with a Plan B or else rush into town and back, grabbing the first dress that caught her eye.

That's if she didn't completely lose her courage first and nix the whole idea.

At this point, that was a very big *if*.

Dear Veronica Jayne,

Today has been a good day. It always is when I get to spend time with family and friends. I don't ever want to take that for granted. Remind me of that if I start complaining about life, will you? It's so easy to forget how many blessings God has showered me with.

I've got a super busy weekend, so I've been spending extra time on our project so I don't get behind. I'm organizing the final presentation with the software. I was blown over by how well your script and my graphics meshed together—better even than we'd planned. I think you'll be surprised when you see them. I'll attach the whole thing to an email once I'm sure I've got things the way I want them.

Excellent work on the script, by the way. The photos would be nothing without that great narration. I know I've said it before, but it bears repeating—I'm so happy you're my partner! Two thumbs up!

Sincerely,

BJ

Ben's gaze slid across the inner workings of Vee's truck, his years of working on engines making it easy for him to spot the problem.

"It looks like your timing belt snapped," he said, his

hands gliding expertly over the engine's surface as he peered here and there to be certain he was making a complete diagnosis of the vehicle. "I'm afraid I'll have to special order some of the parts in order to fix it, so it may be a day or two before you get your truck back."

"You can't just slide on a new timing belt and call it good?" she asked hopefully.

He chuckled. "Not exactly. Let's just say that it's a little more complicated than that. I have to take the engine apart just to reach the area where I need to work. That's going to take some time in and of itself. Plus, with Serendipity being such a small town, off the beaten track and all, we don't keep a lot of spare parts at the shop. That would be too much of a burden on the shop's overhead. We've found that it's easier to order parts in when we have specific requests and know just what we need."

She sighed and smoothed her hair with her palm. "That figures. So what are we looking at? A week? Two weeks?"

"Well, hopefully it won't be quite that long." His gaze shifted briefly to where his nephews crouched, looking through a toolbox full of various-sized wrenches. "You need it for your work, right?"

"Exactly. Not to mention the special occasions coming up. Between the Easter banquet and Easter week services, my dance card is full to the brim. If it's going to be a long time, I may have to try to find some other reliable means of transportation to tide me over."

She groaned aloud. "And it'll be expensive, too, I'm guessing. A month's wages down the drain, right? Do I need to start looking for a third job?" She closed her eyes and raised her hands as if she were being held up by a gun-toting thief. "Just please make it a clean wound. That's all I can ask after the lovely day I've had."

He laughed. "You sound like a cup-half-empty kind of girl," he teased. "I don't want you worrying about time or money. It sounds like you've got enough on your plate as it is. I'll tell you what. How about if I cut you a break? I'll do the work on my own time and only charge you for the parts I use."

Her gaze locked on his, her almond-colored eyes narrowing. He'd never realized how beautiful they were until this moment. His stomach did a backflip as she stared him down. His throat bobbed as he tried to swallow.

"What?" he asked when she didn't speak.

"Why would you do this for me?" she asked suspiciously, her gaze narrowing on him.

Now *that* was a good question.

Why *would* he offer to help Vee? He'd done some really dumb things—like offering to work for free— early on in his dating days. He'd given of himself and gotten nothing back in return, except more dead-end relationships.

But even if he hadn't learned his lesson in that department—not to give too much of himself for free when he stood the risk of being hurt—there was no overlooking one fact.

He and Vee weren't dating. She didn't even like him overmuch.

So what was he doing? And more to the point—why?

Why should he put himself out for her when she was very rarely even nice to him? Wouldn't he simply be laying himself out like a carpet and asking to be walked on?

When the silence dragged on, she apparently decided

that he didn't have an answer to give, or at least not one that either of them would believe. Instead, she wandered to the other end of the garage and nonchalantly peeked under the vinyl cover of a hooded sports car.

His sports car, as it happened. Pride welled in his chest. This beauty was a classic Mustang rebuilt with his own two hands over a period of several months. He'd repainted her a deep navy blue with black trim, and she was custom-made from the engine to the wheel rims.

To say he was proud of that car would be an understatement. It was practically his baby. He'd spent countless hours nursing it to health and making her live up to the vision in his mind. But he'd never once, until now, showed her off to anyone other than his uncle. Even then, he'd only given Uncle Derek the merest glimpse of her. This was the first time he had considered showing her off for real, and his nerves crackled with tension.

"You're welcome to have a look," he said, carefully removing the cover on the shiny blue vehicle, which had been methodically waxed from stem to stern until it sparkled with a keen luster. The tire rims were gleamed silver and the black leather interior had been polished until it shone.

Vee whistled her appreciation and Ben stood up an inch taller, unable to still the smile growing on his face.

"Wow," she complimented, walking slowly around the vehicle, stopping to admire it from various vantage points. "Now *that* is a sports car. I've never seen anything quite so nice. It's really beautiful, Ben. Did you do the work yourself?"

Pride chased ego in dizzying circles in his stomach and curled up into his throat. He coughed into the crook of his shoulder.

"Who owns it? I'm so jealous, whoever they are. I've never seen anyone driving it around here, that's for sure. I would have remembered a car as fancy as that."

For some reason, her comments affected him more than he would have liked. He didn't know why it mattered what she thought. She probably didn't know a sports car from a Zamboni, but her smile was so genuine and her approval so apparent that he couldn't help the pride that welled in his chest.

It was an odd feeling. While there was no question that he was proud of his work on the car, there was something about the fact that it was specifically Vee Bishop's admiration that stroked his ego even more. That, he knew, ought to be cause for concern in itself, but he had to admit he liked the feeling.

"It's mine and I rebuilt her myself," he confirmed. "All the way from the ground up. She's my pet project. Between the auto shop and the fire station I haven't had much time to put into any kind of a hobby, so it's taken me several months to get her this far."

"She's definitely a beauty. You do good work."

"Thanks," he said, choking up again. He settled his weight on the balls of his feet. He was wound up like a top, waiting for her to spin him.

"So why haven't I seen you driving her around?"

"I suppose I was waiting until she was finished to show her off, until she was just perfect. I only drive her late at night when no one is around to see her while I get the engine in tip-top shape. I think she's close to making her debut now."

"I should say so. I'm impressed. I didn't know you rebuilt cars."

"Only this one." If she didn't stop escalating his ego,

his chest was going to pop like an overinflated balloon. As it was, his adrenaline was running overtime, making his pulse buzz in his ears. "I suppose you could call rebuilding her my hobby, of sorts."

"Well, it definitely puts *my* hobby to shame."

"Really? What do you do for fun?" He was genuinely curious, although he couldn't have explained why. Maybe it was that she'd shown so much interest in what he'd done that he felt he ought to reciprocate.

She laughed, looking a little self-conscious, which wasn't like Vee at all. At least, not the Vee Ben knew— the woman who was always in control, who always knew what to do or say in any given situation. The woman who was generally as strung up as tight as a bow.

And the woman who didn't like *him* at *all*.

Or at least he didn't think she did. She didn't usually treat him with the respect she was showing him now, and that put her in a new light for him.

Maybe he was judging her too harshly, based mostly on her outward appearance and attitude. Yes, she sported a tight bun and an even tighter expression, but he supposed that was understandable given her circumstances. She worked in a tough, nearly exclusively male environment at the fire station. Maybe she wasn't as rigid as he'd been given to believe she was.

"Candles. I make candles," she said, shattering whatever preconceived notions Ben had had of her. "You know the ones on the end cap in the craft section of Emerson's? Those would be mine." She snorted. "Pathetic, I know."

Now it was Ben's turn to whistle his surprise.

Landscaping. Candle making. Firefighting. What else did he not know about her?

Vee was a complete enigma. She surprised him at every turn. Whatever else he thought of her, he didn't consider her pathetic in any way, shape or form.

"Not at all," he said aloud. "I bought some of those candles for my mama last Christmas. She loves them. She lights them whenever she takes a bubble bath, and she won't even consider using any others."

Vee murmured something Ben didn't quite pick up, but before he could figure it out, his attention was drawn to his two antsy nephews. They'd been cooped up in the truck too long and they were raring to do something physical.

"Uncle Ben!" Felix shouted from the far corner of the shop. "Can you put us up on the lift?"

"Please?" little Nigel pleaded.

Ben laughed. "Okay, guys, but just this once. We need to get Miss Bishop back to her house. I'm sure she doesn't want to hang around this greasy old garage all day."

"Oh, no, I—" Vee started to protest but then dropped silent, watching as Ben situated the boys on the hydraulic lift, which was generally used to raise cars off the ground so he could work underneath them.

After making sure the boys' feet were safely away from the edges, he moved to the electrical box and flipped a switch. The lift ground to life and the boys squealed in glee.

"Ben!" Vee exclaimed in dismay. She rushed to his side and reached for his elbow before she'd even finished saying his name. "Surely you're not going to—"

"Let the boys take a little ride up the lift? Why not? My uncle used to allow me to take a jaunt up there all the time, and no harm ever came to me. Don't worry. It's

fun. Nothing to be concerned about. Besides, my nephews have done this before. Plenty of times."

"That doesn't make it safe." Now she was starting to
sound like the woman he knew—the one who had an
opinion on everything—an opinion that usually said
that whatever he did was wrong. Vee Bishop pushed her
weight around, tiny as she was, and always thought she
needed to micromanage every tiny detail of what was
going on around her.

"Maybe you're not aware of this fact, but boys like to
have a little danger in their lives," he said. He was still
smiling, but it was starting to feel forced now. "Not, of
course, that I'm suggesting that riding the lift is really
dangerous. It's not. Believe me, I've got it completely
under control. I promise I won't go an inch higher than
five feet. Felix and Nigel climb trees taller than that."

"With cement underneath them?" Vee stepped back,
but she didn't look happy about it. She folded her arms
in front of her and scowled at him. "If they get hurt it's
on you."

Of course it was on him. He was in charge of his
nephews for the day. He wouldn't let them do anything
truly dangerous. They wouldn't get hurt on his watch.

"We'll take you home as soon as we're done here," he
said, grinning when his nephews shrieked with delight
at being carried up by the rising lift.

"If we don't have to go to the hospital first," she
grumbled under her breath.

He spared her an exasperated glance. Really? Did she
not trust him at *all?*

"Fine," she conceded as she met his gaze. "Could you
drop me by my father's house instead? He didn't sound
at his best when I talked to him earlier, and I just want

to make sure he's all right. I can get Eli to take me home after he finishes his shift at the police station."

"Sure thing," Ben assured her.

"If it's an inconvenience I can—"

He didn't let her finish. "It's not an inconvenience. Okay, boys. Get your balance and watch where you're standing. I'm going to take you down now."

The boys groaned in unison, but they followed Ben's directions and situated themselves safely on the lift before Ben brought it down.

Slowly. Carefully.

The whole thing had been perfectly harmless, just as he'd said.

"See?" He flashed Vee a satisfied, and possibly a bit triumphant, smile. "All safe and sound."

Vee shrugged, still appearing unconvinced. Ben pushed back the wave of irritation he felt at the way she wouldn't back down, even now that he'd been proved right. Why couldn't she believe in him, even a little? Why did she always assume the worst when he was involved?

Resolutely, he turned away from her, focusing on the boys. He wasn't going to let Vee spoil the pleasure he felt from spending time with them.

If Vee Bishop wanted to disapprove of him, fine. He wasn't going to let it bother him one single bit.

Chapter Six

Dear BJ,

Today didn't go as planned, but days seldom do, do they? In my experience, God doesn't always have the same agenda I do. It's more than rolling with the punches. It's adapting—trying to see what God wants me to learn.

Sometimes I feel that I hinder myself. My own personal perception of events skews my actions, and often I wonder whether or not I'm walking the right road. I question if I'm doing the correct things at all—taking this Spanish class, moving forward with my life, into mission work.

That's when I have to trust God the most, I guess—and lean on friends like you. Thank you for letting me vent.

In Christ,
Veronica Jayne

Vee couldn't believe Ben had allowed his nephews to ride on the hydraulic lift, even if he had only raised them a few feet in the air. She could not imagine what he was thinking, but she'd been around her own brothers long enough to know that guys often took irrational risks for no apparent reason. It appeared to be in their DNA, passed on from generation to generation.

Like uncle to nephews, for example.

"Would you like to come in for a moment?" she asked as Ben pulled his truck into her father's long, washboard dirt driveway. "I'm sure he'd be glad to have the company, especially the boys. Children always make him smile."

She could only hope that was true. It used to be, but now it was hard to say *what,* if anything, would make her father smile. Her dad didn't find joy in much since his wife's death. He rarely left the house, preferring to sit by the fire with one of his books. He didn't even attend regular Sunday services at the church anymore.

It was a matter of constant prayer for Vee. She didn't know what to do for him or how to reach him, and neither did her brothers.

No matter what they tried, from family dinners to community gatherings, nothing seemed to help. In fact, he seemed to be withdrawing more and more into his shell with each passing day. Vee worried about his health, which appeared to be declining. Where once there was a strong, robust man heading the Bishop clan, there was now a weary, world-worn soul. It broke Vee's heart every time she thought of him.

"You sure he won't mind having the boys around?" Ben reiterated. "They're pretty wound up right now, and I know your father hasn't been feeling well lately."

Vee chuckled. "Believe me, he's used to rowdy boys," she said. "Don't forget, he raised Cole and Eli."

Boys didn't get any rowdier than Cole and Eli. Even as adults her brothers tended to be loud and raucous.

What she didn't say was that she wasn't positive how he'd handle it now. The boys might brighten his day. Hopefully. Otherwise, they'd simply tire him out and send him further into seclusion.

It was a chance she had to take. She would do anything to break her father out of his shell and put him back on the road to healing. She knew as well as her father that grief was inevitable. It was what a person did with it that counted in the long run.

"Just for a moment, then," Ben agreed. "I've noticed that your father hasn't been to Sunday services at church for a few weeks, and I'd like the opportunity to say hello and see how he's faring."

"Dad?" she called, knocking twice before entering the house where she'd grown up. "I have a surprise for you!"

"You know I don't like surprises," her dad growled, his voice as scratchy as the scruff on his chin. Although it was well into the afternoon, her father shuffled into the living room still dressed in his ragged blue bathrobe and worn-out slippers. Vee was embarrassed for him but not about him. Anyone with eyes could see he was still grieving.

He walked hunched over like a man twenty years past his age. His short gray hair was ruffled and his brown eyes cloudy—at least until he saw Felix and Nigel.

"Hey, boys," he exclaimed, smoothing his hair back with his fingers as if that would somehow make him more presentable. "Tell me, who do we have here?"

Ben made the introductions. "These are my sister's kids, Felix and Nigel."

"Kayla's boys. Well, I'll be a rooster's uncle. Just let

me put on another pot of coffee," her father said as they all moved into the kitchen.

"I'll get it." Vee was relieved to have something to do with her hands, though making coffee didn't keep her mind as occupied as she would have liked. Her heart shattered every time she saw her father this way. She felt so helpless. All she could do was pray, and as she scooped grounds into the filter, she silently did just that. At least seeing Felix and Nigel had seemed to have a positive effect on the man.

"I'll bet you boys don't want to sit around the table while the adults chitter-chatter, now, do you?"

The boys' combined protest was enough to convince every adult in the room that they did not want to be holed up in a house with a bunch of boring adults. Vee chuckled at their enthusiasm.

"I've got a big backyard just right for children," her father continued. "My own three kids used to play out back all the time. It was all their mother and I could do to keep those three out of trouble. They were always fighting with each other, falling out of trees, scraping their knees on the pavement..."

Her father's expression took on a distant quality, and for a moment Vee wondered if he even knew where he was, much less that his own daughter was in the room and that she, along with her brothers, were all grown up now. His mental status seemed to be declining with every passing day.

Then, just as quickly as he'd faded out, her father's face brightened and he returned to the present. It was almost frightening how easily she could see the transformation in his gaze.

"Now, somewhere around this old house," he said,

tapping his index finger on his chin, "I've got a ball for you boys to play with. Hmm. I wonder where I put it?"

His bushy gray eyebrows lowered over his nose as he paused, concentrating. After a moment he grunted and nodded to himself, then rose from his chair with a groan and scuttled out to the front hall closet. *Scuttled* was precisely the right word for the way he moved. He reminded Vee of a crab she'd once seen on a beach when she'd visited the Oregon coast.

The top half of her father's body disappeared into the closet as he fished through the coats, and she heard his muffled shout of triumph and delight when he finally found his prize.

"Here we are, boys," he called out, lofting a black-and-white checkered soccer ball at Felix, who caught it easily and without hesitation. The ball must have been the one that belonged to Vee and her brothers way back when. She couldn't imagine why her parents would have kept it all these years, but it certainly came in handy now.

"C'mon, Nigel. Race you to the back!" Felix took off at a sprint.

"No fair," Nigel squealed, darting off after his brother. "You got a head start."

Her father laughed. Actually *laughed*.

Vee didn't think she'd heard that happy sound since before her mother's funeral. A little glow of hope, like the flicker of a candle, warmed her heart, and she offered a quick, silent prayer of gratitude to God for allowing her to witness the moment. Just now, thanks to Felix and Nigel, she'd been given just the tiniest glimpse of hope that her father might finally begin to settle his grief and move on with his life.

Maybe not right away, but Vee prayed it would be

soon. Seeing her father with the boys was a good first step. It's what her mother would have wanted.

Vee poured coffee into three mugs and settled at the kitchen table with Ben and her father. Ben immediately swept her father into conversation, telling him about her truck repairs, bringing him up to date with all the go-ings-on around town and filling him in on the topic of Pastor Shawn's new series of sermons.

Ben was so laid-back and friendly that it didn't take long for him to put her father at ease. It was a good thing, too, because even with today's monumental prog-ress, Vee was never quite sure what to say to her father these days. She was thankful she didn't have to carry the conversation by herself. She was always afraid she'd say something that would upset him or, worse yet, acci-dentally mention her mother and send him even deeper into his shell.

Ben might look like a tough guy on the outside, but Vee had to admit he had a sensitive side. He was kind and gentle to her father without being condescending. It was eye-opening for her to see this side of a man who would reach out to an older neighbor in his time of need.

He was sweet. And perceptive. Almost like BJ.

Vee's throat closed and she almost choked on her sip of coffee. Ben was definitely nothing like BJ.

Or at least, as much as she knew about BJ. The real-ization struck her that BJ was nothing more than words on a computer screen. She had a sense of his personal-ity, and he'd told her about his goals and dreams, but she knew so little about the day-to-day aspects of his life. Did he have nephews, like Ben, who he enjoyed spend-ing time with? Was he a good neighbor, a good friend, to the people he saw every day?

Ben, however—*Ben* was very much a real man. She could see him, hear him, even touch those enormous biceps of his if she was so inclined.

She coughed, trying to force air back into her lungs, but it didn't seem to help. Ben couldn't possibly be half the man BJ was, nor would he ever be. She jammed that frequency of thinking before it could be broadcast any further.

Of course she was thankful for Ben's help. He'd been there to rescue her earlier, with his big old tow truck and amiable half grin. And now he was being nice to her father, which was a big plus in her book.

But the feelings she was experiencing—those couldn't be more than mismatched forms of gratitude, could they? She didn't even like Ben, but at this exact moment, she had to actively remind herself why she disliked him.

He might be acting nice today, but not all that long ago he'd broken her best friend's heart. How could Vee possibly put that aside, even for a moment?

BJ wasn't like that. That was good enough for her.

Or was it?

Her heart stuck in her throat and she almost choked again. What if she was using her quasi-relationship with a cyber-guy to avoid dealing with the real thing?

In some ways, wasn't that exactly what her father was doing? Avoiding reality to shield him from his own grief? She thought back to when she'd first been paired with BJ in her Spanish class, and a shiver passed through her when she realized that their friendship had started up just after her mother's passing.

Yes, BJ was a real person, and she'd connected with him in a very real way...but it probably wasn't a coincidence that she'd thrown herself into getting to know him right at that time rather than reaching out to the people in town.

Her chest felt suddenly heavy with sorrow, another sniper-strike of grief aimed straight at her heart when she wasn't looking.

Was it like that for her father, too? Her mother had been the love of his life. No wonder he couldn't cope.

Vee got up from the table and stared out the kitchen window, watching the boys laughing and talking as they kicked the soccer ball back and forth to each other. She'd had so many good times in that backyard that she could hardly remember them all. Swinging bats and kicking balls with Cole and Eli. Playing cops and robbers and tag and hide-and-seek from the moment the sun rose in the sky until their mother forced them inside at dusk.

What had happened to that innocent feeling she'd had as a child? When had she become so jaded about life?

She recalled how once she'd followed her brothers up the big, spreading oak in the middle of the yard. They'd been trying to get away from her, their pesky little sister, and Eli had climbed too high, trying to balance on a branch that couldn't support his weight.

He'd fallen fifteen feet and had broken an arm and twisted an ankle. She remembered how frightened she'd been to watch paramedics taking him away on a stretcher, thinking it was her fault and that her brother might not come home from the hospital.

She always had been a little melodramatic about that sort of thing. No wonder she'd panicked when Ben had allowed his nephews to ride up the hydraulic lift. Could anyone blame her for being a little overcautious? But it was one thing to be wary of physical dangers—and it was another thing entirely to be cautious about opening her heart to the people around her.

When had she closed herself down to the outside world, like her father was doing now? She hadn't always approached personal relationships with an abundance of prudence and few expectations.

She turned back to her father, who was chuckling at some story that Ben was regaling him with. Ben's attention was definitely helping her father to come out of his shell of misery and grief.

Maybe it was time for Vee to do the same thing.

Chapter Seven

Dear BJ,
I know I just sent you another email a little while ago. I hope you don't feel like I'm inundating your inbox with messages, but I think I've had another revelation about myself, and I wanted to share it with you. You understand me better than anyone else I know, next to God, of course.

I won't bore you with the details, but suffice it to say that after today, I'm going to be making some major changes in my life. I never realized until now that the woman I see when I glimpse at my reflection in the mirror every morning may not be the person others see when they look at me. We've been talking a lot about change, but maybe it's not change at all so much as just reconciling what's on the inside of me with what people see when they look at me.

Anyway, that isn't the only reason I'm emailing you tonight. I wanted to double-check with you to make sure you didn't need anything else from me for our project.
Sincerely,
Veronica Jayne

It had taken Vee an hour to curl her hair into the soft ringlets that now framed her face.

An *hour!*

How so many women did this on a daily basis was beyond her comprehension. Why would any woman put herself through such utter nonsense if she didn't have to? Vee didn't have the patience for this kind of self-torment, not even on her best day. And as long as it had taken her just to *curl her hair,* she wasn't certain this was going to be anything remotely resembling her *best* day.

Even so, she did have to admit to a fairly significant physical transformation. She stared into the mirror and saw someone she barely recognized. She'd brushed the sides of her long, flowing brown hair forward across her shoulders and allowed the rest to stream in waves down her back. She'd carefully lined and shaded her almond-colored eyes with sparkling silver eye shadow the way Olivia had taught her. She snorted at her reflection. She was a caricature of her normal makeup-less self, and she wasn't the least bit confident that she didn't look as silly as she felt.

This was crazy. It usually took her all of two minutes to pull her hair back in a knot and shun everything but the barest mineral foundation on her skin.

And as for plucking her eyebrows—what kind of barbarous personality had invented *that* particular brand of torture? She would rather relive Hazing Week at the fire academy than go through tweezing again, hair by painful hair, until her whole forehead was inflamed and burning red.

She shook her head at her reflection and scoffed. This whole idea was a big mistake from start to finish.

And she'd barely started what was sure to be an excruciatingly long day.

She was *so* tempted to undo all of the progress she'd made on herself, if a person could really call what she'd done to herself *progress*. A still-small inner voice was telling her to quit while she was ahead. The problem was that she was already late for setting up the Easter Banquet and she didn't want to miss another moment of it. Washing the makeup off her face and the curl out of her hair would take time she didn't have.

If she didn't hurry, she wouldn't be able to help with the meal at all. It was her first time serving with the fire department, although she, along with everyone else in Serendipity, had been involved with town fundraising for the event since she was in elementary school. The school held car washes and bake sales every year to help buy supplies for the dinner.

This time she'd be right in the middle of the action— actually physically helping the less fortunate—if she stopped staring at herself in the mirror and hightailed it to the community center.

She left the house without another glance. Less than ten minutes later she pulled her truck into the parking lot of the community center that served as the hub of many of Serendipity's social events. Thankfully, Ben had been able to secure the parts needed to fix her timing belt and had repaired her truck in time for her to drive it to the banquet.

Under normal circumstances she would have elected to walk the short distance from her apartment to the center, especially as nice a day as it was, but there was no *way* she was going to walk that far in heels.

In fact, walking at *all* was somewhat of an issue.

She'd always considered herself athletic and coordinated, but no matter how many times she practiced walking back and forth across her small apartment in three-inch heels, she could not seem to master the teetering-on-the-edge-of-falling feeling those ridiculous shoes produced.

Another "how do they do it" moment. She had a new appreciation for the women who attempted to wear heels on a daily basis.

Score one for the ladies of high fashion.

She'd almost reached the front door of the community center and was about to call out a greeting to a couple of her brother's cop friends who were lounging by the door, but they spied her first before she could get a single word out.

One of the guys, Brody, had been stretched back on a metal bench, his arm extended over the back. His friend Slade had been standing with one foot on the bench, leaning forward with his forearm on his knee for balance. They'd appeared deep in conversation, at least until Vee strolled up, though maybe *stroll* was too generous a word for the actual gait she was using.

More like *lumbering* or *teetering*.

Just not, hopefully, if God was gracious to her, *falling on her face*.

Before she could so much as say hello to the guys, both of the men sprang to their feet like twin Jack-in-the-boxes after the trap mechanisms had been dispatched.

"Let me get that door for you," said Brody, who sprinted over to the set of steel double doors and had thus reached them first. He opened the right door with a flourish and waved for her to go through.

"No, allow me." Slade reached for the opposite door, but when he tugged, it didn't open. He grimaced and a bright-red flush rose to his face, but he recovered quickly.

"At least let me escort you in," he crooned with what Vee presumed he must think was his best swaggering grin. To Vee it looked more like a laughably cocky contortion, which was made even more entertaining by the fact that he crooked his arm and offered his elbow to escort her like they were in a scene in an old movie.

Who were these fools, and what had they done with the police squadron?

"Thanks, guys, but I think I can manage on my own." She probably was being overoptimistic, given the circumstances, but whether she wanted to admit it or not, she was flustered by the way the men were acting. They'd certainly never offered to open a door for her before, much less presented an arm for her to take.

What was up with that?

And then it struck her like a lightning bolt out of the blue.

Zap!

They didn't recognize her.

At least, they hadn't known who she was until she spoke to them. When they heard her voice, the men turned as one, astonishment written on both of their faces, their eyes widening and their jaws dropping.

"Vee?" Brody queried, his tone a mixture of bemusement and disbelief. Mostly disbelief.

"Well, I never," Slade muttered under his breath, following the statement with a low wolf whistle as his gaze followed her figure from her eyes all the way to her toes, and then back up again.

Vee lifted her chin. "What is your problem?"

She should have been ready for this. She squared her shoulders. She *was* ready for this.

The looks on these guys' faces was pretty much the reaction she'd expected from people—at least the part where they stared at her in shock. Frankly, she'd expected that to happen the second they caught sight of her. She couldn't believe that she'd managed to change her outward appearance so much that not only had the guys not recognized her when she'd first arrived, but her appearance had sent them scurrying to one-up each other.

Oh, well. She didn't have time to waste on a couple of knuckleheads like Brody and Slade. She perused the room, trying to find Chief Jenkins. As was town tradition, he and the police chief were responsible for handing out orders and work details to the people under their respective commands.

Instead of finding Chief Jenkins, her eyes met and locked with Ben Atwood's. And unlike the fellows at the door, she was immediately and startlingly aware that *he* knew exactly who she was. There wasn't a moment's doubt or hesitation in his eyes, though he looked at least as stunned as Brody and Slade had been.

Her heart jumped into her throat at the sheer admiration in his eyes. For some reason, that one moment almost made the whole tortuous episode seem worth it.

But only for a second—before someone bumped into her from behind, jarring her enough for her to belatedly come to her senses.

This was *Ben Atwood* who had her heart racing.

How could that be?

Ben was certain his jaw dropped. Even if he'd managed a slick recovery, the astonishment he was feeling in every pore of his being must have been written all over his face.

Who was this vision of loveliness floating across the room at him? His brain was spinning so fast he was sure his eyes must be deceiving him.

No one needed to tell him that it was *Vee* in that gorgeous royal-blue dress. He was perfectly, maddeningly aware it was her. And technically, she was limping, not floating.

But *wow*.

Wow. Wow. *Wow*.

The last time he'd seen her, he'd been rescuing her from her broken-down vehicle. She'd been wearing ratty jeans and a ragged T-shirt, and her forehead had been smeared with grease. She'd looked fresh and innocent and mischievous. It suited her.

But today, she'd cleaned up like…well, like a princess. There was no other way to describe her. He'd had no idea that the thick brown hair she kept so tightly pulled back in a knot at the back of her head could be the long, curly hair that was now cascading down around her shoulders and streaming three-quarters of the way down her back. He'd known that her eyes were beautiful and distinctive, but now they were enhanced by sparkly gray eye shadow and a subtle arch to her brows that called him to her gaze.

If it weren't for the frown lining her face, the transformation from duckling to swan would have been complete.

Not that he'd ever thought of Vee as ugly. Stern, maybe, but not unattractive.

Now she was stunning. He couldn't seem to tear his gaze away from her in her dazzling dress and the high heels that accentuated her lean, womanly figure and surprisingly long legs for a person of her stature. He would never have imagined that under the tiny, no-nonsense attitude was a woman who would turn heads at even the most regal of functions, much less at a simple town banquet.

And there was no doubt that she *was* turning heads. Oh, yes indeed she was.

Men and women alike had stopped what they were doing to gaze at the newcomer in their midst. Observing the crowd, Ben could clearly see that Vee's change in appearance had done a number on them. Vee had known these folks all of her life, but it was obvious that it took most of them a minute to realize it was Vee Bishop under that perfectly flowing hair and dazzling makeup.

For some reason Ben hadn't been in doubt at all. She'd thrown him for a loop, but not that way.

It wasn't long before the whole room was abuzz, with everyone noisily wondering the hows and whys of Vee's transformation. Three of Vee's single girlfriends—cheerfully christened throughout the town as the Little Chicks because of their tendency to speak in high, twittering tones—hovered around Vee, talking over themselves in their excitement to be heard. The moniker Little Chicks fit them—it definitely sounded like chirping to Ben.

And taking the spot closest to Vee was her best friend—who also happened to be one of Ben's ex-girlfriends. Olivia Tate. Jo Spencer appeared at Vee's other side and looped their arms together, exclaiming about how beautiful she looked loudly enough for the entire room to hear.

The women had rallied around Vee quickly, despite

the fact that she was beyond a doubt the most beautiful woman in the room. There was no jealousy or pettiness. All of the girls were supporting her—not that Vee had ever needed any kind of support in the past.

Ben knew that moving into that particular circle, a flock of protective women nurturing their own, would be hazardous to any man's health, especially him with his history with Olivia. Even the other guys appeared to be taking their time to watch rather than approach.

Their loss.

Ben bucked up his nerves, swallowed his amazement and darted forward, taking Vee's other arm before another man could lay claim to it. Olivia moved to the side, allowing him more room in their circle.

As soon as he touched Vee, her deer-in-the-headlights expression disappeared, replaced by a hard-as-nails determination that was completely at odds with the soft ebb and flow of her gown.

"You look just lovely, dear," Jo said, patting Vee's arm. "Doesn't she, Ben?"

"Yeah," he agreed, but the word came out an octave lower than his usual voice and had an odd, husky tone to it. Discomfited, he cleared his throat. It figured that Jo would aim her question directly toward him when he was having a hard time finding his voice.

He felt like he should say more than simply assenting to Jo's comment, but his mind was so jumbled he couldn't think coherently. What had happened to his brain?

After a long, painful pause, he continued. "You look nice, Vee."

Which was the understatement of the century. Idiot. What was he thinking?

He *wasn't* thinking. That was the problem. He felt like hitting himself in the head to restore some mental function.

"Has anyone seen Chief around?" Vee asked, scanning the room and clearly determining to ignore the blatant admiration she was receiving. "I've got to get my orders so I can get busy helping out around here. No sense standing around doing nothing when I can be working."

"Are you kidding me?" Ben blurted before he thought better of it. Unfortunately, his statement was not only foolish—it was loud.

Every woman within hearing distance narrowed their eyes on him. He shrugged uncomfortably.

"I just meant that I wouldn't want Vee to get her dress dirty," he stated defensively. "It's so pretty. I'd hate for her to ruin it serving food."

"I didn't ask your opinion," Vee retorted, her tone icy. "And I didn't come here to stand around gawking, which is what everyone else appears to be doing. This is my first year with the fire department and I'm not about to miss the opportunity to help."

Ouch. Well, that was a slap in the face and probably well-deserved.

Vee might look like a different woman on the outside, but her attitude hadn't changed a bit. Same old tough-as-nails Vee, with a chip on her shoulder the size of a boulder and an attitude to match.

"Of course you're going to be helping," Jo assured Vee in a conciliatory voice, patting her arm for reassurance. "Look, there—I see Chief now."

As a matter of fact, Chief Jenkins was at that moment making his way through the crowd, his astonished gaze on Vee as he moved forward. And even more surprising—Vee's *father* was with him.

"Daddy!" she exclaimed, running up to hug him and plant a kiss on his freshly shaved cheek. "What on earth are you doing here?"

Her father barked out a husky laugh. "The same thing you're doing, I imagine. I offered to put my cooking skills to good use, and I've only just now had a break from the kitchen. I've been cooking since six this morning. Believe me, those church ladies can be real slave drivers when they want to be."

Vee laughed and hugged him again. Ben could see the sheer joy shining from her eyes. He knew how concerned she'd been over the way her father had holed himself up in his house after the death of his wife.

It was great to see him out and about, and it was even better to see the beautiful smile of delight on Vee's face.

"If I may say so, you look absolutely gorgeous, my dear," Chief said when he reached Vee. "Truly stunning."

Vee's smile widened even more at Chief's compliment. If Ben wasn't mistaken, she even blushed.

Vee Bishop. Blushing at a compliment.

Would wonders never cease.

"Thank you, Chief," Vee responded in a lilting tone much lighter than her usual rich alto, but a moment later she was back to her no-nonsense self. "Reporting for duty, sir. Where do you want me?"

Chief's bushy gray eyebrows lifted in surprise. "Goodness, Vee, I wouldn't have expected that you'd want to get your hands dirty, not with your fancy dress and all."

She leveled him with a glare. Ben would not have wanted to be Chief at that moment.

Even though Chief Jenkins was used to being in charge, he actually winced.

"Maybe you could greet people at the door?" he suggested weakly.

Ha! Ben wanted to crow. See? He wasn't the only one who thought Vee's getup wasn't appropriate for a worker bee at a messy banquet dinner.

Vee sighed, clearly frustrated. "What is it with you guys? I came to work, not to watch. What's the problem? Do you want me to run back home and change?"

No, Ben did *not* want her to change—but he had the sense to keep his mouth shut. It would be a shame to see Vee walk out of the community center now and come back dressed in her usual attire of jeans and a cotton shirt. Truly. A real shame.

"I *am* going to help out with the Easter banquet," she continued obstinately.

"Which she is perfectly capable of doing in a dress," Jo added.

Chief's gaze turned to Jo and he immediately nodded his consent. People didn't often cross Jo Spencer, and it didn't look like Chief was going to do so now. Besides, it was very likely that if he argued, he'd find himself ganged up on by a whole horde of women, not just Jo, and no man wanted to be put in that position, not even the chief of the fire station.

"Yes, of course," he offered. "I'm sure we can find you something to do."

Something *appropriate,* Ben hoped.

"I was just going to see if I could help set up tables," Ben said, addressing Vee. "Maybe you could follow along with plates and silverware?" He held his breath, waiting to see if she was going to blow up at him or not.

Surprisingly, she looked relieved at his suggestion. "Sure. I guess I can do that. Then maybe I can help serve the food."

Ben nodded. Obviously it wouldn't do any good to argue with her. The harder any of them pushed, the harder she'd push back.

Maybe he could discreetly lead her into the least messy projects. She didn't have to know he was moving with any particular purpose in mind or that he was keeping a close eye on her.

It was a personal thing.

Because how sad would it be if she got that pretty blue dress dirty? That would be a disservice to all of mankind.

He had to admit that he himself couldn't stop staring at her and reveling in the remarkable change she had made. If he had to work by her side all afternoon to make sure she didn't get food slopped all over her, or if he had to take care of cleaning all the greasy pans himself so she didn't have to, then so be it.

A man had to do what a man had to do.

Chapter Eight

By the time Vee had finished serving hot biscuits during the banquet and had washed down all of the tablecloths with a wet rag afterward, she was nearly ready to call a forfeit to the game.

Not only was she utterly exhausted, but her feet felt as if they'd been in a vise for a week. She was certain she had several blisters forming, and all she could think about was going home to soak her aching toes in a hot bath with fragrant candles and lots of bubbles to soothe her frayed nerves.

She couldn't wait to write to BJ and tell him how the event had gone…the *event* in question being the unveiling of her new look rather than the Easter banquet itself. The truth was, both affairs were a surprising success after everyone got used to the idea that she was wearing a dress and stopped harassing her about it. Even after everyone had turned to their work, she'd notice men's eyes on her from time to time.

Men. Watching her. Simply mind-boggling.

Vee put a hand to the small of her back and stretched. It was all she could do to keep from groaning aloud, but because Ben had not left her side since the beginning of the afternoon, pride meant that she had to keep her aches and pains to herself, even if that meant gritting her teeth until her jaw hurt.

She wasn't about to admit that the dress or the heels in any way fazed her or made her life more difficult. She'd toughed out more agonizingly painful situations than the high heels that were biting into her feet. Hazing Week at the fire academy had been worse.

Hadn't it? At the moment, she couldn't think of anything she'd experienced that hurt worse than the way that her shoes were cutting off the circulation in her feet.

But she could do it. It was mind over matter—at least until she was able get away from the banquet and tear the nasty, tortuous heels from her feet.

She glanced up to see Ben staring at her speculatively, but he looked away as soon as their eyes met.

"What?" she asked, feeling uncomfortable with his overt perusal. Had he realized the direction her thoughts were going? Had her feelings shown on her face?

Ugh. How was she going to explain that?

Ben flashed a half smile and shook his head. "It's nothing."

She shrugged. "Suit yourself."

"But you do look especially pretty today, just so you know," he continued, as if he hadn't just the very moment before told her he didn't have anything to say.

Especially?

Did that mean he thought she was at least sort of pretty *all* of the time? No one had ever called her pretty before, at least not anyone besides her father and mother, and on the odd occasion, her brothers, and now she was hearing it from virtually everyone around her.

It was not only groundbreaking—it was earth-shattering. Yet somehow Ben's remark held more weight with her, more even than all the other compliments combined.

Which was utterly ridiculous, and she needed to stop that little ego-flattering train of thought right now, before it pulled out of the station.

She should know better than to be affected by transient smooth talk just because those types of words had never before been directed her way, especially by a man. Those sweet yet dubious words were coming from the mouth of a man who'd had an endless string of dates on his arm. He'd probably fed that very same line to half of the single women in Serendipity.

After all, he'd dated most of them at one time or another since he'd returned to town from serving in the National Guard. But no matter what she told herself, heat rose to her face nonetheless, and she knew her cheeks were stained a scorching red.

"Thank you," she said after a long pause. She thought she ought to at least acknowledge the compliment, even if it came from the biggest player in town. "And look here—I didn't even manage to get a single smudge of food on my dress," she continued drolly.

It could have been a teasing remark. The circumstances were ripe for a little flirtation. But somehow she'd managed to make it sound catty.

"Sorry," she apologized with a wince. She might have a million reasons to dislike and distrust Ben, but he hadn't done anything on this particular afternoon to warrant her verbal abuse. He'd been very kind to her and had kept her company all day. He'd even been nice to

Olivia. It was probably just for show, but it was a start, or at least it might be.

Ben's smile was as genuine as his starlit bronze-green gaze. "Why are you sorry? In my opinion, you have every right to be defensive. Folks sure acted differently toward you today, didn't they?"

"You think?" There was *catty* again. She might as well have hissed. Rrreer! Fffft!

She took a deep breath and tried again. "I'm surprised you noticed."

She didn't mention that Ben had acted just as *differently* as the rest of them. Maybe more so. Not so blatant or so noticeable, maybe, but different just the same. He'd certainly never gone out of his way to spend that much time with her before.

"It was hard not to see it," he answered. "The guys from the fire station practically fell all over themselves trying to stand next to you in the serving line. And I don't want to think about how the dolts from the police force were acting toward you."

"And yet you won out."

His eyebrows danced. "I'm bigger."

Well, that was true.

"And I hope my motives were better," he added.

This time it was her eyebrows that jumped. Ben Atwood with good intentions? Now that was a laugh.

"How so?"

"Oh, come on, Vee. You have to have realized that after your appearance today, you're going to have dates lined up for the next year at least. You've been hiding yourself behind that firefighter's uniform and nobody knew the truth about just how pretty you really are. Are you trying to tell me that not one single man in the room approached you to ask you out? Don't bother because I won't believe you."

The heat roasting her face rose a few degrees higher. Was it getting hot in here or what?

Because the truth was, Ben was right. To her very great astonishment, a couple of local single men *had* asked for her phone number—not that she'd given it to them. If they wanted to call her, her number was listed in the phone book, the same as it had always been. Besides...

"That wasn't my intention at all," she assured him, wondering why she suddenly felt the overpowering need to explain herself to a man she didn't even like.

"Wasn't it?" The bronze in his eyes sparkled, dancing with the green.

She tossed a wadded-up paper napkin at him. "No, it was not," she stated, emphasizing each word. "I had something to prove to *myself* today. Not to anyone else. Especially not to a bunch of fickle men." Today men had asked for her phone number. Tomorrow, when she was back in her usual clothes, they wouldn't give her the time of day. Things would be back to the way they'd always been, with dull, boring Vee not turning *anyone's* head.

"And did you?" he queried, tilting his head. "Prove something to yourself?"

"In some ways I suppose I did," she admitted, chewing thoughtfully on her bottom lip. "I clarified some things, anyway."

"So you had fun?"

"Definitely. At least for part of the time. I really enjoyed serving the dinner—knowing that I was helping people in such a direct way. That was an incredible blessing, not only to them, but to me and our team. Still..."

"Still?" he echoed when she didn't immediately finish her statement.

She paused and frowned pensively. "You know what bothers me most about today?"

He shook his head. "No. What?"

"What you said earlier—your observation about how folks reacted to me today. I don't understand why people treated me differently just because I was wearing a dress. Something is off with that, don't you think?"

If his stunned gaze was anything to go by, she would have to guess that her statement took Ben aback. She was surprised when he agreed with her.

"Yeah, Vee. I do."

Dear Veronica Jayne,

Did you receive the introductory packet from the Sacred Heart Mission yet? I got mine in the mail yesterday. If you ask me, it looks pretty complicated. There are tons of forms to fill out, and we have to take a psychological assessment. Oh, and of course we have to have a complete physical workup with our primary care provider. I'm not worried about that part, though. I'm in pretty good shape—at least physically. The psychological part remains to be seen, ha ha.

I'm planning to start doing all the paperwork on my next day off. I want to send it in as soon as possible, especially because there's a very short window between now and summer orientation. I know you are just as anxious as I am to get out onto the mission field, and I'll be so happy to finally meet you in person if the Lord leads us to the same mission. What a great day that will be, huh?

I've been praying for you. I know you said you're

going through a rough patch right now. All I can say is that I've been corresponding with you long enough to know you're a good person at heart.

Be brave. Step out of your comfort zone. Put yourself out there. But be gentle on yourself, too. I've said it before and I'll say it again. I don't need to see your face to know what a special person you are. Even your thoughts are beautiful.

Yours,

BJ

Ben gritted his teeth as he strained to brace his palms against the weight bar and push his arms straight over his chest. He was bench-pressing two hundred pounds today, a good ten more than usual, pushing himself to the outside of his physical limits. He blinked the sting of sweat out of his eyes.

If only it was as easy to push his mind to such extremes so he wouldn't have to think.

"Are you trying to kill yourself?" Ben's paramedic partner asked with an amused, almost calculated smile on his face as he watched Ben's struggles from his position as spotter.

"Two more reps," Ben wheezed through his teeth as an alternative to answering the question his friend had not-so-innocently posed. His arms and chest burned with the effort of pushing the bar up twice more, but he was determined to succeed in his efforts, if only because Zach was watching.

Zach helped him return the bar to the rack. Groaning, Ben rolled to a sitting position on the bench.

"I don't know what you're talking about," Ben denied, shaking his head and not quite meeting his friend's gaze. He dabbed at his forehead with the white towel he'd draped around his neck.

"Benching two hundred pounds? That's a bit much even for you, big guy. What if I hadn't been there to spot you and your muscles had seized up on you?"

"But you were there, weren't you?" Ben snapped, scowling at his friend.

Instead of offending him, it only made Zach chuckle all the more.

"Seriously, dude. You've got it bad." Zach's snicker turned into a full-blown laugh. "So tell me—who is the lucky lady?"

"I'm glad I amuse you," Ben retorted. "And I don't know what you're talking about." He really, *really* didn't want to get into this, especially with Zach, whom he considered one of his best friends. The guy wouldn't stop razzing him for a month of Sundays if he learned the truth about what was really going on in Ben's mind.

"Right. So, here's the thing, bro," Zach stated sagely. "The only possible reason for you to be pushing yourself so hard is so you don't have time to think. And if you're trying not to think, it must have something to do with a woman." Zach nodded shrewdly. "Trust me. I've been there. I know from whence I speak."

Ben snorted. Zach actually did have firsthand knowledge where women were concerned. He'd been the town bad boy from the time he was in school until he'd become a Christian years later. Now he was happily married to his high-school sweetheart, Delia, and was the father of two boys.

Unfortunately for Ben, Zach thought everyone should share in his happiness and find wedded bliss themselves. Like marriage was the answer to every problem. Ben scoffed. As far as he was concerned, anything to do with a woman was merely the beginning of all problems.

Vee Bishop being a case in point.

"Who is she? I want a name." Zach smirked and raised a dark eyebrow over his equally dark eyes.

Ben grunted and moved to the inverted sit-up board, hooking his legs over the top beam for stabilization. Then he started performing a furious round of sit-ups, mentally counting as he went.

Twenty. Twenty-one. Twenty-two.

Zach was still hovering, and Ben didn't like the tell-tale gleam in his friend's eye. Just because *Zach* happened to be enamored of the married state didn't mean Ben had to be.

Fifty-seven. Fifty-eight. Fifty-nine.

"Now you've got me really curious," Zach remarked blithely. "I don't buy your original denial, by the way. You answered too fast, and you're fighting too hard."

Eighty-three. Eighty-four. Eighty-five.

Ben's abdominal muscles were burning, but he didn't let up the frantic pace of his movements.

Ninety-two. Ninety-three. Ninety-four.

"You know I can stand here all day, bud. I've got nothing else to do—unless there's a fire somewhere, and you know as well as I do that's not likely to happen."

One hundred.

Ben swung his legs around and stood, facing down his friend with the biggest scowl he could muster. Could the man just *please* leave it alone? But no, Zach was still grinning at him with an I-won't-quit attitude in his eyes.

"Not one woman. Two," Ben growled under his breath but loud enough for Zach to hear him. He didn't know if he was more exasperated with his situation or with Zach being such an utter nuisance.

"I'm sorry. I don't think I heard you correctly," Zach said, cupping his ear, although it was clear from the look on his face that he'd heard every word perfectly well. "Did you just say you're having issues with *two* women?"

Ben grunted noncommittally.

Zach snorted and shook his head. "Well, no wonder you're doing enough sit-ups to kill a lesser man. Not the best idea, dude, trying to deal with two ladies at the same time. Women are pretty possessive creatures. It doesn't pay to cross one, in my experience."

"Tell me about it," Ben groaned, stepping onto the treadmill and setting the controls for an easy jog. "Believe me, I learned my lesson back when I was going out with Olivia Tate. I made the mistake of taking another girl to dinner—just as friends, mind you—but I never heard the end of it. How did I know that the female population has such an extensive, unspoken list of dos and don'ts we men are supposed to conform to?

"I thought I'd gotten over the worst of my problems when I realized that after two or three dates, a girl would expect me to date her exclusively. Olivia and I had 'the talk' and everything about how we wouldn't date other people. But I hadn't realized that for Olivia, exclusive meant *exclusive.* Apparently I wasn't even supposed to acknowledge female acquaintances without first clearing it with Olivia, her best friends, her mother and probably a whole host of other women. Man, did I ever get into trouble with that one."

"Yeah, I remember," Zach said, choking back another

laugh. "Ouch. I think Olivia might still be a little sore about that one."

Ben blew out a breath and grimaced. "Tell me about it. I think we're finally reconciling enough to be friends, but for the longest time she wouldn't even speak to me. She'd burst into tears if I so much as entered a room where she was."

"Her not speaking to you was probably a good thing, if you ask me. Scorned females rank right up there with grizzly bears and poisonous snakes as the scariest things on the planet." Zach brushed his black hair off his forehead with his palm and chuckled. "But you're avoiding the real topic—your problem. *Problems*," he corrected himself. "Two women." Zach shook his head and snickered again. "Really, Ben."

"There's this woman…"

"This much I already know," Zach said. "Get to the good stuff. Do I know her? What's her name? What does she look like? And then we'll get to Woman Number Two. Same questions, same order. I'm dying of curiosity here."

"There's the rub," Ben admitted, shaking his head and snorting. "I don't know her full name, and I definitely have no idea what she looks like. 'She' Number One, that is. I know a little bit more about the second woman."

"Come again?" Zach said incredulously. "Now, let me get this straight. You have a problem with a girlfriend you've never actually seen and whose name you do not know." Zach whistled in surprise.

Ben punched the control to set the treadmill into a full-out run and wiped his brow with the blue towel draped around his neck.

"I didn't say she was my girlfriend."

"But you obviously have some feelings for her or you wouldn't be bench-pressing two hundred pounds."

"I do care about her. It's not that."

"So what's the problem? I don't get it. Given that you don't know what she looks like, I'm guessing you met on the internet, right? But don't people usually post their pictures on those dating sites?"

"Oh, no. It wasn't a dating site." Ben scoffed and shook his head, causing sweat to drip over his forehead and sting his eyes. "You think I'm that desperate?" He paused. "No, don't answer that."

Zach's dark eyes glittered puckishly and his lips quirked as if he was forcing himself to hold back his ridicule, but he didn't say anything.

"I'm taking an online Spanish class," Ben explained. "I thought it would be a good idea to get a second language under my belt before going off on my mission. Anyway, I got hooked up with her, Veronica Jayne, on a group project."

"And you fell for her." It wasn't a question, but Ben treated it that way.

Ben shrugged noncommittally. "Kind of. Well, I mean, I have to admit I've thought about it. She's a really nice girl. We've been privately emailing each other for weeks now, and we have great conversations together."

"*Conversations?* She's a *nice girl?* Seriously, dude?" Zach barked out a laugh. "You are so clueless."

Ben tensed at the insult, almost causing him to lose his balance on the treadmill. He turned it down to a walk so he could cool down—both his body and his temper.

"And it doesn't bother you *at all* that you don't know her last name and have no idea what she looks like?" Zach made it sound like Ben was crazy for not demanding a picture right away. Would that have made any difference in how his friendship with her had progressed? He hoped he was better than that.

"Of course I've wondered." He stopped the treadmill, stepped off and leaned over to stretch his calves. He averted his gaze from Zach's, staring at his own toes to avoid having to see the amusement in his partner's eyes.

"But you never asked for a photograph?"

"I didn't want to scare her away. Besides, if I did that, she'd want a picture of me, and that *would* scare her away. Same with our last names. I wouldn't want her doing an internet search on me. I know it'll happen eventually, but I'll cross that bridge when I come to it."

Zach tilted his head. "Dude, have you looked in the mirror recently? You're not exactly Quasimodo."

"I have a mental picture of her," Ben responded defensively. "She says she works in a flower shop. She's really feminine. I imagine her wearing floral dresses that go down to her ankles, and I'm positive she has pretty hair and kind eyes."

"And a long, hooked nose. And pointed teeth. And don't forget green skin," Zach added, chortling in amusement at himself. The guy was always clowning around, but Ben wasn't in the mood for a joke.

He stiffened, ready to take offense, but then he started thinking about it, and he had to admit Zach had a point. He shook his head and laughed. It was funny. He was taking everything way too seriously.

"In all honesty, I've been thinking about asking her for a picture of herself for a while now, now that we know each other fairly well. I wouldn't say it's a romantic relationship. Not yet, anyway. I can't deny the thought has occurred to me on more than one occasion that it might turn into one at some point. We've been talking about meeting in person once we've committed to Sacred Heart."

"What's Sacred Heart?"

"A Christian stateside mission. They help people in disasters with food and shelter and such and also try to take care of their spiritual needs. Veronica Jayne and I are both applying to serve there."

Zach whistled. "Cool. I knew you were interested in doing Christian mission work eventually, but I guess I didn't know you were heading that way so soon. So how long would it be until you enlist?"

"Not long now. We both want to finish our Spanish course, and then we'll meet in the summer for orientation at a facility they have in Houston."

"But now you don't want to wait that long to meet her."

"No. I don't. I don't think I can because of something Vee said."

Zach raised his brows. "Vee Bishop?"

"Yeah. You remember how she dressed up for the Easter banquet? Blue dress? High heels?"

Zach laughed. "Apparently I don't remember it as well as you do," he teased. "No, seriously. Everybody in town knows about Vee's presto change-o, frumpy-dumpy into super-gorgeous woman that no man could keep his eyes off of. Even people who weren't there at the banquet have heard about it by now. You know how Jo is about spreading the gossip around—especially something as interesting as that."

"Vee isn't frumpy-dumpy," Ben retorted protectively. "I don't know how she felt, but the whole thing made me uncomfortable. I know she was aware of it. People were treating her differently. Better." Ben knew he sounded defensive in his tone, but he couldn't seem to help it.

"Well, I'll be," Zach said, his eyes narrowing on Ben. "I never would have guessed *that* one."

"Excuse me?"

"You have a thing for Vee Bishop. She's Woman Number Two, isn't she?"

The way Zach said it, he almost sounded like one of the elementary-school bullies Ben had had such problems with growing up. *Ben and Vee, sitting in a tree. K-I-S-S-I-N-G.*

Kissing Vee? Ben swallowed the emotion that rose into his throat, not even wanting to acknowledge it was there. He wasn't ready to go where his thoughts were leading him. He didn't even want to identify whatever feeling it was that was swelling inside his chest.

Hence, working out at the gym until his muscles were screaming, though he would never tell Zach that. Veronica Jayne had only been a part of it.

"I don't have a thing for Vee." His denial sounded false even to his own ears.

"Right."

"Okay," Ben amended. "Maybe I do have a little problem with Vee. Ever since the banquet I can't seem to get her out of my mind. The way she looked when I first saw her across the room in that gorgeous blue dress, so slender and beautiful—I can't even begin to describe it. And her eyes…" He shook his head.

"It sounds to me like *other people* weren't the only ones who were seeing Vee in a different light."

Ben sighed and dropped his gaze to his shoes. He was ashamed of himself. "You're right about that. And that's what bothers me."

"That you have feelings for Vee?" Zach picked up a set of free weights and started working his biceps again.

"No. That I didn't *realize* I might have feelings for Vee until she showed up in that knockout dress." Ben's muscles had had enough torture for one day, so he straddled a bench and leaned back on his arms instead of joining his partner with the free weights. "What kind of a man does that make me?"

"Human," Zach answered immediately. "Maybe you knew you had feelings for Vee and you just didn't want to admit it to yourself."

"Maybe. But it still bothers me that I could be so shallow. I thought I was better than that, which was why I didn't mind that Veronica Jayne and I didn't exchange pictures. God isn't concerned with appearances. He looks at people's hearts."

"That's true," Zach agreed. "But God also made women incredibly attractive to men. It's in our nature for us to notice when an especially pretty woman walks by. I don't think there is anything necessarily wrong with that."

"For me, there is. Going all brainless around beautiful women is one of my stumbling blocks. I got into a lot of trouble when I first got back into town after serving in the National Guard and started dating again. All of a sudden there were dozens of pretty girls who wanted to hang out with me—with *me*—and it went to my head. I made a lot of bad decisions and stupid mistakes. Mistakes that ended up hurting people I cared about. I don't want that to happen again, and I'm terrified it might. I've got to reel it in. Do you understand what I mean?"

"Which is why you're so flipped out about this other girl, Veronica Jayne, right?"

"Exactly. I don't want to mess up our friendship because I can't handle it when I find out what she really looks like. What if I don't find her attractive? I know—that makes me super shallow, right?"

"And Vee? She's back to her old hair-in-a-bun, super-tough-attitude self now, you know."

Ben sighed internally. It didn't matter to him what Vee wore. It didn't even matter that she'd always disliked him. He had feelings for her either way. Which was entirely irrelevant, not only to this conversation, but to his life.

"It doesn't matter how I feel about Vee. She can't even stand to be in the same room with me. It seems like she's just barely tolerating my presence when I'm around her, though I think it's been a little bit better lately."

"You've told her how you feel?"

"Of course not. But I can tell you without a doubt that she has some kind of problem with me. I only wish I knew what it was."

Zach burst out laughing, and it took him a moment to contain himself enough to speak. He was holding his belly, snorting and huffing.

Ben rolled his eyes.

"Dude, you really are clueless."

"You think?" In Ben's opinion, *clueless* didn't even begin to cover it.

"Seriously. You really don't know why she doesn't like you very much?"

Ben shook his head and made a bowing motion with his hands. "Enlighten me, oh wise one."

"You just told me what your problem is." Zach flashed a knowing grin.

"And that would be?" Ben was a little annoyed at

the way his friend was dragging this out, but at least it seemed like he had an answer to Ben's problem. Zach did know women. After all, he was married to one.

"Vee's best friend is Olivia Tate," Zach explained, drawing out the words as if Ben would be slow to comprehend.

Which he definitely was.

"Olivia," Zach repeated. "Vee's best friend. Your ex-girlfriend. Just think about it."

Chapter Nine

Vee stared at the blank computer screen and sipped absently at her caramel latte. She was in her usual place in the back corner of Cup o' Jo's Café, but this was anything but a usual day.

She had to break things off with BJ, and she didn't know how she was going to do that.

No, that wasn't quite right. It wasn't as if she and BJ were actually an item, so it wasn't like they were breaking up or anything. But they were both well aware that the potential to become more than just friends had been there since the first day they'd met. They'd even talked about it, making the decision to wait until they met in person at the Sacred Heart Mission to pursue anything further, anything that might be construed as romantic.

But she had to be honest and admit, at least to herself, that even after they'd come to their agreement, she'd harbored these now preposterous-sounding private fantasies about the moment when she and BJ would finally meet in person for the first time...

She's at the first orientation meeting for the Sacred Heart Mission. Seated at the far end of the room, she's scanning through the packet of informational materials she'd been given, excited to finally be pursuing her ambitions. She's finally here, making her dreams a reality. Her heart is pumping, and her mind is swirling in dizzy circles with all the adrenaline pumping through her.

Suddenly it's as if the atmosphere itself grows warmer. More humid. Harder to breathe. She knows instinctively that BJ has entered the room.

She glances toward the door, knowing this moment is going to change her life—change both of their lives. Her eyes meet BJ's, and the world is turned on its axis.

He is the most handsome man she's ever laid eyes on, just as she knew in her heart that he'd be, and better than she could even have imagined.

Reality alters when he smiles, and she knows for certain that they'll be together forever.

She has found true love.

Ridiculous. Pure, utter poppycock.

She had to let it go and get on with her life. Her *real* life.

And that meant being brutally honest with both herself and with BJ. She respected him enough to want to clarify her new perspective directly and without any delay.

She'd been living in this fantasy world of Prince-Charming-rides-in-to-save-the-day for long enough. She hadn't realized the truth about her relationship with BJ until the day Ben had come with her to visit her father, when reality had struck her like a slap to the face. She was using BJ to avoid real life because she couldn't handle the grief she felt after her mother's death.

She was hiding in cyberspace.

And it was time to come back to earth.

She didn't know if it would be a wise idea to remain friends with BJ at all, as much as she liked him as a person. She wasn't sure she could completely annihilate the fantasy, and if she couldn't, she could never embrace the reality.

She supposed she could wait until they met in person at the mission to make any final decisions on the matter. If, indeed, they ended up at the same mission at all. Vee was having her doubts about that, too. Maybe it would be better for both of them if she applied to a different agency and they made a clean break. Perhaps they should simply finish their Spanish project and call it all good between them.

The internet provided a false sense of intimacy. And she was no longer kidding herself—it *was* false. A woman could present herself any way she wanted to be—and Vee had done just that. Yes, in some ways she had been more open with BJ than with anyone else— she hadn't been lying when she'd said that he knew her better than anyone else. She'd felt comfortable showing him parts of her personality that no one else knew about. But she hadn't shown him everything. Veronica Jayne was who she was, but there were distinct differences in how she'd presented herself online and the way the people in Serendipity saw her.

No doubt BJ had done the same. Maybe there were other sides to him beyond the strong, soft-spoken man Vee imagined him to be.

There was absolutely no way to know if they'd even get along in person, much less be romantically inclined toward one another. They'd never even exchanged pictures, though they'd been emailing each other personally for at least a couple of months.

Who did that?

Naturally, she'd pictured BJ to be a handsome man with bold features and strong arms, but for all she knew the guy had a hump on his back.

Even worse, lately when she imagined what BJ looked like, the image of Ben Atwood persistently entered her mind—probably because he was, in fact, the best-looking man she knew. Objectively speaking, that is.

And how messed up was that?

Must. Face. Reality.

"Okay," said a light, lilting voice from the other side of her computer screen. Olivia, of course, with the worst timing ever. "I have *got* to know what it is you were thinking about just now."

Ben.

Vee was thinking about Ben. She certainly couldn't say that out loud—especially to Olivia.

"If you must know, I've been keeping a secret from you," Vee said on a sigh. That ought to pique Olivia's interest enough to keep her from suspecting Vee's mind was anywhere close to dwelling on her ex-boyfriend.

It did. "Oooh! Secrets. I love to hear about secrets. Spill it, girlfriend." She set her plate on the table and slid into the chair across from Vee.

Olivia was the exact opposite of Vee—her tall, graceful body was highlighted with short, thick, pixie-cut red hair she'd gotten from her mother's Scottish roots and emerald-green eyes that had at one time or another enthralled practically every single man in the town. Not only that, but Olivia was as bubbly and outgoing as Vee was reserved and antisocial. Yet somehow despite the odds they'd become fast friends in elementary school and had remained that way throughout their adulthood.

"I'm warning you—this one's a doozy."

"Better and better," Olivia murmured, leaning closer so she could share the moment.

"There's this man…"

Olivia squealed loud enough for many of the patrons sharing a meal at Cup o' Jo to turn and glance in their direction, curiosity written on their faces.

"Olivia," Vee begged, "will you please be quiet about this? I'd rather not have the whole world aware that I have a problem."

"Okay, okay," Olivia agreed, scooting around to Vee's side of the table, pulling her cheeseburger and French-fry-laden plate along with her. "Now, spill the beans. Who is this man, and why have I not heard about him?" She peered at the empty computer monitor as if she'd find the answer there.

"His name is BJ." Vee nodded toward the computer screen. "I met him in my online Spanish class. We're doing a project together on the advantages of knowing the Spanish language when we work in stateside Christian missions."

"Sounds intriguing," Olivia said, popping a French fry into her mouth. "The man, not the topic," she clarified with a laugh. "Although that's interesting, too. So he's going to be doing this stateside mission thing with you? And *habla español* a little bit between you?" She waggled her eyebrows.

Vee nudged Olivia with her elbow. "Cut it out. Knowing how to speak a little Spanish will be very important in the line of work I'm planning to do."

"Of course," Olivia agreed. "You know I'm just joshing with you."

Vee chuckled and nodded. "Yeah. I know. I'm easy

bait. And I have to admit that the whole man thing *is* interesting. Or should I say *complicated.*"

"Hey, Vee." She hadn't seen Ben enter the café, much less realized that he'd approached her table—with Olivia sitting right there, to boot. "How are you doing tonight? And you, Olivia?" he continued, though his gaze stayed on Vee.

His bronze-green gaze held hers, and his toothy smile made her stomach do a somersault. Transparently gorgeous any way she looked at him. And for some reason he was only looking at *her.*

She shouldn't be looking at him at all, especially not with her best friend present. She dropped her gaze to the tabletop and searched for something to say, something that wouldn't make her sound like an idiot. She couldn't seem to be able to form words. The thoughts were in her head, but nothing came out of her mouth. She was afraid if she tried to speak it would come out garbled. Then she really *would* sound like an idiot.

Tension mounted as each excruciating second ticked by. Sweat trickled down the nape of Vee's neck. She didn't know how long it was until Olivia noisily cleared her throat, but it felt like an eternity, and a painful one at that.

"Yes, that's right. I'm here, too, though I can clearly see why you didn't notice me," Olivia said with a teasing laugh that bordered on flirtatious.

Vee stared at her friend in shock. She had expected Olivia to be mad. She would have been if she was in the same situation.

At least Ben had the grace to look chagrined, his lips twisting as he considered what to say.

Olivia laughed again, beaming a hundred-watt smile at Ben, who shifted uncomfortably.

"I think my food's ready," he said awkwardly, brushing his hand back through the dark curl falling down over his forehead. "I guess I'll see you ladies later. Have a good might. Meal. Night," he stammered, then shook his head, turned on his heels and practically ran for his table.

Vee mused silently as she watched Ben stride across the room and slide into a booth with his back toward her. He must have sensed her gaze upon him because he turned and winked at her.

Vee slid an inch lower in her booth, as if somehow that would make her inconspicuous, because at the moment she felt as if she was wearing an enormous exclamation point on her head.

"Well," commented Olivia in a drawn-out syllable. It wasn't a question. Vee shivered.

"Well?" Vee repeated without acknowledging that she had any indication of where Olivia's train of thought had gone. "Do you want to tell me what just happened here between you and Ben, or do you want me to guess? Because if I guess, I can guarantee it's going to be more interesting than anything you can make up on the spur of the moment. I thought you guys weren't talking to one another. *He broke my heart and I'll never fall in love again,* and all that."

"I'm over it." Olivia shrugged. "Actually, I'm more interested in what happened between *you* and Ben."

Vee ignored her. This was not about her. "You're actually speaking to him again?"

"Sure. This isn't junior high anymore. I don't like drama."

Vee had to contain her urge to snort. Olivia Tate was one of the biggest drama queens she knew. But she appeared to be serious about this, so Vee let her continue.

"We live in the same small town. It's inevitable that we'll run into each other from time to time, especially because we both go to the same church."

"That's very mature of you," Vee stated blandly.

Olivia burst into shrill laughter that made a few heads turn. "Really, Vee. You kill me, sometimes."

"Maybe you can get over it, but I can't. I have a long memory. He hurt my best friend, and that's all there is to say about it."

"That's always been a problem for you," said Olivia, suddenly serious. "You always stick up for the underdog." She reached out and gave Vee's hand a squeeze. "My little pit bull. I know you love me, but I'm okay now. When I look back on what happened now, I see that it wasn't all his fault. I need to take some of the blame, too."

Vee's jaw dropped. "He cheated on you! He was going out with another woman after the two of you had decided to date exclusively. How could that be your fault?"

"He definitely took another woman out, but I'm not sure they were actually dating."

"What?"

Olivia shrugged. "He told me at the time that she was just a friend. I didn't believe him then, but now I think he might have been telling the truth."

"Wh-what changed your mind?" Vee couldn't help asking.

"He has. Or rather, his ex-girlfriends have. See, back then I was sure he was playing me false, not just because he had dinner with his so-called 'friend,' but because when I confronted him about it he didn't even try to change my mind. I told him to leave, and he left. I told him never to call me again…and he didn't. I thought that meant he didn't care about me, that our relationship hadn't mattered to him at all."

"What does that have to do with his ex-girlfriends?"

Olivia grinned. "Well, over the years, I've found myself comparing notes with a lot of girls our Mr. Atwood has dated, and I've reached some new conclusions." She paused, clearly waiting for a signal from Vee.

"Fine," Vee said, rolling her eyes at her overly dramatic friend. "I'll ask—what new conclusions?"

"I think he's just really clueless about women."

"But how is that possible? He's dated so many!"

"Yeah," Olivia agreed. "And the reason he's dated so many is because he finds some ridiculous way to mess his relationships up. One girl told me she broke up with him because he'd never call her back after she called him—but she admitted that when she left messages, she'd usually say something like 'Nothing's wrong, I was just calling to hear your voice. You don't have to call me back.' So he didn't.

"Another girl made him go with her when she went shopping. And when she asked him if a dress made her look fat…"

"He said it did," Vee filled in, seeing where this was going.

Olivia giggled. "Let's just say he didn't lie to her. So after our big fight, when I told him to get out and never call me again…"

"He left. And never called you again."

"Bingo. Yes, he hurt me. Yes, he should have known

better. But it wasn't all his fault. You can let it rest. I promise my feelings won't be hurt if you do."

"Do what?" asked Vee, confused.

Olivia winked. "You know."

"Uh-uh. I don't. And I'm not sure I want to."

Olivia merely shrugged and flashed a knowing grin. "You don't want to talk about it. Okay. So tell me more about this cyber-hunk of yours."

"Where to start? His writing flows like music. Like a symphony of words. Mushy as all get-out and sweet as a daisy in the springtime. I'm afraid I got a little too caught up in that."

"What girl wouldn't?"

"In some ways I feel like I know BJ very well, but in other ways I really don't know anything about him. I've never even seen what he looks like."

"You have got to be kidding me. You're getting all twitterpated over a man when you've never even seen his face? Girl, you *are* a mess."

"Tell me about it," Vee agreed with a miserable groan. "But I'm not *twitterpated,* as you put it. Actually, I'm trying to figure out a way to back out gracefully without hurting his feelings."

"But why? Maybe you'll meet him face-to-face and fall instantly and madly in love." She sighed dramatically. So much for not being a drama queen.

Vee met her friend's gaze and lifted her eyebrows. "Can you not see why I have a problem, here? This whole relationship is a sham."

Olivia's shoulders slumped. "I suppose. When you put it that way. So what are you going to tell him?"

"I have no idea. That would be the reason behind the

expression you saw on my face when you walked up."
Vee wiggled the computer mouse to light up the screen.

She pulled up her email. There was a note from BJ.

Dear Veronica Jayne,
We've been corresponding for months now, and I feel
like I know you pretty well. I hope you feel the same
about me. We aren't strangers anymore, are we?

What do you think about exchanging pictures? I'd
like to see what my flower girl really looks like.
Sincerely,
BJ

"Veronica Jayne? *Flower girl?*" Olivia was definitely
getting her jollies at Vee's expense. She was enjoying
this *way* too much.

"Veronica Jayne is my online handle. It also happens
to be my given name, thank you very much. It says so
right on my birth certificate. He calls me his flower girl
because that's what I told him I do for a living—I work
with flowers. Which is also true."

"Kinda. Not firefighting?"

"Me in my firefighter's garb. Now *there's* an attractive image. No, thank you."

"Hey! I'm here to tell you that you rock that uniform.
There's absolutely nothing wrong with you being a female firefighter."

"No, I know that. I was going for something a little
different, you know? Everyone here in Serendipity sees
the no-nonsense firefighter who's just one of the guys,
which is not particularly good for my love life. I guess I
wanted to present a different side of myself, something
a little more soft and feminine."

"Oh, I get it," Olivia responded. "You think that since you've only shown him the 'girlie' parts of you that he won't like the rest. Is that why you want out?"

"That's part of it, I suppose. But it goes the other way, too. He might not like the parts of me I haven't shown him—and I might not like the parts of him he hasn't put on display. Who knows what he's really like in person?"

"I think you should wait and find out. See how things go when you guys meet face-to-face."

"No, I need to do this now."

"Before you've seen what he looks like, even?"

Before she lost her nerve, more like.

"He's offering to send you a picture of himself. Are you seriously trying to tell me you aren't the least bit curious if he's handsome or not?"

"Of course I am."

"Then let him send you a photograph. He was the one who offered, right? You get to see what he looks like, and then you can tell him you just want to be friends or whatever. What's the harm in that?"

"I don't know. I get all jittery when I think about it. What if he's nothing like the man I pictured in my head?"

"So what if he isn't? You said yourself it didn't matter what he looked like."

"But what if he *is,* Olivia? What if he's the most attractive man I've ever seen? What am I going to do then?"

Olivia glanced across the room at Ben and flicked her chin in his direction. "I highly doubt that your BJ guy is going to be the best-looking guy you've ever laid eyes on. I saw the way your gaze lit up when Ben stopped by our table."

"No you did not," Vee responded adamantly. She wanted to crawl underneath the table and hide there. Maybe dig a hole to China and forget learning Spanish. Not only was she struggling with an attraction to a man who no doubt looked at her as nothing more than an annoying coworker at best, but her very best friend Olivia, ex-girlfriend of said attractive man, was picking up on it.

This was bad. Really bad.

"Ben looked at you the same way," Olivia stated as matter-of-factly as if she were reciting the weather forecast. "I wouldn't mind, you know—if you and Ben got together. You'd make an adorable couple."

Vee was embarrassed—humiliated—that her emotions were running so close to the surface. This wasn't like her, and it made her more uncomfortable than she could say.

"And now that he's had some time to grow up a little bit, he's probably less clueless about women. He's certainly gotten smarter about dating every woman in town," Olivia continued. Same song, different verse. "Ben isn't the same fresh boy that he was when he came back to town from the military. He's matured. And you've got to admit he *is* pretty sweet-looking. You two would look so cute together. I really wouldn't mind."

Vee shook her head furiously. "*I'd* mind. Can we please not talk about this anymore?"

"Okay," agreed Olivia easily. "Then let's get back to your cyber-guy. Picture or no picture?"

Vee stared at BJ's email for a moment before pressing reply. She typed in a single word in response.

Okay.

Chapter Ten

Okay.

Ben stared at the one-word email. Veronica Jayne wanted to exchange pictures with him. His heart raced so hard that it roared in his ears.

What did his flower girl really look like? Was she blonde? Brunette? Tall? Short?

More to the point, would it matter? It was time for him to discover if he had any depth of character whatsoever or, as he feared, if he was just as shallow as the next guy, not able to look past a pretty face into something more substantial and meaningful.

Veronica Jayne hadn't attached a photograph of herself, so he assumed she wanted him to go first. He used his mouse to click the folder containing his digital pictures and scrolled through them, searching for a photo of himself that put him at best advantage and that he imagined Veronica Jayne might like.

There was one of him and Zach panning goofy for the camera, their arms slung over each other's shoulders, but he quickly nixed that one. He didn't want to confuse Veronica Jayne by sending her a picture of two guys, he reflected with a startled chuckle. What if she thought Zach was the better-looking of the two of them?

Ben wasn't willing to take *that* chance. Zach Bowden had turned more than a few women's heads in the years before he'd married and settled down. What kind of comparison was there between the two men? Ben didn't even want to know.

He finally settled on a picture his mother had snapped of him on a Sunday afternoon over the dinner table. It was a close-up of his face, and he was smiling his natural smile. It would have to do.

He hit Reply and attached the photograph to the email, then poised his fingers over the keys to write her a short note.

Dear Veronica Jayne,
Well, here it is. Or rather, here I am. I have to admit I'm a little nervous about what you'll think of me. Don't judge too harshly. I'm looking forward to receiving a photograph of you so I can finally put a face to your lovely name. Veronica Jayne. My flower girl.
BJ

"Hey, Uncle Ben," Felix called as Ben's two nephews scampered into the room. "What are you doing? Mom said you're supposed to take us to the church carnival."

Ben closed his laptop with a snap and laughed as he rounded up his nephews and tickled their ribs. "I was just finishing up some work here. You guys are anxious to go to the carnival, huh?"

"Yeah, yeah," the boys answered in unison.

"Impatient little rugrats." He ruffled their hair. "Are

you ready to throw rings at pop bottles and win the cakewalk?"

"What's a cakewalk?" Nigel asked, screwing his face into an adorably bemused expression, his dark brows lowered over expressive eyes. "Do we really get to walk on cakes?"

Ben barked out a laugh. "No, little man. You don't walk *on* cakes. You win one if you're the last person standing. Or sitting, technically. In a chair." The two boys shared confused looks and he shook his head. "It's hard to explain. You'll just have to learn to play it when you get there."

Ben bundled the boys in their jackets and they headed out.

It was only a couple of blocks to the church from his parents' house, so he and the boys walked, enjoying the temperate spring air. Felix and Nigel were both squirrelly from being cooped up in the house all day, and Ben thought it would be good for them to run off some of that energy before entering the carnival, which would be a crush of people in a relatively small area.

He was in excellent physical shape, but it was all he could do to keep up with the little guys, and he gained a new appreciation for mothers who had to herd their kids around day in and day out.

Located on the northeast corner of town on Main Street, the parking lot of the little white chapel was already full to overflowing with vehicles. Festive music streamed from the open doors of the fellowship hall, and he could already hear the joyous sound of children's laughter, which made him smile. Nigel and Felix picked up their pace, dashing into the building ahead of Ben.

"Come one, come all," greeted Jo exuberantly as Ben

entered through the double doors. "Come eager to spend your money for a good cause—new choir robes for our trusty sanctuary choir! Hey there, Ben. Are you and the boys ready to win some prizes?"

Jo sounded like an old-time carnival barker, adding to the already festive ambiance. Ben suspected that in Jo's mind, at least, the *good cause* in question might have been more to do with the kiddos having fun than having anything to do with the state of the choir's worn-out robes.

"Did you see my nephews pass by?" he asked.

Jo waved a hand over her shoulder. "They just went by here, somewhere about the speed of light. Good luck finding them in that throng of people."

It *was* crowded. And noisy. But Ben wasn't worried for his nephews. Townspeople looked after their own, and a couple of extra boys running around was no cause for concern.

Ben had helped set up the booths for the carnival the evening before so he knew what to expect. The fellowship hall had been divided into a series of separate booths draped with colorful cloths and signs and flashing lights—mostly red and green, donations from town folks' Christmas collections.

A rubbery bounce house and a hay maze had been set up in the field behind the church, with an oil-drum train circling the whole thing. Chief Jenkins engineered the train, and he whistled and tooted at frequent intervals just to keep things lively, as if there wasn't already enough clamor in the neighborhood.

"What do you guys want to do first?" he asked as he caught up to his nephews, who were leaning over a booth to watch Riley Bowden, Zach's eldest son, toss beanbags at a cardboard rendering of Noah's Ark. There were several animals painted on the Ark, their mouths cut open for the kids to toss beanbags through. Eleven-year-old Riley was a good shot and two of his three beanbags sailed through the holes into the lion's and hippo's mouths.

Phoebe Hawkins, who was manning the beanbag toss, cheered for Riley as he picked out his prize—a straw cowboy hat, which he planted on his head with pride. Ben congratulated the boy on his good aim.

Ben fished a wad of dollar bills from the front pocket of his jeans, intending to spend every one of them. Each year the carnival had a different charitable goal in mind. After they'd collected enough money to buy the choir some decent robes, whatever was left over would go to the church's food bank. Ben couldn't think of a better way to contribute to the ministry of the church than to fork over a little cash to watch his nephews have a good time.

"Uncle Ben, Uncle Ben," Nigel exclaimed, grabbing his hand and pulling him toward the booth across the way from the Noah's Ark Beanbag Toss. "Look! Gold-fish!"

Sure enough, there were the goldfish, swimming around in gallon-sized plastic bags full of water that were stacked enticingly along the back counter.

"Anyone want to win a goldfish?" Vee's wry chuckle snapped Ben from his reverie. He looked up to find her grinning craftily at him.

He narrowed his gaze on her. "You planned this, didn't you?"

Vee shook her head and scoffed, but her smile remained. "Right. I ran out and bought three dozen goldfish because I knew it would entice your nephews and annoy you."

"I wouldn't put it past you," he objected, but he smiled back at her nonetheless. "How do you win one of these fellows, anyway?"

Vee pointed to a plastic pool half-filled with water in which a couple dozen identical yellow rubber ducks floated. "Pick a winner. Small, medium or large prizes, depending on what's written on the bottom of the ducky you select. You boys want to try?" she asked, addressing Felix and Nigel.

In hindsight, Ben realized he should have been more cognizant of what was going on in each of the booths so he could avoid instant goldfish ownership, but it was too late now, with both of his nephews clamoring to have a go at the duckies. It wasn't like he could say no to them. It would ruin their day. Besides, Ben remembered being thrilled to win a goldfish when he was a kid. He wouldn't deny his nephews the same happy memory.

"That will be two bucks," Vee reminded him, holding out her hand palm up.

Ben peeled two fresh dollar bills from his wad of cash and passed them off to Vee. "I want you to know I am doing this under duress."

"No you're not," she replied without hesitating. "You're doing this because you are a good uncle and you want to give your nephews a day they'll remember."

"If they win goldfish, this is going to be a day *I'll* remember," he groused. "Thanks to you."

"Oh, hush, you, and let the poor boys have their fun." She turned to Felix and Nigel. "Okay, you guys, it's time to play. You each get to pick up only one duck, so choose carefully, all right? Ready? Set? Go!"

Felix plucked his duck out of the water within seconds. Nigel was not quite so hasty with his choice, taking his time to select the perfect duck. Several times he started for one and then changed his mind and pulled his hand back."

"You've got to pick one, Nigel," Ben urged.

Nigel finally made his choice. The boys turned their ducks over at the same time.

"Large," announced Vee in a voice Ben was certain was lined with laughter. "And large. Congratulations, boys, you've each won yourselves a goldfish."

Felix and Nigel high-fived each other.

Vee laughed, and Ben wondered if she was laughing with him or at him.

He groaned, but it was more of an exasperated, dramatic gesture than a meaningful one.

"You've got this rigged, don't you? I'll bet every one of these ducks has an *L* on it."

"Well, that would be very kind of me if that were true, don't you think?" She plucked a random duck from the pool and turned it over, waving it under his nose so he'd be sure to see the *S* clearly marked on the bottom. "But in this case, it's not true. I think you were meant to own goldfish, Ben Atwood."

If it were anyone but Vee, he would have thought she was flirting with him. But it *was* Vee—and Vee didn't flirt. With anyone.

Especially not with him.

So why did his gut tighten in response to her repartee, and why was his breath raspy in his throat? He needed to tread softly here.

"Maybe I'll just feed the fish to Tinker," he remarked mildly.

He'd clearly caught her off-guard with the statement. He hadn't meant it, of course, but it was fun teasing her. "You wouldn't," she said, her voice hitched with hesitation and distress in her gaze.

He flashed her a toothy grin, stepping back and slapping a hand over his heart. "No, of course not. I'm wounded here. Seriously, Vee, do you think I'm capable of fish-ocide?"

"I think you're capable of a lot of things," she said under her breath, shaking her head.

What was that supposed to mean? The woman spoke in riddles. And unfortunately for him, he didn't speak *woman*.

He would have demanded an explanation in plain, understandable English except that several other children were congregating around her booth and she'd turned her attention to them.

That, and the fact that Jo Spencer was yanking at his sleeve.

"It's nearly your turn, dear," she said, loud enough to be heard over the din of the crowd. "Don't you worry a bit about Felix and Nigel. I'll watch them for you. And the goldfish. We can leave them with Vee for later."

"My turn for what?" asked Ben, confused. He'd willingly offered to help set up and take down the booths for the carnival, but other than that he didn't remember signing up for any other duties.

Jo chuckled in delight. "Didn't anyone tell you? No, of course not. Why would they? It was supposed to be a secret."

It sounded to Ben like she was having a running conversation with herself, but he kept an ear out for any vital information she might pass on. "More than one handsome man has been surprised today. Felix, Nigel, come along with your uncle and me. Vee, can you put the boys' names on their goldfish so they can pick them up later?"

"Of course," Vee agreed readily.

"This does not sound good," he remarked as he let Jo lead him down to the end of one row of booths and up another.

"Don't be a spoilsport," Jo scolded. "Now, it's just right outside here."

Ben tensed automatically. Presumably he wasn't going to like whatever *it* was that they were heading toward. Why else would the ladies' church committee, the ones who'd spent so many months planning the carnival, be so hush-hush about it?

"We all wanted this to be a surprise," Jo explained, answering his question as if she'd read his thoughts. "It's going to be the highlight of the day for everyone."

Jo pointed to a spot just beyond the bounce house where—oh, no, it couldn't be.

Oh, yes, it was.

An old-fashioned dunk tank.

Currently, Zach was dangling his legs over the edge of a board hanging well over the tank. He was catcalling everyone within hearing distance, provoking them to take a swing at him. Or a throw, rather. The board was rigged to a twelve-inch-round bull's-eye.

Charlie, one of the younger firefighters, was taking a turn trying to dunk Zach. Three balls later and Zach was still as dry as a bone as he crawled off the board with a triumphant grin on his face.

"See, now?" Jo told Ben. "You probably won't even get wet. And remember, it's—"

"For a good cause," Ben finished for her. "Yeah, I

know. I guess it looks okay. The target is obviously hard to hit."

"Believe you me, the mechanism doesn't spring very easily. My three balls didn't make a dent in it. I had to go and press it with my own two hands to dunk Chance into the tank, cowboy hat and all. You should have heard him bellow."

Ben raised a brow.

Jo shrugged nonchalantly. "We had to try it out to make sure it worked, right?"

"So it's hard to spring the latch?" Ben asked again, not at all sure that Jo was being straight with him.

"It's very difficult, yes. In any case, a little water can't hurt a big, strong, hunky guy like you, can it?"

Probably not, but Ben didn't like the idea of getting soaked just the same. He wasn't even wearing swimming trunks. He wondered who'd put his name on the list and conveniently forgot to tell him about it.

"Your turn, buddy," Zach announced, giving him a friendly punch in the shoulder. "We boys have got to do our civic duty, now, don't we?"

"As long as I don't get wet," Ben replied as he tugged off one of his worn black cowboy boots and then the other. He found a tree a little bit out of the way and put his boots and hat aside. If he ended up getting dunked, he wouldn't be as caught off-guard as Chance had evidently been.

Feeling petulant, he climbed up on the board. He was going to do this for the sake of the church, but he didn't have to be cheerful about his *service* the way his partner was.

He didn't announce himself or hoot and holler the way Zach had done. Rather, he sat silently, staring at the crowd. It wasn't long before there was quite a long line, mostly composed of young women, who wanted to take their turns trying to dunk him. Fortunately, no one was a very good shot, and Ben was beginning to think he was going to come away from the experience dry and unscathed.

"Oh, I'm so doing this." Ben recognized Vee's voice at once.

Terrific. He had a sinking feeling *she* wouldn't miss.

Apparently those around her felt the same way, for a cheer rose up from the crowd as she picked up the first of the three baseballs she'd purchased. She took aim and pitched.

The first one went high and wide. The second was off to the left, barely missing the target and causing a collective groan from the audience.

Ben released the breath he'd been holding. Vee wasn't any better a throw than any of the other women before her. He was as good as safe.

But then her determined gaze met his, and Ben knew beyond the shadow of a doubt that he was going to be unceremoniously dropped into the tank full of water.

"Wait a minute," he called. He was probably only delaying the inevitable, but he wasn't going into that water without getting some kind of satisfaction out of it.

"What does she win if she dunks me?" he asked.

A goldfish, maybe?

Ha! That would be justice in the extreme.

"How about a date?" Jo suggested with a chuckle that suggested that this was a calculated proposal.

The folks crowded around the dunking booth put up a crazed cheer.

Whoa.

Ben hadn't seen *that* one coming.

In a panicked haze, he surveyed the gathering, desperately trying to think his way out of the hole he'd dug himself into, but his brain wasn't keeping up with the pounding of his pulse in his head. There was nothing he could think of, no one who could help him, who could save him from his own foolish big mouth. Everyone so clearly approved of Jo's idea that it would have been beyond disrespectful to act as if he were anything but pleased by the idea. Actually, he thought the suggestion had merit, but he doubted Vee would feel the same way about it.

She hadn't seen that fly ball coming, either, for she had the same distressed expression as when he'd suggested that he was going to feed his goldfish to the cat. Her almond-brown eyes were as huge as a doe's in a hunter's light. Her cheeks were scorching red, which was unusual given her dark complexion.

"No, that's all right. No dates, please." Vee held her hands up as if she were being robbed and backed away from the counter. "I don't need a prize, and I really don't think a date would be a good idea."

Wow. Now *that* stung.

It was the equivalent of his asking her out and her turning him down right in front of the entire community; and although it hadn't been Ben's idea in the first place—exactly—he didn't care to be humiliated in front of his friends and neighbors. Pride burned in his chest.

How could she?

He didn't realize Vee still held the third and final baseball until, a good ten feet or so from the booth, she suddenly spun around on her heels and fired the ball at the target.

Ben heard a metallic *thwump,* and the next moment he was underwater.

Freezing cold water.

By the time he splashed around and finally got his bearings to surface again, Vee was gone.

Vee stayed around long enough to see the satisfaction of her baseball hitting the mark and Ben disappearing underwater, but then she quickly hurried off before someone in the crowd could suggest she collect her *prize*.

What was Jo thinking? She knew the history between Ben and Olivia. Surely she had to know that Vee—

Her feet suddenly refused to move of their own accord. She felt like someone had slapped her in the face.

She knew exactly how that statement ended, and it wasn't good.

Surely Jo had to know that *Vee hadn't forgiven Ben.*

Heat burned her face and she forged ahead, picking up her pace and leaving the church grounds far behind her. She headed down Main Street, making a right toward the park.

She ought to be ashamed of herself. She *was* ashamed. Just the other day Olivia had made it clear that she was willing to let go of her past with Ben, even though she was the one who had been directly hurt.

Who was Vee to hold a grudge when she wasn't even the wronged party? And what about the wrongs she'd done, herself?

Ben had certainly reached out to her on more than one occasion, extending the hand of friendship, which she had brushed aside time and time again. And now she'd humiliated him in front of the whole town.

Not good.

She owed him an apology. A big one.

"Vee, wait!"

Vee froze, her whole body tensing when she heard Ben's voice.

Why had he followed her? To chew her out as she knew she deserved? Yes, she needed to apologize to him, but at this very moment she *so* wasn't ready for this. She hadn't even had time to pray about it, much less consider her words.

"Wait up just a second," Ben called again. He jogged to her side. He'd clearly been running. His breath was coming in low, ragged gasps. He was soaking wet, from his slicked-back black hair to the bottom of his blue jeans.

And he was barefoot.

"You don't have any shoes on," she pointed out, realizing only afterward that she was stating the obvious. Not only that, but it sounded like she was scolding.

He scowled down at her.

"*What* is your problem?" he demanded. "What did I ever do to you?"

She cocked her head. It had never been about what Ben had done to *her*. But clearly he didn't realize that. Olivia was right—he truly was clueless about women. For some reason that made it a lot easier to let go of her anger. He wasn't the callous playboy she'd taken him for. He was just a sweet, naive guy who sometimes did the wrong thing, even if it wasn't on purpose. "You really don't know, do you?"

He shook his head fiercely, confusion gleaming from his eyes. "Obviously not."

"Well, then, I've wasted an awful lot of effort and

energy giving you the cold shoulder, and it appears it was all for nothing."

"What?" He moved back a step as if she'd pushed him. He ran his fingers through his wet curls.

"Oh, nothing. I just realized I've been carrying a heavy burden God never meant for me to carry."

His brow lowered. He actually looked concerned for her, though why he should care after the way she'd treated him was beyond her. She'd not only dunked him into a tank of cold water, she'd been the one to put his name in the hat in the first place—a fact that he was probably unaware of. She was the reason he'd been picked for the dunk tank at all.

What had she been thinking?

"Is there anything I can do to help?" His voice was so rich with sincerity and disquiet that it yanked at her heartstrings. If he was any sweeter, he'd have to change his name to *Chocolate*.

"Why are you being nice to me?"

Of course the question came out sounding defensive. When had she become so cynical? She tried again. "I don't understand you. You should detest me for the way I've treated you."

His gaze widened, and his eyes shimmered with an emotion she did not immediately recognize.

"Vee," he said from deep in his throat. "Do you really not know, honey?"

He reached out tentatively and stroked her cheek with the pad of his thumb, then ran his fingers across her jaw.

She knew she should turn away, but no man had ever looked at her the way Ben was looking at her now. No man had ever touched her with the combination of strength and gentleness he was showing her. No man's fingers had ever quivered as they slid across her cheek, showing vulnerability within that strength.

His other hand joined the first, tenderly framing her face, tipping her chin up with his thumbs.

"Vee?" he said again, but this time it was a question.

She wasn't certain just what she said in that moment. She was pretty sure it wasn't a real word. Probably more like a strangled sigh.

She pressed her palms to his chest. His breath was warm against her cheek and he continued to hold her gaze, but he didn't move a muscle.

Was he waiting for her to push him away?

She didn't. Instead, she tangled her fingers in the wet cotton of his shirt and pulled him toward her, standing on tiptoe until his mouth met hers.

Warmth flooded her senses. Her heartbeat pounded in her ears. The world spun around her and there was nothing but Ben.

Only Ben.

His kiss was tender. Searching. Wonderful.

And it scared her to death.

Vee broke away with a cry of dismay and darted off in the other direction as fast as her shaky legs could carry her.

This time Ben didn't follow her.

Chapter Eleven

Ben wasn't the kind of man to kiss and tell, but he was in a world of trouble, and he didn't know where to turn for help. He was so confused he couldn't even bring himself to return to the church to pick up his nephews. Instead, he'd called Jo Spencer and asked her to bring them—and his hat and his boots—by the house.

Even now, after a restless night's sleep, his head was still swimming.

What had possessed him to kiss Vee Bishop? Talk about a gigantic step in the wrong direction.

Not that he regretted kissing Vee. At that second, and even now as he thought about it, he had very much wanted to kiss her. He still did.

He just *shouldn't* have.

Kissing Vee complicated every part of his life. It wasn't anything a cup of coffee could cure, but he thought going to Cup o' Jo was a good first step. Maybe Jo would have some good advice for him, or perhaps a jolt of caffeine might set him straight, though he highly doubted it.

What did a man do when he was headed down the

wrong road? He'd made a mess of this whole thing. Vee might never speak to him again.

And then he had Veronica Jayne to consider. He'd only just sent her his picture. She might interpret that to mean something more than it was, which of course he hadn't considered until after he sent the photograph. What if she thought he was leading her on?

He'd made that mistake in the past with women, and whatever happened, he didn't want to hurt Veronica Jayne. She was special to him, and he cared for her, even if it was something completely different than what he felt for Vee.

He was no longer caught up in wondering what Veronica Jayne really looked like, and he wasn't madly checking his email to see if she'd sent her photograph. He simply didn't feel for her the way he felt for Vee, even if he was unable to put words to exactly what his feelings for Vee were.

Honestly, the last thing he should have been doing was pursuing a relationship with *any* woman right now. He could not be in a less-stable position than he was at this moment—in a transition phase on his way to mission work. That was his calling. He couldn't just drop it and suddenly become the kind of man Vee would want in her life.

Not that he knew what kind of man Vee wanted, or if she wanted a man at all. The truth was, he had no idea how Vee felt about what had happened between them, other than the fact that she had freaked out and run away.

And that wasn't exactly a good sign, was it?

He'd definitely caught her off-guard. He'd caught *himself* off-guard.

What was he going to say if he had to talk to her?

Obviously, he would have to talk to her. Eventually. He wasn't a man of words. He preferred action—only in this case, it was *action* that had gotten him in trouble.

With an inward sigh, Ben entered Cup o' Jo and walked up to the counter to order a double espresso—the strongest thing they served.

As always, Jo was behind the counter waiting on customers. She was always about, setting the tone of the café to be like a second home to her customers and friends. She made everyone feel welcome, and no matter what kind of day Ben was having, she always managed to make him feel better.

Jo had a never-ending set of interesting T-shirts, a different one every day of the week. Today her shirt proclaimed If It's Broke, Fix It.

Ben frowned. That was definitely a skewed version of the old cliché.

Jo set his cup of coffee before him with a speculative look on her face. She was only quiet for a second before speaking her mind.

"Did you fix things, dear?" she asked bluntly.

Ben raised a brow. "I'm sorry—fix what?"

Jo shook her purple dishtowel at him. "You know perfectly well what I'm talking about. Between you and Vee. I could tell there was something going on there. First you take off after her during the carnival. You didn't even bother to dry yourself off with a towel. Now, I don't mind one whit that you called me in to help with Nigel and Felix yesterday, but if you think you're keeping me in the dark with what's happening between you and Vee, you've got another thing coming."

Ben downed his espresso in two gulps and choked on the bitter aftertaste.

"Well, did you get a chance to talk to her?" Jo was nothing if not straightforward to a fault.

Ben's face flamed. *Talking* wasn't exactly what happened between him and Vee. Not that he would tell Jo that.

"A little bit," he answered vaguely.

Jo leaned over the counter and tapped him on the shoulder with a closed fist. "Well, then, talk a little bit more, son. Make the effort. I promise she will be worth it."

What was she talking about? Despite the fact that Jo was like a second mother to him—or maybe because of that—he definitely did not like the feeling that the woman was inside his head.

He slid the mug over the counter without meeting Jo's gaze. Maybe if he didn't quite look at her…

"Thanks for the brew," he said, turning away so she wouldn't see the confusion and angst in his eyes. Clearly she was reading something into nothing—or was that nothing into something?

Spinning around turned out to be an even greater problem because Vee had just walked in the door with Olivia. They were both dressed in sweats and running shoes. Vee's hair was in a ponytail, not a bun, which startled Ben. The swing of her hair made her look so— *feminine.* She'd clearly been working out—her face was flushed and wisps of hair that had escaped her ponytail framed her heart-shaped face—yet she looked so lovely, all ruffled and not quite put together.

His heart jumped into his throat. She noticed him just seconds after the moment he saw her. Their gazes locked and held while Ben's mind spun wildly, searching for the right words to say in the singularly most awkward moment of his life.

"Hey, Vee. Olivia."

So smooth. Cary Grant could take lessons from him. If he could have slapped himself upside the head without anyone noticing, he would have.

"Did you enjoy the carnival?" Olivia teased, picking up the conversation and running with it. "I heard the water was nice and cold."

Ben could almost see the layers upon layers of emotional barriers going up around Vee.

Obstacles he didn't know how to cross.

He made a choking noise. Clearly, he wasn't able to *fix* the problem at all. He didn't have the vaguest notion how women thought.

He tried to look nonchalant, to force casual words from his lips. He really did. But there was nothing there. His head was whirling and his thoughts were screaming and he knew if he didn't leave that moment, he would make an utter fool of himself.

"Ladies," he rumbled from deep in his throat. He planted his cowboy hat on his head, tipped it to them with a nod and tried very hard not to run as he passed by them, heading for the exit and the fresh air he so desperately needed.

A man had to breathe, after all. And around Vee Bishop, that was impossible to do.

"He did *what?*" Olivia screeched, reaching for Vee's elbow and shaking her with great enthusiasm.

"Can you please lower your voice?" Vee whispered coarsely. "In case you didn't notice, Ben is sitting right across the room from us." Ben had stepped out of the café for a moment, but now he was seated in the back corner opposite her, slumped behind a computer screen.

Olivia snickered. "Oh, I noticed, all right. It was hard not to, with you two acting all weird around each other."

"Can you please, *please* not make a big deal out of this? You are going to make me sorry I told you anything." Vee buried her head in her hands.

"Oh, like you could keep something as monumental as this from me. Not going to happen. I already knew something was brewing between you and Ben, but I had no idea the soup was done. How long have you two been an item? Was it just after the carnival or have you been keeping it under wraps for longer than that?"

"You have the oddest metaphors," Vee commented, chuckling despite the fact that her best friend was putting her on the spot. "I'm begging you not to make this—" she paused slightly "—*episode* into more than it is. Ben and I are *not* a couple, nor do I think we ever will be."

Olivia lifted a brow. "Really?"

"If we were—and I'm not saying that's even a possibility—you'd be the first to know."

"I want to hear details. Play-by-play, girl. I want to know it all. I'm still in shock to learn that he kissed you."

"*You're* in shock," Vee responded with a groan. "I'm completely stunned. I don't know *how* it happened, let alone *why*."

"Well, duh. I know why."

"How fortunate for you," Vee replied dryly. "You were there at the carnival when Jo suggested that I win a date with Ben if I dunked him, right?"

"Oh, yes. And you *sooo* dunked him." Olivia laughed. "People are still talking about it. Adding ten feet to your throw. That was pure genius, Vee. Pure genius. Everybody thought so."

"Everybody but Ben. My actions were foolish, that's what they were. I left right afterward, and then I started feeling badly about the way I've been treating him, especially back at the dunking booth. I wanted to apologize to him, but I wasn't ready to talk to him when he came chasing after me. I hadn't even prayed about it."

"Dunking Ben wasn't a big deal, hon. I'm sure he doesn't hold it against you."

"Maybe not, but don't you agree that I ended up humiliating him in front of all of our friends? I made such a big deal about *not* going out with him that it made it seem like I thought he was a bad guy, someone I would never date. How awful was that?"

"It was only because you were flustered. And you had good intentions, even when you were turning Ben away. You were thinking of me, being loyal to me. That's a good character trait when taken in context. Surely he understood that when you explained it all to him."

Vee's face flamed and she choked on her coffee.

"We didn't exactly get to that part."

"So are you telling me he just dashed up from behind, whirled you around and planted one on you? How incredibly romantic." Olivia sighed deeply, resting her chin on her palm. Her gaze turned dreamy. In Vee's opinion, Olivia was enjoying this whole situation far too much for her liking.

"How *appalling,* you mean. I can't even look him in the eye. And just in case you hadn't noticed, he's clearly avoiding me, too. It's pretty obvious that he thinks that kissing me was the wrong thing to do. It was a mistake that never should have happened."

"There is nothing at all obvious happening here. You're reading way too much into his every single move. He may look like a big lug, but Ben is a very sensitive man, Vee. He feels deeply, but he doesn't always show it. You know how guys are. They keep everything locked inside. I have a good notion that he's infatuated with you and isn't sure what his next move should be. I mean really, how do you follow a dramatic kiss like he gave you?"

"I haven't a clue."

"Maybe he's just giving you space to process what happened. Maybe he's getting his nerve up to ask you on a proper date."

Vee inhaled deeply and darted a glance at Ben. His gaze was squarely on the computer screen in front of him.

How did she feel about all that had happened? Did she dare put a name to it? Label or classify it? Where, exactly, were her emotions pointing when it came to Ben Atwood?

And more to the point, how did *he* feel about her?

Awkward.

That's how Ben was feeling. Completely out of his depth.

He slunk down a little lower in his seat, wishing he could disappear or at least find a way to get out of the café without having to pass by Vee again. He was still staring at an empty computer screen. When he'd sat down to write an email, he'd come up blank. He'd quickly decided that soliciting advice from Veronica Jayne was a bad idea. He didn't want to hurt her feelings.

That said, he didn't know *what* to do.

It was almost as if he were in high school again, getting flustered when the girl he liked walked past. Only this wasn't high school, and he'd already *kissed* the girl he liked.

He didn't know whether that was an act of courage or flagrant foolishness. He'd sought God's will, but so far had come up empty-handed. If the Lord was directing him, he must be missing the clues.

He had his life here in Serendipity, but his dreams and his future lay in stateside mission work. His attraction to Vee Bishop grew stronger every day, but what good could come from that?

She was too intense and independent a woman to expect her to change her plans to suit him, and he wasn't the kind of man who could leave his wife behind at home while he was off doing mission work. And that was assuming his attraction to her was reciprocated at all.

She *had* kissed him back—he was positive of that. Actually, she'd more or less initiated the kiss. But he could analyze the moment to death and never figure out how she felt about him.

Then there was Veronica Jayne, his mystery flower girl. He held no illusions now that they could try to date—not with the strength of his feelings for Vee. But he still hoped that he and Veronica Jayne could remain friends after their class was done.

He'd been praying and praying that he would someday be as strong on the inside as he was on the outside, but spiritual growth was a lot more difficult than physical growth. Building muscles on his biceps and chest was a cakewalk compared to trying to sort out his current emotions.

The one thing that he did know was that he was falling for Vee—hard. He didn't know whether she returned the sentiment, and he definitely didn't know how God would have Vee fit into his future, but there it was in black and white.

Now he needed to make a plan and make it work. Vee wasn't going to make this easy on him. For one thing, she was completely immune to his charm, or whatever it was that other women saw in him. She wasn't flirtatious like they were—not that he knew what to do with a flirtatious woman any more than he knew what to do with a scrupulously unsociable one.

How could a man feel so completely hopeless and yet utterly hopeful at the same time?

Only a woman could do that to a man.

One woman. Vee.

Ben wiggled the computer mouse to bring the screen to light again. He opened his email account and quickly scanned down the list, wondering if he'd find the familiar moniker that usually awaited him.

Veronica Jayne.

Except there was no email from Veronica Jayne. Not a word and not a picture.

Had he scared her away by pushing their friendship forward too quickly? Had he shaken her up by sending her his picture?

It figured. He was somehow managing to make a mess of *all* the relationships in his life.

It just figured. With a growl of frustration, he closed the browser and stalked out of the café without so much as a backward glance.

* * *

"Did you ever check your email to see if BJ sent you a picture?" Olivia queried with a sly smile that bespoke more than a little curiosity.

"I thought you were trying to get me to see the good side of Ben Atwood. I can't do that and worry about BJ at the same time. Not that I'm admitting to feeling anything for Ben, mind you."

"Of course you're not. You're going to be as mule-headed about Ben as you always are with everything. And just so we're clear, my main goal in life right now is to make you see that Ben is a good man and deserving of a chance. But that said, it never hurts to have a backup plan, don't you think?"

Vee felt like Olivia had pushed her in the chest.

A backup plan? Is that was BJ was?

If she was being honest, she had to admit that he might have been so, at least at some point. Perhaps that's what he always had been, the guy she'd had in her cyber back pocket in case the real thing—a face-to-face relationship with a man—never materialized.

But now Ben was in the picture, whatever that meant, and she and BJ were talking about exchanging pictures. This was all getting far too real for her and far too complicated for her liking. Sure, they'd talked about meeting each other at a stateside mission someday, but that *day* had always been some distant, unspecified date in the future.

She had mixed feelings about the whole thing. Half of her was scared to death to see what BJ looked like. The other half didn't really care at all—because, to be honest, her heart was leaning elsewhere. What did it matter what BJ did or did not look like when she couldn't keep her mind off Ben?

Her heart roared in her ears. She definitely wasn't ready for *that* kind of honesty yet. She couldn't even look Ben in the eye. That did not bode well for any kind of real relationship with Ben, but no matter what happened on that front, she knew without a doubt that she could never have any kind of a relationship with BJ while she felt this way about another man.

It saddened her to think there would be no more emails to look forward to, no more bright spots in her day just knowing BJ was out there somewhere, possibly thinking of her just the way she had been thinking of him.

As a friend. A supporter. He'd definitely been those things.

She sighed. What was the old proverb? All good things must come to an end? She supposed that applied to mythical internet relationships, too.

"Hello? Earth to Vee. Are you reading, Vee?"

"Huh?" Vee snapped out of her reverie to find Olivia waving a hand in front of her face.

"That's what I thought. You aren't paying any attention to me at all. You're staring at Ben."

She snapped her gaze back to Olivia's. "Was not."

"Were, too. Deny it all you want, girlfriend, but you've got a thing for him."

"I thought we were talking about BJ."

Olivia barked out a laugh. "Did anyone ever tell you how contrary you are? When I mention Ben, you want to talk about BJ. When I suggest we see what the elusive BJ looks like, you want to talk about Ben."

"I am not contrary," she countered, then realized that simply by answering she was proving Olivia's point.

"So you'll check your email to see if BJ sent his picture? And you'll look at it if he did?"

"You aren't going to let this go, are you?" Vee muttered morosely.

"Have you ever known me to let go of an interesting tidbit of gossip?"

"This isn't gossip."

"No, it is not. It is *way* better than gossip. More interesting, by far," Olivia assured her.

"Fine," Vee snapped.

"Fine? You mean you'll look at the photograph?"

"No. I mean *you'll* look if it's that interesting to you. I don't even want to know what BJ looks like anymore."

"Because you've already fallen for Ben."

Vee sighed dramatically. "Do you know that you exasperate me sometimes?"

Olivia grinned like the Cheshire cat. "I know. And you love me for it."

"Actually, I love you in spite of it, if you must know."

Olivia reached in front of Vee and wiggled the computer mouse, bringing the screen in front of the two of them to light.

Vee's stomach clenched as she opened up the webpage for her email, then typed in her password to pull up her new messages. Maybe BJ hadn't written. Or maybe he hadn't sent a photograph like he'd said he was going to.

She glanced at the screen and sighed. Sure enough, there was a message from BJ, complete with an attachment.

She really, *really* was not ready for this. There was no way she was opening his letter. Not now, at least.

She hovered the pointer over the *X* that would close the browser.

"Oh, no you don't," Olivia reprimanded, laying a hand over hers. She really was pushy when she wanted something, Vee thought sullenly. This was one time that she didn't appreciate that character trait in her best friend.

"I can't do this." She knew Olivia wouldn't buy it, but she had to try to sell it nonetheless.

"Fine." Olivia's tone was a cross between enjoyment and exasperation. Mostly amusement, bless her heart. "Then I'll do it for you. Scoot over and hand me that mouse."

Vee thought about arguing, but what was the point? Besides, if she deleted the email without looking at BJ's photo, there would be a teeny, tiny part of her that would always wonder what she'd missed. Olivia was right. Seeing BJ's photograph would offer her a measure of closure so she could go on with her life. That said...

"I can't look." Vee braced her elbows on the table and pushed her palms against her eyes, completely darkening her vision. "Promise that you won't keep me in suspense too long," she squeaked. "Just take a quick look at the man and put me out of my misery."

"No problem. I'll fill you in on the general details, and then you can decide if you want to have a peek yourself. I'll give you all the good stuff. You know what I'm talking about. Tall. Short. Big. Little. Handsome. Troll."

"Olivia!"

"Kidding. I'm kidding. No, not really. I'm not. Who better than me to discern if a man is right for you? Your best friend since kindergarten. I know you better than anyone. I'll point you in the right direction."

"You're pushing Ben at me," Vee felt led to point out.

"Exactly."

With her elbows braced on the table and her palms tightly covering her eyes, she heard, rather than saw, the abrupt change in Olivia's demeanor as her best friend swept in a high, squeaky breath and exclaimed in surprise.

"Oh, my. Oh my, oh my, oh my."

Vee groaned and pushed her palms more tightly against her eyes, as if that would somehow make this situation go away. "What is it? Does he have scales?"

"Um, not exactly," Olivia answered slowly. "No, I definitely would not say that."

"What, then? Is he a modern-day replica of Clark Gable, so unbelievably gorgeous that he instantly took your breath away and made your heart leap out of your chest?"

Vee expected Olivia to break into laughter at her measly attempt at humor, but she sounded surprisingly sober for one who had only moments earlier been pushing Vee to take a look at her mystery man.

The mood had changed. Vee felt it in every fiber of her being. Every muscle tensed, every tendon stretched, until she was shaking from the effort of merely being there.

"You're getting warmer," Olivia offered after a painful pause.

"Well, that's good to know," Vee replied, as tongue-in-cheek as she could manage. "So he's not dreadful to look at, then?"

"Not at all." *That* answer came quickly. Maybe too quickly.

"So describe him to me. I'm dying here."

"You could just look."

"I could, but why spoil your fun?" Actually, Vee was still battling her own fear. It wouldn't help her to stretch it out any more than necessary, but she couldn't help but try.

"Okay, then." Olivia started out slowly, drawing out each syllable. "Broad shoulders, dark hair, nice eyes."

"Nice eyes? That's kind of vague, don't you think? What color are they?"

"They're kind of a mixture of colors. They're hard to describe with words. You'll just have to open your eyes and see for yourself. And Vee? Leaving personality aside, and past history, who is the best-looking man in Serendipity?"

Vee felt the tension leave her shoulders. Olivia was obviously talking about Ben. If BJ was anywhere near as handsome as Ben Atwood, Vee had nothing to fear in looking at his picture, except the terrifying notion of him ever finding out what *she* looked like.

Boy, would he be disappointed. But that was not going to happen, since she had no intention of sending him a picture back—especially now that she'd learned BJ was a handsome man—it was all good.

"Vee?" Olivia queried. "You didn't answer my question."

"Ben. Ben Atwood. He's the best-looking man in town," she said, low enough that others nearby would not overhear. "I know that's what you think, too. So does BJ look like Ben, then?"

"Yeah, about that." Olivia hesitated again.

"Well, does he?"

"Yes. Yes, he definitely looks like Ben."

Vee did *not* like the way Olivia's voice sounded, all high and squeaky and strangled. An awful possibility filled Vee's mind to explain why she was having such difficulty.

Ready to face the truth at last, or at least unable to deny it any longer, she dropped her hands from her eyes, already knowing what she was going to see when she looked at the screen.

Or rather, *who*.

"No way," she croaked, shaking her head fervently.

No. Possible. Way.

"This cannot be happening to me. Olivia, there must be some kind of mistake."

"Think of the odds," Olivia agreed, sounding as astounded as Vee felt.

Ben Atwood, staring out at her with his easy, charming half smile, his luminous bronze-green eyes—the ones no words could adequately describe—making her heart roar in her ears until she could hardly hear anything else.

Vee couldn't process it. She just couldn't.

"Ben can't be BJ," Vee hissed in a harsh whisper, desperately leaning toward Olivia's shoulder, half for support and half so that she would not be overheard. "Turn off that traitorous machine before someone else sees his picture on there! This is not right. There must be some kind of horrible mistake."

"Like what, Vee? How would BJ get his hands on a picture of Ben unless he *is* Ben?"

"I don't know, but there must be some other explanation. Something. Anything."

She knew that there wasn't another explanation for this phenomenon, just as deeply and absolutely as the fact that she hadn't had a *single clue* that BJ was Ben before this very moment.

How could she have worked with him every day, held conversations, even kissed him, and *not known?* It was unfathomable.

"Maybe there's another man in this town," Olivia suggested, "using Ben's picture because he's the better-looking one. Maybe he's trying to pass himself off as Ben because he's really as ugly as a rock."

"It's not another man in Serendipity," Vee admitted with a groan. "Anyway, BJ could never be ugly to me, no matter what he looked like."

Ben. Not BJ. That would take some time to process.

"No, it's doubtless *not* another man. I'm sorry, Vee, but I can't think of any other scenarios, probable or otherwise. So what are you going to do about it, now that you know it's Ben on the other end of the line?"

She wanted to scream, but she was in public. Maybe later, into her pillow at home.

"*Do* about it?" she whispered weakly, hardly able to speak. "I don't know."

Her heart sunk. What *was* she going to do about it?

"You have to do something."

"No I don't," Vee replied just a bit too quickly. "I don't have to do anything about it at all. I can simply delete the email and pretend I never saw Ben's picture. Simple as that. End of story."

"Really? You think you can do that?" Olivia peered at her speculatively and then shook her head. "You think you can just pretend it never happened, that you never discovered that BJ and Ben were one and the same? Do you think you can work alongside Ben every day and never give away any indication that you and he were ever a cyber-item? And what about your class with BJ? Aren't you working on a project together?"

"You make it sound impossible," Vee complained grumpily. Which, of course, it was. Even if she could ignore Ben in person, she could hardly ignore BJ. Half his grade was their combined project. She took the computer mouse away from Olivia, who hadn't yet closed the browser. Not only was Vee afraid someone else might see the telling photograph, but she simply couldn't stand to look directly at Ben's smiling face a moment longer.

No wonder Olivia couldn't describe the color of Ben's eyes. They defied explanation, at least any kind that could be put into words.

"Honestly, I think it would be impossible. I know I couldn't do it, even if I tried. I'd be bound to slip up eventually and say something that would tip him off."

That was Olivia, though, who, bless her soul, tended to chatter. Vee was more hush-hush about things. She'd more than likely be able to pull it off.

Except for the fact that she'd blush to her toes every time her eyes met Ben's, and how obvious was that? Vee wasn't a blushing woman any more than she was a talkative one, so her turning the color of an apple at inopportune moments would be a dead giveaway.

Oh, what was she going to do?

"Maybe you could just send him your picture back? Throw the ball into his court and let him decide what to do with it? If nothing else, he'd be able to experience the same shock you are feeling."

Vee thought that was an excellent suggestion, for about one second, until she started thinking about the ramifications of such an act.

First of all, she'd have to find a photograph to send him, and she did *not* take good pictures. Not that it mattered, but she had her pride. Second, the wait would be excruciating. She'd be on pins and needles every second after she hit Send.

And what if he decided never to speak to her about it at all? Could she really handle working around him and seeing him around town knowing that he knew that she knew that…

This was getting *really* complicated.

Impossible, more like.

Why had she ever, *ever* thought she could conduct any sort of relationship online, romantic or otherwise? Had she really believed it would somehow be easier than conducting her affairs in person?

The whole situation would have been funny if it wasn't so serious. She certainly wasn't laughing now.

"Maybe you should just come clean with him," Olivia suggested. "Just tell him the truth—that you were surprised to learn it was him when you received his picture, and you're sure he'll be as flabbergasted as you to discover you've each been emailing someone who lives in the same town—who works for the same fire department, to be exact."

"That's going to go over well." Vee couldn't even imagine how she would start *that* conversation.

"Maybe you two will eventually laugh about it," Olivia suggested.

"Somehow I don't think he'll find this funny." Not any more than she did. He'd probably think it was much, much worse.

She was on the winning end of this equation. Plain Jayne meets Hunky Paramedic. No contest there.

Yeah, no. That wasn't going to happen. She could not stand the humiliation of coming clean on this one.

"Remember, he did kiss you," Olivia reminded her,

as if she had somehow deduced where Vee's thoughts had taken her.

That was true. Vee wondered how she'd forgotten about Ben's kiss, even for a moment. Technically, she'd kissed him, but he hadn't seemed to mind.

Which only served to complicate matters even further, if that were possible.

She didn't know how to feel about what had happened between them, only that she'd been surprised at the intense feelings he stirred in her. She'd always thought she disliked him, putting it mildly; and maybe she had because of what he'd done to Olivia.

But now she'd let that go. And that she *was* attracted to him, though she had initially tried to deny it.

Given that new bit of insight, there was no way bringing the current situation to light would be a good idea for anyone involved. Heartache, maybe even heartbreak, was the very best she could hope for.

But what else could she do?

Delete her email account?

No, she'd still have to work with Ben. And she couldn't leave BJ in the lurch without finishing her end of the project. Different solution, same problems.

Quit the fire station?

How was that fair? Because she knew about the online relationship and he didn't? That just didn't seem right.

Maybe she should just pack up and move.

To Siberia.

To be a tiger trainer.

She thought that was her best idea yet. Out of sight, out of mind and out of country.

If only it were that easy.

"What am I going to do?" she groaned to Olivia. It was a rhetorical question, obviously, with no answer whatsoever, and she'd already asked it several times this afternoon.

There was no more time to think about it. The high-pitched *beep, beep, beep* of her emergency pager broke into her thoughts.

She was needed at the firehouse. There was some kind of emergency situation.

Her problems with Ben would have to wait.

She had a job to do.

Chapter Twelve

Ben was already at the station when the call came through, so he was a first-responder to the location. According to the operator, a leak in a gas stove had caused an explosion in the kitchen of a farmhouse a couple of miles south of Serendipity. The whole unstable house was coming down at an alarming rate.

As with nearly all of the emergencies in the tri-county area, Ben knew the folks involved. The Salingers were part of Ben's church family. They had four children under ten—two boys ages six and nine, a three-year-old little girl and an infant son.

Ben's adrenaline was pumping full steam ahead as he hit the siren to the ambulance and flipped the switch for the flashing lights, even knowing his skills as a paramedic would probably not be needed. The neighbor who'd called it in said the family had gotten out of the blaze safely and were standing by for assistance.

He was more worried about the structure of the old farmhouse itself and the way its loss would affect the family. The Salingers must be terrified and heartbroken as they watched their home burn to the ground. Ben sent up a quick prayer thanking God for the Salingers' safety and asked Him to watch over them and comfort them in their time of need.

Vee was standing near the back of the fire truck just ahead of him, her right arm looped around a spit-shined silver handle made exactly for that purpose. Her face looked serious underneath the wide width of her helmet. Her brow was low and her jaw was set. As always, the woman meant business.

Ben gripped the steering wheel harder. He had the eeriest feeling that she was looking directly at him. That there was a question in her eyes that she was expecting him to answer.

And how unlikely was that? He was starting to imagine emotions where there weren't any. Going mental, and all over a woman.

Sure, they both needed to confront their issues with each other, but now was definitely not the time to do so, and she knew it as well as he did. Thinking she was staring at him was all in his head.

He averted his gaze and concentrated on the road before him. Zach Bowden, sitting beside him, tapped a pencil against the clipboard he was holding and then tucked the writing utensil behind his ear. Usually his partner had something witty to say to lighten the mood. Often he'd describe humorous or entertainingly dramatic situations he'd encountered with his wife or his children.

Today he was unusually silent. He'd obviously been Ben's partner long enough to realize something was amiss. He noticed Zach giving him several speculative sidelong glances.

Zach, however, wasn't the type to stay silent for long. Somehow Ben knew that when Zach finally spoke, it wouldn't be a tale about something his family had gone through recently.

"Are you okay, buddy?" Zach finally asked. "Did you ever get a photograph back from that—what's her name? Veronica Jayne?"

Ben didn't answer, choosing instead to keep his attention on driving.

"So that's how it's going to be, is it? I guess your silence is all I need to know to answer my own question. I can clearly see that your mind is elsewhere."

"I'm fine," Ben ground out, exasperated by his partner's incessant prying. Guys weren't supposed to have these kinds of conversations. Zach had been married too long.

His answer was probably fudging the truth a little bit. He really wasn't *fine*. Ben knew that Zach wanted a real answer, not just the off-the-cuff reply he'd given him, but that was all Ben had to offer right now.

"And?" Zach prodded.

"No, I have not received an email from Veronica Jayne, not that being fine and receiving word from Veronica Jayne are in any way related. And the reason my mind is elsewhere is because I'm praying for the Salingers."

"And not at all because Vee Bishop is currently in your direct line of vision?"

Ben was glad it was dark so that Zach couldn't see him color. He knew that the warm flush to his face would have him cherry-red by now.

Zach chuckled as if he could see Ben's discomfiture. "That's what I thought. You and your lady problems. I knew you were a little off your game tonight. Delia and I went through some rough patches, too, but now look at us, happily married with two beautiful sons. It can't get any better than that, partner."

Ben didn't bother trying to point out to Zach that a couple could only experience a rough patch if they were a *couple* to begin with.

Besides, he didn't want to talk about Vee.

"Can we pray for the Salingers?" he suggested, not entirely for the right reasons but close enough. "Out loud?"

By the time the fire tanker pulled up to the burning house, the scene was absolute chaos. The police had been called to the scene, and they had their hands full trying to contain the crowd. Some folks were there for the sake of the family, and others strained for a decent view of the fire, one of the most exciting things to happen in months.

It was amazing how quickly word spread in Serendipity. Half the town must be there. There weren't many true emergencies in town, and Vee knew folks in general tended to be oddly drawn to such tragedy and trauma.

Most, out of the goodness of their hearts, were there to try to help the Salingers however they could, but attempting to maintain crowd control when the fire department was trying to fight a fire only added to their responsibilities.

Vee caught her police-officer brother Eli's eye and nodded a quick greeting before turning to her work. Every person on the detail had a specific job to do. Chief Jenkins shouted orders while some of the men hooked up the fire hose to the tanker and began blasting the low-level flames.

Vee's job was a little less physical but equally as important as fighting the fire with water. She was the fire-fighter in charge of assessing the scene. First, she had to ascertain that all the people and animals who might have been in the building were safe and clear of the edifice. After that, she'd evaluate the fire itself, both in terms of the extent of the flames and the possible structural damages to the house.

Unfortunately, in Serendipity, where many folks still lived in primarily clapboard houses, structural damage was the rule and not the exception. Vee anticipated that the house would quickly be completely consumed in flames given the magnitude of this particular blaze.

She'd make a thorough tour of the fire site as soon as she was able, and then she'd make a report back to Chief Jenkins, but first she needed to find the Salingers and make sure they were all safe and unharmed. Ben and Zach were waiting at the site in case anyone needed any kind of medical assistance.

Between the dark of the moonless night and the amount of smoke pouring out of the building, it was difficult to see the nose in front of her face, much less figure out where the Salinger family was amid the enormous group of Serendipity locals.

Suddenly Vee heard someone scream, a fierce shriek that cut through the murky air like a knife, stabbing Vee right in the gut. She turned in the direction of the sound and began running, peering to the right and left of her to see if she could locate the source of the noise through the billowing smoke.

A distraught Emma Salinger forced her way through the crowd and ran into Vee's arms, nearly plowing her over. She grasped Vee's jacket and yanked hard on it, urging her toward the burning house.

"My baby, my baby, my baby, my baby," she repeated over and over, shaking Vee with every syllable. Emma had a frenzied look in her eye.

"Emma," Vee stated firmly, making sure she was loud enough to be heard over the din of the crowd, the trucks, Chief Jenkins barking out orders and the firemen shouting information to one another. "Look at me. Honey. Emma. Look. At. Me."

The hysterical woman only cried louder. "My baby! My baby!"

Vee's mind was spinning. Had the infant somehow been left inside the house when everyone had evacuated the premises?

"Where is Preston?" Vee asked.

Kent Salinger appeared at Vee's elbow, his infant son tucked protectively into his shoulder.

"Here's the baby," he answered for his frantic wife. "Honey, Preston is right here. Everything is going to be all right."

Vee gritted her teeth. How could he even say that? They were safe, but the Salingers had no place to call home anymore.

"No," Emma insisted, ignoring her husband and gripping Vee's jacket with renewed fervor. "No. Not Preston. It's Crystal."

Crystal, their three-year-old daughter.

"She's not with you?" Kent asked, starting to sound as panic-stricken as his wife.

"She was," Emma admitted and then crumbled to the ground. "She was with me. Dear God, save her."

Vee followed the woman down, crouching before her. "Emma, where is your daughter?"

"She ran back in the house." Emma choked on a sob. "Calliope was in there. I couldn't stop her."

"Who is Calliope?" Vee asked, confused.

"Crystal's favorite doll," Kent answered over his shoulder. The man had already slid Preston into Emma's weak arms and was at a dead run for what was left of the front door of the house.

Vee's pulse roared in her ears as her adrenaline burst through her veins. The entire house was engulfed in flames. Kent was crazy if he thought he could survive entering the dwelling with no protective clothing or training in dealing with fires. He'd never make it out alive, much less rescue his daughter.

Vee dashed forward and dived for Kent, hitting him behind the knees and knocking him squarely to the ground with a jolt so hard it knocked the wind out of her and probably out of him, too. Kent was already struggling underneath her, trying to get away.

"Let me go," he screamed, thrashing his legs. "I've got to get Crystal."

His heel met Vee on the chin and she was knocked flat on her back. Though she could see the gush of blood that poured down the front of her jacket, she could not feel the pain.

"Kent," she screamed at him, grabbing at one leg. "You can't do this. Let me. I'm trained for this. Trust me. I *will* get your daughter out safely."

Or die trying.

Chief Jenkins appeared at her side and wrestled Kent to a standing position, keeping a firm hand around his upper arm. Ben rushed forward to grasp Kent's other arm. Chief and Ben were both large men, and though

Kent tried, he could not break the firefighters' combined grip.

"You're bleeding, Vee," Ben said.

"It's nothing but a superficial cut." She wiped her chin with the back of her palm.

Vee knew this was her moment. She wasn't wearing her SBCA gear, the tank and mask that would allow her to be able to breathe in the inferno. Her duties this evening, liaising with the family and the community and assessing structural issues, shouldn't have required her to carry the heavy equipment around, so she'd elected not to gear up with them. It had never been an issue before, and she hadn't thought twice about it.

She was thinking about it now.

She had a decision to make and no time to make it in. It was now or never. She had to save that little girl.

Taking one last glance back at the rest of the Salinger family, who were huddling together crying for their daughter and sister, she pressed her visor down over her face and dashed for the building.

She could hear Chief Jenkins yelling at her to come back, heard him issue her a direct order *not* to enter the building. The structure was caving in. It wasn't safe for anyone to dare a rescue, especially without the proper breathing apparatus.

Vee knew that despite the odds, Chief Jenkins would have organized a team to try to save little Crystal, but by then it would be too late. The entire house was already engulfed in flames. She couldn't live with herself if she didn't at least try.

Chief would be furious when she returned, and she would no doubt be suspended from the force for her actions, and rightly so, but she would deal with those ramifications afterward, when Crystal Salinger was safe. Her mind was entirely focused on getting in and getting herself and that girl out of that house alive.

Just before she plunged through what was left of the front door, she heard Ben's voice calling to her, a terrified bellow that was halfway between horror and rage.

"Vee! Vee-ee!" His deep, tinny voice echoed through her consciousness at what seemed to be an unimaginable distance, but she could not stop now. Not with a little girl's life on the line.

As soon as she broke through the door, she immediately dropped to her hands and knees, crawling to avoid the worst of the smoke. Her lungs already burned, and she knew she wouldn't survive long without her breathing apparatus. She tugged the top of her collar over her nose and gritted her teeth, trying not to breathe any more than was necessary.

Her firefighter training kicked in full force, right along with her adrenaline, as she scrambled toward what she hoped was the little girl's bedroom. She was working off of zero information. She didn't know when the girl had entered the building, or where, or where she might have thought to have gone after she'd entered the house.

"Crystal! Crystal!" She tried calling the girl's name, but with her collar muffling her voice and the fire roaring around her she knew the three-year-old would never be able to hear her. She couldn't see her hands in front of her face because of the flames and the billowing smoke. The poor girl must be terrified, assuming she was still conscious. She might have passed out already. Vee wouldn't even consider the alternative.

She moved as close to the sides of the room as she dared, feeling her way forward. She didn't want the walls to cave in on her, but she needed the structure to guide her through the house. This was a shot in the dark, grasping forward and to her sides and hoping beyond hope that her gloved hand would meet the little girl's body.

Vee prayed frantically as she methodically swept one room and then a second. She knew she didn't have much time left to get out of the house before it came down around her. The girl had even less, having been exposed to the smoke for a longer period.

Just inside the third bedroom she thought she heard a small whimper.

Was she imagining it? Did she want to find little Crystal so badly that her ears were hearing sounds that did not exist?

No. She heard it again. Directly in front of her. A terrified little squeak, not much more than a murmur. How Vee even heard it over the roar of the fire was nothing short of a gift from God.

Vee scrambled forward, almost falling over the little girl, who was huddled in a small ball in the center of the room, her arms tucked over her head and a little rag doll with red yarn for hair poking out from between her knees.

Vee knew her firefighter's uniform might frighten the already terrified little girl. Lifting her visor was risky, but she'd already gone about as far out on a limb as was possible, anyway. It would be far less difficult to get them both out alive if the child wasn't fighting her every step of the way.

"Crystal," Vee shouted, not wanting to scare the girl but needing for her to be able to hear. "My name is Vee. I know you're scared, honey, but I'm here to get you and Calliope back to your mommy and daddy, okay?"

The little girl nodded and clutched her doll to her chest.

Vee wrapped Crystal's arms around her neck and grasped her wrists with one hand.

"We're going to take a little horsey ride, okay, honey? You just hold on tight and I'll get you out of here."

Crystal wasn't heavy or awkward to carry. With all the adrenaline coursing through Vee, she could barely feel the girl's weight at all. Vee crawled on her knees with her one free hand, heading straight back to the one opening she knew would be her best opportunity for breaking free of the house.

It seemed an eternity before she could make out the shape of the front door. A couple of times her grip slipped on the little girl's wrists and she'd had to stop and readjust Crystal's position on her shoulders. Her lungs burned from the smoke and from holding her breath. She could only imagine how the little girl felt.

Chief had evidently ordered a couple of the men to widen the doorway with their axes, so she didn't have to worry about either one of them being snagged by any protruding pieces of wood.

They were almost there. Almost…there…

And then they'd made it. Two firefighters met her just inside the door to help her scramble the final few feet out of the entranceway.

The moment they were free of the door, Zach gently took Crystal from her and carried the child to the ambulance, where her family anxiously awaited.

Vee didn't even realize she was still crawling on her hands and knees until her gloved palms slipped out from underneath her on the wet grass. She sprawled to the earth, taking sweeping gasps of air, though it was still acrid with smoke. It was better, at least, than what she'd been facing in the building.

It was only through God's grace that she and the child had made it out alive.

"Thank you, Jesus," she said aloud as she groaned and rolled over onto her back. Even though she was lying flat on the ground, her vision blurred and her head spun in dizzy waves. Every muscle in her body ached as if she'd been pummeled in a boxing ring, especially her chin where Kent Salinger had kicked her. The adrenaline was fading, and she could feel the pain of it now.

She closed her eyes, trying to steady herself, searching for the willpower to roll to a sitting position. She was in enough trouble as it was, even without admitting she'd been hurt in the process. Chief would be furious.

But it wasn't Chief who first appeared at her side. Large, muscular arms scooped her up under her neck and knees as if she weighed nothing. She was pulled into a close embrace, surrounded by strong biceps and a rock-hard chest.

Ben.

He was like a fortress around her, shielding her from further harm. She removed her helmet and pressed her cheek to his chest, able to hear his rapid heartbeat even through his paramedic's jacket. She knew she should refuse his help, force herself to get down and walk on her own two feet, but she just couldn't bring herself to put up any resistance. For what might have been the first time in her life, Vee Bishop didn't fight her own need to be held.

Chapter Thirteen

Ben was quivering so much his teeth were chattering. Hopefully Vee couldn't tell how shaken up he was feeling. She'd been through enough without her seeing how much her daring rescue had affected him.

The thought that he might have lost her before he'd had the opportunity to tell her how he felt about her made him sick to his stomach. That even *he* hadn't known how he felt about her until she'd made the mad dash into the Salingers' home after Crystal was beside the point.

Crazy woman.

Wonderful, brave, and completely insane Vee Bishop. The lady who'd somehow slipped in and stolen his heart, and the woman he now knew he couldn't live without.

Ben had been walking in her direction when Kent Salinger had broken for the house, and he'd watched in amazement as Vee had tackled him to the ground. To see a woman a little more than five feet tall take down a man who was well over six feet and a good hundred and eighty pounds was a sight in itself.

But then she'd run into the house herself to save the

girl. Ben would have gone after her, except he didn't dare let go of Kent.

"Crazy woman," he muttered aloud as he strode back to the ambulance with Vee tucked safely in his arms.

Vee moaned. Ben wasn't sure whether that was in protest to what he'd said, or whether it was because she'd been injured in some way. There was blood all down the front of her jacket and a large, gaping cut on her chin.

One thing was for sure—she wasn't feeling 100 percent. Otherwise, she would have been all over him for saying that she was crazy.

"Almost there," he whispered, brushing his cheek against her hair. She reeked of smoke, but that didn't keep him from inhaling deeply. She was alive, and that was all that mattered. The smell of smoke was an acrid reminder to thank God that Vee was still here with him.

He wanted to blurt out how he felt about her, now that he'd finally figured it out himself. But he'd wait until she'd recovered a little bit before he blasted her with a whole new shock.

He reached the foot of the nearest fire truck just as she murmured, "Put me down, please."

Gingerly, he set her down on the ground, supporting her by the shoulders. "Are you able to sit?"

"Of course I can sit," she answered briskly, though her bold statement was interrupted by a coughing attack and she didn't immediately let go of his forearm.

"Easy does it. You're probably dizzy from all the smoke inhalation. Let me get you some oxygen and take care of that cut for you."

She protested, but he ignored her. Thankfully Zach had thought to leave a tank behind for Ben to use with Vee. With great care, he took her helmet from her tightly clenched fist and set it aside and then placed an oxygen mask over her mouth, careful to avoid the cut. He didn't think she'd need stitches, but he cleaned it up for her.

"Lady, don't *ever* do that to me again." His eyes met hers and his heart jammed in his throat. "You had me really worried there for a while."

"Crystal?" she choked out.

"She's good. She and her family are already on their way to Mercy Medical Center with Zach and Brody. She doesn't appear to have any external injuries, but they'll check her out to be certain and then treat her for smoke inhalation. They'll probably keep her overnight for observation, but thanks to you and your crazy stunt, that little girl is going to have a long and happy life."

"Zach and *Brody?*" she queried tremulously. "He's a cop. I don't understand. Why didn't you go with them in the ambulance? You know a lot more about medical issues than Brody does."

He leaned forward until his forehead was touching hers. "Are you kidding me? And leave you here without any support? Not in this lifetime. Besides, even a big lug like Brody can drive an ambulance. Don't worry. Zach is taking good care of Crystal."

Her eyes misted. One lone tear fell, but she quickly brushed it away with the back of her hand.

"My eyes are watering from all the smoke," she explained with a soft hiccup. Her voice was husky with emotion, but he imagined she would no doubt write that off to smoke inhalation, too.

He caressed her cheek with his palm and brushed a soft kiss against her forehead. "You did a very brave thing today, honey."

"She did a very *stupid* thing today." Chief Jenkins

strode around the corner of the fire truck and glared down at Vee, his hands pressed against his hips. He was a formidable man on the best of occasions, but right now, with steam practically sizzling from his ears and his face streaked with black from the smoke, even Ben took a step back. "What were you thinking, Bishop?"

"Crystal," Vee answered weakly. "I had to save Emma's baby."

"You disobeyed a direct order! Not only that, but you didn't even use the common sense God gave you. You knew that house was about to come down around your ears. You, of all people, know how to assess structural damage in a fire. What you did was not only reckless, but it put your fellow firefighters at risk trying to help you. You're suspended from active duty until further notice."

Vee shook her head as if she didn't quite understand Chief's words to her. Her eyes were misty again, and Ben thought she might break into tears at any moment.

Vee Bishop. Crying.

Clearly the poor woman was in shock. Ben stepped forward, blocking Chief's view of Vee.

"Look here, Chief," he started. Ben ignored the fact that Chief had turned his dominating glare upon him. Better that than for him to continue hovering over Vee.

He reached for Chief's elbow and pulled him aside. "Now, I know Vee disobeyed a direct order," he started.

"Yes, she did," Chief barked. "And don't try to talk me out of suspending her. She knew the consequences when she made the decision to run into that house on her own."

"But she did save the girl." He was stating the obvious, but that had to count for something, didn't it?

"That's irrelevant. People in our line of work have

to obey orders, keep the chain of command. Otherwise you've got utter chaos."

"I know," Ben agreed. "But don't you think you can give her a bit of a break right now?" He leaned toward Chief and lowered his voice. "I think she's in shock. She needs medical attention. I *know* she inhaled a lot of smoke in there, and I haven't really been able to assess her for external wounds. Kent Salinger gave her a good clip on the chin with the heel of his boot."

Chief adjusted his helmet, drawing it lower over his brow. After a moment, he nodded.

"Do what you have to, Atwood. See that she's properly cared for. We'll deal with this later."

"Yes, sir."

"And you," Chief said, stepping around Ben to hover over Vee and point an accusatory finger at her, "promise me you won't do anything else foolish until we have ourselves a little talk back at the station tomorrow."

"Yes, sir," Vee replied weakly.

"Make no mistake about it. We *will* have that talk," he promised. "Don't you go thinking you're out of the woods yet, Bishop."

"Yes, sir," Vee said again, then sighed heavily and sank back on her shoulders.

"Are we good, Chief?" Ben queried, squatting down beside Vee to support her shoulders. He brushed a tendril of hair from her forehead that had escaped the knot at the back of her neck.

"Take care of our girl," Chief said and then turned on his heels and marched away, shaking his head as he went.

That was exactly what he planned to do. Not just now, but for as long as Vee would let him.

"Take it easy there, honey," he murmured, shifting

on his knees so he was cradling her in his arms. "Don't worry about Chief Jenkins. He's just a little overwrought from trying to fight the fire—and from nearly losing Crystal Salinger and the best firefighter in his unit. He'll come off his high horse once things have settled down around here."

Vee squeezed her eyes closed and pinched her lips together. "You heard him. I'm suspended from the department."

"We'll see," he murmured.

Not on his watch. He'd find some way to keep Vee from the repercussions of her actions if he had to band the entire fire department behind her to do so. Chief couldn't fight everyone. And anyway, Ben guessed that Chief Jenkins wouldn't be quite so angry once he'd had the opportunity to cool off.

He sat silently with her for a moment, reveling in the fact that she was in his arms. Even with her hair unkempt from the helmet and her face smudged with smoke, she was the most beautiful woman he'd ever known.

His heart swelled and closed up his throat when she leaned backward and their gazes met. She didn't say a word, but her glinting eyes spoke volumes.

Gratitude. Tenderness. And…something more? Or was he just imagining what he wanted to see there?

The world around them might as well not have existed at all. He was keenly aware of Vee—the way she looked, the way she smelled, the way she sounded as her breathing increased through the oxygen mask. None of it should have been the least bit romantic, but Ben wouldn't choose to be anywhere else but here with Vee in his arms.

He desperately wanted to kiss her again, to discover

once and for all if the emotions he was reading in her eyes were real or just a figment of his overactive imagination, his deep desire that she reciprocate his own feelings. This time, she would have no doubt of his intentions.

This time *he* had no doubt of his intentions.

As if reading his mind, she twisted in his arms, tilting her head toward his. He reached around to the nape of her neck and slid his fingers over the elastic that kept the oxygen mask attached. Carefully, oh so slowly, he loosened the mask and slipped it over her head.

"Vee, I—" he began, his voice in a low timbre he didn't recognize.

She stopped him with a finger to his lips. She shook her head and then ran her palm across his cheek and behind his neck, pulling him closer, tilting her mouth up to his.

So there was no need to say the words, after all. She felt as he did, that they should be together.

Vee was his. He had only to prove it with a kiss.

He tilted his head, taking his sweet, sweet time, his mouth hovering over hers until he heard her gasp in anticipation. Her warm breath mixed with his, intoxicating him.

His gaze flicked away for just one second, but it was enough to change his world. His eyes alighted on her helmet, forgotten for the moment and tipped upside down. Her name was written inside, in bold, permanent black ink marker.

Veronica Jayne Bishop.

Chapter Fourteen

Knife, meet heart.

Broken trust was a sharp weapon, and it hit Ben right in the chest, its ragged edges cutting deeply.

He scrambled backward, jumping to his feet, nearly knocking Vee—*Veronica Jayne*—over in the process.

"Wha—?" she mumbled incoherently, her eyes heavily lidded and her full lips half-pursed, poised for a kiss.

The initial pain and shock Ben felt at seeing her name turned to humiliation and then anger in a matter of seconds, rolling from one emotion to another like a snowball gaining both strength and momentum as it spun down a hill.

"I'll bet you and your friends had a good laugh at my expense, didn't you?" he bit out, spinning on his heels so that he didn't have to look at her.

"I don't know what you mean." She sounded perplexed and bewildered and a little hurt herself.

Like she had any right to be.

"How could you?"

"How could I what?"

"Don't play dumb with me, *Veronica Jayne*."

"What did you just call me?"

"Veronica Jayne. That's your name, isn't it?"

"Well, yes, but—"

"You must really think I'm an idiot."

"No, Ben. I never once, not even for a moment, thought that you were an idiot."

"And yet I played your little game. I told you all my deepest secrets so that you could make fun of me with your friends."

"I never laughed at you." Now she sounded angry.

Angry? What right did she have to be angry? That was *his* emotion.

"I didn't know."

Really? She was going to try to *lie* her way out of this now? He narrowed his eyes on her and tilted his head, daring her to continue.

She blinked several times and her gaze dropped away. How much more obvious could she be?

Guilty as charged.

"I really didn't know, Ben," she continued, her voice cracking under the strain of speaking. "I only found out just moments before the call for the fire came in."

"What does that matter?" he snapped. "You should have told me right away. You should have told me as soon as you found out."

He wasn't at all convinced she was telling him the truth about when she'd discovered he was the BJ she'd been emailing. It was gut-wrenching even to consider that she might have known all along. That she had played him like a puppet, making him into a fool.

He certainly felt like a fool.

And even if she hadn't known, as she was claiming, she still should have come forward the moment she'd discovered the truth. But Vee Bishop apparently didn't care for the truth. And anyway, he'd known all along that she didn't care for him. Whatever grudge she held against him, she'd paid him back for it—with interest.

"I can't believe I fell for you. F-fell for your ruse," he stammered, correcting himself. "Well, I have got news for you."

He turned back to her, crouching down and tilting his head so their lips were as close as they had been in the moments before he'd seen the name in her helmet.

She sat frozen to the spot. He couldn't even feel her breath this time, but he knew his own was quick and ragged, and his heart was pumping overtime. There was only one thing left for him to say.

"Game over."

Vee folded the last of her shirts and tucked them into the suitcase lying open on her bed. That was it, then. Everything she needed to leave Serendipity behind.

And with it, her heart.

She couldn't believe that she could get this close to happiness and then have it be ripped out from underneath her. Every time she closed her eyes, she remembered Ben—his forehead touching hers, how strong his arms were around her, the warmth and anticipation of his lips hovering over hers.

The fury that scorched his face when he had learned the truth about her.

And what could she say? She *had* known that Ben was BJ. That she'd found out only moments before the emergency had been called seemed irrelevant. Ben would never have listened to any rationale she might have given for not coming clean with the shocking news.

He was convinced she'd betrayed him.

And wasn't that partially her fault, too? No, she hadn't deliberately deceived him, but she'd spent years holding on to a grudge, refusing to follow God's commandment to forgive. After the way she'd treated him for so long, could she blame him for thinking she'd play this kind of cruel trick on him?

She moved to her sock drawer and scooped the entire contents of the drawer into her arms and then tossed them haphazardly into the suitcase, using the socks to fill the nooks and crevices of her suitcase.

Oh, Ben. They *knew* each other, both as Ben and Vee and as BJ and Veronica Jayne. They'd shared their thoughts, their feelings, their deepest hopes and dreams through their email letters. They'd shared a kiss as Ben and Vee—and she'd thought, in that moment before he'd seen her full name on her helmet, that there would be more than just one simple kiss between them, that she'd read a lifetime in his bronze-green eyes.

She'd believed the unbelievable. And how stupid was that?

She was in love with Ben Atwood. If Ben was BJ, all the better, right? And she was Veronica Jayne. That should be a good thing. Inside her heart, she really was that person—the one he'd said he cared for. The one he'd encouraged in the Lord more times than she could count.

And now—thanks to one big, tangled misunderstanding—it was all ruined.

She had to look toward the future—toward the Sacred Heart Mission, where she'd be out of Serendipity and out of Ben's life. He'd never leave her heart or her mind, but hopefully her leaving would make things easier on him.

That was the least she could do, with the mess she had made of both of their lives.

"Are you out of your mind?" Zach spotted Ben while he did bench presses—two hundred pounds. Benching the heavy weight was getting easier. His life was a blooming disaster and it didn't look like it was going to get better anytime soon, but all the angst had done wonders for his workout routine.

Not that that was any comfort to his heart. How was he going to live without Vee?

"I've been benching two hundred for a while now. It's no big deal."

"I wasn't talking about the weights. I was talking about the woman. You are seriously just going to let her walk out of your life?"

"She isn't going anywhere that I know of. At least not at the moment."

Their Spanish project was finished, on his side, at least. Just this morning, he'd emailed her the final presentation for her to accept or reject, as she pleased. He was done with it.

And then, who knew? Eventually, she was headed for stateside mission work.

What would happen to the plans they'd been making? He sighed inwardly. It would be best for all involved if he scrapped the whole thing—started over and applied for a completely different mission. Working alongside Vee would be pure torture for him now.

"So what are you waiting for?" Zach prodded, taking the bar from him and placing it in the rack. "Until you can bench two-fifty?"

"I'm not waiting for anything. I'm done with it."

"Then you're an idiot."

"Thank you very much," Ben said with more than a little bitterness in his voice. "I think we've already clearly established that point. I was played, and I fell for it." His flower girl. Having difficulty finding herself. Letting her hair down. The clues were all there, and he hadn't seen them. How stupid could he be?

"Fell for *her,* you mean."

"Whatever."

"So, I repeat, what are you going to do about it? How long is it going to take you to admit that you need her in your life and you're willing to forgive her for whatever it is that you think she's done to you?"

"What do you mean, what I *think* she's done to me?"

"I mean you haven't really given her the benefit of the doubt, and I think she deserves at least that much. From what you've told me, she said that she only learned it was you right before we got called away for the emergency. She wouldn't have had time to digest the shock, much less figure out a way to tell you anything."

Ben grunted and rolled to a sitting position. He didn't want to admit that his partner might have a valid point.

"What if the roles were reversed? What if she'd been the one to send her picture to you?"

"So what if she had? I would have spoken up right away and let her know I was BJ."

"Would you really? Because if it were me, I would have been reeling from the shock of finding out. Of all the women in the whole wide world, of all the places she could be living, she's right here in Serendipity with you—and not only that, but you guys even work at the same fire station together."

"What are the odds?"

"Exactly. Which is why I think Vee deserves a chance. She's a good woman, Ben, and I think deep down in your heart you know it. You have to admit, you've had your share of dating disasters. But maybe this is why none of those women worked out—so you'd be free when the right one came along. I can't think of a better person for you to end up with."

Ben moved to the free weights and started his biceps curls, not even bothering to keep a count in his head.

"Stop meddling," he protested in a low voice.

"Okay, I'll shut up. But consider this. You really liked Veronica Jayne. You and she seemed like really close friends. You understood each other. You had the same goals and ambitions and dreams. Friendship is really important in a relationship, take it from me."

"Apparently I *am* taking it from you," he growled.

"I'm not finished. So on one hand you have Veronica Jayne, and then on the other hand there is Vee—you two have sparks flying so high that the fire department would have a hard time containing you."

That much was true, which was why Ben thought it was a good idea to stay as far away from Vee as possible. He wasn't sure he was going to be able to keep his resolve once their eyes met or he saw her beautiful smile.

"What I'm saying is this—Vee and Veronica Jayne are one in the same person. How much more of a blessing are you looking for, buddy?"

Ben felt like he'd been flash-frozen. He dropped the weights to his side and stared openmouthed at Zach.

"She made a mistake—fine. Is it really unforgivable? Is holding on to your grudge worth losing your chance of being happy? You love her, you dolt. So go get her, and stop being so stubborn."

Zach was right. What was he doing lifting weights with a sweaty guy friend when he could be in the company of Vee—Veronica Jayne?

He hadn't given her the benefit of the doubt. Trust went both ways. He'd been so shocked by the revelation that Vee was Veronica Jayne that he hadn't given her a chance to explain. She was probably as stunned as he was by the discovery. Maybe she should have told him, but like Zach said, it was a mistake. He'd made plenty of his own.

Letting her go would be the biggest mistake of all.

He had to find her. Now.

"I'm out of here," Ben said, wiping the sweat off his forehead with the towel draped around his neck.

Zach laughed. "It's about time."

Ben quickly showered and dressed and headed straight for Emerson's Hardware. It was early in the day, but he hoped he'd be able to catch Vee alone so he'd be able to talk to her and clear up this whole mess once and for all.

As he walked, he tried phoning her cell, but she wouldn't pick up. She'd probably blocked his number. She obviously didn't want to talk to him—not that he could blame her after the way he'd reacted.

That only strengthened his resolve to make things right. And then he would kiss Vee senseless and prove to her once and for all that as Ben and as BJ, as Vee and Veronica Jayne, he was in love with her.

When he got to Emerson's, he went straight to the gardening department, but she wasn't there, so he asked for her at the front desk.

She'd *quit* Emerson's Hardware just the day before.

The news struck him mute. No two weeks' notice. No explanations about where she was going or why she had decided to up and resign so suddenly. Just an apology and a farewell.

She was leaving.

A dark pit grew in the center of his stomach and filled with raw dread. Vee couldn't leave. Or more accurately, she couldn't leave *him,* though he'd certainly given her no reason to stay.

He jogged as fast as his legs would carry him over to her apartment. He had to catch her before she left for good.

But he ran into a dead end there, too. Her rent had been paid until the end of the month, and her apartment had been emptied. No forwarding address. No hints as to where she might have gone.

He was winded and his heart was pumping overtime, but that didn't stop him from making a sprint for Vee's father's house. Surely she would stop in there to say goodbye. And if she wasn't there, she would have to have told her father where she was going or at least how to get in touch with her.

"I'm sorry, son," her father said when he opened the door to Ben. "Vee only told me she'd be in touch after she was settled. I wish I could tell you more. Here, though—she left you this note. Maybe that has a clue to where she is."

Ben took the folded piece of lined notebook paper and opened it, holding his breath as he scanned the contents. It was short and to the point, with beautiful, measured handwriting that for some reason reminded him of the emails he shared with Veronica Jayne.

Dear Ben,
I know that nothing I can say will change what happened, but I want you to know how truly sorry I am for the way things went down.

Since I don't know whether you will even speak to me or not, I'm leaving you this letter, which in a way seems oddly appropriate. I want to let you know that nothing that happened between us was make-believe. What I felt for you—feel for you— is and will always be real.

For what it's worth, I really care about you.
Love,
Vee

Stunned, Ben left Vee's father's house and walked aimlessly, eventually finding himself in the park. He slumped onto a bench and held his head in his hands.

What was he going to do now? She evidently hadn't told a solitary soul where she was going. She was running away, not only from him, but from everything she knew and loved.

There was no question that he would go after her. He just had to figure out where she'd gone. It wasn't going to be easy. But then memories flashed through his head of long conversations via email of plans for the future.

Maybe finding her was going to be the simplest thing in the world.

Chapter Fifteen

Vee sat at a desk in the far end of the classroom, staring out the window, watching children running around on a playground. They all seemed so energetic. So innocent. So carefree. So happy.

She sighed. She should be examining her syllabus for the class ahead. The introductory training manual for the Sacred Heart Mission was enormous. It was a week-long class, and Vee imagined it would be quite demanding.

She'd been through the fire academy, so she wasn't too worried about mastering the material, but she needed to keep her mind where it belonged—here at the mission and not home in Serendipity, where Ben was probably at the station, kicking back with Zach and the other guys, eating his *secret* chili and not giving her a single thought at all.

The mission teacher moved to the front of the room and started writing his lecture notes on the whiteboard. Vee closed her eyes. This ought to be one of the most exciting moments of her life—beginning the training she'd waited for years to do.

She had to cling to that—the external goals she'd

set. The calling she felt from God to help other people. She had to do something, and this was it. She opened her eyes, determined to make this work despite how her heart ached.

She had read the first paragraph of her syllabus when there was a noise at the door on the other side of the room.

"Excuse me. Pardon me. I'm sorry. I guess I'm late."

Suddenly, it was as if the atmosphere grew warmer. More humid, making it hard to breathe. Vee's heart leapt into her throat at the same time she tried to sweep in a breath, and the result was audible.

She would know that deep, rich voice anywhere.

She glanced across the room, unwilling to believe what her ears were telling her.

Ben was there—with his dark curly hair and his luminous green-bronze eyes and his biceps so huge they were straining through his black T-shirt.

Their eyes met and locked. Her world tipped, turning sideways on its axis and making her head rush in a dizzy loop while her heart pounded maddeningly in her chest.

What was he doing here?

Ben—her BJ—was the most handsome man she'd ever laid eyes on, better even than she could have imagined.

His eyes glimmered as he smiled his charming half smile, and she was certain every woman in the room grew just a little bit giddy. Somehow she knew, though, that his smile was only for her.

"Ben," she choked out as he strode across the room, not even bothering to excuse himself when he bumped a couple of desks.

"Vee." That was all he said before he framed her face

and kissed her. This time there was no doubt of his feelings. He was pouring out all his emotions right here in front of everyone.

And Vee wanted to be nowhere else in the world but in his arms.

"Vee," he repeated, kissing her once again for emphasis. "You left without saying goodbye."

"I didn't think you'd want to hear it from me."

"I don't."

She frowned, confused. "Then why are you here?"

"I don't want you to say goodbye, Vee. Ever. We can both stay here and complete our introductory courses for the Sacred Heart Mission, but first I have something to say. I love you. Will you marry me?"

Vee would have suspected that she'd heard wrong had the entire class not broken out shouting and clapping. There was no mistaking that.

But the sound faded as her eyes met Ben's and she read the love shining in his gaze. He meant it. He wanted to marry her—Veronica Jayne Bishop, for all she was both on the inside and the outside. He knew her—everything about her, just as she knew about him. And she felt the same way.

"Vee, honey?" Ben said with a nervous chuckle. "You're kind of leaving me hanging here."

Vee laughed along with him, her joy bubbling over. "Of course I'll marry you, Ben, or BJ, or whatever your name is today. I've been waiting for quite some time to tell you that I love you with my whole heart."

Ben whooped and pulled her into his arms, kissing her again, more fervently this time. He kept repeating the same line between kisses.

"I love you. I love you. I love you."

Vee couldn't hear those words enough.

"Um, excuse me," came a deep voice from the front of the room.

Ben and Vee turned as one, without letting go of each other.

It was the teacher who'd spoken. He had a wry smile on his face. "We're all really happy for you, and congratulations are definitely in order."

"Thank you, sir," Ben responded.

"However," the teacher continued, "do you think you could continue this happy reunion later, after my class is finished?"

Ben and Vee laughed and slid into adjoining chairs, his warm fingers still clasping hers across the aisle. It was then that Vee knew they would never be parted again.

* * * * *

Dear Reader,

Thank you for joining me for another heartfelt romantic adventure in Serendipity, Texas. If you happened to have missed the other books in the Email Order Brides series, the titles are *Phoebe's Groom* and *The Doctor's Secret Son*. You can find these books and many others of my backlist available for order from online booksellers in both print and ebook format.

In *Meeting Mr. Right*, both Vee and Ben struggled with their identities as adults because of traumatic bullying instances in their childhoods. Our past is so firmly etched into our hearts that sometimes it's hard to let go and learn to live in the present. But unless we focus on what's going on around us in our day-to-day lives, we're going to miss out on many opportunities to see God working in our lives and to discover new occasions to love and serve one another.

I hope you've been encouraged by Ben and Vee's story and that it's been a blessing to you. My thoughts and prayers are always with the readers of my stories, and hearing from you is a great treasure to me. Please email me at debkastnerbooks@gmail.com or leave a comment on my fan page on Facebook. I'm also on Twitter (@debkastner). Hope to see you online soon!

Keep the faith,

Deb Kastner

We hope you enjoyed reading
this special collection.

If you liked reading these stories,
then you will love **Love Inspired**® books!

You believe hearts can heal. **Love Inspired**
stories show that faith, forgiveness and hope
have the power to lift spirits and change
lives—always.

Enjoy six new stories from
Love Inspired every month!

Available wherever books and
ebooks are sold.

Love Inspired®

**Uplifting romances of faith,
forgiveness and hope.**

THE WORLD IS BETTER WITH

Romance

Harlequin has everything from contemporary, passionate and heartwarming to suspenseful and inspirational stories.

Whatever your mood,
we have a romance just for you!